DESTINED TO LOVE

Both of them had dreamed of this. They had been lovers long before they touched.

"Why are you always running? What is it that frightens you?" Brannoc asked her.

"Nothing," she said vehemently. "Nothing frightens me."

His hands ran down her arms, peeling the blanket from her. She did not resist.

"You are my fate, Phaedra," he whispered. "The dreams have guided me to you. Will you fight me?"

"Fight?" But there was no chance to save herself with words. Brannoc lowered his head and covered her mouth with his own.

Her pulse was pounding. At his voice, his touch, all the wanting in her flooded to the surface.

"Phaedra." His voice caressed her name, and she shivered.

"Let me love you," he whispered, his lips moving in her long, fragrant hair. "I have waited so long."

Phaedra flowed like water beneath Brannoc's lips and hands. She opened her mouth to him, secretly rejoicing as his plundering tongue overtook hers.

PAGAN DESIRES

Veronica Ashley

Zebra Books
Kensington Publishing Corp.
http://www.zebrabooks.com

ZEBRA BOOKS are published by

Kensington Publishing Corp.
850 Third Avenue
New York, NY 10022

Zebra and the Z logo Reg. U.S. Pat. & TM Off.

First Printing: October, 1997
10 9 8 7 6 5 4 3 2 1

Printed in the United States of America

In memory of my grandmother

WERE NOT THE GODS RESPONSIBLE FOR
THAT, WEAVING CATASTROPHE INTO THE
PATTERN OF EVENTS TO MAKE A SONG FOR
FUTURE GENERATIONS?
—HOMER
THE ODYSSEY

THE SOUL OF A MAN IN LOVE IS FULL OF
PERFUMES AND SWEET ODORS.
—PLUTARCH

One

Phaedra Acominatus trembled in her sleep. Her shallow, uneven breathing broke the stillness of the night like cries for help, but no one heard her. Night's infinite arms could not hold or comfort the sleeping seven-year-old. Phaedra hugged her knees to her chest and curled tight as a bud, upsetting a gilded book which tipped and tumbled over the edge of the divan. A silk sheet followed, spilling soundlessly onto the mosaic floor of peacock blue and Nile green. Near the carved foot of the divan stood a bronze brazier. It cast a pale, flickering light, smudging the darkness, hinting at the delicate perfection of her face and the paleness of her skin, which in the sunlight appeared as pure as the feathers of a swan.

Phaedra winced. A lock of blue-black hair fell across her face. Her eyelashes fluttered as she struggled to awaken. But she could not. The dream had her now . . .

Packs of wolves were moving across the Byzantine Empire and entering the city of Constantinople. Someone must have let them in through the Golden Gate, for the city walls were impenetrable. The walls surrounded the city on the landward side like the flexed, muscular arms of a waiting giant. Phaedra thought the great walls were invulnerable to attack, that they'd been blessed by the Holy Virgin. But in the dream, the walls didn't stop the wolves. They moved right into the city.

Phaedra saw them clearly, a sea of beasts lit by a pale, full moon. They were as mythic in size as any of Homer's creatures. Their wet, matted jaws seemed large enough to devour small children whole. They were the color of old metal left in the rain, of deep dirt torn from the earth with sharp tools. Crimson amulets hung from chains around their brutish necks and swayed against their matted fur as they moved their heads from side to side. They lumbered with graceless purpose through streets Phaedra knew.

The wolves moved up the Mesê, the great Middle Street in Constantinople. Their ears looked like pointed traps, ready to capture sounds of fear. They crossed the Augusteion market, eyes glistening in the moonlight. Their attention roamed greedily as they lumbered past the marble colonnades, the gilded statues and the shops of silver, perfume and jewel vendors. Their claws clicked against the white marble pavement and echoed ominously through the deserted market. Phaedra felt the crushing heaviness of their paws. It seemed her body was the street and they were trampling her. She listened to them with every pore of her body as they moved toward the palace. She heard their hunger, a deep, rumbling, caged fury lodged in their throats, and she shuddered, knowing they would not stop until they lapped up pools of blood and feasted on flesh.

The wolves stopped before the Bronze Gate of the palace. A hundred pairs of blazing eyes looked up briefly at the gate's roof of gilded bronze, shining like a nimbus of holy gold. Then the wolves looked down at Phaedra! Their menacing gazes flared at her, for somehow she stood before the gate. Her heart jammed her throat and knocked the wind out of her. The closest wolf had only to leap and it would have her in its jaws. The beast snarled at her, baring a ridge of teeth as slick as newly honed blades. Its eyes glittered like steel lances, prodding her to move. She stepped back, but the cold bronze gate barred her escape. The wolves advanced. The sound of their hunger rose into the night, until it was a roar in her ears. She fell to the ground, and screamed.

"Come along, Phaedra."

"Coming!" Phaedra answered her father. She patted the mare's shiny black coat one last time before jumping off the gate of his stall. The light was filmy and golden inside the imperial stables, and Phaedra's eyes shone with delight as they swept over the stately Arabian horse. It was her horse, a gift from her father, who'd been teaching her to ride the last few weeks. She thought this last lesson had gone well. Hadn't her father remarked that she sat tall in her saddle, "like an Amazon Queen"?

The stomping and snorting of the other horses broke her reverie. She looked around at the mosaic of light and shadows, the spun gold of hay against the weathered wood of the stables. There was nothing in her eyes that hinted of the horror of her dream. Only the faint lines between her brows seemed to suggest the battle of will behind her expression of happiness and serenity.

Phaedra returned her attention to her horse, Nike. The smell of grain, horse and heat filled her nostrils. She wiped her sweaty brow with the back of her hand and smiled. Tomorrow her father was going to introduce her to the historical teachings of Xenophon, one of the most respected Athenian cavalrymen who'd ever lived.

"Phaedra!"

She detected a slight note of impatience in her father's deep voice and jumped into action. She said good-bye to her horse, swung the gate closed and, after straightening her leather tunic over her linen breeches, ran through the stable to join her father outside.

General Nicephorus Acominatus swept his daughter into his arms. "What have you been up to, little minx?"

Phaedra met her father's twinkling, grey-blue eyes. "Nothing."

"Nothing?" he repeated in mock horror. "Why, do you remember the last time I caught you doing 'nothing'?"

Phaedra laughed, clamping her hands over her mouth. She remembered it well, her best prank ever. She'd hidden a garden snake in her nurse's bed.

"Phaedra, Phaedra, Phaedra," he sighed.

His daughter beamed, revealing two missing teeth. He hugged her. "Toothless little minx, don't you know how special you are to me?"

"Yes," she laughed, pushing her long, loose hair behind her ears. She glanced at the thin, white scar on her father's cheek, an old wound inflicted during a battle with the Seljuk Turks. She continued in a more serious tone. "My nurse says all your talk will give me a big head. But what's wrong with that? I should like a big head, Father. A head like a giant so that I might gaze out on the entire empire and watch for enemies!"

"A giant, eh?" He smiled and nodded, knowing full well that the delicate-looking creature in his arms was a warrior at heart. If only she could armor herself against the dreams, he thought.

But were they only dreams? Gently, he tried to wipe away the dark smudges beneath her eyes, even though he knew they were the markings of another sleepless night. Phaedra's mother, Cassandra, had had the power to see into the future. Her dreams had been like bits of polished brass, reflecting events of a time waiting to become fully alive. It grieved him that Phaedra could barely remember her mother. The child had been two when Cassandra died. But if the child had inherited her mother's gift of sight, then that, plus her pale, beautiful skin and golden eyes, were signs that Cassandra lived on through her only daughter.

The scar on Nicephorus's face tightened as he clenched his jaw and mulled over a thought. There were men in the world who craved to control such powers and use them for their own ends. But how could he keep watch over Phaedra if he was off protecting the empire? Not only would she need the head of a giant, but she would have to learn to fight like one, too.

He would save those lessons for another day. With a playful grunt, Nicephorus kissed his daughter on her forehead. Phaedra squirmed in his arms. Needing no further signal, he lowered her to her feet and watched her run off toward the group of men waiting for him in the center of the sandy field. They were his men, members of his cavalry regiment, garbed in military dress. They had just finished practicing their maneuvers for the day. His attention sharpened as Phaedra closed the distance between them. Furrowing his brow, he quickened his step. He knew Phaedra regarded his men as her brothers, easy targets for her little sister games.

Nicephorus Acominatus, Strategus, or General, was Greek by birth, with ancient Roman patrician blood, and his profile was worthy of an imperial coin. Clean-shaven, the broad planes of his face seemed chiseled by a sculptor. His short black hair was streaked with silver. He wore armor of solid silver wrought and gilded. Like his men, he had on the classic military kilt of the long vanquished West Roman legion. A cloak of Ionian blue draped his back, and buskins of gilded leather covered his feet and legs. A tall man, he stood a full head and shoulders above most of his officers. Despite his size, the might of his muscled arms and the deadliness of his strategic intellect, he carried himself gracefully. A court scribe had once referred to him as the Leopard.

When he wasn't with his daughter, Nicephorus enjoyed spending time with the officers under his charge. They had been busy preparing for the campaign against the Normans, who were recently reported to be in northern Greece, Byzantine territory, and led by Bohemund, son of the wily Robert Guiscard who had carved an empire for himself out of Byzantine lands in Italy. Practicing military maneuvers, there had been little opportunity for Nicephorus to relax with his men. Nor would he get his chance now.

The field shimmered with heat, blurring the line between sand and blue sky. Beads of sweat fell from Nicephorus's brow. Narrowing his eyes, he noted that one of his officers had scooped Phaedra up onto his horse. He smiled. His men were finally learning how to keep the little minx out of mischief.

"General!"

The shout stopped Nicephorus. He turned and watched a short, stocky man in a white tunic run toward him. The man was holding a tablet of paper and flapping his arms like a chicken. The general moaned and smiled all at once.

"Gabriel!" Nicephorus shouted in greeting.

The man was running forward at such an awkward angle that he would have run right past the general had Nicephorus not put his arms out to stop him.

"Oh, my!" the man panted. The beard around his mouth was wet with spittle, and the curls of his beard were as wiry and black as the hair on his head. With Nicephorus's arms steadying him, he fought to catch his breath.

"Dear me!"

"No rush, Gabriel. Take your time."

"Oh. Thank you, General." Gabriel wheezed, then coughed. "I was wondering if you'd permit me to make some sketches for my book," he inquired, tapping the tablet of paper. He was still breathing heavily. He looked up into the general's face. "It's for Emperor Alexius's mosaic. You've heard of my commission?"

"Who hasn't? The entire empire knows the great artist Gabriel is designing a mosaic for the palace. But what do I have to do with it?" Nicephorus questioned, already knowing the answer.

"I'm planning to include illustrious members of the court."

At that, Nicephorus dropped his arms to his sides, letting

Gabriel go. As the man wobbled, the general placed his hands on his hips and bent over to stare him in the eye. Nicephorus knitted his brows into an expression of gloom and doom. "And you mean to include me?"

Without a blink, Gabriel nodded.

Nicephorus's expression was stony. "I thought I made it clear to you that I didn't want anything to do with it?"

"You won't even notice I'm around."

"I doubt it," Nicephorus muttered, walking away.

Gabriel was unoffended. In fact, he smiled, because up until now the general had blatantly refused to even acknowledge his presence. Nicephorus was the only military officer in the empire who hadn't jumped at the honor of being portrayed in the mosaic. "But after all, this is no peacock, but the Leopard! Gabriel thought aloud to himself as he followed Nicephorus.

Gabriel positioned himself next to Phaedra, the only person who smiled at him. He set to work immediately, studying the general on and off as he made short, fast strokes with his bit of charcoal.

Nicephorus stood in the midst of his men. The cavalry regiment was comprised of Greeks, Armenians and Cappadocians, plus Celts and Goths, mercenaries, because there was a shortage of native soldiers. This lack of local manpower could be traced to the policies of past emperors, who had been fearful of military overthrows. They had robbed the army of honors and privileges that had once attracted warriors.

But no matter their origin, all the men in the regiment spoke Greek, the empire's official language. Most of them shaped the words with hesitant tongues and spiced it with bold laughs. Each man had been handpicked by Nicephorus. As Strategus, he was required to pay their wages. In return, he had their allegiance, and the regiment bore his name and wore his colors.

The air hummed with their vitality, as if the rippling muscles beneath their leather armor gave off waves of energy. Their life force beat with the strength of pounding hearts conditioned to withstand the onslaught of charging mounts and sword thrusts. But when Nicephorus began to speak, his officers' attention sparked. They looked up at their general with respect and pride in their eyes. Each man had taken a personal oath to obey Nicephorus without question, even if it meant following him to hell.

Phaedra would have marched to the underworld and back, too, if it meant being with her father. She still believed that someday they would ride and fight side by side in battle. Why not? She was, after all, an Acominatus. But for now, until she grew into the Amazon her father already envisioned, she would be content to place him at the center of her world.

Nicephorus looked at the men gathered around him. While his eyes held the promise of a smile, the bronze planes of his face were still and serious. Phaedra had told him about her dream and, with it firmly etched in his mind, its symbolic message perfectly clear, he said, "We go to fight off the Normans! The barbarians snap at the greatness of the empire and look at us with greedy eyes. Their small minds twist and turn, devising ways to attack our flanks and drag us down. They make war amongst themselves. We will win by turning them against each other. We will cut them down and protect the glory of Constantinople!"

"They're like wolves, are they not?" The silky and elegant voice caused a sudden, reflexive start among the men. Everyone turned to look, for they all knew its source, and it was not one of them.

Their attention centered on Emperor Alexius Comnenus, the rebel general the army had helped to the throne only one year ago, when they had taken the capital by storm, ousting Emperor Boteniates from the throne. The former general was dressed for battle too, for he intended to lead the empire against the barbarians. His garb was rich with color and jewels. His armor of wrought gold caught the sun and sent sparks flashing into their blinking eyes. A mantle of imperial purple was clasped at his shoulder and held in place by a brooch set with rubies. His feet were shod in scarlet buskins. And upon his head gleamed a gold crown dripping with pearls.

Moving as one, Nicephorus and his men prostrated themselves at their emperor's feet, touching the sandy ground three times with their foreheads. Their leather armor creaked as they rose, following the lift of his hand.

But the emperor wasn't looking at them. His gaze was centered on Phaedra. Eyes downcast, she was sitting very still on the horse.

Emperor Alexius looked away from the girl as Nicephorus crossed his arm over his chest in the ancient Roman salute. As the rightful heirs to the Roman legions, the military still clung to the ancient customs.

Alexius took a step towards Nicephorus, and the arc of men parted immediately to let Alexius pass. He was short, compact, broad-shouldered, with a presence that commanded grave obedience.

"Phaedra dreams," the emperor whispered. His brown eyes, sharp with interest, noticed how the men near him stiffened protectively when he mentioned the girl.

Phaedra's father clenched his teeth. The slaves must have been eavesdropping at the door while Phaedra recounted her dream to him. His daughter already had a reputation as the "Dreamer of Dreams."

Nicephorus towered above the emperor. He had to look down to meet his gaze. Alexius's face was a mask. Nicephorus forced a smile.

"Basileus," said Nicephorus, using the Greek word for emperor. He swept his arm to one side, and escorted Alexius away from the men and Phaedra. "My daughter has a poet's imagination. And ever since she discovered Homer's *Odyssey* on my shelves, that imagination has been especially vivid."

"Homer?" the emperor chuckled. "Yes." He stroked his beard which glistened with oil. "Perhaps you'll bring her to the palace, so that I might hear this dream." Alexius swept the general's face with a quick, sharp gaze, but Nicephorus held his expression still.

Alexius looked up, squinting into the sunlight, and smiled inwardly to himself. As the Basileus, he was also the Protector of the Church, the Chosen of God, and the Thirteenth Apostle. Nevertheless, the mystical side of Christianity and life intrigued him. He believed dreams and visions were inspired paths to knowledge. Hadn't the great Emperor Constantine experienced a celestial vision on the eve of battle? It was reported that Constantine had seen a cross of light, emblazoned with the words "In Hoc Signo Vinces" meaning "In this sign you will conquer." Constantine had also dreamed that Christ was the true ruler of the universe.

In the heavy silence, Alexius lowered his gaze to the gold sun brooch holding the two ends of Nicephorus's cloak closed. The emperor squinted as he turned thoughts over in his mind. Phaedra's dreams interested him greatly. The girl's mother, Cassandra, was said to have been a descendant of the great Spartan queens. He had read that the women of that ancient pagan time had special powers. His eyebrow arched. Perhaps the daughter had the gift of prophecy as well. If so, she could be of use to him, and the empire.

"Basileus, the dream was very upsetting to her," Nicephorus said bluntly. He saw the emperor's brows slam together, but despite the warning, he could not stop speaking from his heart. "I beg your tolerance, but she is only a child. Repeating the dream will stir it all up again and she'll be condemned to relive it. As her father . . ." Nicephorus stopped, catching himself just as Alexius raised his hand and nodded in understanding.

But as the emperor turned to leave, Nicephorus caught the unsympathetic glance he cast Phaedra's way. Nicephorus bristled. Christe! the general swore to himself. She's only a child! The general frowned as he watched Alexius move away, his Tyrian purple robe rippling gently in his wake.

She was only a child, yet her own father was duty-bound to abandon her again. Nicephorus squeezed his hands into fists. He sensed this campaign against the Normans would be a long and vicious one. The barbarians were fools, but stubborn and strong. He sighed and, feeling the shifting movement of his men around him, remembered he was not alone. He ran his hand back through his short hair, looked at Phaedra, and started. His daughter was staring at him with huge eyes, as if she'd heard every word of his conversation with Emperor Alexius, and had read their thoughts as well. As much as he yearned to drive the barbarians out of the empire, and preferably to hell, he wished he and his daughter's lives were not a painful series of good-byes.

Two

"Phaedra? Where are you, child?" A woman's voice, high pitched with worry, floated in the wind.

Nothing short of a magic spell could help locate Phaedra this time. She was tucked away in a secret place, like a pearl in an oyster, deep in the palace garden. She sat reading among the ruined pillars of a pavilion, a marble column at her back, where she was well hidden by a dense ring of cypresses. She wore a silk tunic the color of clouds that puffed when the wind sneaked up her hem. Around her, the effect of nature's benevolent touch was as evident as her destructive hand. Wildflowers bloomed where the earth had been lunged apart, and a lush green canopy of vines, fingered by streams of hazy, golden sunlight, clung to the stunted remains of once stalwart marble columns.

Phaedra didn't look up from the open book balanced on her knees. Her eyes, golden like honey, burned with serious intensity, giving her an air of maturity beyond her seven years. Homer's epic poem had hypnotized her. Strung together like a jeweled necklace, the Greek words led her on a great adventure. With every quick turn of the page, Constantinople drifted further and further away.

A teasing spring wind sprayed her long black hair across her cheek. Calmly, she brushed the strands aside again and again. Lured into a world more real than the columns around her, Phaedra paid no mind to the wind's playful game, nor did she hear the approaching footsteps on the pebbled path on the other side of the trees.

"What I said about Strategus Nicephorus Acominatus is the truth, I tell you!" thundered a voice.

"Humph!" another voice grunted.

Phaedra jumped at the intruding sounds, then clutched her book as it tottered on her knees. What was this about her father, she wondered. He was in Greece, defending Byzantine lands from the barbaric Normans. He'd been gone for eight months. Was he coming home?

Holding the volume to her chest, she peered through the screen of cypresses, but saw nothing, not even a tinge of color. Nervously, she pressed her back into the marble column. She wanted to melt into it. She could not see out, but what if they could see in? From the blunt tone of the one voice, she knew the men thought they were completely alone. They would be sorely angry if they were to learn otherwise. Her body curled tightly, she held her breath and listened.

"But there's been no official word," someone replied. Phaedra narrowed her eyes as if this would help her hear better.

"You'll have it on paper soon enough," the gruff voice snorted.

Have what, Phaedra wondered.

"How did it happen?"

Someone sighed heavily. "They tell me Nicephorus ordered his cavalry and archers to retreat."

At this, Phaedra's face knotted in a scowl. She had a mind to kick the liar in the shins. Her father would never command such a thing! Unless he was planning to trick the enemy.

"It was a ruse, you see," the harsh voice continued. "It was a trick to lure the enemy into an ambush. Our emperor's men had been waiting for the Normans all along."

Phaedra's face glowed with a knowing smile.

"But I don't understand," came a silky whine.

Fool, snickered Phaedra, leaning forward again, eager to grasp the next words. Obviously, the man with the high voice knew nothing about battles.

"I find it difficult myself." The other voice sighed. "No doubt all of Constantinople will, too." He paused. "Normans!" He spat. "Thick-skulled and stinking in their foul skins, but Christ, how they fight!"

"The ambush should have succeeded, but I've heard that the barbarians fought back with such vengeance, our men fell before them like sheaves of wheat."

Phaedra's hands froze. Impossible, she thought. No army could survive an ambush launched by her father. Didn't these simpletons know that? She strained forward, waiting for the liar to speak again.

"The barbarians took Nicephorus hostage," he said. "Imagine, the Leopard a hostage! The barbarians asked for our General's weight in gold, and Emperor Alexius paid, and still they murdered him!"

Phaedra felt the sky come crashing down around her, and she flung her arms around the column to hold herself up. "Please," she prayed, tasting blood on her lip. Her head dropped like a dying flower and rested against the cool marble. "Please let this be a dream. Please," she begged, raising her moist eyes to heaven, "let this be a dream." She squeezed her eyes shut and prayed, and for a moment, she had the sensation that she was rising into the air.

Phaedra slowly opened her eyes. She held her breath. The birds flew among the vine leaves just as before. She nudged the earth with her toe. This was not a dream! A soft moan escaped her lips and, like a wounded animal, she slipped to the ground.

"Did you hear something?" questioned a voice behind the trees.

"No." There was a pause. "It was probably an animal."

Tears spilled down her hot cheeks. Her body trembled as she sought to control herself.

"I know nothing of military things," said the silky, pompous voice. "But, speaking as a man, I think he would have made a good emperor."

"You speak treason."

"I speak the truth, my friend. You know as well as I that his men would have done anything for him, including securing him the right to wear the crown. By a force of arms, of course."

"I suppose you're right." One of them sighed. "But there's no use thinking about it now. He was struck down in cold blood by a barbarian. And not just any heathen, mind you, but the son of Robert Guiscard, wily bastard! You'll remember old Guiscard carved out an empire for himself in the Byzantine lands of Italy. Apparently, the son, Bohemund, learned much at his father's knee, including how to spill another man's blood onto his sword."

"Bohemund. The name suits the beast."

Bohemund. Phaedra's lips tested the foreign name. Her stomach clenched as if she'd eaten spoiled meat.

"Were I Nicephorus's son, I would hunt this barbarian Bohemund down and kill him."

"You," the other mocked. "Why, you ride like a girl and prick yourself on your own dagger!"

"I would at least try!"

"Enough, enough," Phaedra cried to herself, pressing her hands over her ears. She sat crouched on her knees, looking nothing like the high-spirited girl who liked to race her father's cavalry soldiers. She looked pale and vulnerable.

"Yes, yes, what son would not want to avenge his father's murder? But the Leopard has no son." The man paused. "Enough of this. Let us go and drink to our friend, eh? What do you say? The Bearkeeper's Tavern, or the Gold Chariot?"

"You choose. Hmmm. What of his daughter? A pretty thing, wild though, with a stare that could cut through your bones. My wife swears the girl's the image of her mother Cassandra, only with black hair. What do you think will become of her?"

"I don't know." Their voices were fading. "He was a good friend to the emperor, so no doubt he will . . ." and the voices trickled away.

Silence descended like a shroud. Phaedra rocked back and forth, hugging the book to her chest. She didn't know how much time had passed, but when she finally looked up, the light on the leaves was gold, and the wind had cooled. She stretched, her arms stiff and sore as if she'd been working the earth.

They had to be wrong, she thought, clenching her jaw. She dried her swollen eyes with one fist, then the other. There was probably a letter from her father waiting for her at home right this minute. The idiots had gotten her father confused with someone else. She froze. Her mind clung to that thought. Yes! Yes! That was it. She felt as if a great stone had been lifted off her heart. Anxious to get home, sure she would find a letter from her father, she crawled on her hands and knees through the confining ring of cypresses, clawing her way through the dirt and branches, a wild and desperate look in her eyes.

Phaedra knew where to look for her nurse, at the Court of the Gold Lion, where the woman loved to sit and gossip. Once Phaedra found her, they would go home and everything would be just as it was this morning.

Nervous energy drove Phaedra as she walked up the narrow and steep path. Twice she took the wrong turn and unexpectedly ended up on a parapet overlooking the Sea of Marmara. The second time, she stood there for a little while, clutching the marble rail. How many times had she watched her father ride and sail off to battle? Every time he had returned to her. His coming home was as natural and expected as narcissi blooming in spring.

She took a deep breath and turned her thoughts to Sharif, the ex-charioteer her father had hired to look after her. Sharif would tease her mercilessly about this, if he ever found out. He was of the same mind as her father. Both thought women worried far too much, and that it was bad for the humors. "Let Sharif tease me," she thought. "I'll pull that curly beard until he begs for forgiveness!"

Her wan little smile struggled to turn into something hopeful and bright. She tapped her book against the railing. The broken rhythm was answered by the cries of gulls.

Minutes later, outside the red and green pebbled Court of the Gold Lion, Phaedra lurched to a stop.

"Aghia Sophia! Phaedra, where have you been?"

The wail snapped Phaedra out of her thoughts. She watched her nurse running towards her.

"I was reading," she answered truthfully in a husky voice. She looked up at the pinched face looming above her. Her nurse Zoë was blonde, with pretty doe eyes, and a thin-lipped, stingy mouth.

"Reading? Look at you. Why, your good tunic is ruined!"

"I fell." Phaedra looked down at herself. Her garment was stained with earth, and the delicate fabric was snagged where the branches had poked her. But she didn't care.

The nurse cocked her head to the side and stared pensively at the child. Her eyes widened. "You've been crying! Are you ill, Phaedra?" She tipped the girl's chin up. "Did you have another dream?"

Phaedra jerked her head away from the woman's touch. "I'm fine!" For a second, she forgot about the conversation she'd just overheard and narrowed her eyes at her nurse. She should have never told this woman about her dreams. Shortly before leaving to fight the Normans, her father had hired her as a replacement for the last nurse, who had run screaming from the house one night. Phaedra had hidden a snake in the woman's bed. And the nurse before that had deserted wordlessly, but for the same reasons. Phaedra had meant no harm, they were only pranks. Had she been a boy, the women wouldn't have batted an eye at the jests, but because she was a girl, they'd thought her difficult.

Phaedra had believed Zoë was cut from a slightly different cloth than her predecessors. For one thing, she wasn't afraid of snakes. But when Zoë confided that she was a descendant of a great prophetess, Phaedra, like a silly goose, told her about the dreams. Zoë said that the wolves represented the pagans' desire to destroy the Church of the Nazarene and return to ancient rituals. With that ridiculous revelation, Phaedra's respect for Zoë's prophetess abilities had dwindled like rain water down a sewer drain. The wolves obviously represented the enemies of the empire! Even she, a child, knew that.

Zoë frowned at the disapproving look on Phaedra's face. Unconsciously, the nurse stepped back. She had to remind herself that the girl before her was only a child. She steadied herself, forced a smile and gently said, "Why don't you come sit next to me and I'll send for a cup of honeyed water?"

"I want to go home," Phaedra said loudly. She was not ready to tell Zoë about the conversation she had overheard.

Zoë bristled. The girl's self-possession unnerved her. She looked around at the people who strolled by, staring. Phaedra did too, and noticed many of them pointing at her and whispering. She lowered her eyes to the gilded book in her hand and pretended to ignore them. She looked up again and saw they were still staring. Her skin prickled. Her stomach churned, and she felt like screaming at them to stop.

In a hushed voice, her nurse said, "We'll leave in a little while, Phaedra. The empress wants to see you first."

"Why?" she pouted. This was not going as she had planned.

"How should I know the wishes of an empress?" Zoë snapped.

Phaedra narrowed her eyes but said nothing. She squared her shoulders and walked past her nurse, holding the book like a sacred relic in her arms. She plopped down on the fountain's rim. She felt the cool, smooth stone through her tunic. As she made herself comfortable, she caught her nurse shaking her head in disapproval. Bouncing, Phaedra shifted her position, turned away from that sour face, and looked into the water.

The rectangular pool was so still and clear, she could see down to the blue and purple mosaic tiles which were no larger than her nails, laid out in a circular pattern. She looked across the pool at the statue of a bronze lion. A steady stream of water gushed out of its roaring mouth. She looked down again. Then her eyes widened, for upon the turquoise stillness was the image of an eagle, its wings spread as if posing for a painter. There was no eagle flying above her, and the silvery blue sky was cloudless.

Her hair fell forward as she hunched closer to the water, but the image of the eagle rippled away. Before she had time to think, another picture began shifting and shaping the surface of the pool. Her heart stilled as her father's noble face and a strong figure appeared on the surface, and . . . something else. Wolves!

She started at the image on the water. She thought she heard the cry of an eagle. She swung around and looked across the pool. The lion's mouth moved! "Kill him," she heard the statue say.

"Phaedra?"

The girl jumped off the fountain's rim, dropping her book in the water, and collided with the empress. She steadied the girl, then dipped her lily hand into the water to retrieve the book.

"Oh, dear." The empress looked at the wet book in her hand. She shook her head and daintily held the book away from her body so it wouldn't drip on her crimson and purple silk tunic. Then she looked at Phaedra. Her blue eyes widened, taking in the sight of the girl gasping for breath. The child's skin was deathly white, her eyes huge and haunted.

"Mary, Mother of God! What is it, child? The book? Surely we can find you another!"

Fighting to catch her breath, eyes round with terror, Phaedra looked up into the empress's concerned face. The pearls dangling from her crown swayed and tinkled softly as she tilted her head to one side. Phaedra blinked. Now the empress seemed to be standing on her head. Phaedra felt cold and hot all at once. Her insides heaved and she thought she was going to be sick. She slumped back onto the fountain's stone rim, unaware that by doing so, she was being disrespectful. She heard someone gasp, faintly, as if from a great distance.

The empress set the book aside on the fountain's rim and leaned over the girl. "Are you all right, Phaedra?"

Her voice sounded so far away. Phaedra swallowed. "Yes, Illustriousness." She did not recognize her own voice.

"Phaedra?" The empress tilted the girl's chin up with a delicate touch. "You know . . ." The empress stopped, unable to continue with those amber eyes staring up at her so. Why, a person could drown in such a gaze! The empress swallowed as she saw tears well up in Phaedra's eyes. She stood up straight and stepped back, lifting her wet hand to her uncovered throat. "Why, the girl already knows," she thought to herself.

Phaedra read pity in the empress's drooping eyes and, in a shattering instant, she knew it was true. Her father was really dead. "My father's . . ." A rush of pain strangled the word in her throat. She heard the wretched sob of some animal, unaware that the sound came from her. Through a curtain of tears, Phaedra saw the empress close her eyes and lift her face to the sky in prayer.

"Then it's true. Bohemund murdered my father." Phaedra choked on her words and turned to look into the water. "A son would be expected to vindicate his father's murder." She spoke as if in a trance. "So must I."

The empress opened her eyes with a start. She stepped closer. Her reflection swayed above Phaedra's on the surface of the pool. "Dear child. No one expects . . ." She stopped, cut off by the reflection of Phaedra's calculating stare. "But you're just a girl, Phaedra."

That mealy-mouthed tone! Why, it sounded just like her nurse! Insulted, Phaedra stiffened, and for a flashing moment, the feeling cut through her grief and prodded the fiery, honor-bound Acominatus part of her into action.

"And the barbarian is just a man," Phaedra said. Her eyes were suddenly wild with revenge. "And all men have weaknesses, do they not, Empress?" But she didn't care about an answer. "Someday I will make my father's killer wish he'd never been born." Her sharp voice wavered, as the pain locked within her breast clawed its way free again. She put her open hand over her heart. She'd seen women do this in times of sorrow, but now she knew why. It was out of sheer horror and terror over the hurt.

Phaedra's tears streamed hot and furious down her cheeks. She felt the empress backing away. Good, Phaedra thought, tasting the salt of streaming pain. She didn't want the empress to see her cry anymore.

As the empress mumbled a prayer, and Zoë nervously shooed away curious Byzantines, Phaedra sat crying into the pool. She couldn't see past the flow of her tears. She couldn't see that the pool's calm was now distorted like pieces of broken glass.

Phaedra was sure the pain she felt in her chest signaled she was dying. It was like a knife gouging and probing around the wound in her heart. She collapsed forward. Her head felt like stone! "Oh, Father! Father! Why? Why?" she cried, gripping the fountain's stone rim for support. She didn't think that the ghost of her father would answer, or God, for that matter. She was searching her soul for a reply.

But there was none. She heard nothing but a far-off muffled roar. It was the sound a shell makes when it's pressed to the ear. It was the cry of a soul trapped in a cave, cut off by water.

Three

In the most luxurious public bath in the Zeuxippus district of Constantinople, women who had overindulged in one too many goblets of wine the evening before now lounged about. They treated their bloated condition by sweating it off in the caladarium, the hot room. Later they would eagerly offer up their languorous bodies to the able hands of slaves, ready to massage their flesh with almond oil until it glistened. Those with overripe, dimpled thighs would have their legs wrapped in seaweed, a method used since ancient times to draw out impurities and smooth the skin. Those who delighted in sweets would expect miracles from the mud packs applied to their blotchy complexions. The mud from sacred mineral springs was the best and, therefore, the only mud used at Zeuxippus.

But of all the therapeutic rituals, the one which everyone relished was the exchange of gossip. Whether dimpled or taut, wrinkled or smooth, the women gorged themselves on these juicy tidbits. It fed their curiosity and peppered the day's boring diet of mundane affairs.

The caladarium was steamy and noisy. Maidens and matrons, lounging in towels or bathing, devoured news of the Christian barbarians from the West, smacking their lips as if they were savoring ambrosia. The barbarians were on their way to recapture Jerusalem from the Seljuk Turks, who had overtaken that most holy of holy cities, the jewel of the Byzantine Empire. The Emperor Alexius of Byzantium had appealed to the West for help, for freelancers and mercenaries to increase the size and might of his own armies. They had come, but they'd also descended like a plague of locusts on the suburbs of Constantinople.

Only the leaders had been permitted into the city. Their physical attributes were already the stuff of legend. Women who had actually seen these Christian fighting men tossed about description after description, which fell like ripe plums into the waiting hands and greedy mouths of the idle. The mosaic walls and marble columns rang with high-pitched voices. Exclamations and hearty laughter rolled like tidal waves across the steamy, scented pool, drowning out all private thoughts.

Except for Phaedra's. Separated from the enclave of women by deep water, she lifted herself half out of the pool and rested her arms on the edge of cool tile. She propped her chin on her hands and narrowed her eyes in concentration. There wasn't a wave strong enough to pull her away from the tide of her thoughts.

What was Alexius going to do about these barbarians from the West, she wondered. Something had to be done. She'd recently learned that another Christian knight's army would soon be joining the barbarians already camped on Constantinople's doorstep. One didn't need to be a military strategist to see the danger of having two barbarian armies joined outside the city walls.

Phaedra knew the comings and goings of these iron men, partly from her conversations with the emperor's fourteen-year-old daughter Anna. The princess had confided that she was keeping a chronicle of events, as she wished to write a history about the empire in the style of the great court historians. The girl was recording it all: Duke Godfrey of Bouillon's raid on the countryside, the Franks' attack on

Constantinople on Holy Thursday of Easter Week, and the Normans' brutish measures to secure basic provisions. Although they'd brought enough metal and arms to fight until the Second Coming of Christ, it seemed they'd arrived with little in human comforts save the clothes on their backs.

Imagine that, Phaedra smirked, unsurprised. After all, they were an undisciplined lot, worse than animals. Although she'd yet to meet one of these barbarians face to face, those who had dealt with these men claimed that their greed far outweighed their devotion to God. They were on a holy mission all right, a holy mission to fill their own coffers! She'd use her father's sword and defend Constantinople herself if the western wolves proved foolish enough to attack the city again!

Phaedra tensed. She felt her anger knotting a path across her shoulders and down her back. She lowered her palms to the pebbly blue and green tiles and exhaled a long, deep breath. She willed her thoughts to flow with the gentle waves caressing her body. But her eyes remained cool and focused on the curtain of steam around the pool, as if she expected an armed barbarian to come lumbering through the caladarium at any moment.

Even Poseidon would have been wary of the fierce look in her eyes, but probably not for long. No doubt Poseidon would soon shift his attention to her more comely attributes, like to her mouth, curved full and generous, her eyes, gold like honey, and to her hair, jet-black. Her skin was a pale cream that beckoned to be touched. Even the gentlest caress would have discerned the muscular strength beneath the soft skin.

The silky perfection of her skin was the envy of every sallow, ruddy, olive-skinned woman in Constantinople. Indeed, Phaedra took great pains to protect herself from the sun. But it was her faithful administration of a complexion cream that made her skin appear as if it was eternally lit by the moon. She'd come across the recipe for the cosmetic after her father's death, while going through his papers. She attributed the cream to her mother, Cassandra, whose beauty was said to have rivaled the goddesses of pagan times.

Scented steam weaved fingers around Phaedra's pale, firm limbs, wide shoulders and tapering back. And all the while, she was contemplating the death of a barbarian, a very specific wolf named Bohemund. Twenty-one years had passed since Bohemund had murdered her father. Honor demanded that she avenge his death. Honor demanded that the wolf pay for his deed.

A wanton peal of laughter cut through her thoughts. She slipped down into the water, pushed off from the side and scissored along the bottom of the pool toward the echoes of laughter. She broke through the surface, rising like a sea nymph. She quickly walked to the pool's edge, thinking that there was only one topic that made these women laugh so heartily, and that was men.

Men were all they ever talked about here. It was as if once they shed their clothes, they shed their minds as well. They were naked in the truest sense, for their minds were bare of all intelligent thoughts. The corners of Phaedra's mouth turned down in displeasure as she rested her hands on the pool's cool tile surface.

"Barbarian!" a woman shouted, the word riding high. Phaedra tensed, lifted her head and looked over her shoulder at the laughing bathers.

"Well, you know what they say! That their prowess in battle is matched only by their prowess in bed," said a blonde woman tartly, reclining on the shallow pool's steps.

"They take what they want, when they want it," explained another. "Imagine. A torrid night, better yet, afternoon, between the sheets. Even my lover's appearances are scheduled! As for my husband, he saves his passion for his accounts. He looks at his money the way he used to look at me." She shrugged bitterly.

Someone cleared her throat. A woman with hair the shade of honey dipped her hand into the pool. Phaedra recognized the widow Demetria. Rumor had it that her late husband had encouraged her to make love to other men so that he could watch. Phaedra's gaze swept the pack of naked women, thinking the rumor had probably started here.

One thought triggered another, and feelings caught in Phaedra's throat. She swallowed and blinked. There had also been a rumor about her own husband's death. A year ago, the gossipmongers had feasted on the lie that her husband Jason had died while they were in bed, making love. She felt her heart lurch beneath her breast and tears burn behind her eyes.

Phaedra and Jason would have been married seven years. They'd met in Athens. Jason, a member of the nobility and a scholar, had been searching for ancient scrolls. She'd been deciphering botanical manuscripts that contained formulas for perfumes and cosmetics. She'd been thinking about starting a business, since her inheritance was running out. Had she been a man, she would have joined the empire's elite cavalry unit. However, as that avenue of independence was closed to her, Phaedra had decided to follow in the footsteps of a Byzantine princess who'd actually sold cosmetics through the palace apothecary. The emperor had offered to support Phaedra, but she had graciously declined, wary of giving him power over her life.

But with Jason, there'd never been a question of giving up anything. He was intelligent and witty. He'd never married, having spent too much time away from Constantinople, tracking down scrolls and books. But he'd genuinely loved women. After they'd spent a delicious day and night in bed, Jason had asked her to marry him. He'd called her his "swan."

The memories were all too clear. And painful. Seeking the solace of the quiet water, she let herself sink beneath the surface of the pool. Within a few heartbeats, she rose up again, just in time to hear Demetria's droning, husky voice.

"Imagine feeling those commanding arms around you,"

Demetria said, her lips wrapping around each word as if they were a piece of sugar candy.

"The press of their thighs."

"Judging by their size," rationalized a small girl, "why, they must be . . ." To Phaedra's relief, the girl coughed as if she'd swallowed the wrong way.

"Ummmm." Someone finished for her. "Sweet death."

"They are indeed magnificently figured." The matter-of-fact tone lured Phaedra's attention. She turned to her left. Not far from her sat a silvery-haired matron, her hand clenching her towel close to her thin body, her painted toes submerged in the steamy water.

"Never have I seen such men in the land of the Romans," she said directly to Phaedra. She looked over at the others. "As tall as the emperor's special guards, the Immortals. With great powerful arms and legs. And eyes with the power to strip a woman." At this, the more modest women crossed their arms over their breasts, as if such a man were watching them now.

A tall, voluptuous woman stepped out of the pool. She turned slowly to the bathers, in no hurry to cover the brassy red curls that blanketed her womanhood. "Indulge yourself with your fantasies. I know how it feels to straddle such a man." The women became quiet. Even the water seemed to listen, for not a ripple marred the surface. "I have taken one of the Immortals of the Varangian Guard to my bed."

The women gasped. Phaedra shook her head.

"He touches me with more than his eyes." The redhead grinned lasciviously at the old woman. "Like the Normans, he is descended from the Vikings. And I assure you, such men burn with an unquenchable flame." The woman raised her arms, and allowed a servant to wrap a towel around her.

Lewd questions and answers echoed in the marble pool's grotto as Phaedra climbed out, stepping carefully between outstretched legs. She rolled her eyes at the gluttonous women who greedily consumed the red-haired siren's intimate and explicit tales. These women were the descendants of Christian noblemen, and all they talked about was a man's prowess in bed! Barbarians yet!

Impatiently, she grabbed a towel from an attendant. With it clenched in her hand, she stalked through the archway that led to the tepidarium, passing mosaic walls which depicted the myth of Io, the beautiful daughter of the king of Argos. Fragments of glass, in colors to rival the glory of Eden, formed patterns and shapes. Here was Zeus making love to the beautiful princess. And in a few steps, there he was turning his lover into a cow, so that he could keep his tryst a secret from his wife, Hera. Poor Io was left to fend for herself. She roamed the earth as a cow, forever tormented by a pesky fly which had been sent by the ever-wise, all-seeing wife.

Phaedra flicked her gaze over the mosaics. "Gods and barbarians," she muttered under her breath. "The bane of women's existence!"

Phaedra threw herself upon a cushioned massage table. She lay on her stomach, propped her chin on her hands, and stared at the slick white marble wall before her. She felt warm oil, scented with almonds, trickle down her back, then the even, steady strokes of skillful hands massaging her.

Phaedra felt disdain for the women's talk of virile, handsome barbarians. What fools these women were! The barbarians knew nothing of science or literature, and their ignorance most certainly extended to poets like Homer, dramatists like Euripides and Aristophanes, and the historian Herodotus and geographer Strabo. Had they read Aristotle and Plato? She strongly doubted it. The barbarians were uncivilized. Murderers.

One murderer in particular had stolen his way into her dreams years ago. He was the reason she'd learned how to fight. He was a Titan with a scarred, twisted, sneering face and large, deep-set eyes. His loins were covered with animal skins, and his chest, arms and back were matted with hair like a wolf. He stood, straddling the fallen bodies of men, with a long and wicked sword, dripping blood, raised in his hand. There was treachery and brutality in the very shape and sound of his name . . . Bohemund.

Soon, the barbarian would no longer be a dream, but a beast of flesh and blood. Coldly, she reviewed what the emperor's daughter Anna had recently told her about Bohemund. The barbarian had decided to join other western princes and knights in the march to rescue Jerusalem from the Turkish infidel. And he was due to arrive in Constantinople at the month's end. Why, he was practically being delivered into her hands, Phaedra thought. She would finally get her chance to avenge her father's murder.

Phaedra's lips curled into a smile as dangerous as the cold curve of a scimitar. Her eyes glinted with the faintest hint of a challenge.

Four

The white marble walls and floor of the changing room had a pale pink cast. The room shifted with brilliant colors as newly-arrived patrons removed their silk and woolen tunics. Bathers merged into this shifting sea. Pink, olive and cream-colored, their skin glistened with captured heat and perfumed oils. With the help of attendants, they changed into their garments. Contented sighs mingled with whispers and salutations, marking the ebb and flow of movement.

Phaedra stood before the niche in the wall. Her hair, which had been dried between sheets of silk, was a cloud of curls. With the help of an attendant, she dressed herself in a black silk tunica talaris or undergown. Over this drifted another layer of black, shorter in sleeve and hem length than the tunic, decorated with bands of pearls, as were her black silk slippers.

The attendant was buckling the jeweled belt around Phaedra's waist when a voice rang out.

"Phaedra! Mother of God! You're still wearing black?"

Phaedra looked up and watched a tall woman stride quickly across the changing room, paying no attention to those who had to jump out of her way. Her gold tissue gown was a flame-color that brought out the fire in her sleekly coiled hair.

Kasia was aggressively beautiful, and the royal set of her shoulders and the lift of her chin suggested that she knew it. Her perfect brows arched. "Don't tell me you're practicing for the nunnery?" Her painted mouth curled in amusement.

Without betraying her thoughts, Phaedra smiled. "Hello, Kasia. You're looking extremely satisfied with yourself. Did your jewels triple in value this morning? Or did you just find a great bargain on a big, strapping slave?" Phaedra looked straight into Kasia's eyes. She lifted her long, loose hair as the attendant draped her cloak over her shoulders.

Kasia's nostrils flared as though she were piqued by Phaedra's remark. But those who knew Kasia well, knew it meant she was pleased. Phaedra watched as the slow, luxurious, sphinx-smile Kasia was known for shaped her mouth.

"He's very big," Kasia confided. Her eyes darted about the room to take account of the eavesdroppers pretending not to hear.

"This calls for a celebration!" Phaedra exclaimed as the attendant placed a headband, decorated with dangling silver coins, upon her head. A long veil of white silk hung from the back of the circlet. "I know you've been looking long and hard to find just the right man," she said as she worked the headband down to the middle of her brow. She turned and thanked the attendant for her help.

Kasia rolled her eyes. "Enough about my wickedness. Tell me, when will you start adopting a few bad habits of your own? All this . . . this black." She lifted a fold of black and let it fall. "I think it's time to put these widow's clothes away, Phaedra. Although they highlight the paleness of your skin, and make you look ever so much the wounded swan, enough is enough!"

"Widow." The word brought the memory of her husband's death flooding back. An onslaught of images swept through her, making her senses reel. "Oh, Jason," she thought, closing her eyes.

Phaedra began to move away, the little silver coins tinkling, but Kasia gripped her arm, and said firmly, "It's been over a year." Phaedra turned away and caught a group of women staring at her. However, not one of them was able to look her in the eye. Their focus flew to the floor and ceiling, and to each other. Phaedra returned her attention to the beautiful hand, thin and pale, clutching her black sleeve.

"Thank you, Kasia. I'd forgotten how long it had been," Phaedra answered. Her cynicism controlled the tremors beneath her breast. A tear had the audacity to well in her eye. Phaedra willed it to disappear, but Kasia's sphinx-eyes caught its fragile glimmer.

Kasia let Phaedra go and watched as the black silk figure moved through the corridor and to the door. Then, as if she had thought twice about her actions, Kasia gathered her skirt and followed Phaedra, stopping her at the columned entrance.

"I'm giving a celebration tonight. At my villa."

Phaedra sighed, watching the street before her and the stream of people moving in the shadows cast by the walls of the baths. "Not yet. I can't." She swallowed the knot of grief in her throat and lifted the edge of her veil to conceal her face.

"You can!" Kasia urged. "It's time."

Shaking her head, Phaedra tore herself away.

Kasia tightened her lips in annoyance as she watched Phaedra cross the street. Just as Phaedra began to climb into her chair, an old woman in an ancient but clean gown, approached. Kasia's attention sharpened. A fortune-teller, no doubt, she thought. The city was full of them. So long as they were registered with the city, the authorities left them alone. Kasia's green eyes narrowed suspiciously as the crone reached for Phaedra's hand and raised it, palm up. The fortune-teller scanned the hand briefly before looking into Phaedra's face. Then the old woman did the oddest thing. She bowed her head to Phaedra! As if Phaedra were a queen!

Curious, Kasia gripped the side of the entrance and continued to spy, but nothing happened. The crone said a few words, Kasia couldn't hear them above the noise of the crowd, Phaedra wrenched her hand free, and then turned to

climb into her chair. The crone simply stood in the middle
of the street, nodding like a creature possessed. Then, as if
feeling meddling, intrusive eyes, she turned and caught
Kasia's emerald-bright gaze in her own.

Kasia's eyes flashed, recognizing an opportunity. Without
blinking, she moved into the street and cut a path through
the crowd.

The chairbearers took hold of the poles and lifted the chair
into the air, but Phaedra barely noticed as it rocked slightly
from side to side. The old woman's last words rang in her
mind over and over like a chant: " 'There is no way to escape
your destiny, Dreamer of Dreams. The Dragon draws near.' "

Dreamer of Dreams. Phaedra slumped back against the
pillows. No one had called her that in years. She'd been a
child the last time she'd heard it. And what was this about a
dragon? She pictured the beast portrayed in illuminated
manuscripts, the serpentine trunk and tail, eagle's feet and
wings, lion's forelimbs and head. Was her destiny tied to
this? The image wavered in her mind like a pennant against
the sky, and then it was gone.

"Humph!" She let out an impatient sigh and drove the
name Dreamer of Dreams from her mind. She sat up and
turned slightly to punch a comfortable hollow in the mountain of brocade pillows that supported her back.

She hated being carried about like this, but women of
standing simply did not ride, or walk about the city like men.
Women of gentle birth were sequestered within gilded cages,
hidden behind veils. Always veils. Everywhere veils. They
were another thing she hated. She took a deep breath. At
least her chair was scented. She'd filled the smaller pillows
with dried rosebuds and cedar shavings, so every time she
leaned back, the scent was released into the air.

Phaedra drew back the curtain and peeked out. They were
crossing an open square, the Augusteion. Named by Emperor

Constantine in honor of his mother, the Augusta Helena, it was paved in white marble. It blazed beneath the noonday sun and made everything above it shimmer, from the towering palaces dedicated to God and the emperor, to the colorful crowd. She shifted forward to get a better look, taking care to conceal most of her face. They passed bearded monks lost in their private conversations, mercenary soldiers off duty, and patricians, members of the nobility, in their white and purple robes. A flash of blue silk and a man's face, framed by bushy eyebrows, caught and held her attention. Gabriel. She smiled and dropped the curtain that hid her from view.

The artist Gabriel was known throughout the empire for his mosaics. His brows were just as noteworthy. They were like two little shrubs that had never been pruned. They arched over his brown eyes and were as gray and as thick as his curly hair. His stocky upper body had long since fallen and settled around his middle. He was plump as a partridge and dressed in a blue silk robe with silver trim. Phaedra smiled again. Gabriel was rich now. She'd heard the palace mosaic alone was responsible for netting chests full of gold coins, and he hadn't even completed it yet! It was too crowded and noisy to hear the conversation he was having with the men at his heels, craftsmen and fellow artists probably, but Phaedra imagined it had something to do with mosaics, perhaps the mosaic in the Imperial Palace.

She clutched the side of her chair as it lurched to a stop to let a string of camels pass. As she watched the crowds swallow him up, Phaedra reminded herself to invite Gabriel for dinner. He was one of the few people who had known her since childhood. But it had been months since their last visit, right after Jason's death. "It would be good to see him," she said to herself.

"The shop!" She poked her head out and told the bearers to proceed to her perfume shop, The Swan. But just as she opened her mouth to do so, she changed her mind. She remembered she'd promised Alexander that she would be home in time for the afternoon meal. She smiled at the thought and relaxed against the pillows.

As Jason's adopted son, Alexander was destined to carry on the Ancii name. But he wasn't a son to Phaedra in name only. She'd raised him as if she had been the one to give him the gift of life.

The shop will have to wait, she mused. But as she breathed the sweet fragrance within her closed chair, her thoughts turned to The Swan. After marrying Jason, she had continued to develop fragrances and cosmetics for her own shop. Jason's wealth had provided them with more than enough to live on, so the risk of failing and losing everything she owned had been greatly alleviated. However, she was determined to make The Swan a success. Jason had encouraged her. He had thought highly of her need to challenge herself. And the shop proved to be just that, a challenge. And a very profitable business venture, too. It was known primarily for its fragrances, but its complexion creams and cosmetics were also popular. Both men and women considered these items necessities, items which enhanced a person's looks, or at the very least, gave the illusion of beauty.

Jason had been so proud of her! Alas, by the time she could prove that The Swan was a success, Jason had taken ill. Phaedra nursed him the best she could, following the physician's instructions. She even consulted a herbalist traveling from Cathay. The emperor's own physician attended Jason as well. The emperor thought highly of the noble Ancii and considered him a friend. But the illness caused the virile, potent man to waste away to skin and bones right before her eyes.

Even though he had been 55 to her 25, Jason had never been an old man. He had seen and done things, and had shared it all with her. He had traveled to the most distant mountain peaks to learn the secrets of the land and the sky, and the experience had changed him. It was as if nature had bestowed upon him a crown of white hair to herald his wisdom. He had never considered Phaedra to be anything less than his equal, and he had never backed down from her temper. Her narrowed, flashing eyes had intimidated the manliness out of the younger men, but they had never held him at bay.

Phaedra hugged herself as memories, and the strength of four men, carried her closer to home. They left the marketplace behind and turned into side streets that snaked up and down the hills. It was quieter. The cacophony of noise that accompanied the push and press of merchants, soldiers, citizens, and street vendors leading their animals to market was now just an even lull. Multi-storied houses, with overhanging balconies that jutted out like chins toward their neighbors, shut out the light.

Suddenly, a dark feeling of dread washed over her. She felt hot. She pulled the front of her gown away from her clammy skin, and waved the air before her face with her other hand. Her stomach clenched and rolled. She swallowed and fought the premonition that needled her in the ribs like a bony finger. "I'm just anxious to get out of here," she said to herself, closing her eyes for a moment. When she opened them, she found her vision slightly askew, as if the chair bearers had decided to carry her on her side.

"Christe!" she whispered. "Not now."

As if it had been waiting for this, her acknowledgment of doom, the vision came. And the sounds. She saw riders on horseback, two men with broad backs and heavy shoulders. They were driving their mounts hard. Their thighs and legs seemed to melt into the animals' flesh. Wordlessly, they urged their mounts . . . where? She heard them, the sound of hooves shattering stone. The breathing of the beasts was heavy and thick. Their eyes were dark and wide, bordering on madness. The images cut and flowed, but she never saw the faces of the men.

She couldn't think. All she could do was react. She squeezed her eyes shut and furrowed her brow, as the vision, like a bolt of pain, ripped through her body and drove clear through to her soul. Then, as suddenly as it had started, the vision disappeared. Breathless, Phaedra slumped back into the mound of tasseled pillows.

The fortune-teller. The thought came unbidden. The fortune-teller must have stirred something up.

She felt the chair stop. The squeak of metal gates told her she was home, and she gulped a sigh of relief.

"Mother! Mother!" A boy looked up, jumped from his perch on the rim of a fountain, and ran toward the chair bearers as they moved into a private courtyard. A bear cub, which had been playing beneath the boy's feet, bounded after, whining a gravelly growl.

The boy looked over his shoulder. "Shush, Brutus!"

No sooner had the chair touched the ground than the boy yanked the curtains aside. Phaedra tapped the boy's nose as he poked his head inside her chair.

"Cook made us our favorite!" the boy said in a rush. "Come on! Come on! I'm so hungry I could eat an elephant!"

"Oh, well then . . ." Phaedra laughed, and the darkness that usually followed one of her visions was swept aside by Alexander's excitement.

"Here, let me help," Alexander offered.

"Thank you, Alexander." She stood and bent over to kiss the boy's head. Alexander was tall for a boy of seven. In another few years, Phaedra was sure he would be able to look her right in the eyes. He had hair as black as her own, but his curls were looser and constantly standing every which way on his head. Black brows and long dark lashes framed his large brown eyes. There was a slight hook to his nose and his mouth was rarely still as his thoughts, ideas, and hundreds of questions tumbled out in breathless streams. He was slightly built, but quick and agile. And he rode like a Trojan prince. It was as if the blood of her father, and the heritage of cavalrymen, had somehow been passed through to him.

Phaedra looked at the bear cub rolling at her feet. She knelt gracefully and brushed her hand through the cub's thick and shiny black fur.

"Hello, Brutus." Phaedra had noticed Brutus months ago in an iron-barred cell beneath the Hippodrome, where the bearkeepers sheltered the animals used to entertain the crowds during the chariot races. He had been a runty thing. The bearkeeper could not afford to feed all of the bears in his care. The cub would have died, or been fed to the lions, had Phaedra not taken the animal off the keeper's hands. His large, callused fingers had closed greedily around the gold solidus she had given him for the privilege of rescuing the bear.

She glanced at her personal maid, Helena, but quickly returned her adoring gaze to her son. Phaedra felt Helena frown. The woman could always tell when her mistress had had one of her spells.

"Can we spend the weekend in the country, Mother? Sharif has promised to teach me how to shoot a Turkish bow!"

"The country?" Helena echoed, arching a brow. The ribbons of her braided hair, decorated with ivory and gold beads at the ends, fanned the air as she shook her head. "The country isn't safe with those barbarians lurking about! No place is safe except that which lies protected behind the city gates and walls. The sooner our Emperor Alexius moves them out of Constantinople, the better!"

Alexander scoffed and puffed up his thin chest. "Why, I'll protect you from the barbarians, Helena!" He lunged, attacking an imaginary giant with an imaginary sword.

"Where is Sharif?" Phaedra inquired as she pulled the cloak from her shoulders. Placing it in Helena's waiting arms, Phaedra looked around, her gaze sweeping through the courtyard, over the fountain and the terra cotta pots sprouting plants of basil and mint, past the myrtle tree that stood like a sentinel beside the kitchen door. Out of the corner of her eye, she caught Brutus bounding toward the opened gates.

"Alexander, keep an eye on Brutus."

Alexander heaved a sigh and glanced quickly at the wandering bear. Since Brutus didn't appear to be causing any mischief, Alexander neither moved from his post, nor dropped the subject of his lessons.

"Can we, Mother? You know . . . go to the country?"

The incident with the fortune-teller suddenly crowded in on happier thoughts, and Phaedra automatically nodded. "Yes." She paused. "Maybe a visit would do us all some good." Then she turned to go into the house, but out of the corner of her eye, she caught the bear cub bounding into the street. She wheeled around. "Brutus!"

Alexander turned and sped off after the bear cub. But in that same instant, Phaedra felt the earth begin to tremble. The sensation rippled up from the soles of her feet. In her next breath, she heard the thundering clatter of hooves on stone and sensed the mighty weight of the beasts drawing closer and closer. She froze, stilled by an image that suddenly flashed before her eyes. "Mother of God!"

Within heartbeats, the startled whinnying of a horse jarred Phaedra into action. "Alex!" She ran toward the gates, her white veil flying behind her. She slid to a halt, clutching the iron gate to keep from falling, her eyes riveted on a black stallion with iron-shod hooves, which glinted like dagger blades, striking dangerously close to the bear cub. But Brutus stood his ground. His head was thrown back in a fearsome gesture and he was growling heroically, sharpening his claws on the air. Alexander, who stood still as stone, simply stared up at the horse, but Phaedra saw the look of intent in the boy's eyes. Were he to rush at the bear now, the excited animal would rip him apart with his claws.

Phaedra knew that if she called out to Alexander, she might further alarm the animals. She cast a quick glance at the horses and their riders. One look told her that the man on the black horse was a Greek cavalry officer. She could tell from his steel cap, with its stiff crest of feathers, and his yellow cloak. She couldn't see the other rider who was mounted on a white horse—she could only sense his presence. It was the rider before her, on the black horse, who alarmed her. Although his face seemed familiar to her, she knew by the murderous glint in his eyes that he saw no one, nothing, save the bear cub.

The man pulled back hard on the reins. His legs squeezed the sweating flanks and brought the beast buckling to submission. The horse danced back, away from the bear and boy. It snorted and reared again before heeding the yank of the reins.

Now the Greek pulled a whip from his saddle. Phaedra took a step toward Alexander to bring him back to safety, but then she glimpsed the weapon coiled in the rider's hand. His gaze was locked on the bear. He brought his arm back to deliver a blow, but just as his arm arched, the rider on the other horse moved to stop him.

It was Phaedra's chance. She dashed to Alexander and threw her body between the boy, the bear and the horse. The whip ripped down with a lightning crack and caught her on the arm.

"Mama!" Alexander shrieked.

Phaedra lurched back. A bolt of pain tore up her arm. She looked at her sleeve. The whip had reached out like a talon, tearing the fabric to shreds. A crooked red gash ran the length of her forearm.

Gritting her teeth against the throbbing pain and cradling her arm, she cocked her head in a gesture that ordered Alexander to move toward the gate. Her eyes followed him as he flew to safety. Brutus bounded after him.

When they were safe behind the gate, Phaedra turned her attention to the riders and stormed toward them. Her narrowed eyes blazed with fury.

"Damn you to hell! What business do you have riding as

though this street were your own personal racecourse! And how dare you raise your whip to a citizen of this city!" She could feel the heat flooding her face. "Get off your mount," she yelled at the man, swinging her arm down at her side for emphasis. "Explain yourself to me!"

"Phaedra?" The man's voice was very gentle. The Greek coiled the whip around the pommel of his saddle, then jumped to the ground. He removed his helmet and, tucking it beneath his arm, approached Phaedra. She clenched her jaw at the sight of the man approaching her. He was tall, swarthy, with black curly hair and deep-set black eyes.

"How dare you!" Something slammed shut in her eyes. Her body remained taut, ready to inflict the first blow if Strategus Vinicius Maximus so much as stepped too close.

The man wasn't stupid. He read the look in her eyes and lurched to a halt a full two arms' lengths away. It was as if she'd magically erected a wall between them.

He bowed. "My apologies. But the bear frightened my horse."

"A bear cub," she corrected, "scared your great war horse?" She looked at the black beast, standing still, his reins in the other rider's hands. For the first time, she looked at the man who had ridden at Vinicius's side like a dog out of hell.

But all she could see were his eyes. His head was wrapped like an Arab's in a drab brown headcloth, and he had one end pulled across his face, concealing his nose and mouth. His eyes, however, were a deep blue.

Phaedra and the rider's eyes met and held. For a dizzying moment, she had the distinct feeling that she knew who he was, or, at least, knew of him. The memory of a dream flickered in her mind. And then it was gone.

The rider, too, continued to stare. For a brief moment, he cut his gaze to Vinicius, and seemed to measure the distance between man and woman. Then he returned his attention to Phaedra, catching her gaze just as she was about to look away. Fine lines appeared at the corners of his eyes as if he were smiling.

Phaedra felt the presence of his smile behind the cloth. She caught the judgmental look he gave Vinicius and now she was certain the man was looking at her differently, appraising her. Without looking away, she reached for the veil so she could cover her face, but his bold gaze seemed to take such delight in her modest reaction that, out of spite, she let the veil slip between her fingers. Go ahead and look, she thought as she tilted her chin up.

Hearing Sharif's heavy gait behind her, Phaedra looked away and found her friend posed in an intimidating stance that was all chest and chin. She forgot the stranger.

"Sharif! Everything's all right," she said. She looked back at Vinicius and nailed him with her gaze. The man shifted his weight from one foot to the other.

"Seems Vinicius and his friend think they own the streets of Constantinople," she muttered under her breath. "As they are wont to race through them and trample everything that crosses their path."

"Again, my apologies, dear lady," Vinicius said, bowing low. His eyes lingered on the bloody arm of Phaedra's gown. He frowned. "But we are on imperial business."

The Greek looked back at the mounted rider and, lifting his arm in a grand gesture, explained, "Brannoc was sent ahead of his lord's army to prepare for a meeting with Emperor Alexius." Vinicius turned back to Phaedra and lowered his voice to a whisper. "A barbarian! But, believe it or not, this fellow speaks Greek."

Phaedra looked up at the barbarian, taking care not to meet his gaze.

Vinicius continued. "How barbaric can he be, eh? Perhaps I can convince him to fight for our emperor?"

"If it's official business you're on," boomed Sharif, "then you'd best be on your way, General." Sharif drew his eyebrows together and glowered until Vinicius began to move away.

Vinicius bowed again, then took his leave. After accepting the reins from the barbarian, he rose into his saddle. "Lady," he said, and he lifted his arm in salute. At Phaedra's nod, the Greek dug his heels into the horse's flanks, and both riders started off at a trot. But as the barbarian passed, Phaedra caught the glint of silver spurs. Whoever he was, the man was a knight. Phaedra shook her head. Why was he trying to pass himself off as an Arab?

She felt Sharif's hand on her shoulder and turned away from the riders to go inside the courtyard. She winced, reaching for the iron gate, and paused for a moment. She realized the vision had come true. Two riders had ridden through the street. Only now she knew their faces, Vinicius and the man with the blue eyes, the one the general had called Brannoc.

What did they have to do with her? She looked up at the black gate, her gold eyes searching the arabesque decorations as if the answer were hidden within the curls and arcs of metal.

"The Dragon."

Phaedra turned sharply, looking for the fortune-teller, for it was the old woman's voice! But there was no one standing in the courtyard with her. She felt a fluttering in her stomach, but she chose to ignore it. Clenching her jaw, she slammed the metal gates closed. A bone-jarring clang echoed. It could have awakened the dead.

Alexander was determined to beat Sharif at backgammon. The boy's eyes were locked on the leather board. They were playing in the villa's central courtyard, in a garden open to the sky. Its boundaries were lined by white marble columns on all four sides. The tinkling music of the fountain and the steady whine of the spinning wheel beneath the portico were the only sounds to be heard.

Leaning against a cool marble column, arms lightly crossed over her chest, Phaedra watched the players in silence. Her wounded arm, dressed with a healing salve and bandages, throbbed steadily, but the ache was not enough to kill her pleasure. She noted the humorous gleam in Sharif's brown eyes as they contemplated his serious opponent.

Alexander was sitting just like Sharif, hunched over the table, his hands clasped together, elbows resting on his knees. Phaedra could read how grown-up her son was just by the way he sat. This was not a fidgety boy who bit his nails. This was a man. Even his mouth had lost its boyish sweetness. Phaedra saw the sardonic curl at the corner of his lips suggesting he took secret delight in plotting the defeat of his opponent. She'd seen that look on grown men, warriors on the field.

Phaedra arched her brows and took a deep breath. In the blink of an eye, Alexander had become a man, or so it seemed to her. How could it be? She searched her memory for other clues, moments when she had sensed the man within.

After Alexander's roll of the dice, he turned to her, knowing she was there, and flashed her a grin of such uncontainable joy, she knew the boy within was still the master. He had been trying on a new role, as if it were a new tunic. The boy turned back to his game.

Phaedra glanced up. The heat of the setting sun was tinging the sky orange-red. She bit her lip. In a few hours, Kasia's guests would be gathering at her villa. "Should I go?" Phaedra asked herself.

Recalling the package that one of Kasia's slaves had delivered that afternoon, Phaedra turned away from the players, and walked into the hall. Its walls were an earthy red, accented by a border of black and white tiles in a Greek key pattern. The floor was white marble, the ceiling gilded gold. Cedar doors on her left opened onto the tricilinium, the dining room. She moved past the entry and didn't stop until she came to the exedra, her office.

Books and rolled maps from her father's library lined the office walls. The only other visible reminder of her father was a leopard skin which commanded the white wall behind her desk. Phaedra knew the skin made visitors uncomfortable. It made people think The Leopard was right there in the room, watching them.

Cradling her wounded arm, she moved soundlessly across the hall. She proceeded to climb a stairway which led to and opened onto another hall, lined with sleeping chambers.

Phaedra closed the door to her sleeping chamber, leaned against it, and stared at the white canvas package. It was on her bed, which was set upon a dais and covered in cream-colored silk. Ivory drapes adorned with pearls hung loosely at the bed's four corners.

Knowing Kasia, anything could be in the package, she thought. She crossed the room, her black tunic trailing over the white and cream tiles of the mosaic floor. In the corner stood a tripod floor lamp of black metal and brass. A little bronze brazier was posed on the floor next to the bed.

Jason had chosen the ivory and cream colors to set off Phaedra's beauty. "The Swan," he called her. Many artistic interpretations of this graceful bird graced the villa. However, none approached the splendor of the fresco which commanded the wall facing the bed. The fresco had been a wedding present from husband to wife. An artist from Alexandria had captured the Greek myth of Leda And The Swan. It portrayed Zeus disguised as a swan with wings raised in majesty, black eyes gazing down at the beauty Leda on a bed of green earth. Her arms were curved away from her naked body in a yielding display of active desire. Her hair, black as night, rippled as if in a breeze created by the movement of wings.

Phaedra opened the package, peeling away the wrapping to see what Kasia had on her mind. Finished, Phaedra knotted her brow and twisted her mouth. A square of white fabric lay on the bed. Phaedra touched it. The silk was more air than cloth, as if it had been spun by dream weavers. Delicately, she lifted it. It was a pleated gown of some ancient Greek design, created from a silk so fine it was sheer.

"Is Kasia's gathering just a prelude to a Greek love orgy? Or am I to play the sacrificial virgin?" she said out loud, shaking her head. She held the sheer garment out at arm's length. "For a private evening of seduction, perhaps. But a feast?"

Phaedra knew that only Kasia would be so bold as to appear in public in such a thing! She snorted. "The woman thinks I have nothing to wear. Thinks I'd show up in black. I should! Just to spite—" Phaedra stopped in mid-sentence. By God, Kasia had done it! Phaedra didn't know when she'd decided to attend Kasia's banquet, but it was obvious that she had made a decision.

Phaedra wrinkled her mouth in ill humor. She felt as if the swan were watching her. She turned to the fresco and, lifting the gown, asked, "What do you think?" She cocked her head as if she were expecting an answer. "Might as well attend naked? Yes, I see your point."

She spread her fingers and let the fabric slip onto the bed. She vowed she would render Kasia speechless before the night was over.

Five

Kasia's pursed lips broke into a slow, silky smile as she watched Phaedra emerge from her carriage. The light of the new moon illuminated all. Phaedra wore a close-fitting, hip-length tunic of pleated pomegranate silk that melted into a skirt. The round neckline and the hem were embroidered with gold thread. Her ebony hair was pulled away from her face with gold combs and left to run down her back. Her belt, a gold design as delicate as cobwebs, closed with a buckle etched with the outline of a swan caught in flight.

The moon revealed the frown lines around Sharif's mouth (he had insisted on escorting her this evening), and the eagle look in his eyes as he studied everyone who approached the villa. An air of controlled panic surrounded Helena who had also refused to let Phaedra travel alone at night. Unlike the Church's patriarchs, Helena didn't believe that widows should go so far as to renounce earthly desires and offer their lives to Christ. However, Kasia had a reputation as a courtesan and a spy for the emperor, and the maid hoped that Phaedra knew what she was doing. Leaning out of the carriage, her brow creased with worry lines, Helena watched her mistress enter the villa. As she turned away, Helena caught Sharif's disapproving glance. She moved her lips in a prayer and yanked the chair's curtains closed. They would remain here until Phaedra was ready to leave. Sharif's orders.

Kasia's servant helped Phaedra remove the cloak draped

loosely over her shoulders. Kasia approached, arms extended for an embrace. "Although widow's black becomes you, tonight's garments set you afire," she pronounced appreciatively. Kasia looked Phaedra up and down. The transformation from widow to temptress took Kasia's breath away. Like the sun and the moon, Phaedra was just as unattainable, Kasia sighed to herself. But already she could sense the men readying themselves for the chase.

"I want you to keep the white silk I sent," Kasia commanded. "Consider it a gift."

Phaedra fought the smirk that threatened to break her composed expression. She cast a casual glance over Kasia's costume. The woman was wearing a sheath of gold silk so sheer that the rouged rose of her nipples could be seen by even those with failing vision. A gold belt, slung around her hips, flashed with amethysts and emeralds. Her arms were bare and her hair was gathered loosely in a serpentine curl, laced with strands of ivy and olive leaves.

Kasia led her friend to a couch, where a senator and a mercenary from the elite Varangian Guard sat. Phaedra assumed the large warrior was Kasia's latest lover. She smiled and sat down, making herself comfortable.

Turning, Phaedra saw Vinicius. He cleared his throat and said as if by way of introduction for all to hear, "This is Sir Brannoc. Watch what you say. The man knows Greek better than I."

The blue eyes held Phaedra and, for a moment, she felt cut off from everyone in the room. She knew who he was. This was the man who had ridden at Vinicius's side earlier that day. He'd had his head and face covered with a headcloth, like an Arab. She saw the glimmer of recognition in his piercing gaze and felt her heartbeat quicken.

He looked away, then back at her again. Her golden eyes were fixed on him. His eyes lingered, as if to savor the way she looked and commit the sight to memory. She sat straight as a queen, her legs curled on the couch, her elbow resting on the couch's curved arm. In the light, her skin looked as pale a pearl, which the burning hues of her dress accentuated. For a moment, he delighted in her throat, the long, proud line and the way the jewels and gold beads of her earrings brushed her collarbone.

He parted his lips and drew a shallow breath. Her mouth held him now, and the look about his eyes softened as if the thought of tracing her mouth and kissing her had suddenly crossed his mind. She took a startled breath.

"Sir Brannoc? Why don't you sit . . ." Kasia caught the warning scowl on the Varangian's face, ". . . next to the Lady Ancii." Kasia pointed at the empty place besides Phaedra. "And Vinicius, you'll sit here, to my left." She leaned over and patted the senator's arm. "I hope you don't mind sharing your couch with the empire's most noble young general." The senator reluctantly made room. "I'll introduce you to everyone later. I'm starving," Kasia announced, her eyes following Brannoc as if he were a platter piled high with all her favorite meats.

For fear of appearing rude, Phaedra didn't want to alter her position on the divan. Only, he was so large, she felt he would need the space. But as she began to curl her legs in, he said, "Please, don't move on my account. You look so comfortable."

She noted that across the table, the poet's attention had been captured as well. It was Brannoc's voice, warm, deep and paved with a resonance that a poet could appreciate. It made her think of lazy mornings and weathered bronze. He spoke with an accent, but his Greek was flawless. As he sat down, servants appeared to fill his cup.

"I apologize for this afternoon. You're all right?" he inquired politely, his eyes on the goblet, his finger circling the wet base.

"Yes," she answered. Her eyes settled on his hand, large and pale bronze from the sun. Her brows drew together in curiosity at the blue tattoo which encircled his wrist. She couldn't tell what it was.

"And the boy? The bear?"

"Fine." She raised her face to him. He had a handsome face, chiseled and lined, with a strong sensual mouth.

"A bear's an unusual pet for a city dweller."

Her eyes flickered at the unexpectedness of his statement, but she answered readily enough. "The bear keeper would have killed him."

"Aahh, you have a soft spot for animals." The crinkling around his eyes told her he was amused.

"Some animals," she answered huskily.

She looked away and caught Vinicius watching them. She lowered her gaze to her plate.

"The Greeks think these pilgrims and princes marching to save Jerusalem are barbarians, no better than animals. Am I correct?"

Her brows rose a trifle. The shift in mood caught Phaedra unaware. Without moving her head, she glanced at Brannoc out of the corner of her eye, then looked over her shoulder, away from him, hoping to catch a servant's attention.

But Brannoc was not to be put off. "Would you save these poor western pilgrims?" he pressed.

Phaedra sat perfectly still, then looked at him directly. There was no laughter in his face now. "You seem to have little regard for our emperor Alexius, who is directing this campaign against the Turkish infidel. And none at all for Constantinople's citizens."

"True."

"Then why are you here?"

"The women of Constantinople are reported to be the most beautiful of all." He watched her arch her brow cynically. "I wanted to see for myself."

Phaedra pulled away slightly and stiffened against the back of the couch. Brannoc smiled to himself and watched her toy with her earring.

"And they all smell like flowers," he said, his rich, deep

voice like music. "Why, Constantinople must be the Garden
of Eden!"

Phaedra reached for her goblet. She was just about to take
a drink when he said, "And you are jasmine."

Her lips froze against the rim of her cup. He continued.

"The Hindus call it 'Moonlight of the Grove.' Arab men
don't trust women who wear jasmine."

Phaedra caught his cool blue gaze over the rim of her cup.
Then he turned his attention to the servant who was holding
forth a platter of grilled scallops. She sipped her wine.

Phaedra straightened and blinked as if she'd been forcibly
awakened from a deep sleep. She started to push a wayward
curl from her face. That's odd, she thought. At first she
couldn't put her finger on it. Suddenly, she felt as if she were
being borne into the air.

In a corner of her mind, Phaedra knew she wasn't really
flying, and that thanks to the wine, she was imagining the
whole thing. But she didn't want the feeling to end. What if
she had the power to alter her shape?

"Christe!" she swore in her next breath. The thought frightened her. She'd rather face ten men in battle than have that kind
of power. She felt a chill creep under her skin and closed her
eyes against the dizzy spell that was making her senses spin.

A sweeping rush of sound, like great wings, caused her
to open her eyes again. She gasped in disbelief, for not only
was she high above the table, but gathered beneath her were
animals, sitting where the guests had been!

She heard her heart pounding like a drum, and she had
the vague sensation that her limbs were not quite her own,
but she paid the feeling no mind, as it took all her concentration not to take flight from the scene beneath her.

Kasia was no longer Kasia, but a brown asp, with flicking
tongue and large luminous eyes. And she was coiled within
the olive branch wreath. The Varangian had been transformed
too, but he was a lion. She gazed in wonder at all the other
beasts: a bear, horse, pig and cow. Vinicius was a hawk, the

senator an ass. The only guest unchanged was the fortune-teller!

Brannoc. The name slipped into her mind and crouched there. Hesitantly, she looked. Her eyes widened in terror as they settled on the beast sitting in Brannoc's place. *It was a dragon,* a great winged beast breathing smoke. As if knowing that he was being watched, the dragon looked from side to side, then up at the ceiling. For a heartbeat, she felt as if she were spiraling down to come face to face with the beast. She heard a scream, but didn't realize that it had escaped her lips.

In the next instant, Phaedra felt hands shaking her. She jumped and realized Brannoc was holding her up by her shoulders. Brannoc. Not the dragon.

Brannoc tightened his grip around her arms, as if he could sense her knees turning to water. "I have you. You're safe," he reassured her in his deep, commanding voice. However, his eyes were alight with worry. All the blood seemed to have drained from her face, giving her a deathly pallor.

"The night air will do her good," said the fortune-teller. "Air and moonlight is what she needs."

As if the old woman had taken her by the hand, Phaedra turned and walked quietly away from the table. Like winged Mercury, Vinicius went to her, reaching her side with lightning agility, catching Phaedra at the dining room's entrance. He put his arm around her shoulder and led her away.

In the mosaic-tiled hall, Phaedra squirmed away from Vinicius's touch and moved quickly into the courtyard, her skirt rippling soundlessly in her wake. The general ignored her rebuff and pursued her into the night.

"Are you all right, Phaedra? What happened in there?"

"I'm fine," she mumbled. Chilled, she hugged her arms to her chest. She looked around. Kasia's garden was built over a series of terraces overlooking the sea. Torches illuminated the trees and descending walkways. The breeze carried the sweet scent of night-blooming lilies.

A shiver danced up her spine. What's happening to me,

she asked herself. Now I'm seeing animals, dragons, yet. One would think I was some strange hermit who had nothing but rocks for company!

Poised at the top of a short flight of stairs, Phaedra took a deep breath, closed her eyes and ordered the animal image lingering in her head to leave her in peace. But the dragon was as finely etched in her mind as if it had been sketched by an artist with an eye for detail. Lifting her skirts, she flew down the stairs.

"You really shouldn't scare people like that!" Vinicius's voice followed her. "It makes people talk. As it is, people already think—" He caught himself and stopped.

Phaedra's black brows arched. Twisting the silk skirt between her fingers, she turned at the bottom of the stairs to look up at him. Does he know about my visions, she wondered. Feigned curiosity was reflected in her eyes. "What are people thinking, Vinicius?" she inquired.

Now that he had finally captured her attention, Vinicius descended the stairs slowly, all the while studying her in the moonlight. He noticed how the gold combs had loosened, and now hung in her tangled hair. Her skin was pale, but there was a faint blush of color on her cheeks, and her lips were deep red, as if she'd bitten them.

She studied him carefully, too. She and Vinicius had known each other since they were young. Their families had owned neighboring estates in the country, and they'd been childhood enemies. He'd grown into a handsome man. He was tall, with black curly hair, a long, straight nose, and a piercing gaze. She knew there were plenty of women eager to wed him, that all he had to do was crook his little finger and they would drop themselves into his life.

He stopped before her and crossed his arms over his chest. He loomed above her. She had the impression that he loved to stand over women.

"What are they thinking? They think you have . . . powers," Vinicius said. "And that you've created magic potions for your fragrances, because the scents make men behave like love-sick fools."

"Humph! How imaginative to blame men's bumbling ways on a fragrance," she mocked, although to herself she was breathing a great sigh of relief that he hadn't mentioned her dreams. "Tell me, these people . . . are they not also afraid of their own shadows?"

She turned her back on him to continue on her way. A pensive reflection dulled her eyes momentarily. Magic? Potions? She was drifting into dangerous waters. It was one thing to be thought of as a crazy old crone who told fortunes, but quite another thing to be a member of the nobility accused of following the old, pagan ways. She could lose everything, she could lose Alexander.

"No. Never. I can protect myself," she said under her breath. She followed the pebbled walkway across the terrace.

"Don't you think you should be concerned?" Phaedra didn't stop, but shook her head. "They're saying it's the work of the devil."

She snorted a laugh to prove she was mildly amused. But as she continued on her way, removing the gold combs from her hair, her thoughts turned to another matter, Brannoc and the dragon.

Phaedra shook out her hair. There was only one thing on her mind, one matter she wished to discuss. Spying a stone bench set within a copse of yews and myrtles, Phaedra moved toward it and sat down, making sure Vinicius could see her, hoping he would follow.

She heard the brush of Vinicius's heavy step on the gravel walk and waited, looking out over the sea.

The general stopped in front of her and leaned casually against the marble rail, blocking Phaedra's view. She took her time to meet his gaze. Slowly, she lifted her eyes from his sword belt to his flat belly, then up to his chest and shoulders, muscular from years of fighting and handling horses. Finally, her gold eyes met his. He grinned.

Keeping her voice low, she asked, "Tell me about this barbarian . . . Brannoc."

Vinicius flinched. "Brannoc?" He looked at her closely and furrowed his brow, wondering why she was interested. She didn't have that moonsick look on her face, an expression that would have told him that she thought the barbarian handsome, so he decided her interest was not of a romantic nature.

Phaedra leaned forward. "He's a knight. That much I know."

Vinicius sat down next to her. "The man's a born warrior, a beast from what I hear."

"A beast?"

Vinicius nodded.

A beast with a keen sense of smell, Phaedra thought, recalling how he'd recognized her fragrance.

"Claims he's Welsh, but he's been fighting the Moors in Spain," Vinicius continued. "Now there's a story about how that all came about, but he hasn't told me yet. He followed a war leader named Roderigo del Bivar, El Cid to the Arabs. Perhaps you've heard of him?" Phaedra shook her head. "No? Well, he's become somewhat of a hero in his lands. But, anyway, Brannoc and El Cid parted company a year ago. Brannoc joined up with another Christian knight."

Phaedra looked up at the moon. "He speaks passable Greek for a beast. Where do you think he learned?"

"I don't know. I've also heard him speak in the Arabic tongue."

She cocked her head, turning to look at him. "Then he's obviously spent time in the courts of the Arab caliphs, not a far-fetched idea, considering the Arabs have held Southern Spain for over 350 years." She paused. "Welsh? Spaniard? Arab? Who is he?"

Vinicius scrunched his brow in thought. "There's something about him . . ." He paused, caught up in his private thoughts. "It's as if Brannoc could read another man's mind just by looking into his eyes. In other words, he's a dangerous man." He shrugged. "Maybe it's nothing. He's good with horses, though. And his animal's a beauty."

"Arabian," Phaedra said matter-of-factly, remembering the white stallion.

"Yes." He looked at her with admiration in his eyes. He didn't know many women who could tell one breed of horse from another. Wary of his next impulse, he rose quickly to his feet and walked away from his post by the rail, brushing his hand against the leaves on the trees.

"Now, if you ask my men, they'll tell you that he's a sorcerer."

Phaedra's attention sharpened. She looked over her shoulder at him. "Why would they say that?"

"His wrists." He caught the question in her eyes. "Haven't you noticed? Around each wrist is the tattoo of a serpent, or maybe it's a dragon, for the creature has wings."

The Dragon. Phaedra exhaled a long breath and turned back to face the sea. Was Brannoc the Dragon in the fortune-teller's prophecy?

"What is it?" Vinicius asked.

She shook her head. She couldn't bring herself to look at him for fear she'd give herself away. She tightened her fingers around her combs until the points dug into her palms.

"Phaedra?"

She didn't look.

"The man serves—" he paused. "Bohemund."

Her heart stopped. She straightened, a part of her wondering if she'd heard correctly. "Bohemund?" she echoed.

"Yes."

Anger blazed beneath her breast as readily as if she'd just drawn a sword in her hand. Her muscles tensed, hearing a dark call to action. And all thoughts of dragons, visions, and the mutterings of the fortune-teller vanished like puffs of smoke.

Her throat tightened. She caught Vinicius's knowing stare.

Like most citizens of the empire, he knew how her father had died. How could anyone forget when "The Song of the Leopard," sung in taverns from Salonika to Jaffa, kept the story alive?

Phaedra's expression was calm. Bathed in the moonlight, her face was as pale and quiet as a deathmask. There was no hint of her passion for vengeance, no clue that she'd kept the fire of revenge burning in her belly for over twenty years. Without saying a word, she rose to her feet and looked out over the water and the silvery pattern of moonlight upon it. The surface seemed to twist from side to side, as if a great beast were moving just beneath. She permitted a thought to wash over her: There is no way to escape your destiny, Dreamer of Dreams. The Dragon draws near.

"The Dragon *is* here," she said to herself. "And he will take me to Bohemund. It is our destiny!"

Six

Constantinople. She was older than Troy. A city poised on a cliff. The center of the east-west caravan routes, famous for her silks, spices, gold, jewels and perfumes.

Byzantium's backbone was its center of trade, a market that stretched along the city's natural spine and built along the Mesê, the great Middle Street. Like a string of Indian pearls, shops like The Swan decorated the Mese. The street was as broad as a parade ground, broken by squares containing statues of emperors and empresses. It stretched from the Bronze Gate that led into the Palace, down the heart of the city, away to the north to the mainland.

The shops were set within colonnades of white marble. By royal decree, the perfumers' shops were allowed the most prominent locations in the Augusteion Square, close to the Imperial Palace, so their fragrances could sweeten the air.

A mosaic of a white swan identified Lady Ancii's shop from the other perfumers set beneath the marble portico. It was mid day. The smell of the salt sea drifted on a breeze.

Inside The Swan, the cool, dim light brought relief from the sun. Women in silk browsed among the displays of cosmetic brushes, kohl-sticks and hair pomades in squat terra-cotta jars. Those who had come to purchase the famous perfumes waited patiently for assistance. There was no rush. The air was lush with the promise of heightened beauty. As the shopkeeper and his son dabbed the fragrant oils on their customers' wrists, scents escaped into the air, creating an earthly paradise.

As befitted this temple, father and son spoke in hushed, reverent tones that suggested all women were queens. They moved in front of tall cedar shelves which lined the walls bearing glass, alabaster and onyx flasks. Here was The Swan's treasure, perfumes, scented oils and unguents that flooded the shop with customers from as far away as Cathay.

Phaedra was sequestered off in a back room, hidden behind a blue curtain. Dressed in her black tunica, she sat at a cedar table, staring at the bronze shell she used for mixing. It was empty.

Before dawn had risen, Phaedra had left home for this room, her sanctuary. Her complexion was paler than usual, more luminous without the tints from cosmetics. Her hair was a wild tangle, a curtain of black.

Around the room stood large earthenware jars filled with almond and sesame oils. The light from a wall sconce barely touched a spider spinning in a corner near the table's edge. Phaedra watched the spider work, her thoughts spinning fragrances, old and new, out of air.

She stopped. Pagan Desires. Brannoc.

The two thoughts, side by side, brought a smile to her lips, though it held no mirth. The perfume and the barbarian. They were connected, woven together. She could feel it in her bones.

She sat up with a start, thinking the light had grown brighter. A plan, fully grown, came to her. What better way to beguile a man from his allegiance to his lord than by having him fall madly in love with you? Use Pagan Desires to bind the Dragon to you! Ensnare him and he will open the door for you to destroy Bohemund.

If any of Phaedra's scents were "magical," it was Pagan Desires. It was inspired by a blend she'd found in her mother's book of herbs. Written on parchment leaves in Cassandra's hand were blends descended from her mother and all the women before her. One of the fragrances was said to have originated with Helen, Queen of Troy.

Had Helen worn it the day Paris kidnapped her, Phaedra wondered? Had the Trojan War been launched over a woman because of her perfume? Of course, Helen had been golden-haired and beautiful. "Helen of the white arms," was how Homer had described the princess. Scented from head to toe, such a woman must have been irresistible.

Phaedra was fingering the bronze shell when she caught her reflection. Her dark hair, large eyes and full mouth. She didn't think she was beautiful, like Homer's fair Helen, but perhaps Pagan Desires would give her the illusion of being a great beauty.

No, she believed in Pagan Desires and the mantle of magic it wove around all those who wore it. She'd known Pagan Desires was unlike any other scent the moment she created it. One month after Jason's death, she'd locked herself in her workroom at her villa in the country. Working with her oils, she'd felt as if someone had been guiding her hands, her thoughts, her senses. Pagan Desires wasn't as provocative and forward as the others. Its intent went deeper, to the soul. At the heart of its essence was a yearning, a longing for something Phaedra hadn't been able to put into words.

Perhaps it was a love potion, she mused, recalling Vinicius's comment from the evening past. And for a moment, she let herself believe that her perfumes were as powerful as Vinicius had suggested. Somehow, she had to make Brannoc fall in love with her. She needed to play Helen of Troy. After all, this was a war, of sorts. But unlike Helen, Phaedra planned for this battle to be waged at home, in Constantinople.

Phaedra pushed her hair behind her ears, then reached across the table to a jewelry box. She'd bought it from a monk who had boasted about its sanctity, claiming it had held a finger bone of St. Agnes. Phaedra had found the box beautiful and the bone about as saintly as a chicken's. Now, using a key which hung from a gold mesh belt around her waist, she opened the lock and removed a small journal. It was her mother's herbal notebook. Closing her eyes, she breathed in the scent of the mother she never knew, almonds and vanilla, two of the ingredients found in her mother's famous complexion cream. The journal was no bigger than her hand. The leather cover was worn at the edges, softened by time.

Phaedra raised the journal to her lips and kissed it. Reverently, she placed it on the table and opened it to the first page. She brushed her fingertips across her mother's handwriting:

> What is real is not only what we see on the surface—
> there is the magical as well.
>
> > C. Acominatus

> The soul of man in love is full of perfumes and sweet odors.
>
> > Plutarch

> I am the rose of Sharon,
> and the lily of the valleys.
> > The Song of Solomon

These were Phaedra's prayers. Every time she set to work, she recited these words like a special incantation. Unseen treasures were hidden within the pages of this book. Phaedra bowed her head to the power and creativity of her mother and the women who had come before her.

As she turned the pages, Phaedra could not help noting that she was running out of some of these ingredients. There were oils she could create herself, but the cinnamon from India, myrrh, saffron and aloes were running low. Caravans from Arabia and the lands of the Euphrates had been disrupted by the Seljuk Turks, and those that made it to Constantinople were commanding exorbitant prices for their very precious cargo. The coming war with the Turks some were calling The Crusade, for possession of Jerusalem, would tip the balance even further. The Crusade would make it even harder for her to replenish her supplies. What was she going to do?

"Ahhh, dear Lady. Welcome to The Swan." Simon's booming voice caught Phaedra by surprise. Her gaze flew to the heavy curtain that guarded the room's entrance. Why was he talking so loudly?

"You seek the fragrance your friends call Athena? Yes, of course we have it!"

Phaedra laughed. She had been contemplating a new formula for Athena, since the violet scent was not completely to her liking. But Simon had insisted that it was popular. He claimed it reminded women, the matrons especially, of their youth and young loves.

Phaedra shrugged. Simon knew more about women than she would ever know in three lifetimes. A small man with a wizened face and piercing black eyes, Simon could tell what fragrance a woman would buy the moment she stepped over the threshold. His son, a delicately boned youth with ink black hair and his father's eyes, was not yet his father's equal in this respect, but he showed promise.

Phaedra locked the herbal notebook away and stood up to leave. While rising, she noted a change in the air. She scrunched her nose and sniffed. It was a smell charged with elements—earth, wind, animal and water. It was the scent of a coming storm.

"Hold! You there!" Simon shouted. "Just what—"

In the next instant, a sword point jabbed through the curtain. She jumped back as the blade ripped the cloth with a long hissing sound, revealing a giant barbarian. He stood, sword in hand, staring at her. He was wearing the red cross of the west.

She grimaced. The man's face was brutally ugly. A mass of puckered, scarred flesh marked the site of one eye. Another scar twisted his mouth into a permanent sneer. Obviously pleased by her reaction, he smiled. The look on his face grew more frightening.

"Christ! Another one!" Simon shouted. The barbarian didn't turn around, but continued leering at Phaedra.

"You're frightening my customers!" As if she were used to such inconvenient disturbances, Phaedra swept past him.

Out in the shop, she stopped short, seeing that the man had company. There were four more barbarians. They reminded her of bulls sharing a cramped pen, their muscles straining from holding back their charging energy. The shop's customers had backed up against the wall.

Phaedra caught Simon's eye and took a deep breath. Every day since the western armies' arrival, groups of barbarians had been invading the city on sight-seeing ventures. The emperor only permitted a handful of them at any one time to enter the city without a Byzantine escort.

Regardless of their number, they wreaked havoc everywhere they went. At The Swan, the number of destroyed perfume flasks was up to six. Precious oils and their glass containers damaged due to the clumsy handling by the oafish barbarians. She now saw the number was about to increase. One of the barbarians standing near the entrance was reaching for a terra cotta vase on a high shelf.

"Don't touch that!" Phaedra ordered, just as the man's paw closed around the vase. She suddenly saw something that made her reel with surprise. A shape in leather and a blue cloak filled the entrance, blocking out the light. It was Brannoc. His hair was unruly and long, bound by a circlet about his brows. She was drawn by the stone at its center, pale and milky, like the moon.

There was no resemblance to the dragon beast of the evening past. He was just a man. However, there was something about his sudden appearance that made her feel hunted. Brannoc tilted his head to the side, studying her as his fingers took the vase from the other man.

"You are the owner of The Swan?"

She had forgotten how beautiful his voice was. "Yes."

Brannoc followed Phaedra's gaze and called the man away with his free hand. No one else moved, not even the barbarian who had removed the vase.

Brannoc stepped forward and bowed low to Phaedra. When he straightened, he stood still, his eyes steady upon her. She returned no expression at all.

"Are these your men?" she asked. Her tone was tight with authority. She felt everyone's eyes upon her.

Suddenly Brannoc's gaze warmed with mirth. But if he thought he was going to disarm Phaedra with his smile, he was mistaken, for she stood straight. He looked around and seemed to appraise the shop, drink in its value. He stopped and lifted his nose slightly, like an animal who has caught a promising scent.

His eyes narrowed, brows crinkled together. "Of course." He breathed in deeply, looking up into the air as if to catch a glimpse of something. "Jasmine. And roses. Sandalwood. Myrrh. And violets."

"Last night you remarked that we Byzantines looked at you as being no better than animals. Perhaps if your men had manners, our opinion of you would change." She paused for a reaction, but Brannoc was lost in thought.

"Shall you tell him to sheath his sword, or shall I?" She gestured to the man behind her.

Brannoc's finger cut the air and the barbarian's sword rasped into its leather scabbard.

"That's better."

Brannoc turned and with a sharp gesture, dismissed his men, tilting his head toward the door in case they'd forgotten where it was. Creak of leather and clang of steel, and they were gone. As the last of the men vanished, Brannoc turned back to Phaedra. The shop seemed to expand and everyone breathed audible sighs of relief. Phaedra walked to the shelf and adjusted a vase.

Before Simon's son returned his attention to work, he muttered, "Those men scared away two of my best customers!"

Brannoc shot him a thunderous look, but the youth was all bravado now that there was only one barbarian left. "You can't bully me. I know why you're here."

"Shush!" Simon quieted the boy. Phaedra looked. Simon renewed his conversation with a customer.

Phaedra busied herself, fussing with the perfectly arranged flasks, while listening to Brannoc move about the shop. Why won't he leave? What does he want?

Unknowingly, Phaedra had removed a flask of perfume from the shelf. She was turning it in her hand when Brannoc came up behind her.

"You have a gift, Lady Ancii."

Phaedra's fingers clenched around the flask lest she drop it. Brannoc moved to stand beside her.

"You have created a temple to beauty," he said, caressing the word.

She looked sideways then met his gaze.

His eyes released her. He studied the bottles before him. "You have a reputation in the court of Cordoba. It is said the creator of The Swan's fragrances is a sorceress because of the spells they weave."

The compliment didn't lure her. It was his mention of Cordoba. "The court? How do you know of such a thing?" She knew he had fought on the side of the Moors, but she wondered if Brannoc would tell her the truth.

"The Caliph was my lord for a time," he answered easily, as if such an arrangement, a Christian knight in an Arab caliph's household, were the most natural thing in the world.

He continued. "And they are especially fond of jasmine."

She tensed. The way the word had rolled off his tongue, she was sure he was teasing her. She remembered the evening before, when Brannoc had fussed over her jasmine perfume.

"They, Sir Brannoc?" she inquired. "And what do you like?

Have you, too, been bewitched by one of The Swan's fragrances?"

He laughed under his breath.

"Perhaps your time would be better spent shepherding your men out of some new folly?" She paused. "Besides, I am busy," she added, nudging a flask of perfume into a tight spot on the shelf. But just as she did, he put his hand over hers, claiming her and the perfume, sending a shock of heat up her arm as if the Dragon had breathed his fire upon her.

Her eyes didn't stray from the dragon tattoos around his wrists. She couldn't move now even if she'd wanted to, for her feet had grown roots, and she was as solidly planted as a vine. Even though his grasp was light, covering her hand, she could feel the power of him drumming through her. And yet, it was as if she'd known his touch all along, had even enjoyed it in times past.

Phaedra shivered. Brannoc's warm hand had relaxed on hers. The gesture was slight, but she felt the pressure ease. She slipped her hand out and ventured a glance behind, wondering if anyone had caught the overfamiliar gesture. No one had been watching. There were only two customers, and they were both being attended to by Simon and his son.

Brannoc removed the perfume Phaedra had been touching and studied the seal stamped in the red wax. "Pagan Desires," he read aloud. He looked at her, his face open with interest.

Phaedra felt her cheeks flame. Oh, this was splendid, she noted to herself. Of all The Swan's perfumes, why did he have to choose this one? This was not what she had planned!

He nudged the seal open with his thumb and held the flask beneath his nose. Phaedra could smell the scent as well, its rose, jasmine and vanilla veils, which dropped away, revealing a soft musk like ripe plums. She swallowed hard as a slow smile rose on his face.

"Jasmine." His eyes teased her.

"Among others," she said with flawless calm, stopping him

there, or, at least attempting to halt the words she sensed on his tongue.

But it was not to be. Her eyes narrowed as she watched him step closer. She pulled away, tucking her chin, as he bent over her to whisper in her ear.

"I doubt that even the saintliest of men could resist a woman who wore this scent. Although you, Lady Ancii, are in no need of its powers to inspire such desires."

His breath was warm, the words flirtatious. Unconsciously, she brushed her cheek with her hand.

"Your silver tongue will stand you in good stead here in Constantinople. Perhaps you'd like to put it to practice elsewhere?"

He drew himself upright. "I've seen everything I want to see."

Phaedra pretended not to hear. She reached for the perfume in his hand so she could return it to the shelf.

"I'd like to buy this," he said, pulling it away from her. He met her startled gaze. "It's the least I can do."

Phaedra watched in stunned silence as he crossed the shop to pay Simon. He now owned Pagan Desires!

With the perfume in hand, he bowed to her. "I am your slave, your servant. Ask me anything and it is yours," he promised.

The thought of her perfume in the barbarian's possession vanished for a moment. Anything, she mused. Her eyes glinted like sharpened bronze. Bohemund. Bring me Bohemund.

The gleam in her eye gave her away.

"I see you already have a task in mind," Brannoc keenly noted.

Phaedra veiled her eyes. Oh, yes. She had something in mind. And when the time came, Bohemund would be helpless. Brannoc and Pagan Desires would see to that.

She smiled a slight, edged smile. "Enjoy your day in Constantinople, Sir Brannoc. But take care your men do not make it a short stay."

Seven

"Blasphemers!" screamed the holy man, standing on top of an Ionic column in the middle of the Taurus market. He whipped a willow branch against the rail that enclosed the sixty-foot-high platform he lived on. However, far beneath him, the majority of citizens moved along, their minds focused on business. Only a few glanced up to see what the noise was about.

"Blasphemers!" he yelled again. "Repent now. The end of the world draws near!"

Phaedra rolled her eyes. "Madman," she muttered under her breath. She was on her way to buy olives and goat cheese for the evening meal. She'd dismissed her chairbearers, preferring to walk after sitting in the back room, having taken an inventory of her oils and supplies. She had servants to attend to such tasks as the shopping, but she'd needed a diversion.

And now she had one. Daniel, the holy man, lived like a bird on his perch, never sitting or kneeling, eating only what his disciples sent up in a bucket, berries, nuts, never cooked food. His white beard reached his ankles, covering his nakedness. War with the Turks had flushed the hermit from his cave. Now his home was the air above Constantinople, and he made his presence felt with his fire-and-brimstone warnings, his foreshadowings of death and destruction.

"Whore! Jezebel! Daughter of Satan!" Daniel thundered.

Phaedra felt Daniel's eyes on her. His mad, hateful eyes were burning her back. She did not stop.

"You! You who hide behind widow's black! Concubine to the devil!"

Phaedra felt other eyes turning her way. People stopped and stared openly, until there was a crowd, the answer to Daniel's prayers. Spurred on by the growing attentiveness of Constantinople's citizens, Daniel spumed with hatred.

"Sorceress! What magic potions have you created today to bend men's minds to fornication?"

Enough! Phaedra stopped and glared up at him. He was outlined against the setting sun, his body was gilded red-gold, his arms thrown wide to his sides in the sign of the cross.

"Yes, harlot," he pointed. "God knows your sins and the blackness of your soul. Pray with me and save yourself from eternal damnation!" He wiped his mouth, frothing with excitement.

"Pray, sinner, sorceress, pray. It is you who have lured the beasts of the West to come hither," he accused. "Because of you, darkness will swallow Byzantium. The end is near," he screamed, throwing his arms to the heavens.

The crowd's mood blackened. There was a hint of menace in people's eyes, and the whispered words shared between strangers caused them to become allies against a common evil, the power of a she-devil who was bringing dark destruction to their world.

"Pray!" Daniel ordered.

"Pray yourself, false prophet," she answered loudly.

As if her coldness had been carried on the wind, Daniel's teeth chattered and he hugged his arms to him. "Oh, pagan whore. Murderess!"

Someone bumped her, and she turned with a jolt. She felt a sea of anger and discontent. It was moving toward her, threatening to harm her. Hushed murmurings. Voices filled with venom. Someone bumped her again. Her veil slipped aside, revealing her face.

"Whore of Babylon, you dare to unveil yourself before God? Seize her!" he yelled. "Destroy the pagan idolater before she destroys us!"

Phaedra tightened her hands into fists. Suddenly, she was seized from behind. Hands pulled her back by the shoulders, and there was a voice in her ear. "You're in danger here, Lady Ancii. Lady Ancii? Come with me."

She shrugged to be free of the weight. The grip tightened, and squeezed her like a vise. Again, the voice. "Come."

Phaedra frowned, recognizing who it was. Brannoc. But she did not take her eyes off Daniel until the barbarian yanked her back, off her feet.

"Now," he gritted.

Despite his size, the crowd barely shifted to let them pass. It swallowed them. It was as if he had the power of the mage and could disappear into air. It was not air but steel that kept Phaedra's arms manacled to her sides. She twisted in his grip. She had no feeling left in her arms.

"Let me go!"

He whispered, "Alert them again and I may have to kill a man or two. Then you'll be forever in my debt, Lady."

She opened her mouth, a quick retort shaping her lips, but it died there, muffled beneath his palm. Before she knew it, he'd lifted her off the ground as easily as if she were a bag of air, and carried her away.

Stubborn women make heavy bundles. Phaedra purposefully stiffened, increasing her weight tenfold. When Brannoc grunted, she had to smile. Served him right for treating her like a piece of baggage.

Brannoc carried her uphill, following a twisting street flanked by buildings so close together that they overhung the walkways. He set her down in a shadowy alcove carved out by two corner walls.

Clutching her veil, Phaedra turned on him. "What do you think you're doing?"

Brannoc lurched back, as if a fire had just erupted before him.

"Saving your foolish neck," he answered gruffly.

"From what?" Her voice was high. "Who?" The puzzled look in her eyes gave way to comprehension. "Daniel? That fool—"

Brannoc raised his finger to his lips. The gesture stopped her cold. Both listened as the sound of footsteps on stone drew near. Although hidden from view, neither one of them moved. The footsteps passed. Silence.

"Didn't you see what was happening? That fool was turning the crowd against you," Brannoc explained, but all it inspired was a frustrated sigh from Phaedra. He continued. "I've known plenty of fools who have robbed men of their lands and their inheritance. The stoning of a pagan wench is nothing," he argued.

Her glance was mocking. She turned to the side to move around him, but his arm shot out to block her way. He rested his hand on the stucco wall behind her. She sighed into the silence and stubbornly refused to look at him.

"You shouldn't be walking alone."

"I don't need an armed escort," she replied.

"I wasn't volunteering, if that's what you were thinking." He paused, saw the spark in her eye and continued. "Besides, I'm unarmed."

She noted his tattoo. "I suppose your dragons offer enough protection," she mocked cynically.

"In a manner of speaking, yes."

She frowned. It wasn't the answer she was after, and yet, deep in her bones she knew he spoke the truth. But how could it be? Why did she care?

Suddenly bold, she said, "They say the dragons are the markings of a sorcerer."

"Your holy man denounced you as a sorceress," he countered. "I'd say we are well-matched, wouldn't you?"

"Humph! Then you are as big a fool as Daniel."

He leaned toward her. At first she thought it was because he couldn't hear her, but as he shifted his weight to his hand on the wall, she saw what he meant to do. He was going to trap her with his body. He looked down on her.

She stared straight ahead at his white surcoat. It didn't have a cross. The wind sprayed her loose hair across her cheek, veiling her eyes and mouth from him. She was suddenly glad to be shielded from his scrutiny.

But it didn't last. Brannoc brushed her hair to the side and, running his finger along her jaw, gently nudged her face up to look at him, his forefinger under her chin.

She met his gaze and held it easily. She was aware of everything and nothing. The curve of the wall at her back, the scented heat of Brannoc's body, the blue of his eyes, and his strong mouth. And his power. Jason had been a powerful man too, but this, this was different. Wilder. Darker. It was a power born as much by instinct as by intellect.

Jason. Brannoc. Christe! She'd woven her husband and this barbarian together in her head! Damn him!

She tensed.

"No." Brannoc softly implored. His eyes begged her not to fight him, not during this moment in time. She swallowed hard and, without understanding why, she let the power of his plea lull her to feeling safe here in the shadows.

She wanted to strike him for making her feel that way. She wanted to kiss him. She wanted to run far away and cast all thoughts aside.

"The Swan." A whisper like burnished bronze. It held no question, yet thousands of questions echoed in his voice.

He moved his hand from her chin. His thumb slowly rubbed across her lower lip. She could almost taste him. She trembled with the desire to take his finger in her mouth.

No! Not now! Suddenly, she wrenched free of his hand.

Brannoc stepped back, a searching look in his eyes, and moved to stand in the street. Hands on his waist, he turned away from her.

Palms flat behind her on the wall, Phaedra struggled for control. She stared at the barbarian. This was not the time to begin her campaign to seduce Brannoc, she thought to herself. Let it stop here, with no more than the memory of his hand on her face, her mouth. Harmless. She bit her lip and looked away as his gaze settled on her again.

"I'll escort you home. Wait here while I see about procuring a sedan chair for you."

Brannoc didn't know Phaedra well, otherwise he never would have left her. For as soon as he turned the first corner, she flew in the opposite direction. In a flash, she was gone.

Phaedra told no one about her encounter with Brannoc. But that evening, alone in her chamber, she stood before the swan fresco, studying it as if it held the answer to her wild rush of feelings.

Here she was, plotting a seduction. The problem was, she was beginning to enjoy it. She couldn't explain the sudden shift in thoughts, but she knew the idea was as mad as a maiden's midnight dance. She couldn't allow it. She dared not, she told herself vehemently. She only needed Brannoc to destroy Bohemund. The blue-eyed barbarian meant nothing to her!

The light's flames flickered behind her, bathing the fresco's naked image of herself in a light that made her think of Jason and lovemaking. With a deep breath, she remembered the feel and the scent of his hair and his chest, silky tight with curls, each one a tendril of heat . . .

She was all desire, reliving that image. Despite her calculating attempt to dismiss her feelings, they kindled a wildness deep in her belly. Did she have the strength, the power to seduce Brannoc in order to get what she wanted? But could she control him? His desires?

Could she control herself?

She read the desire in the swan's eyes, the lascivious gleam painted, transfixed, unreal. Brannoc was real. His gaze the moment he'd touched her mouth, had been hungry. She trembled, suddenly cold in her night shift.

Hesitantly, she reached out to touch the curve of a painted arm. But just as her fingers reached the wall, she pulled back as if she'd been burned by a tongue of flame.

On Easter morning, Daniel looked out over the square and preached that he had seen the risen Son of God. It wasn't the first time he'd made such a claim, but he did it with such conviction that he stopped many citizens on their way to the Church of the Holy Wisdom, Santa Sophia. Of course, news about Daniel's encounter with the "pagan enchantress" had spread quickly, like all delicious pieces of gossip, adding to his notoriety, appealing to those people who preferred the provocative to the miraculous.

According to Daniel, Christ had stood on the column's rail and looked down upon the city with mournful eyes. Daniel had kissed Jesus' feet where the nails had pierced his flesh.

Daniel coughed, clearing his throat, and repeated Christ's words for the benefit of his audience. "The Goliaths of the North and West who have journeyed to Constantinople possess far darker souls than the heathens they go to fight against," Daniel said with deep, godly voice. " 'Shall we pray for the barbarians' souls?' I asked Christ. 'No!' He said. 'Banish them now. Lead them out and deliver Byzantium from evil. Amen.' "

"Amen!" the audience beneath the column chorused. Crossing themselves, they waited hungrily to hear more about this miracle. As Daniel preached, his voice covered the square like a canopy. He was nothing but skin and bones, but the holy words of his miraculous vision had given him the might and weight of ten men.

News of Daniel's warnings about the barbarian mercenaries and Christ's heeding words reached the emperor. Daniel's vision couldn't have come at a worse time. Three barbarian knights were staying at the Imperial Palace: Hugh of Vermandois, Godfrey of Bouillon and his brother, Baldwin. They'd all heard about Daniel's vision. Their anger could have felled trees, such were their rantings and ravings. They were men of God! They were fulfilling God's will!

Over the next two days, news spread to the knights' armies lodged outside the city and across the Golden Horn. To the common soldier, this was just another plot by the crafty Greeks to belittle the westerners and rob them of glory.

Kasia had filled in all the details for Phaedra. Kasia knew everything about these Goliaths from the West. Kasia even knew the exact moment Bohemund of Taranto had marched through the Golden Gate. So had Phaedra. But whereas the former had witnessed it firsthand, Phaedra had felt it in her bones.

It was the third day after Daniel's miraculous visitation. Phaedra was waiting for Kasia to join her in the royal vestibule at the Imperial Palace. Both of them had been invited to a special assembly to witness the barbarian princes swear their fealty to Emperor Alexius.

A mosaic of the Byzantine Empire, gaping with white, unfinished splotches, covered one wall. It was a luxurious expanse of space in a room that could house full grown palm trees. Scented plaster had been used, so the air spun with myrrh, rose and musk. The marble floor was so slick, visitors had to walk carefully, lest they fall and embarrass themselves.

The mosaic faced white marble columns, hung with filmy draperies, overlooking a courtyard and the sea. Phaedra was standing so close to the columns, the draperies nearly touched her as they puffed with warm breezes.

Phaedra didn't serve the empress. She served a darker mistress, revenge. Now, after years of waiting, her father's killer would finally be within her reach. The nightmares and dreams, full of a young girl's imagining, would soon root themselves in reality. How close had she come to capturing the barbarian, she wondered. Were his eyes the cold blue of Viking waters? Did he look like a wolf?

Such musings were part of her dark, dark game. It didn't really matter what he looked like. His death was the more important issue. She held his fate as lightly as a chess piece within her palms.

She looked at her hands now. Were these hands capable of murder? When the time came, would she use her dagger? Or poison? She could even create a poisonous perfume. She had the knowledge, the power. Such blends were said to work remarkably well and slowly, leaving no trace.

A boat captain's cry, and the faint surf of shouts lured her outside. The air was warm, wild and sweet with the scent of lemon and apricot. Beautiful water. Dangerous, too. For centuries, the water had carried warriors on her back, bronze men with the promise of gold and land glinting in their eyes like dagger points. Shielding her eyes from the sun, Phaedra imagined Agamemnon and Odysseus's ships moving across the water, bows pointed like lances in the direction of Troy. Now the sea had brought another type of warrior on her back.

Bohemund. What would someone like Homer have made of him?

Two-faced marauder on the wine-dark sea.

The last time Bohemund had stepped foot on these shores, he'd been the enemy. Now he was Byzantium's ally. An ally! Defender of the Byzantine people! The gall! Now there was a switch to make a cynic proud.

Her thoughts were interrupted by Kasia, who urged her to the vestibule. There, before them, was Gabriel's unfinished mosaic.

Something caught her eye, a design in the mosaic where Gabriel had depicted Constantinople.

As she stared, her eyes widened with recognition. The image gripped her heart. There was no mistake. Gabriel had a dragon and a swan in the mosaic. There! A dragon swooping above the city. And a swan in the water beneath Constantinople.

A dragon and a swan.

Her heart hammered beneath her breast. Something clawed at her belly. Why did he have a swan and dragon in his mosaic? What did they mean to him?

"Phaedra?" Kasia's tone arched with interest. She placed her hand on Phaedra's arm, startling her. There was a wild look in Phaedra's eyes. Kasia gave Phaedra's arm a consoling little squeeze, then left, pausing in the vestibule's doorway for a backward glance at her friend.

The ceremony was held in the Audience Hall. The room was long and shadowed, its ceiling supported by marble columns. Mosaics decorated the walls here, too, but these were purely decorative.

Set above the court on a scarlet, carpeted dais was the emperor Alexius Comnenus, chosen of God. He wore the imperial purple over a cloth of gold tunic. His gold throne was carved with lions and mythical winged beasts. He was waiting for his guests, his new allies from the West.

Phaedra was so close she could see him perfectly, the tanned face, short brown beard and large brown eyes, but she could not see past the serene expression that molded his handsome features. His face was like a shield. Phaedra had known it most of her life. But even though his face betrayed nothing, his broad shoulders and commanding bearing revealed he was a soldier who was used to the weight of swords charging into battle, leading men to their glory or their death.

This was no battle, and yet a clash of men, dreams, and

desires was surely about to make itself felt. However, an observer wouldn't think so from the look on Alexius's face. He stared straight ahead. He was like an icon, oblivious to the people around him.

Although he was short, Phaedra knew that the throne and dais worked in his favor. The barbarians will think he's as tall as one of the Viking guards, she thought. That is, if they're able to see beyond the emperor's crown. The crown was aflame with jewels the size of walnuts, and probably was worth more than all the land in Frankland. The smaller gems were worth a country of castles.

Before the throne, guarding Alexius, stretched a half circle of the mightiest warriors of the Byzantine Empire. These were the Scandinavian axemen of the Varangian Guard. Phaedra noticed Kasia's lover among them, marble stiff and unblinking beneath his scarlet cloak.

Suddenly, the entrance went dark with men. A captain of the Imperial Guard entered first. The barbarians followed in their white surcoats, the symbol of the red cross marking their right breasts, uniting them.

"That is Godfrey of Bouillon," Kasia whispered to Phaedra as a tall, broad-shouldered giant with red-gold hair walked past. He was pleasing to look upon and, like his captains, he wore a surcoat which lay open on its sides. It was belted and embroidered with a red cross.

"That one," Kasia pointed with her chin, "the one built like a bull, is his brother Baldwin."

Phaedra followed Kasia's gaze to a man as different from Godfrey as night was to day. The brother was dark, with jet-black hair. This was the one who'd been trained for the Church. His walk was haughty and proud, his chin held at an angle that suggested he was thoroughly enjoying the pomp and luxury of the ceremony.

"Hugh of Vermandois, brother to the King of the Franks," Kasia emphasized with a cynical sneer.

This prince, too, was like a tree. Imposing. He was fair

complexioned, with full, fleshy lips and a long, beaked slope of a nose that he held high, as if he were balancing something on its tip.

One by one, the knights of the cross advanced and knelt before the throne. To acknowledge his fealty to Emperor Alexius, each man pressed his hands together, as if in prayer, and placed them between Alexius's jeweled palms. When finished, each moved to stand behind the throne.

Phaedra leaned close to Kasia and whispered behind her hand. "Do you think they realize what they've just done?"

"That they've just sworn to restore Jerusalem and all former Byzantine territory to Alexius?" Kasia smiled deviously as she said, "They'll come out of this with nothing!"

Like most Byzantines, both women knew that by taking such an oath, the knights promised to restore to Alexius any captured province or city which had once belonged to the Byzantine Empire. This included all the lands as far west as the Straits of Gibraltar, all of Italy, North Africa, Egypt and, of course, the Holy Land. All of it.

Murmurings erupted all around them. The mood suddenly became focused and charged with fear. Phaedra's hands hardened into fists.

"The Normans," someone whispered.

Bohemund.

Turning as one, the witnesses looked at the door. To the jingle of spur chains, the Normans rumbled in. There was no mistaking Bohemund from his men. He was at the front, leading, shoulders pulled forward as if he were already on the attack.

"Christe," Kasia sighed appreciatively, drinking him in like a draught of nectar presented by the gods, taking note of his hair, the color of the desert sun, short and curly, down to his wide shoulders, deep chest and slender waist. It was a long sigh, a long drink. Phaedra cut a disapproving glance at Kasia before giving the barbarian her full attention.

Her amber eyes were almost black with anger and contempt. She drew herself straighter, lifting her chin, and silently damned him to hell.

As if he'd heard her, Bohemund caught Phaedra's eyes in his. They were an icy blue, devouring. He raised one eyebrow at the proud, haughty, beautiful face turned to him, and opened his mouth in a grin, like a leering wolf.

Phaedra felt Kasia clutching her arm. She watched Bohemund for a second more before realizing that she, too, was being watched. She turned with a start. Brannoc was looking at her. She felt he knew exactly what she was thinking.

She tore her gaze away and concentrated on the scene taking place at the dais. Bohemund was placing his clasped hands between the emperor's. With that simple act, the barbarian swore his fealty to Emperor Alexius and vowed to serve the interests of Byzantium. She watched, knotting her hands into fists lest she reach for one of the soldier's weapons and use it to murder him now.

And all the while, she took secret delight in the role he had given her, that of nemesis, agent of his doom.

Eight

Sharif had promised Phaedra he would allow her to practice her charioteer racing skills in the Hippodrome, just as long as she made one small concession. He demanded she dress as a man, for women were forbidden from such practices as chariot racing.

But before she even had the opportunity to mount a horse, the captain of the Imperial Guards approached them.

"Lady Ancii." He bowed slightly. "By order of Emperor Alexius, I'm to escort you to the Imperial Palace immediately."

What could Alexius want with her, she wondered?

"Surely the captain doesn't think it wise that I go dressed as I am?" she replied, drawing attention to her manly attire. "Allow me to retire to my home where—"

The captain cut her off with more than a smile. "The emperor is quite aware of your present condition."

She turned away from the captain, putting her hands on her hips, and looked up at Sharif.

"What shall I tell Alexander?" Sharif asked.

"That I've gone to visit an old friend." Phaedra caught the flicker of worry in the charioteer's eyes and gripped his arm to reassure him that all would be well.

Calmly, Phaedra left the horses in Sharif's care and led the way off the track, walking far ahead of the captain. She could feel his eyes on her back. She knew he was shaking his head. She knew what he was thinking, that her masculine choice in clothes was the sign of an unwell mind.

To avoid attention, they followed the stairwell which linked the box to the Imperial Palace. The serpentine passage was dark, lit by torches which gave them the shadows of ogres. Once inside the palace, the captain ushered her into a gold and blue chamber and left. Phaedra took a deep breath. And waited.

"Charming."

The word curled through the quiet as a statement of fact. No criticism rolled in its wake. Phaedra looked over her shoulder, in the direction of the voice. Emperor Alexius was standing in a shaft of sunlight. Seconds before, she'd been completely alone. She'd heard nothing. It was as if he'd fallen from the sky and been borne by a band of sunlight.

His gaze swept her thoroughly, taking account of her attire. "My lord," she said softly. Alexius wasn't wearing his crown. He wore his authority like an invisible mantle. He took a step toward her, then halted, as if he'd suddenly remembered that he was the emperor and she should come to him.

Phaedra quickly crossed the room, dropped to her knees and kissed the embroidered hem of his purple gown. She looked up at him and met his gaze. His eyes were soft, benevolent, amused. He held out his hand to help her up, and she took it. He felt cool to her touch, like wax. She sensed a tense familiarity between them, as if he were her father, and she the prodigal daughter returned.

He shook his head. "Chariot racing? Where do you get these ideas?" He squeezed her hand in his before releasing it.

"It was Sharif's idea, actually."

"Your skill has much improved," he whispered.

She clenched her jaw at the thought that he'd been spying on her. She tilted her head to the side and waited.

"However, I strongly advise that you stay away from the Hippodrome for a time. You've usurped the men's sacred territory. I can already hear their whining protests droning on and on in my ear."

"You 'advise' me only?"

"There's no need for stronger words between us, is there, Phaedra?"

His patronizing tone needled her. The silky sound of her name put her on alert.

She stepped back and did the unthinkable—she turned her back on the most powerful man in the civilized world. "You didn't bring me here to chastise me, did you?"

She heard the hem of his tunic brushing along the mosaic floor, moving away from her.

"Quick, like your father." He paused. "I was happy to see you at the oath-taking ceremony," he said finally.

Aahh, here it comes. "Why did you invite me?"

"I thought the daughter of the Leopard would be interested."

Where was this going, this dance, she wondered? But it was always like this between them. With the emperor, she always had to give more weight to the words left unsaid.

"Ceremonies bore me!" she announced to the room. If the columns had been alive, they would have arched back in horror.

"But people don't." He took a quick breath and continued. "How shall I put this? I hear Daniel has taken a special interest in you."

A look of confusion crossed her face. What did Daniel have to do with the ceremony? "He's been living far too long with his head in the clouds. It's addled his brain," she said.

"He has quite a following."

"A following of sheep."

"God's sheep, nevertheless. Perhaps you should consider leaving the city."

Phaedra whirled around and stared after him. "What?" The word sliced the silence between them. How could she leave now, when she was so close to destroying Bohemund?

Bohemund! The Emperor knew of her blood vow.

"It's for your own good," Alexius said. His look was calculating. His eyes were slitted like a lizard's.

She cut across the chamber, her soft leather boots and voice killing the quiet. "No. It's not me you wish to protect, but someone else." She paused. "Bohemund."

Alexius moved his hand in vague acknowledgment that she was right. "You wish to destroy him. Am I correct? To avenge your father's murder." He stopped, then plunged. "But I need him, Phaedra."

The room reeled, and for a moment she thought she was going to be sick. She clutched her stomach. "You need him?"

"His battle skills are legendary."

"You mean his gift for lying and trickery!" She found she could still command her voice. She made no attempt to keep her anger out of it. "He tricked you out of the empire's gold and murdered my father!"

"Phaedra." His tone inspired caution. "Perhaps a stay in the country would calm that temper. At least until the barbarians are well on their way."

"No," she whispered, shaking her head. This was a nightmare. She would have thought the emperor, of all people, would have supported the death of that beast. After all, any fool could see that Bohemund was a threat to the security of Byzantium.

"You can't mean . . ."

The emperor swiped the air with his fisted hand. "He will bring down the Turks and regain Jerusalem for me."

Phaedra saw her plans for revenge crumbling into dust. Ablaze with anger, she couldn't even see that she was crossing a line and committing treason.

"And do you really think he will give Jerusalem back to you? Hand it over on a silver platter, my lord?" she asked, her voice bristling with cynicism. "He deserves to die," she added venomously.

"I need him alive! Let him be. I'm thinking of your welfare," he said again, running his fingers through his beard, watching her eyes widen. "He is as well-guarded as I. In fact, one of his men—Brannoc, I believe is his name—has thwarted two attempts against Bohemund's life. He's killed two would-be assassins already. Surely he'll kill you, too, if he discovers your intentions."

But Brannoc was not going to be a problem, she wanted to tell him. Pagan Desires would see to that. She mustered all the self-restraint she could. "I am unworthy of my emperor's concern," she said humbly.

"Of course I am concerned!" he protested. "You are as dear to me as my own daughter," he professed, placing his hand over his heart. "But for the empire's sake, you must stay away from the barbarian."

"I will not betray my oath."

Alexius swore under his breath and circled her. "You're trying my patience, Lady Ancii."

"I've just begun. I've sworn an oath. I will keep it or I will die trying," she vowed, following him with her gaze.

"You will heed my orders."

She shut her eyes against his command. He was so sure, so confident that she would yield to him!

Anger suffused Phaedra's skin with a deep blush of color. She could feel a power flexing inside of her, ready to lash out. Her rage knew no bounds, and she was sure that were she to walk through her shop now, flasks and bottles would crack and pop in her wake.

A small glimmer of reason held her back from signing her death warrant. Her anger had to be mastered, or else it would destroy her.

She opened her eyes. She resisted the idea of telling him

about her vision, but now, for some reason, it felt right. She remembered that when she was a child, the emperor had always been interested in her dreams.

"The barbarians march to their deaths. I've seen it," she said coolly.

Lured by the power of a word, Emperor Alexius turned slowly. "Seen it? So, the Dreamer dreams."

Pricked by the sharp knife of memory, she stopped. She recalled the emperor asking her father about another dream, a dream about wolves.

"I know the secret of the most ancient of rituals. I can tell you how this journey will fare," she promised.

He cocked his brow. "Now?"

Answers whirled through her mind. "When the moon flares in the sky." She paused to give him time to think. "But if I do this, you must give me something in return."

She looked hard at him. He stared back. His lips tightened. "Anything," he replied.

He was Herod playing to her Salome. She would reveal all, drop the veils between this world and the next, but she had to have one thing.

She crossed her arms over her chest. "After Bohemund takes Jerusalem, he is mine."

"Ha!" His laugh was a slap. Nevertheless, she pushed forward.

"He will try to rule in his own name if someone doesn't stop him. He will sit on the throne of the most ancient, godliest of cities. As long as he lives, he is a threat to you and the empire!"

"This means you'll have to make the journey with them."

Phaedra dropped her arms to her sides. "So be it!"

"I can't let you go."

"You must."

"You're willing to leave Alexander? The shop?"

The mention of her son was like a splash of cold water.

She blinked, but continued on the path that she had set for herself long ago.

"Bohemund sealed my fate years ago."

The emperor's fingers brushed her cheek, and she had to tense her shoulders to freeze the shiver his touch inspired.

"Such beauty. The Swan will perish in the desert," he sighed.

"The woman will not," she answered, looking him in the eye. And in a breath, Phaedra knew he had agreed to her plan.

"Very well then. Perform the ritual for me," he said. "And after Bohemund takes Jerusalem, he is yours."

But Phaedra caught the flash of heat in his eyes. She dismissed that animal glint for anger, but in her bones she knew she was clinging to a lie.

Nine

Phaedra found the fortune-teller at the entrance to the Baths of Zeuxippus. The old woman was standing quietly in the shadows, as if she had been waiting for Phaedra. The apple-green mantle tucked around the woman's face and shoulders made her skin look as translucent as an onion. The milky-blue eyes that met Phaedra's were quick and sharp. They saw through the younger woman's appearance of calm, to the desperation and urgency that lay beneath the surface.

"I need your help," said Phaedra. "I need you to help me master my dreams."

The old woman's eyes sparkled merrily, making Phaedra feel like a child who has finally set her stubbornness aside. "But you are already mistress of your dreams," she remarked. "You are Cassandra's daughter. You are the Swan."

Even above the noise and shouts of citizens passing on their way to the baths and market, Phaedra heard the crone clearly. But she shook her head, dismissing the words. "No. I cannot. They control me."

The crone sighed in the face of Phaedra's desperation. Or was it pity she felt, that here stood a young woman of such beauty and power, and she did not even know it?

The old woman patted Phaedra's arm. "Very well," she said. "Come with me." And with a nod of her head and a curl of her finger, the fortune-teller plunged into darker shadows. Phaedra followed.

* * *

They wound in and out of streets that coiled like snail shells. Phaedra had long lost track of where they were. Only by placing a hand on a cool stone or brick wall was she able to reassure herself that she wasn't dreaming. But after a long descent, Phaedra gave a start, as if she had fallen asleep, for both she and the fortune-teller had come to a dead end. And the only way out was down a crumbling, narrow flight of stairs, clinging to the side of a house before falling away, down into a hole, a cave.

"Hell," Phaedra thought to herself, peering into the hole. Water, she thought, as she realized that the stairs led to an underground water reservoir. There were more than thirty of these wells beneath the city and the surrounding countryside. They'd been built to make sure the city always had a plentiful water supply. Water was a matter of life and death. A city could not withstand a siege without it. And Constantinople was always looking over her shoulders for threatening signs from her neighbors.

The fortune-teller led the way, descending the stairs as swift and sure as a mountain goat. Phaedra bunched her cloak in her fist and followed quickly. She stepped into a sea of absolute darkness. She heard the slap of water. The sound reminded her that she was alive, for the darkness was so oppressive, she felt as if she'd been swallowed by the jaws of death.

The hairs on the back of her neck rose. Where had the fortune-teller gone? Phaedra reached out with her entire being, but only the water and her thumping heart answered. Defying the dark, she took a step. And another. Just as she was about to take another step, a whoosh of firelight leapt high into the air, and spread a halo around the fortune-teller.

With her torch held high in the air, the old woman looked like a Homeric guide from the spiritual world. A deep shudder rocked Phaedra. She felt cold to the bone. The old woman moved away to plunge the torch into a bracket in the stone wall. Phaedra looked around. They were standing on a slab of stone surrounded on three sides by water that shimmered deep and black in the light. Stone columns grew out of the water, like a forest of trees.

There was a boat with oars tied to the side of the landing. Phaedra knew it was for them. She looked off into the distance, where the darkness rose like a black wall, and wondered where the old woman meant to take her.

Wonder of wonders. There was a whole other world tucked between the city and the reservoir. The fortune-teller lived in a rock house, chiseled beneath street level and tucked into a wall. It was as if an architect had carved it out as a private sanctuary.

Phaedra climbed three shallow steps to the wooden door. She paused on the threshold.

"Enter," coaxed the fortune-teller.

But Phaedra couldn't move any further. Resting her hand on the door, she let the old woman pass and enter first.

Her hesitation surprised her. It wasn't fear that kept her from crossing. It went deeper than that. It was as if an invisible wall stood before her, keeping her back, stopping her from moving forward. She could hear the fortune-teller inside, clucking to herself.

"You desire to see the future?" asked the crone over her shoulder. "And master it? Then come. Come!"

Phaedra pushed her shoulders forward and, ducking her head, stepped inside.

A low, dank, whitewashed room rushed out to meet her. Frescoes decorated the walls, but her eyes didn't linger. She spotted a cauldron bubbling over a fire in the hearth. Soot-stained timbers crisscrossed the ceiling. Spider webs drooped in veils like crystal beads. She could feel the cold of the stone floor creeping up her legs.

As the fortune-teller lifted the lid off the black pot, releasing the pungent odors of spices and lamb, Phaedra noticed that the frescoes depicted the Garden of Eden. The black lines and colors had faded with age, and years of smoke had dulled and grimed their beauty. The animals and flowers looked out into the room like ghosts. Removing her cloak, Phaedra stepped closer and saw a bear and a boar, peacock and fawn, lion and python, eagle, and a white swan and a dragon.

Suddenly the Dragon was in the room, standing behind her, breathing down her neck, fingering her hair. She gasped, turning with a start, but there was no one. As she turned back, she caught the fortune-teller's shrewd glance. Had the old woman felt him, too?

"You understand the power of the beast. Your knowing will serve you well on your journey to Jerusalem," the crone reflected sagely.

Phaedra didn't question how the woman knew about her journey. She accepted it as naturally as breathing.

The magic had begun.

Sitting comfortably on a stool with a lyre-shaped back, Phaedra waited for the fortune-teller's instructions. She couldn't believe the transformation the woman had undergone since their arrival. The fortune-teller stood tall and regal in her home and, without her cloaks, she did not look fragile. She wore her thick, silver hair in a braid which crowned her head. There was color now in her cheeks. And her blue eyes were warm and offering. The fine lines around them were like rays of light, marking her as a wise woman.

Phaedra had learned that the fortune-teller's name was Maia. It was a name that washed over her lips like a wave.

Phaedra leaned forward, elbows on her knees, as Maia threw juniper on the fire. The smoke weaved, conjuring green forests. Maia bound a branch of hazel to her forehead and, standing before the hearth, raised her arms above her head, palms flat to the ceiling.

Maia's shadow wavered on the walls. There was no light save for the red-gold of the hearth and a bronze bowl. The bowl looked as old as Troy. It was beaten, worn and dented. What was it for, she wondered?

No sooner had she asked than an image answered. She saw herself packing the bowl for the journey, taking great care to wrap it in white linen. The tightness in her chest, the dizziness and sickness that usually marked her visions, did not torment her now. The image was so real there, when she looked down, she found her palms were slightly raised, as if she'd been holding the bowl between her hands.

An eerie feeling was stealing over her, frayed with fear, for these were mystical mysteries she was about to learn, ancient powers which had been invoked by her mother and now the woman in front of her. Was she worthy of such knowledge, Phaedra asked herself? Would she know how to master it? Or would it master her?"

She will teach me to control this power. And revenge will be mine.

She breathed in deeply and waited for instructions.

Between Phaedra and Maia lay the bronze bowl filled with rainwater. An arm's length away, laurel leaves burned on a copper plate, sending plumes of smoke into the room. Phaedra was sitting as straight and stiff as if she were wearing armor.

The fortune-teller sensed that a wall was growing between them. There was nothing Maia could do now but, in time, the burning magical laurel would slip past Phaedra's defenses like a drug. The scented smoke would unlock the door, freeing Phaedra's mind.

"Surrender," Maia whispered, "and claim the strength that is yours."

Confusion knotting her brow, Phaedra looked at the fortune-teller. But to surrender is a sign of weakness, Phaedra thought to herself.

"No," said a voice inside her head. And even though the fortune-teller's mouth had not moved, Phaedra knew the words had come from Maia.

"To surrender," the fortune-teller said, "is to finally set yourself free."

The fortune-teller watched the firelight play across Phaedra's face, softening it, warming it with an embrace of gilded heat. Moved by the sight, perhaps thinking how like Cassandra the daughter was, Maia reached out and held Phaedra's face between her hands. At the old woman's touch, something broke inside of Phaedra. The wisdom of age brushed aside the stubborn blindness of youth, and light flooded in.

"Yes," whispered Maia, feeling the change too. "Now open your mind and let it flow, and the visions, the dreams, will be free to come, to be shaped and ruled by you."

Leaning forward, Phaedra stared into the water at her reflection. Then, as the firelight danced, the shadows shifted on the liquid surface. Her surroundings blurred . . .

A room slowly appeared through the ripples. Phaedra saw that it was nothing more than a large tent, a pavilion, really, but it was lavishly hung with draperies and spread with thick carpets, each one an island of color.

The water settled.

"What do you see?" Maia asked. Her voice seemed to come from a great distance.

"A tent," Phaedra answered.

It was empty. Then, through an opening, the tall figure of a man appeared, casually folding back a flap and striding into the tent as if it were his own. She could tell by his size, clothes, white tunic and trousers, that he was a knight from the West. A sword hung at his side from a low slung belt. The man's hair was lion colored.

Phaedra's eyes widened in recognition.

Brannoc.

As the image rose sharp and clear, questions raged. What magic was this? How had Brannoc figured into this?

Just then the tent erupted with soldiers, who rushed in with swords raised in their hands. Brannoc whirled to face them, hand on the base of his sword. She heard the steel sing as it slid from its scabbard. Brannoc swung his sword in defense. She felt the force of metal striking metal as if she were wielding one of the weapons herself. Her muscles tensed and her right arm braced for the fury of attack.

Unknowingly, she had leaned forward to get a closer look at the image. Brannoc moved as gracefully as an animal. Hilt and blade seemed an extension of his arm. For the first time, Phaedra understood the mystical connection between a warrior and his sword. The attackers were no match for him, and one by one, they fell.

As Brannoc fought, a shadow slipped into the room. Phaedra tensed, watching the assassin peel out of the darkness. She heard herself calling out to warn Brannoc.

"Turn! Behind you! Now!"

She damned her helplessness and watched spellbound as Brannoc turned to face the shadow. But it was too late. A lance shot forward, piercing Brannoc in his side. He roared in outrage and pain, and even the fire in the hearth responded with a plume of red that lit the surface as the Dragon fell.

Ripples broke the image on the water.

"No!" Phaedra lunged forward on her hands and knees, but the water splashed over the sides of the bowl.

The water was not the only thing to mock her. The realization that she'd feared for the barbarian's safety felt like a dagger in her ribs. She froze. How could this be? Why did she care what happened to this man? Why? Of course, she needed him in order to destroy Bohemund, but was that reason enough to care?

She sat back on her heels and looked up at Maia, but her eyes were closed.

"Why do you resist the Dragon? He is not your enemy."

"Why should I see him now? Surely there are matters of greater importance that I need to see?"

Maia's eyes flashed open. "Foolishness does not become you," she said, and Phaedra felt her cheeks grow hot with embarrassment. Maia stiffened. Frustration edged her words. "With the power of sight comes the responsibility of using your waking mind. Why do you think your first vision, which you called up with no help from me, was of the Dragon?

She'd done it herself? "I had been thinking of him."

Maia shook her head. "Because he's an important figure in your life," she softly corrected.

Maia waited before venturing into Phaedra's silence. "Look into the water."

"Coward," she told herself. Finally, she looked.

Again, the room fell away and it was as if she were alone with fire and water. The surface moved like silk kissed by a warm breeze. The image of a hand appeared. Large, powerful, a soldier's hand with long tapering fingers. As the image spread across the water, a wrist appeared, then a tattoo, dark blue, a serpent with wings.

She saw Brannoc holding out his hand to someone. Ah, another hand, that of a woman's. It was small, pale, strong, with oval-shaped nails. It slipped easily inside Brannoc's hand. He lifted the woman's hand to his lips and kissed her palm.

At that moment, a flash of heat snaked up Phaedra's arm. At that moment, she saw herself standing before Brannoc, her hand in his, her open palm warm with his kiss that moved clear through to her soul.

She was wearing a white, filmy sheath tied at her shoulders, and her hair hung loose and long down her back. Brannoc towered above her, dressed for battle, his hand thick around her wrist. With her free hand she traced the outline of his mouth. He curled a fistful of her hair and used it to draw her closer to him. At the last moment, she used her hand to stop him. But he only laughed, forcing her head back, and brought his mouth heavily down on hers in a crushing kiss.

Phaedra breathed in sharply, and the room swirled. She felt the savage, hungry press of Brannoc's lips as surely as her reflection in the water. Time and place blurred for a moment, and she was in Brannoc's arms. His lips were hard and hungry, his beard soft. The flame of his tongue branded her. As she returned his kiss, a luxurious heat filled her mouth and poured over her body.

"Brannoc," she moaned against his lips.

She put her arms around him to draw him closer. They kissed long and deeply, mouths open, each one savoring the taste of the other. His hand had dropped to her lower back, and now he smoothed her sheath down the length of her. At first, his touch was light, but the caresses turned rough as if his hands had minds of their own. He used his mouth to halt any protests she might have had, and continued kneading her flesh. He hugged her hard to him when she tore her mouth free and cried her pleasure.

His mouth swooped to her exposed neck and began a trail of kisses that did not stop until he was between her breasts. With reverent care he cupped them, shaping her, stroking her gently. She slipped against him, unable to bear the weight of his passion. He draped her back over his arm as he loosened the ties at her shoulders. He pushed the tunic down her arms, over her hips and completely off, freeing her for his touch and gaze. He caressed her face between his hands and kissed her tenderly, before dropping to his knees like a supplicant before his queen.

He placed his palms on the insides of her thighs and stroked her skin. He followed with his mouth, tasting her, teasing her. She gasped when his hand finally captured the treasure he'd been after. Then his mouth. With a groan, she twisted her fingers in his hair and yielded herself to him. Her mouth opened in a wordless scream as she arched with her need. The burning that drove deep inside her increased.

Before the water, Phaedra arched violently. Hot with yearning, she cried out as he made love to her with his mouth. With utter abandonment, she moved against him. The tension in her womb spiraled deeper and deeper until, poised in a wondrous moment, she felt as if she were rushing up to meet the sky.

The first thing she became aware of was a popping noise. It was the fire, bits of wood and embers crackling orange flames. She peered into the darkness. Maia was gone. Shaking, she rose to her feet.

Phaedra hugged her arms to her chest. Standing quietly and alone, she was flooded with longing, a longing kept behind walls and denied release.

Until now. The feeling so overwhelmed her she couldn't move. Locked with longing, she hugged herself tighter still. She had seen the future. Brannoc was to be her lover.

Any pleasure she might have felt over that union she dismissed in her next breath. Of course they were to be lovers. It was what she had wanted, she told herself. And what man could possibly resist her fragrance, Pagan Desires? None, if she was to believe the bawdy tales she heard from her customers. The perfume was irresistible.

Bohemund would be hers, and she would be able to avenge her father's death.

She shrugged her shoulders with a matter-of-factness that belied her spirit, for her heart continued to beat wildly with anticipation and desire. "He will be my lover," her heart whispered to her blood.

Night's purple hour robed Constantinople. In the garden of her villa, Phaedra held a compress to her brow, hoping the cool, lavender-scented cloth would soothe her head. With her free hand, she knotted the hem of her silk gown which was the color of a plum.

The pounding ache had followed her home from Maia's, that place between heaven and earth. Even bathing in rose-wood and comfrey oils had done nothing to ease the relentless stamping pressure, or, for that matter, mask the smell of laurel. She could still smell the pungent smoke the old woman had used to cloud her thoughts and make way for the visions. She tasted the bitter smoke on her lips.

"Mother! Mother! Come quick!"

Phaedra lowered the compress and turned her head. Alexander was running through the lamp-lit hall, heading toward her in the atrium's garden.

"What is it, Alexander?" She thought Brutus had run out of the courtyard again.

Alexander rushed across the garden and didn't stop until he crashed into her knees. As Phaedra steadied him, he blurted out, "There are soldiers at the gate. And one of them's dying!"

Phaedra rose at once, dropping the compress on the stone bench. "Where's Sharif?" she asked, rushing out of the night and into the villa.

"He's with them now," Alexander said, running past her to lead the way.

While Alexander ran through the open door and into the courtyard, Phaedra could see Vinicius and Sharif struggling to support Brannoc.

The vision! She recalled she had just seen him injured in her vision.

She heard Helena come up behind her.

"Dear Mother in Heaven and all the saints!" Helena screeched as the men moved to get a better hold on Brannoc, revealing his blood-soaked tunic.

Phaedra didn't have to look to know he was wounded in his side. She noted the long, deep gash at his waist. His white surcoat fell in tatters, caked with dried and fresh blood. He hung between the men, his head slumped forward to his chest. He looked like a beast that had been hunted down for sport. His powerlessness made something catch in her throat. She tried to swallow.

Vinicius's eyes caught hers. "I'm sorry, Lady Ancii, but I didn't know where else to take him."

"Who is he, Mother?" Alexander cried out excitedly.

"A barbarian, judging by the looks of him," Helena replied.

"Shush, Alexander. He's a soldier for the emperor." Phaedra threw Helena a scathing look.

"Bring him inside, Vinicius, Sharif," Phaedra commanded, placing her hand on the charioteer's arm.

She was now staring at Brannoc, who'd lifted his head at the sound of her voice. He held her gaze. Even though his pain had to be pulling him into unconsciousness, Phaedra detected a fierce glimmer in his eyes.

He's still fighting, she thought to herself. For a moment, she recalled the vision, played it again in her mind's eye. Once again, he was in the tent, fighting his attackers, falling to the assassin who wielded a lance.

She gave a start and stiffened as Brannoc's eyes opened a little wider, as if in acknowledgment of her thought. But before she could say anything, he slumped forward in a faint.

She reached out and felt the pulse at the base of his neck. He was alive, but his heart was weak.

"Helena?" Phaedra whispered. "Please set up a cot in my study."

The thought of a barbarian under the same roof was too much for the woman. Her beaded braids shook as she exclaimed, "Surely you don't intend to let him—"

Phaedra cut Helena off with a stare that could have turned her to stone.

"At once, my Lady."

As Vinicius and Sharif carried Brannoc inside, Phaedra turned to Alexander.

"Alex, I need your help. There's gauze and bandages in the chest next to the desk. Bring them to me. I'm going to clean and dress his wound in the dining room."

"Yes, Mother," and Alexander raced off on his important mission.

They pushed a silk divan away from the dining table, and eased him down, propping his back against the bolstered arm. Were it not for his wound, Brannoc could have been mistaken for a drunken guest. But it was hard not to notice the stain of blood spreading, hungrily devouring the white threads of his tunic.

Phaedra knelt before the divan. As he was still armed, she unfastened the brass-studded belt which held his scabbard, all the while remembering the vision and the sound of flashing steel as he had drawn his weapon to defend himself. She noted the leather scabbard was decorated with crimson bands, and every inch was covered with twining shapes and symbols in gold thread. A winged serpent guarded the blade. The sword was light, equal parts metal, fire and air.

Handing scabbard and belt to Vinicius, she said, "Take these to the vault for safekeeping, General. Make sure Alexander doesn't touch them."

Only after she'd removed his weapons did she notice a small, embroidered leather pouch hanging from a cord around his waist. She untied it, slid the cord through her fingers and gingerly felt the pouch. Something hard moved beneath her fingertips, but before she dared to look inside, Vinicius returned.

Using Sharif's dagger, Phaedra ripped away the blood-soaked cloth to expose the wound. As she worked, cutting and gently moving the cloth to the sides, she forgot the men behind her. Only when her fingertips peeled back a piece of skin and cloth, fully exposing the wound, did someone gasp, reminding Phaedra that she wasn't alone.

She moved closer and peered at the wound. Gingerly, she touched the perimeter. It needed stitching. It was dangerously

deep, but she noted it was clean. He'd been wounded by a
lance. But she already knew that.

"You haven't asked how it happened," Vinicius said over
her shoulder.

"Sharif, bring me the gauze and bring Alexander to help
Helena."

After taking some of the gauze and doubling it, Phaedra
pressed it into Vinicius's hand. "You can tell me how it happened later. Right now, I want you to hold this against his
wound to stop the flow of blood," she directed. Vinicius's
eyes and mouth had grown as wide and round as a fish.
"Keep your hand on it, General, until I return. I need to
prepare a few things."

Brannoc was awake and alone when Phaedra returned with
a tray topped with healing waters and salves for cleansing,
an embroidery needle and thread for stitching the wound.
She also carried a goblet of wine mixed with herbs to dull
the pain. Like a dutiful patient, Brannoc was holding the
gauze pressed against his naked side. He had somehow managed to remove his tunic. His hair hung past his shoulders,
but it did not shield him from her appraising eyes. His chest
was wide and gold from the sun, and his shoulders and arms,
they could have moved mountains. His chest rose and fell
with each breath, and for a moment, she felt as if he'd inhaled
all the air in the room and left her none.

At her step, Brannoc looked up. His eyes were no longer
drowsy and wolf-like, but wide and alert. She caught herself
remembering her erotic vision and felt the heat rise in her
cheeks. His stare deepened.

She dropped to her knees before the divan and set the tray
down, all without saying a word. She held the goblet out to
him.

"This will help ease the pain," she said, noting the paleness
of his face. She carefully avoided looking in his eyes. After

he'd taken the wine, she lost herself in the process of cleansing his wound.

"General Vinicius was feeling faint, so he went outside to get some air," he said.

A wry smile on her lips, Phaedra said, "I thought he'd outgrown his fear of blood by now. As a child, he would faint at the mere sight of a bead of blood on his finger." She paused as she lifted his hand and the gauze to examine the wound. "What will he do on a battlefield?"

"War will drive his apprehension away. There's no room for fear when you're fighting to stay alive."

Softly dabbing a mixture of aloe and lavender water on the wound, she said, "I'll need to stitch this closed."

He closed his hand over hers, stopping her for a moment. She did not look up.

"I'm used to having my wounds treated by butchers. Your fingers move like feathers across my skin. It is a welcome change, Lady Ancii."

She stared at her hand in his until he let her go.

Silence fell. It was a quiet scented with healing herbs and flowers, unspoken words fragrant with possibilities.

"Why did you run away?" Brannoc asked at last.

Startled, she stopped and looked up from her work. "What?"

"The encounter with Daniel, the holy man who called you a pagan."

She returned the aloe and lavender compress to the tray and picked up the threaded needle. Gently pressing his skin together, she began to stitch the lance cut. Brannoc didn't flinch.

"I didn't run away."

"Oh? That's strange. When I returned, I'd swear you were gone."

"I was quite able to find my own way home."

"You like to take risks." It was an observation that came to his lips as he watched her delicately and neatly stitch his skin as if she were working on a tapestry. He smiled at her handiwork.

Without looking up, she replied, "I can say the same of you. How did this happen?"

"But you already know," he whispered.

It can't be possible, she thought over and over again. He knows about the visions?

Her gaze slowly moved up his naked side, chest, and shoulders to his face. His blue eyes held her as intimately as any embrace.

"No."

He must have instinctively known that she would move away, for he grabbed her upper arm, stopping her. But in the next breath, he had to let her go as Vinicius had returned.

"Feeling better, I see?" He stopped to stand over them both.

"Did he tell you he was attacked by five men? The sixth did that to him," he gestured with his chin, "and got away."

Both answered.

"Yes," she said.

"No—" Brannoc denied.

Vinicius arched his brows. "Well?"

Directing a gaze at the barbarian spiced with warning, Phaedra spoke up.

"You spoke of it in your sleep," she said, luring him into a lie.

Brannoc scratched his chin. "Ah."

"I don't think he should be moved, Phaedra," Vinicius said. "As you're already preparing a room for him, I assume you agree that he should stay," he said.

A room? Christ, yes she was preparing something for him.

"I—" she started. The Dragon? Stay here? That was impossible.

"Well, I don't," Brannoc announced. He moved to get up. But before Vinicius or Phaedra so much as said a word, Brannoc slumped back, clutching his wounded side. His breath hissed between his teeth.

"That answers it. You'll be safe here, with the lady Ancii, Sir Brannoc. No one will think to look for you here. I'll inform Bohemund myself."

With one mind, Phaedra and Brannoc looked up at Vinicius.

"You've thought this through." Lured by his icy tone, Phaedra looked at the barbarian. There was something fiery and suspicious in his glare.

"The emperor cannot afford to lose Bohemund's most trusted and able captain and bodyguard." Vinicius paused. "I've made arrangements for the villa to be guarded at all times. And I beg your indulgence, Phaedra, but you must not leave the villa unescorted."

"What?" Alarmed, Phaedra rose to her feet. "Am I and my family to be prisoners in our own house?"

"It's only temporary."

Phaedra confronted Vinicius, forcing him to step back. "You yourself said that no one would look for him here. This is uncalled for, General!"

Vinicius scratched his chin. "Emperor's orders, Lady Ancii," he added formally.

Infuriated by Vinicius's order of protected captivity, she temporarily forgot who it was she was forced to be held captive with. Then she remembered.

Two days passed and Phaedra became aware of a subtle but pervasive change in her home. She felt as if she'd grown a shadow, an immense, dark presence. It was wild and deep. She had only to reach out to touch it and it would close around her, like ink-black water. If she didn't know better, she would have thought it was the devil following her, or one of his fallen angels.

Brannoc had eased into the easy rhythm of Phaedra's

household, sleeping and healing beneath the leopard skin, amusing Alexander with tales from his travels, winning over Sharif with a knowledge of horses equal to the charioteer's. Helena had changed her mind about him, too, after noting his calm, soothing eyes and fine manners, which she likened to those of a Greek patrician.

But he'd disrupted Phaedra's rhythm. His presence filled the villa. At night she could hear the walls straining to contain him. By day she was running into him at every turn. Their hands and bodies would graze, sending shocks of heat through her. She knew he'd felt it, too, by the way he held himself, close to her, breathless, waiting.

She tried to make herself invisible. But like a moth to a flame, he drew her to him. And if she wasn't tending his wound, she was thinking about him, remembering the visions, the one that had come true and the other that had yet to be.

Over and over again, she caught herself staring out over the sea, wondering how a vision could feel so real. For it was real to her. Her skin knew his touch. The memory of his embrace, his lips on hers, his mouth whispering his desire for her. He unsettled her with such fierceness she could not even look into his eyes for fear of letting the veils slip and exposing her thoughts.

On the third day, she rose and found Brannoc and Alexander in the garden. They were hunched together in a pool of golden light, their heads close, looking down at something. She stood quietly watching, and for a moment she thought of Jason and the pleasure and pride he would have felt for this glorious, raven-haired child.

Brannoc rose and, as if knowing she was there, turned to Phaedra. He smiled a grin that expected nothing in return.

When Alexander saw his mother, he cried out for all Constantinople to hear, "Look, Mother! Brannoc has tattooed my arm!"

In an instant, he was standing before her, proudly holding out his arm so she could look at it. She managed to smile in light of his joy, but felt it waver and crack. She ran her finger over the blue stain of a winged serpent that curled around his forearm three times. A dragon!

Her fury was immediate, roaring through her like a fire set to kindling. She knew if she rubbed hard enough, the stain would come off on her finger, but she didn't. Not now. She glanced over Alexander's head to Brannoc. His arms were crossed, his own tattoos visible, permanent, guarding his heart.

"Yes, I see," she said, each word a spark.

Alexander looked up at her, confusion in his eyes. His mother was supposed to be as excited as he was over his tattoo!

"Alex," she started more gently, "go and tell Helena that we'll be eating out here today."

"Don't you like it?"

"Yes, I do. Now please, go and tell Helena."

Pouting, Alexander walked away, dragging his feet. Phaedra stalked across the garden.

Looking up into the barbarian's face, her temper flaring, she lashed, "How dare you! You've no right to mark my child with your pagan symbols!"

"And what pagan symbol is that?" he asked. The taunting glimmer in his eyes fed her.

She waited a moment before answering. "The serpent."

"Dragon," he corrected, whispering, sending a chill up Phaedra's spine.

"Call it what you will, you have no right to mark my child."

"The dragon will protect him. Just as it will protect you."

Phaedra felt her knees turn to water. She wet her lips with nervousness. What was happening? Why was he speaking of protection? What had she and Alexander to fear? She said abruptly, "What are you talking about?"

"You knew of my coming."

Phaedra swallowed hard. She felt cold. She was shaking from head to foot. She whispered, "No, no." She looked up at him, not knowing what else to say or do.

Lost in a circle of quiet and denial, they did not hear Sharif approach. Only when he cleared his throat did they look up to see him standing awkwardly on the fringe of the courtyard.

Sharif's eyes passed back and forth, measuring the sliver of distance between them. "Forgive me, Lady, but, for some reason, the guards have been ordered to leave." His bushy brows arched. "I imagine this is General Vinicius's doing."

"Vinicius had nothing to do with it." But she could not bear to leave the comment unadorned. "We are well protected."

There was no thanks in her voice, but a muffled heaviness, as if she were speaking from behind a fortress wall.

"There," she whispered out loud in the darkness of her room. She listened closely. It was as if the villa were holding its breath and waiting for something to happen. As her eyes adjusted to the blackness, she pictured Leda and the swan on the fresco before her with such clarity, her room could have been flooded with sunlight. She saw the naked figure yielding, desiring, her black hair moving to an unseen breeze. And there was the god Zeus, disguised as a swan, the fierce heat of his lust in his black eyes betraying his identity. His white wings were spread wide, caught in mid-beat, open to the inevitable. He would have her. Phaedra thought of feathers against flesh, stroking the wildness in Leda until her life force spiraled up and lunged into flight.

"Come to me."

"Desire me."

The voices made her shiver, like the tips of feathers up her back. She could feel her body moisten and swell, the desire unlock in a place she'd thought had no more feeling.

Not since Jason.

Holding her breath, she looked about the room, even though she knew she was alone. Swallowing her disbelief, she rose from the bed and, draping a soft blanket over her shoulders, set out to see . . . she did not know what.

Brannoc saw Phaedra before she saw him. She was standing between the white columns of the garden, looking up at the moon, unaware that the light was sifting through her cotton gown, revealing the length of her limbs as purposefully as if quiet hands were turning back the cloth. Her black hair hung long and heavy, tousled by sleep. Her lips looked swollen, as if someone had been kissing her.

He shifted his weight and the chalky stones beneath him rubbed and grumbled. Her gaze flew, locked on him, and widened with alarm. He watched her gather the blanket around her shoulders. It hid nothing from him, and he had to smile.

She clutched the blanket between her fingers and walked around the courtyard, the columns serving as bars that separated her from the partially clothed, long-maned beast in her garden.

The beast spoke. "I'm sorry to have startled you. I could not sleep, and the moonlight lured me away from my thoughts." He turned in place, watching her watching him.

The white gauze bandages split his torso in half like a river cutting between hard ground. His shoulders were wide and well-muscled, as were his arms, no doubt from wielding the heavy swords and weapons the westerners loved so much. His white woven chausses hung low, nearly to his hip bones. His thighs looked mammoth beneath them. He was all white and gold, save for the blue tattoos. And the blood.

She watched as a red stain suddenly showed through the bandages.

She moved to take a closer look, the columns unable to protect her and keep him at a distance.

She frowned at the thought that he might have torn the stitches and opened his wound. Looking down at the blood pooling up through the cloth, she said, "You might think you're healed, but you're not. This is going to take time." She looked up into his face. "You should be resting. What will your liege lord say when you return to him still bleeding like that?" she asked. "Might he not think I tried to kill you by making you worse?"

"I'll tell him I did die, and that were it not for my stubborn healer, I would not have bothered to leave Hades for the living."

She sighed loudly and, turning away, said, "Come inside so I can tend to your wound and apply fresh bandages." But as she moved, he caught her by the arm, stopping her.

There. All at once, she heard the sound of a breath being drawn and held in, felt the touch of his hand, smelled the healing power of lavender and oils and jasmine on the night wind. She was locked, a fortress barred, until he turned her around to face him.

His mouth was so close she could taste it. His lips moved.

"Why are you always running? What is it that frightens you?"

A spark. "Nothing," she said vehemently, "frightens me."

He ran his hands down her arms, peeling the blanket from her. She did not resist. Taking her hands, he wrapped his fingers around her wrists. Pinned by the Dragon, she could feel her pulse throbbing in her neck and temples. She looked up at him, arching her back as he stood so close.

"Phaedra," he whispered hoarsely.

Held by his desire, she felt a sensation like trickling oil around her hands, and looked. The dragons around his wrists were alive.

Ten

Phaedra blinked, thinking that the moonlight was playing tricks. Spellbound, she watched the dragons raise their heads and hiss. Their wings trembled. They were sea-green and blue, delicate things, more diaphanous than a butterfly.

She drew a long breath as she watched them coil around her wrists, leaving a wet, cold sensation in their wake. They turned up and around her bare arms, tickling her, weaving circles that made her dizzy to watch. Finally, they stilled between her elbows and shoulders.

The clouds moved across the moon, a veil of sudden darkness descended, and the dragons were gone. Knotting her brow, confused, she looked again at Brannoc's wrists and stared, for there they were, quiet, still and blue.

She shivered, her mind fighting against what she had just witnessed, urging her to rationalize, to blame the moonlight, the wine she'd had at dinner, anything!

Brannoc caught her distress and, holding her hands, smoothed her knuckles with his fingers. A flash of heat snaked through her hands, up her arms, and spread like a blanket over her. She lifted her face to him then, just as he raised her hands, and brushed his mouth over one, then the other.

"You are my fate, Phaedra," he whispered, his breath catching in his throat, the bronze resonance of his voice moving through her. "When I was given the sign of the Dragon,

I was told that someday I would be called on to serve and protect someone. That there would be a sign. For years I thought that person was El Cid. But it was not so. Nor is it Bohemund, although my sword is pledged to defend and protect him. I joined his army because I knew he planned to journey to Constantinople on his way to the Holy Land. Throughout the journey, I dreamed of a swan." His hands tightened as he felt her trembling.

Phaedra felt as if she were about to fall or take flight. He too had dreamed? It could not be! How? Why? She listened with every pore of her being as he continued.

"The dreams have guided me to you, the Swan," he said. "It seems we are to be bound together. Will you fight me, Phaedra?"

"Fight?" But there was no chance to save herself with words. Brannoc lowered his head and covered her mouth with his own.

Her pulse was pounding. At his voice, his touch, all the wanting in her flooded to the surface. She could do nothing but let him kiss her, feeling the strangeness, the familiarity of it, stirring her down to her soul. His lips suggested the pleasures to come.

Then, with a fierce hunger, he crushed her mouth, demanding satisfaction. His mouth was hot, hard, wicked. Yes, he'd done this before, kissed her as if there were no tomorrow and all the passion he felt had to be released this moment. He thrust his hands into her hair and played with the silky black mass.

The vision! She panicked.

"Yes!" She gave a start as Brannoc's voice entered her mind. But he was there in front of her, she thought, his steadying hands on her shoulders, his mouth branding hers so she would know the feel of him forever.

Just as Maia had instructed, Phaedra relaxed. She opened her mind and shaped the dream.

Both of them had dreamed of this. They had been lovers long before they touched.

Phaedra flowed like water beneath Brannoc's lips and hands. She opened her mouth to him, secretly rejoicing as his plundering tongue overtook hers and his arms went around her, pressing her so that all his body became known to her, its hardness and grace, its contours and need. His large hands moved on her, stroking, cupping, eliciting moans that dared to pass Phaedra's lip when his caresses descended to shape the curves of her flesh. The feel of his hands on her could not have been more intimate.

She'd expected this, this tide of feeling the vision had foretold, but she was overwhelmed by his needs. And her own. Of their own volition, her arms rose and wrapped around his neck. Her fingers ran through the length of his mane. It was the gentlest of ministrations, but it brought a moan to the beast's lips. He moved his mouth to her neck and whispered her name over and over to her skin.

She loved the heat of him, his hair beneath her fingertips, his breath on her neck as he taught her throat the feel of her name. With no warning, he lifted her up in the moonlight and stood her on the stone bench. The mosaic tiles felt cold and cut into the soles of her feet, but the sensation left as soon as she saw the fire and burning need in his eyes.

With the light guiding him, he brushed her hair back over her shoulders. Then, with one sure movement, his hands tore the white cotton shift from her shoulders. Meeting her eyes and holding her gaze, he slid the fabric down her arms, over her breasts, and let it gather and drape around her hips.

He didn't touch her. He stepped back and circled her until he stood behind her. The moon spilled light across her white shoulders. There were stars in her hair. He reached out and tangled his fingers in it. She arched back as if it were the most exquisite sensation. He noted the weave of muscles her hair could not hide, her tapered waist, the curve of her hip. He became very still.

She caught her breath. His hands caught the rise and swell of her breasts. Within her mind, she leapt back in time, and beheld the vision of herself entwined in his arms.

There was a whispering in the trees. "Surrender," it said. Brannoc looked. Had he heard?

"I have waited so long," he whispered, looking up into her face.

Drawing strength from somewhere deep inside, she held her hand out and drew him to her, initiating the fiery spark that struck whenever they touched.

"Brannoc," she whispered as if in a dream.

The vision unfolded. He stepped toward her and kissed her stomach, leaving a trail of feathery, teasing kisses. He tasted her, licking her skin that grew taut and tight beneath his lips as her breaths came sharp and shallow. She held his head against her and moaned to the moon.

Her shift did not resist the tug of his hands on her hips. It drifted to the ground. He scooped her buttocks in his hands and drew her forward to his waiting mouth. He kissed her lower, deeper and opened her with his tongue. And she became lost within her longing.

Brannoc lifted Phaedra, trembling and wet, and carried her into the villa. A wet sheen gilded her flushed, naked body. He set her down in the study. A bronze lamp turned their bodies to gold. Phaedra watched Brannoc move to the desk and pick up an alabaster vial. There was something familiar . . .

He carried it to her, lifting the top, releasing a scent into the air, and then she knew.

Pagan Desires.

The perfume she'd intended to use to seduce the Dragon was now being used to seduce her.

Like an animal, he crouched before her and began to anoint her body with the perfumed oil, starting with her ankles and the backs of her knees. His fingers ascended, tracing patterns across her lower back and stomach. She could tell he was enjoying the silence and control of the anointing by the glimmer in his half-hooded eyes, the pleasure around his mouth. As she was plotting how she would avenge him for this, he reached her breasts, and for the first time, he touched her, licking her with his tongue, but leaving the nipples unscented.

He anointed her wrists, the base of her neck, the indentations behind her ears. The room expanded with the smell of rose and jasmine and their own heat. She felt a tightening in her womb. She reached for her lover to fill her. He captured her hands, held her back against the wall, and pinned her wrists above her head beneath the weight of his arms. She shivered, feeling the leopard skin at her back, feeling his chest rub against her breasts, turning her nipples to points of fire.

She closed her eyes, and in the dark she saw the fresco, her painted self and arched with a longing too long denied.

They fell to the bed.

Until this moment, Jason had been the only lover she had ever had. Now her body and mind melted, and she moved like a flame within Brannoc's embrace, becoming one with the Dragon. She had the sense that she was coupling with a deep, dark wildness that was as much a part of her as it was a part of this barbarian from the West.

With an urgency that would embarrass her later, she drew him into her. He welcomed her touch and her need, but he had a mind of his own and thought to prolong this coupling he too had foreseen in his dreams. Calmly, he kissed her mouth, neck and shoulders, shushing her demanding whimpers, then finally mastering her with his rhythm. They grew together, their scents rubbing, mingling into each other's flesh. The pulse of blood, the heart hammering, his, hers, became indistinguishable.

Here was the mystery and mastery of life, a force that drove him above her. He dove and dove, groaning. Phaedra writhed beneath him as if to fly away, but he anchored her, forcing upon her wave after wave of pleasure from which there was no escape. Crying aloud, she fell upward, and at the crest of her pleasure, heard his savage moan.

Love me again, she thought.

Words unspoken, but heard. She clasped his face between her hands and kissed him hard, this creature of fire and water.

He tore his mouth free and, rising, moving above her, looked down into her face. "Again, lady," he grunted, smiling. "I don't remember this part of the dream."

She licked her lips, wrapped her fingers around the serpents which guarded his wrists and felt the ascent beginning once more. "Neither do I," she mouthed, moving beneath him.

She let go of him and found the pleasurable places in his back that made him arch and smile. She fingered his hair and drew him down to her again. She breathed his name into a kiss and banished thoughts of dreams.

Brannoc was gone when Phaedra awoke the next morning. Staring at the ceiling, she listened. The villa was silent. She turned onto her side and pressed her face into the place where he'd lain. She drew a long breath. The bed was lush with his male scent, the bloom of perfume mixed with her own heat, and the dampness of their shared pleasure.

She sat up, taking no care to cover herself, and, from the bed, saw he had left the alabaster vial that contained the love potion, Pagan Desires. She arched her brow. The perfume had weaved a spell last night, she thought. But it hadn't worked quite the way she'd intended. The perfume never got a chance to set the trap and lure Brannoc. There hadn't been a need.

Here's the magic, she thought, rising and moving to her desk. She picked up the vial and palmed its coolness. She closed her fingers around it and revered the perfume as if it were a talisman with the power to unveil a new world.

Eleven

Phaedra and Alexander rode far ahead of the soldiers the emperor had sent to escort them out of the city and into the country. Mother and son wore trousers and leather tunics. Short blue cloaks rippled from their shoulders. Sharif was not far behind them, but Helena, confined to a sedan chair, was separated by a great distance owing to the marching pace set by the soldiers. There was a second sedan chair, as it had been assumed that Phaedra, being a lady, would prefer to travel in sheltered luxury. It had not gone to waste, however, as Alexander's bear cub Brutus had preferred its roomy space and pillows to his cage.

There were no packs of clothing or food, as the estate, which had been in Jason's family since ancient times, had everything they would need. Phaedra traveled with one thing only, the vial of Pagan Desires. The perfume was packed in an embroidered leather pouch at her belt. Alexander had his bow slung over his shoulder, for Sharif had promised to teach him to shoot.

It was warm. The fields were gold with growing wheat and the sky was a serene blue. The horses had found an easy rhythm. Out of the corner of her eye, Phaedra proudly noted Alexander's skillful handing of his horse, a dun-colored mare, but full grown. Alexander had finally gotten his wish of going out to the country, and he was crowing with joy. His happiness made up for the cloud of gloom that had gathered above Phaedra's head when she'd heard of the emperor's orders to leave the city. Rumors that she'd brought a barbarian back to life had fueled Daniel's scandalous sermons. Someone had painted "Pagan Whore" on the wall around her home.

Phaedra's enemies had increased on another front as well. A few of her customers had turned on her after learning that Pagan Desires would no longer be sold at The Swan. News of the perfume's unavailability had traveled like a swarm of bees, stinging courtesans and noblewomen alike. No longer would their husbands and lovers find them attractive, sensuous and worthy of their love, they complained. Their marriages and love affairs would be ruined! Without the silken ties created by the love spell of Pagan Desires, they were only women. Powerless.

Simon, The Swan's shopkeeper, hadn't questioned her about her decision. In fact, it was as if he'd known that something had changed within her. As for her customers, to hell with the lot of them, she thought. Fickle women. Sharks.

What a time they must be having with this at the baths, she thought. She scowled, thinking about it, thinking about them. She looked hard into the distance and tried to forget.

But deep down, she'd been waiting for something to pull her away from thoughts regarding Brannoc. She would often catch herself thinking of the barbarian, listening for his horse in the courtyard, casting glances over her shoulder while arranging vials and flasks in the shop. Night after night she would awaken, dreams floating about in her head too vivid *not* to be true. She felt his hands on her. His mouth . . .

Digging her heels into her stallion's sides, she leaned over his neck and horse and rider soon took to the air. Alexander, fearless, and fiercely believing that his mighty steed was the son of Pegasus, Alexander the Great's magical, winged horse, was not far behind.

* * *

They arrived at the estate at nightfall, just as candles were being lit to welcome them home.

The villa was situated between Constantinople and Adrianople, in Thrace. It was surrounded by a fertile valley watered by springs fed by the Maritsa River, situated near the site of an ancient city that no one could remember. The land had been in Jason's family since the time of the emperor Claudius. Since then, it had been occupied by Jason's Roman ancestors, confiscated by Goths and Bulgars, then re-inhabited by more Romans. The land was rich with tales. Jason used to tell Phaedra and Alexander that, in the evening, if they listened carefully enough, they could hear the earth sighing beneath the weight of all that knowing.

The land knew how to care for itself, but the work of farmers and irrigation techniques had made it truly rich. There were orchards aplenty, protected by a thorn hedge. They bore pear, mulberry, cherry, apple, pomegranate and three varieties each of grapes and figs. There were olive groves and various herbs and vegetables.

Phaedra, Alexander, Sharif and Helena gathered in the dining room to eat the light meal that had been quickly prepared for them.

Candles lit the room, and the flames danced and wavered across the glass. Phaedra and Alexander shared a couch in the Roman style, while Helena and Sharif sat stiffly on wooden chairs. They helped themselves to the fresh goat cheese, loaves of golden bread, olives and barley cakes sweetened with Ancii honey, and figs. There was wine for everyone. Even Alexander was permitted a sip from his mother's silver goblet.

The housekeeper, a jowly Thracian with one continuous dark eyebrow across her brow, oversaw everything. She was still wearing the scowl that had appeared when she discovered Brutus in one of the sedan chairs. A large key dangled from her girdle. It opened the storeroom underneath the kitchen. Every time Phaedra finished a bit of cheese, the housekeeper filled her plate up again, clucking all the while, commenting under her breath that her mistress was "skin and bones, skin and bones." Helena, who was prone to defend Phaedra against the overprotective, well-fed housekeeper, was too busy feeling her aching muscles and massaging her backside to fight. Even Phaedra was too tired to fuss. She simply regarded the multiplying food on her plate with weak smiles.

The mix of night, the day's ride and fatigue worked like a sleeping draught. After numerous yawns, Sharif and Helena left to seek sleep in their rooms. On the divan, Phaedra drew Alexander close to her. She held him, smoothed his hair off his forehead and listened as his breathing changed. She knew he had fallen into a deep sleep. She kissed her son's brow and stared out into the night. She was tired, but like a lookout on duty, she stayed awake. Lately, her dreams had become dangerous. They were gold with heat, kisses, Brannoc's hands moving over her body, and pagan desires realized.

Rosy-fingered dawn was just beginning to paint the sky when Phaedra saddled one of the horses. She wore creamcolored trousers beneath a short, saffron-colored tunic cinched at the waist by a wide leather belt. The sleeves were short, exposing her pale arms. On her feet were leather boots, dusty and scuffed from the previous day's ride.

Phaedra's black hair was parted in the center, and wound into a thick coil at the base of her neck. Gold earrings shaped like dolphins dangled from her earlobes.

She heard Sharif's heavy footstep behind her, but did not turn.

"And where are you off to?" he inquired.

Phaedra looked over her shoulder and watched Sharif approach.

"Achilles is getting fat," she said, facing the horse again, patting the glossy black flank. "He needs to be exercised."

Hearing his name, the stallion's ears perked up. Sharif had named all of the horses after warriors and princesses in the Iliad.

Sharif noted the bag of arrows and bow slung across the saddle. He raised a thunderous brow and caught her glance.

"In case I decide to hunt," she shrugged.

"There have been reports of bands of deserters from the cross-bearers' armies in the area."

With a sideways glance, she retorted, "If they're so stupid, then they shouldn't be a problem. Besides, I have this," she said, patting the dagger jammed under her belt. It had a ruby set in its pommel which had belonged to her father. The ruby shone in the light like a bright, wet wound. "And I'll have my bow with me."

But her comment inspired nothing more than a grumble from Sharif. She heard him scratching his stubbly jaw. Ignoring the lowering, gray eyebrows, she snatched the reins out of his hands.

"Just a ride around the estate," she assured him in her most agreeable voice. "I'll be back before Alexander gets up." And with that, she vaulted into the saddle, reined Achilles to the right and cantered out of the courtyard. Achilles's hooves sang on the stones.

She rode as if the devil were after her. Over green land, ripe as olives, and through gold stubbly fields she flew. She sat hunched forward, low, clinging to Achilles, a warrior who attacked the earth with his hooves. It was a radiant day, splendid as honey. The light was moist. Phaedra and Achilles bathed in the golden waves of its shine.

They flew around the perimeter of the estate. They were a spark on the horizon, an arrow aimed at nothing.

Far from the villa, Phaedra reined Achilles. The horse whinnied, snorted and twitched his ears in disapproval. Her hand was light, but commanding. Her thighs pressed his sweating flanks. He slowed to a canter, then a walk. He shook his head as he stole a glance at his mistress.

In the grove, horse and rider halted. The leaves and branches made a patchwork of the blue sky. The gold of the day lost its shimmer. Here it was quiet and green.

Phaedra slid to the ground. A pool of water, fed by an underground spring, lay before her. The stallion stepped boldly into the water and drank. Phaedra followed, lying on her stomach and drinking deeply.

Achilles snorted in her hair, showering her with a spray of water. Phaedra laughed, batting the black muzzle away. A sudden reckless thought stole into her mind. Rising to her feet, she pulled her hair free of its pins, unfastened her belt, and removed her tunic and trousers. After tossing her garments into a heap by the pond, she dove into the crystal water. Achilles watched, blinked and turned away in boredom to graze.

She swam between long sea grasses that twined around her limbs as if they wanted to keep her there. She glided easily through the cool water, rising for breath. On the murky bottom she turned on her back and stilled, moving her arms to keep her place in the water. Looking up, she saw the surface as a mosaic of green and gold. She scissored up and broke into the sky, head first, imagining the gold and green breaking over her like glass.

As she smoothed her wet hair back, she had the startling sensation that someone was watching her. Her neck prickled. Beads of water along her spine turned to knife points. She stayed crouched with her knees bent, to hide her nakedness. She squinted into the grove, looked right and left, but she saw nothing.

Behind her, Achilles neighed and stamped. Phaedra whirled, using her arms to push herself around in the water. Her eyes widened as an intruder squatted to regard her at eye level.

"O Queen, I do implore: Are you divine or mortal?" Brannoc inquired gently, quoting Homer's *Odyssey.* His eyes shimmered with amusement, taking in her startled amber gaze, long wet hair and white shoulders. Her gold earrings sparkled with beams of sunlight. "I have a mind to join you and see for myself," he said wickedly.

She treaded back in the water, away from the blond-haired figure in the red cloak.

"Man of many wiles," she replied. Her words brought a smile to his lips, although it was not what she intended. "What are you doing here? No one knows of this place."

"I'm flattered to be called Odysseus. But tell me, what lured you so far from home? Surely it accommodates a bath? For these parts, I hear," he said, glancing about him, "are full of dangerous men."

"Humph," she retorted. "And one of them is standing before me now."

"Dangerous? I?" He threw back his head and laughed. "How so?"

"Begone, Sir Brannoc. Shouldn't you be protecting someone?"

"That is why I'm here, Phaedra," he said seriously, his voice as calm and silky as deep water. He rose suddenly and whipped his cloak from his shoulders. "But first I would like to wash off the dust of the road that has caked my garments," he said as he unstrapped his sword belt.

"What are you doing?" Incredulous, Phaedra watched him pull his tunic over his head and toss it over her clothes. She felt the blood rising to her face.

"Your secret pool seems to be big enough for two." He grimaced, hopping on one foot as he yanked off a boot.

She stood up, for a moment forgetting the shallowness of the pond at the edge. "Are you mad?"

Brannoc froze, perfectly balanced on one foot, as his gaze feasted on the body so temptingly revealed. "Most assuredly not," he answered with an appreciative grin.

Phaedra felt his eyes on her and cursed him as she dropped like a stone back into the water. She'd not let her body rule her mind.

He turned away and pulled off his trousers. She watched him and felt herself grow warm with longing at the sight of his tall, powerful body. He turned to face her. Their eyes locked. She turned away, but she saw enough to blush hotly.

She heard the water splash with his dive and panicked, sensing that he was coming right at her. She turned again, unconsciously pushing her arms out to keep him away, but, she looked. He wasn't there. She scanned the water. The surface was as smooth as silk.

She wrinkled her brow and, just as she began to worry, watched him surface like a great sea creature, on the far side of the pond.

Her shoulders dropped. Oh. He'd only wanted to refresh himself after all, she thought to herself.

Feeling awkward, on the edge between anger and flight, she stayed in the water. She was angry for permitting herself to believe that he'd wanted her. And she, for the briefest of moments, had wanted him.

He raised his hand and waved to her. She forced a smile.

"Now perhaps I can be left in peace," she muttered under her breath. But even as she said the words, their falseness jarred her. She wanted him!

She splashed through the water, dove and scissored along the green and murky bottom.

Hidden by cattails, resting her head on her arms on the loamy bank, Phaedra didn't hear Brannoc until he was behind her, whispering in her ear.

"I'm a fool to be jealous of the water. Yet it needs no permission to touch you. Whereas I, alas . . ."

Phaedra shivered at the sound of his voice. She felt his hands on her shoulders and let him turn her around to face him. His thumbs smoothed the bones and hollows of her neck. She watched his hands, saw the dragons and looked up. Her thoughts kept her still. Her mind wrestled with the identity and the mission of the man before her.

Who was he? A knight to El Cid. A barbarian who'd sold his fighting arm to travel with Bohemund. A wanderer guided by a dream. Brannoc was not born to magic. At least Maia hadn't intimated that he had such powers. But there was a power in him, on him, she thought, thinking of the dragon tattoos and how they'd come to life. And she had no doubt that he could use that power as easily as if he were drawing a breath of air.

Brannoc met Phaedra's silence with an arched brow. It did not smoothen when she looked him straight in the eye and spoke up.

"Muse, tell me of the man of many wiles,
the man who wandered many paths of exile
after he sacked Troy's sacred citadel.
He saw cities—mapped the minds—of many;
and on the sea, his spirit suffered every
adversity—to keep his life intact,
to bring his comrades back . . .
Muse, tell us of these matters. Daughter of Zeus,
my starting point is any point you choose . . ."

Brannoc laid his finger against her lips to stop her. "You know enough."

She turned away from his fingers. "I want to know all."

"In time," he said, placing his hands behind her on the edge of the bank. Phaedra leaned back against the earth, deliciously trapped between the land and his body. Brannoc moved, rubbing his body up the full length of hers, bringing a gasp to her lips.

She closed her eyes and marveled at the slow silky contact, at the proof of his desire, and melted in the heat of his arms.

"Life is to be lived, not discussed," he whispered.

"No—"

And her answer vanished, blown away by his lips that softly brushed over her mouth, teasing her, before claiming it hard against his. He gathered her in his arms. Without prelude or preparation, he lifted her by her buttocks, ran his hands down the backs of her parting thighs, and drove himself into her.

Phaedra arched back, her bruised mouth open to the air, her body flooded with sensation. Clinging to his shoulders, she met his gaze, caught the heat and yearning in his blue orbs and was nearly undone. She felt his hands on her thighs controlling her, pulling her away from him only to grip her back and impale her again and again.

She wrapped her legs around him to keep her body still. She kissed his chin, stroked his beard with her cheek, then moved to the soft spot behind his ear. She inhaled the natural fragrance of him, and licked his skin. She felt his hands moving up her backside, caressing her, his fingers marveling at the silkiness of her skin. When he could take no more of her teasing kisses, he clasped her head between his hands and stopped her with a deep, burning kiss.

She moved in his arms, building sensation on top of sensation until she could bear no more. Tearing her mouth free, she almost screamed aloud her bliss. The tightness, the purposeful heat held her now, then it threw her, to be lapped up by waves.

She heard his soft laughter as she opened her eyes.

"Impatient and greedy creature." He held her close, breathing in the natural scent of her, the veil of Pagan Desires, and smoothed her hair down her back. He felt her smile against his chest.

"I would not be surprised if you never wanted to make love to me again," she apologized.

"On the contrary," he answered.

His voice was like a stroke of heat. She looked up at him, and understood that he was eager to possess her again.

Brannoc withdrew from her, gathered her in his arms and

carried her out of the water. He set her down near their clothes, keeping his hands firmly on her hips.

Wet, dripping, she lifted her face to him, her eyes full of mischief. She said, "Shall we see how impatient and greedy the mighty Brannoc can be?"

Before he could answer, Phaedra slid between his hands to kneel before him. She moved her palms up his wet thighs as she covered his stomach with kisses. He groaned from the teasing assault of her hands and her lips moving over him. Her tongue followed the path she had laid with her kisses, and then she took him in her mouth.

He moaned as if it were the first time a woman had ever caressed him with her mouth and made love to him like this. Yet the hands in her hair commanded her, eversogently, to continue.

Just when she thought he would relinquish control, he pulled her away and joined her on the ground.

"Enough," he growled, capturing her in his arms. He straddled her and moved his hands over her body, luxuriating in the silky feel of her arms, shoulders, the moon-perfection of her breasts beneath his caressing fingers. She trembled beneath his touch and his gaze. There was no hiding from him. She watched him, this towering warrior, blond and gold to her black and ivory.

When she lifted her arms to touch him in return, he took her wrists firmly in his hands and lowered them to the ground above her head. Only then did he cover her with his body. Her actions thwarted, she struggled, but stilled when his lips tasted hers. She parted her lips and offered all she had to give.

His heat consumed her. She arched to receive him as he thrust into her. Lost in a private world, they moved possessed by a dark wildness that whirled and eddied up from the earth and threw them toward the sun.

* * *

Her head rested on his chest. His arms encircled her, one hand in her hair. She felt warm, languid, like a ripe plum waiting to be eaten. She felt safe and protected, not just by his strength and power, but by the magic represented by the dragon tattoos. She didn't understand why, but the thought calmed her.

She stroked his beard, playing with it, taking pleasure in the feel of it against her palm. She felt him shiver and heard his sigh.

She laughed into his shoulder.

A bird flitted above them. "Fly," she thought she heard it cry.

"We need to go." She started to move, but his hand tightened on her shoulder, making her still.

"I'm coming with you," he said.

She rose onto her side to look at him. Between breaths she realized that he had to return to the villa with her, and that his path was linked with hers in more ways than she could ever dream. "I know, Brannoc."

His eyes narrowed with a burning question, but he kept it to himself.

They dressed swiftly but without haste, as if to prolong the morning and create more time so that they could love again.

Eyes filled with mirth, Brannoc watched Phaedra struggle to slide her boots over her wet feet. He was strapping on his belt when he froze. He turned his head in the direction of the path through the trees and pursed his lips together in thought.

To Phaedra, he looked as if he were listening with his entire being. She stopped fussing with her boots and quietly asked, "What is it?"

He turned to her, raised his finger to his lips to signal quiet, and looked back into the trees. His fingers then moved quickly at his sword belt, finishing the task of securing it.

Phaedra rose to her feet and followed Brannoc's intense

gaze. A flock of birds suddenly broke from the trees and flew above them in alarm. She heard leaves rustling, branches breaking, and the stomp of horses' hooves. The sounds all merged together and echoed a warning.

Phaedra swallowed. She looked down at the hilt of her dagger showing through her belt and, as she lifted her gaze, caught Brannoc silently watching her. He looked behind her, to where the horses were tethered. They were saddled and ready to be ridden.

He moved to her side as quietly as a panther. "The bow," he whispered, directing her attention to the weapon hanging from her saddle. Somehow he knew enough not to ask whether she knew how to use it. The bow's presence seemed evidence enough of her skill. "Hide in the trees and use it as you see fit."

He watched her take off across the grass without a sound. Appreciation over the way she moved flickered in his eyes. He saw her lay her hand on the black horse's muzzle, and whisper a word into his ear. A frown crossed his face as his own horse began to stamp and snort, but in the next instant, Phaedra was beside him.

Both horses remained steady as she removed the bow and the quiver of arrows. A grin began to shape his mouth, but he caught himself, steeled his reaction and, hand on sword hilt, turned to face the intruders.

Hidden by branches and leaves, Phaedra pulled an arrow from the case slung across her back and laid it over the bow strings, point facing the ground. She raised it in front of her even before she saw anyone appear out of the trees.

There were eight of them, northerners judging by the paleness of their skin and hair. Two of them were leading horses, and they were all heading right toward Brannoc, who stood with his legs in a wide, commanding stance, as if he owned the land beneath him. He had not drawn his sword.

One of the men yelled something that made them all laugh. Phaedra winced at the thick, brutish sounds that came from his mouth, but Brannoc understood and answered back. The men stopped in their tracks and a few of them regarded each other nervously. One among them stepped forward, brandishing a sword. Brannoc drew his sword from its scabbard in a gesture so bold, his size seemed to increase threefold. The man froze, lulled by the weapon's slide and metallic slither, which sounded like a song of death. The blade winked in the sunlight.

All of the men were within her range, but she had her eye on the one who had stepped forward, a leader or fool, she couldn't tell which yet. She narrowed her eyes, clenched her jaw. She stood still and quiet, an armed statue that would have been fit to grace the Augusteion were it not for the fact that the figure, hair and face were those of a woman. Her arms were raised before her, one hand firmly on the bow, two fingers pulled back on the string and feathers.

She heard the fool spit out some guttural war cry. It must have pricked a nerve, because they all drew their swords and began to circle Brannoc.

It was all the signal she needed. In a blink of an eye, two men cried out and fell, her arrows piercing their backs. Brannoc never gave her a backward glance, but immediately went on the offensive, striking out at a startled barbarian. The man gathered his wits in time to parry the blow, then lashed out, forcing Brannoc back. Both hands wrapped around the hilt, Brannoc brought the sword up, impaling the slow-moving man on the tip. With a tug, he freed his sword and the man fell to his knees.

Phaedra missed her third mark, for he had suddenly moved into the water. He came up behind Brannoc, who was engaged with two other men. Quickly, she readied another arrow, turned, aimed and caught one of Brannoc's attackers in the thigh. In an instant, she had another arrow ready and was pulling back on the bow string, when someone grabbed her from behind and carried her, struggling, out of the trees.

At her cry, the intruders stopped. Brannoc froze as well.

His eyes narrowed dangerously as he watched Phaedra twist and turn in the arms of one of the intruders. The man must have noticed where the deadly shots were coming from and gone to investigate.

Phaedra was thrown to the ground like a bag of stolen gold. As one of the barbarians kept his eye and sword on Brannoc, the others laughed as if a woman with a bow and arrow was the most ridiculous sight they'd ever seen.

Incensed over being caught, furious at their obvious enjoyment of her plight, Phaedra rose to her feet, brushed the hair off her face and drew her dagger. The seriousness of her actions elicited heartier laughs.

"Fools," she cried recklessly. "I wager there's not a man among you who can take me!"

Brannoc swept Phaedra with a measuring gaze. But a poke in his side snared his attention and he looked hard at one of the men. The barbarian gestured to Phaedra and asked what she had said. He told them, and the guffaws split the sky.

A muscle twitched in Brannoc's jaw angrily. "Phaedra," he warned, disapprovingly. "Drop the dagger."

"I know what I'm doing," she answered fiercely. Phaedra's chin was set, stubborn, and the light in her eyes was deadly.

"Come on," she yelled, waving the blade before her.

One of the barbarians, pudgy and pink, with silver-yellow hair, made a big show of sheathing his sword and swaggering up to her. His fellows clapped him on the back and one of them thrust his hips obscenely.

The barbarian crouched before her. He opened and closed his hands in a clear invitation to step forward and attack him.

"Watch his eyes, they'll tell you everything," she remembered Sharif saying to her.

Pig eyes, she thought to herself, unafraid. Patiently, she waited for him to make what she was sure would be his first blunder.

She was not disappointed. He lunged at her, moving as slow as an ox, and she caught him with her dagger point in his side, ripping away his tunic, pricking his skin, before gliding out of his way. The laughter of his fellow soldiers brought a sneer to his face. He bared his teeth, knotted his fists, and barreled into her, knocking her off her feet. He threw himself on top of her and pinned her dagger arm to the ground above her head. But with her free hand, Phaedra grabbed him hard by the crotch. He yelled and bucked. Phaedra kneed him in the groin and pushed him off with her feet.

No one was laughing now. Clutching his privates, the barbarian rose on wobbly legs and came at her again with a growl. She side-stepped him nicely at the last moment, then brought her arms down together in a crushing blow to his neck. He fell face first, sprawling to the ground, and she leapt on top of him, pinning one of his arms behind his back. She jerked the limb up, making him cry out.

The men were spellbound, their eyes wide with wonder that a woman had felled one of them. It was at that moment that Brannoc, seeing a way out of their predicament, struck the man who had been lax in guarding him. He lunged to take on the remaining two. But when they turned and saw what had befallen their friend, they ran for the trees, leaving their horses and their other friend to die at a woman's hand.

Phaedra jumped to her feet, kicked the man in the shins, and ordered him to follow his cowardly friends.

She was rubbing her arm when Brannoc said, "You are a wonder, my lady."

He looked up at this woman he was sent to "protect" and drank in all of her, from her tousled, rumpled clothes, to her ivory skin, glorious hair, and her proud, stubborn, beautiful face.

She turned away as he reached out and drew her stiff, unyielding body into his arms.

"Wonder of wonders," he whispered into her hair, "but the Swan is a trained mercenary. If only you could ride at my side on this journey to save the Holy Land, then I know I would live to be an old man."

She smiled into this chest. "Oh, but I am going to the Holy Land," she thought to herself, biting her tongue to keep from blurting it out.

She felt him press a kiss into her hair. "Tell me, while I'm protecting you from—what, I don't know—who will protect my heart from you?"

A brush of a laugh escaped. "You speak as if I had the power to destroy your heart."

He tilted her face up to look at him. "You do, Phaedra." He kissed her gently, deeply, with a need that drove clear to her soul.

Twelve

Brannoc grabbed Phaedra from behind and kissed her. They were alone in the vaulted chamber of the villa. Rays of bronze red slanted through the narrow slits in the wall like arrows shot by the setting sun.

By some stroke of luck, they had evaded the watchful eyes of Sharif and Helena. The pair had been shadowing the lovers for two days, ever since Brannoc had accompanied Phaedra home to the villa. Sharif had been greatly distressed by the news of the attack, and relieved that Brannoc had been there to "save" Phaedra. But when the barbarian didn't leave at the end of that day, the charioteer threw himself into the role of Phaedra's guardian and stubbornly held to it.

Meanwhile Helena, well, after all, Brannoc was a barbarian. And his tattoos frightened her. She made the sign of the cross every time she caught a glimpse of them, which was often, because she could not help but seek their strangeness. Alexander, however, was too absorbed with riding, archery lessons and Brutus to take much notice of the time Phaedra spent with Brannoc.

Now, alone in the misty dark of this ancient room, the sun bleeding in through the high windows, Brannoc pulled Phaedra back into his arms and, bending forward, kissed her neck. He breathed in her scent. Playfully, she slapped his arms, which were curled like mighty snakes over her breasts. His kisses traveled up her neck. She tilted her head away from his mouth, exposing more of her neck, and reached back with one arm to pull him closer.

The gesture made him bold. He cupped her breasts and began caressing her through her cream silk tunic, brushing his fingertips over her already taut nipples.

"Phaedra." His voice caressed her name, and she shivered. How could the sound of her name render her breathless, and fill her with strength all at once? What was he doing to her? How could this be?

Brannoc had allowed his hands the freedom they had so longed for, the freedom to caress her body. He fondled her breasts, then smoothed his palm over her hips and stomach. He sought the warmth between her thighs. With a hungry groan, he drew her hard against him, one hand between her legs, the other fondling a breast.

"Let me love you, Phaedra," Brannoc whispered, his lips moving in her long, fragrant hair.

She turned in his arms. Her gaze never left his as she stepped back, unclasped her silk tunic and let it fall to the stone floor. She pulled her white linen undertunic over her head and sent it falling to the ground as well. Her eyes challenged him as clearly as words.

But Brannoc did not obey the fiery glint of desire in her eyes. He stood back and drank his fill of the sight presented to him. His frank, open admiration fanned her desire, but when he began to walk around her, the heat of his gaze became too much for her to bear.

"What is it, barbarian? Can't remember what comes next?" Her teasing masked her own trembling longing.

"Alas, your mouth must be taught better manners." And his thick tone held the promise of a lesson she would never forget.

He disrobed quickly, all the while feasting his eyes on her pale beauty. Naked, he caught her hair in his hands and kissed her until she forgot who she was. There was no space within that sensation for anything but the kiss itself. The demanding press of his lips, the warmth of his breath, the wicked flame of his tongue. She lifted her arms and soared.

The chamber swirled around them and it was as if they were both dreaming the same dream. She matched him kiss for kiss, tasting him, branding him with her own heat. What blazed between them was as fierce, bright and primitive as fire. They kissed with a passion born from naked need.

He lifted her in his arms and carried her to a table of stone no one had touched for decades, and set down his offering. Long ago, in another time, flowers, honey and libations of water mixed with wine had been set on its surface as offerings to the god Zeus and his kind. The polished gray stone held Phaedra now. Its coolness was a shock to her robe of heat. But as she lay back and opened herself to Brannoc, his fire centered deeply in her, the weight of the room, and the hush of sacred mysteries bore down on her and whipped all else into oblivion.

The lavender was knee-high in the fields. At the edge of the rows, Phaedra and Brannoc lay on a soft, wool blanket. A lunch of grapes, figs, bread and cheese was spread out around them. They were far enough from the villa to have some privacy. And yet, if Helena squinted hard enough, she could have just made out their heads poking above the lavender. Clouds, gray and billowy with the promise of rain, crowded the blue sky.

Phaedra nudged a grape past Brannoc's lips. She was lying on her stomach with a book, *The Odyssey,* opened before her. He was beside her, on his back, and had been listening to her read aloud to him.

Nothing existed outside of the world they'd created for themselves over the past seven days. It was a realm devoted to the senses. Even the commonplace took on new meaning. The sun didn't shine. It bathed her, sanctified her like holy oil. Figs tasted different. The flavor grew in her mouth into an unbearable sweetness.

Scents made them shiver with pleasure. The smell of Brannoc's skin against her own, which was now always perfumed with Pagan Desires, was enough to start a liquid fire. Brannoc's bold and giving smile and eyes could provoke wanton images in her head.

They craved the briny sea juices of oysters. They ate honey by licking it off each other's fingers, the sweetest it had ever tasted. They made love with their mouths, hands and eyes. Scents made them shiver with pleasure. Words had the power to inflame.

Now, with her voice, she painted images across their sky.

> "Then Zeus-borne Helen hit upon this plan:
> Into the wine that they were drinking, she
> now cast a drug that undid every grief
> and rage, obliterating any memory
> of misery. Whoever drinks of this,
> once it is mixed within his bowl, forgets."

She stopped. If only such a potion existed, she thought to herself. Then I wouldn't have to destroy . . .

She blinked, as if she'd been suddenly released by a spell. Fool, she chastised herself. There is no forgetting your destiny, your role of avenger. You must never forget!

Unbeknownst to her, Brannoc had opened his eyes and was now regarding her serious expression thoughtfully. He noted her clenched jaw, gritted teeth and the cold stubborn gleam in her eye.

"Why did you stop?" He began to finger a lock of her hair.

Phaedra started and looked at him. The question creased his brow.

"Imagine a potion that could make you forget," she said.

"Imagine? Your customers seem to think that The Swan's

perfumes are capable of that, and more. The potion that makes me forget is Pagan Desires," he said, rising to suddenly kiss her on the mouth.

She gave him a wan smile, indicating the seriousness of her thoughts, and Brannoc checked his glib mood.

All seriousness, he asked, "What do you so desperately wish to forget?" But his tone sounded patronizing to her and she lashed out.

"Is there nothing you wish you could change? Forget?"

His eye flicked at the unrest and passion of her questions, but he answered readily enough. "Of course."

Phaedra closed the book with a thud and looked into his face. The skin of a grape had gotten caught on his beard. Removing it, she asked, "Tell me."

Brannoc gave a grunt resonant with boredom, but Phaedra felt it was feigned. She sensed the turn of deep thoughts behind his eyes.

His chest rose and fell with a deep breath. His mouth was grim. "My mother was the daughter of a great chieftain. I am bastard born. And my grandfather, being the bastard he was, and ashamed of my birth, left me to die near a river's edge." He paused. "I would change that," he said stiffly.

"How did you—"

He cut her off. "I spent the first half of my life questing for the truth of my birth and existence. I had no home then. My sword was my friend and the only thing I believed in was my power to bring death to my enemies."

"You fought with El Cid?"

Brannoc pursed his lips together and nodded. But he didn't have to speak for Phaedra to know that behind his eyes loomed rage and pain. It was contained in an armor of scars worse than any she would ever see on his flesh.

An image flashed before her mind's eye. It was a younger version of the man before her, a boy, walking beneath an ornate archway carved with arabesque and decorated with blue and white tiles of flowers. He emerged in a garden with a stone fountain rising at its center. It was so real, that she could smell the flowers.

"I was a swordsman to al Muqtadir and his sons. The Arabs taught me the poetry of life. And love. He had a library that I called The Temple. You could lose yourself for days inside it, not because it was a maze, but because you wanted to get lost. Hide. And I did . . . for a while."

She turned onto her side, and cradled her head on her hand. As she traced the tattoo on his wrist, she asked, "Where did you get this?"

"My homeland."

"Why dragons?"

"The dragon is a Celtic symbol of power and wisdom." He sat up suddenly, and Phaedra jerked out of his way. He did not look at her. "Any other questions?"

Nonplussed, Phaedra said to his back, "Tell me about the dream. The one that brought you to me."

He turned to her. At last, a smile broke free.

In the next breath he was pressing her back against the earth. Lately he'd been proving to her that the earth made as fine a bed as any within four walls. Nuzzling her throat and breathing in her scent, he moved to further her education again.

"We are living my dream," he whispered.

His hand moved under her tunic and smoothed her skin with the graceful purpose of an inrushing wave.

The darkening sky rumbled and thunder rolled as Phaedra pivoted on her heels, and squinted into the distance, forcing herself to look between the trees, hoping to catch sight of her son's dark head.

Alexander and Brutus had not been seen since midday. They'd casually plopped down beside Brannoc and Phaedra on the edge of the lavender field and had helped themselves to lunch. After promising to play close by, Alexander ran off, and the bear had bounded after him. The clouds had promised rain, but not the doom Phaedra now felt to her bone.

"Alexander!" Phaedra's cry died, muffled by a sudden roar of wind that came slamming across the valley. She swore under her breath and looked up at the sky. The clouds were ink black, but now and then a flash of lightning shone through the swirling masses. Thunder echoed up through the ground. She caught Brannoc's gaze and looked away. Sky and earth were getting set to battle. And her son was somewhere, out there, on the battlefield.

The rain came without introduction, falling in heavy gray sheets. The war was on.

They split up into teams, Sharif and Phaedra, Brannoc and Helena. But it was pointless. Phaedra couldn't even see her hand extended in front of her, much less keep an eye out for her son.

"Alexander!" she yelled again and again, but the wind and thunder batted her cry and planted it deep. Her throat ached, but she would not give up. She was soaked to the bone, but felt nothing. Rocks and pebbles cut into the soles of her sandals, tripping her, but she felt nothing. Raw fear bruised her all at once, with a hold like the talons of a great winged beast. Her hands trembled with it. Her heart beat to its whim.

She stopped and shut her eyes in the streaming rain to pray. She focused her entire being on an image of the Virgin and Child in the Church of the Holy Wisdom, The Sancta Sophia. Lightning cracked. She jumped, and there was Maia behind her closed eyes. The old woman's wise, ancient face filled Phaedra with light.

"He's here. Show him to me! Please!"

But no image came. Her tears mixed with the rain as she walked on. She tripped on a rock, and fell flat, but as she picked herself up, her hand clutched something.

Her fingers sensed its significance even before she lifted it up to see. It was a metal chain with a holy pendant of the

Christ child. It was Brutus's collar. Alexander had insisted on the holy medal, claiming Brutus, like all God's creatures, deserved to be protected, too.

"Alexander!" she screamed with all her might, and even the elements could not stop the others from hearing her. Brannoc, Helena and Sharif stopped in their blind paths and turned their heads in the direction of her cry.

A whimper, the faintest of sounds, stole through the downpour of rain, the boom of thunder, and even the wild beating of her heart in her ears. Phaedra froze and slowly crouched on bended knees. With blind hands, she reached out in front of her and felt the tree trunk before she saw it. She could have broken her neck had she tripped over it, but there was no room in her mind for the realization, as she was focused, searching for the source of that small sound.

There it was again! She moved quickly now, to her right, feeling her way down the trunk's crevasses and ridges until she came to its end. On her hands and knees, she peered into the hollow that nature had carved out, and there was Alexander, holding Brutus, who whimpered again.

"Alexander!" His name came out soft, for she'd temporarily lost the power to speak.

"Mother?" his voice cracked.

She reached in and pulled him to her. Even in the darkness and the rain, she could make out his bright smile. Gathering him in her arms, she felt relief wash through her.

But on the ebb of that wave was a sadness that engulfed her. Even later, in the quiet of the villa, knowing boy and bear were safe and sound, she could not be rid of it. Even in Brannoc's arms, she could find no peace. She could not escape the naked truth. In a few weeks, she would be leaving Alexander to join the cross-bearers on their journey of God. She would be leaving Alexander. Her son.

* * *

The next day, the pink blush of the dawning sky seemed like a gift, a great shell tossed up from a distant shore and left behind by the storm.

Emperor Alexius Comnenus, by divine right, had the power to create his own gifts, such as a double-strand necklace of pearls and pearl earrings, with gold filigree tassels that fell to Phaedra's collarbone. The jewels arrived with the dawn, by imperial messenger. And with them was a summons, written in sacred red ink, to appear at the Imperial Palace the next day. There was the matter of a "ritual" that needed to be performed. Although the royal decree didn't mention the pearls, Phaedra knew the emperor would expect her to wear them. Each perfect, lustrous globe carried his command.

The Audience Chamber's thick purple draperies flung the room into darkness. The flames of a hundred candles danced the length of the room, creating an eerie aisle of light. Through the cream silk veil that hid her face, Phaedra made out the figure of the emperor at the end of the row of light, seated on his throne.

Two scarlet-robed eunuchs soundlessly appeared out of the deep shadows at her sides. They slid the black cloak off her shoulders and lifted the veil, revealing her face. She felt their eyes widen with approval as they removed the silk veil, but it was the sight of Emperor Alexius Comnenus that held her interest. Slowly, stiffly, he pushed himself into a standing position, supporting himself with his hands. It was as if he were unsure he could count on his legs to support him. And in that instant, Phaedra felt him relinquish a bit of his power into the room. And it became hers.

Phaedra lifted her chin and narrowed her eyes slightly. She was aware of his eagle gaze sweeping slowly over her, missing nothing.

Maia's bronze bowl was set before her on the ground,

where she now knelt. She caught the emperor's silent command. The doors closed. They were alone now.

Phaedra closed her eyes and summoned Maia to guide her. Something in her mind opened. It was as if Maia had said. "Surrender, and claim the strength that is yours." Instinct guided. Opening her eyes, she gracefully began to create a new mystical ritual for the emperor.

Alexius sat back in his throne as Phaedra unpinned her hair and removed the circlet of laurel leaves above her brow. Crushing two between her palms, she let the pieces fall into a bowl where they sparked, then flamed into orange curling tongues of fire. Smoke rose from the bowl, bathing Phaedra's face. Closing her eyes again, she drew the smoke inside of her and watched it move through her body before setting it free.

She began to move to an inner music. She opened her eyes, and the silent teachings of Maia worked through her. She picked up the pitcher and poured the water into the bowl. The sound of water spilling and rising filled the chamber. And when it grew quiet again, Phaedra sat back on her heels and looked into the water.

Alexius, unaware of what to do, kept silent until he could not bear it any longer.

"Tell me what will become of the iron men and their journey," he inquired heatedly.

Phaedra's kohl-rimmed gaze silenced him. Slowly, the surface of the water stirred. Soldiers appeared bearing the sign of the cross. Some were on foot, others were mounted on galloping steeds. Trumpets and battle cries blared beneath a whirlpool of hot yellow light and dust. And as she stared at them, a shudder, unlike any physical sensation she had known before, ran through her body.

Alexius looked down from his throne to see into the water, but saw nothing save the reflection of candlelight. "What is it?"

The thundering pummel of galloping horses, the jangle of

bridles and reins, screams and yells of "Death to the Infidel!" filled her senses.

"I'm riding with them, a cavalry unit. Northmen. Greeks. We're riding hard, fast . . . I see them, the Saracens coming over a hill before us, heading toward us. Their shrill cries and drums unsettle our horses. I reach for the bow slung over my shoulder and my bag of arrows. I shoot. The arrow flies. The soldiers aim and fire, too. But the Saracens keep coming," she said dumbfounded.

Whirl of visions . . .

"Knights on foot, covered in steel, bellowing as they wield their long swords and iron maces. Cursing and grunting as their enemies fall before them. There is no mercy," she said, grimacing. "They smash and sever heads and limbs, oblivious of the blood, their own wounds, the cries and noise, the heat and the flies. Birds circle above, watching, waiting.

"Their God protects them, until . . ."

The water went black, then moved again, suddenly alive with the image of naked soldiers, their arms and legs pinned to the ground, roasting beneath the sun, crying out for mercy. Crucified Northmen, their yellow hair matted with their own blood and that of their enemies, scream as they are sliced open like cantaloupes. Sounds of confusion, horses screaming, drums signaling to retreat as the iron men fall victim to their own brothers. Their eyes are wide with horror, surprise and disbelief.

And the children, the women, wives of the fools who believed God would take care of them and their families, and that no harm would come to them. All are cut down like harvest wheat.

The water bears the sweet and musty stench of blood. She sees herself. She is filthy, spattered with blood. There is dried blood under her nails, and her tunic is torn open like a harlot's.

"What becomes of Pelecanum? Dorylaeum? Antioch?" came a voice through the mists.

"Pelecanum . . ." her voice wandered as she focused on a yellow-walled city on the water. "It falls," she looked up with unseeing eyes, "to you."

Alexius settled back more comfortably and placed his fingers together.

She continued. "Dorylaeum. Treachery opens the gates. And Antioch falls to Bohemund."

The room spun and she did not hear the emperor slam his fists against the gilded arms of his throne. She hugged herself, for to feel was to know that it wasn't happening. Yet.

She wanted to close her eyes and shield herself from the darkest image of all, the loss of hope in the eyes of battle weary men. But their self-made hell scared her. She saw the pain on their thin, scarred faces as the realization of their fate dawned. Where was the glory? The land of milk and honey? There was only gore, blood and guts, and the senseless deaths of innocent people.

She closed her eyes and relief flooded through her, but only for a heartbeat, because a voice in her ear urged her to look again. And she did.

"No!" She moaned as the water came alive with wolves. She saw a sea of wolves, their wet, matted jaws snapping at the air and their searching eyes blood red. She felt their crushing weight and heard their hunger. She felt their tongues swell as they caught the scent of blood.

The next vision was of herself, trying to run away from the wolves. But she could not move. The water revealed that her wrists were bound behind her back and secured to a stake of wood as tall as a tree.

Phaedra confronted the fear she saw in her own eyes reflected to her. She heard the crackle of heat. Somewhere close. She saw orange flames rising around her. She clenched with panic. No! No! On the water, the wolves lurched back and howled as she struggled to free herself. The smoke rose around her in billowy capes, smothering her. There was the heat, the fire licking close beneath her feet. A shrill scream shot through her, like an arrow on its way to its mark. "Phae-dra!"

"Phaedra! Phaedra!"

She felt hands on her, pulling her to her feet. Maia's bowl tipped and blood spilled across the mosaic floor. Again a scream, her own this time, rising from the depths of her being.

Alexius held Phaedra's limp body in his arms. He carried her quickly across the chamber. He angled his way through the draperies toward the sunlight and the marble courtyard that overlooked the sea.

Concern knotting his brow, he carried her to a sun-warmed marble bench and cradled her within his arms. Beads of sweat trickled beneath his crown and down his back. He wasn't tired. He was still a strong, virile man. Nevertheless, his heart was pounding. He steeled himself from looking down at the woman in his arms, and kept his gaze on the cool sea beyond painted silver by the sun.

The weight in his arms called to him, and he looked. Phae-dra, the daughter of his most esteemed friend and general, daughter of the seeress, Cassandra. He'd wanted to be a fa-ther to her, too, but she had denied him. She didn't have to suffer alone. He was her emperor. He would have loved her.

"Dreamer of Dreams, what did you see that has brought you to this?" he whispered. And with a mind of its own, his hand moved to stroke her white neck.

Touching her was like opening a door to a room he had been barred from entering. Now that he'd crossed the thresh-old, he let his gaze wander over her body as if he was seeing her for the first time.

Her emerald silk gown was pulled tight across her, mold-ing the swells and curves of her breasts. He swallowed as he watched his hand descend to caress her. His fingers trem-bled at the exquisite feel of her perfumed softness. He bit his lip as he brushed her nipples with his fingertips. He moaned softly at the sensation, at the sight of such beauty lying open and ready, ripe, perfect, and his.

At that moment, Phaedra's eyes blinked open and she found herself staring up into Alexius's face. Her amber eyes saw the heat and obsession of passion beneath his imperial facade. His eyes were large and brown, unblinking orbs of an eagle. All the evil in the world seemed centered in his eyes.

Then she felt his hand on her breasts.

Phaedra jumped with a start and flew out of his arms. Heart hammering, she fought for breath and stayed the fainting spell whirlpooling through her head. She gazed out anxiously at the water before turning to confront him.

Alexius rose. He looked weak, small, but dangerously aware. His voice checked her immediate flight, barring her like a cage.

"What you saw here today must never be repeated to anyone. Do you understand?" He moistened his lips. "Phaedra," he said when she didn't answer.

But she would not give him that satisfaction. She knew that what she saw in his eyes would haunt her. She also knew that he wasn't referring to her visions.

"I promise you nothing!" And with that, she turned on her heel and left him standing in the sun, his hands knotting with frustration, anger flushing his face.

Phaedra flew across the marble courtyard and through the groves of mulberry trees that fed the palace silkworms. At the edge of the trees she stopped to take a breath. She clutched her stomach and fought to suppress the queasiness rumbling beneath her hand. Even though she knew the emperor wasn't following her, she looked back, over her shoulder. There was something about this part of the palace garden. . . .

The memory brushed by, causing her to shiver. Set within the terraces and gardens beneath her was the lion palace. It was in this garden that she'd first heard about the death of her father. It was here, beside its fountain, that the empress had tried to comfort her. And she, still a child, had promised to avenge her father's murder.

Now she would have her chance! Gathering up her gown, desiring above all else to put the garden far behind her, she hurried up the flight of stairs and did not notice the man looking down at her from the landing until she ran into him.

The man's arms reached out to stop her. "Whoa!"

Phaedra looked and, gasping, lurched back from the tall red-haired figure of Bohemund of Taranto. She tripped and would have fallen back had he not reached out to grab her again.

He was so close that she could see the gold hairs in his waves, discern the light like chips of pewter in his eyes. Bohemund relaxed his grip, the better to enjoy the soft skin beneath his fingertips. He bared his teeth in a wolfish grin.

"What have we here?" he said in clumsy Greek. "A palace nymph out for a breath of air?" He paused, arching one eyebrow dramatically. Peering over her shoulder, he wondered aloud, "Or are you returning from a tryst with your lover, beauty?"

Heated, hateful words caught in her throat, rendering her speechless. Unnerved by her silence, she struggled fiercely to be rid of the weight of his hands on her. But he would not let her go.

"Let's have a look at you." He lifted her off her feet and set her down an arm's length away from him. His large hands inhibited her flight. His eyes moved over her more thoroughly than hands and lingered long on the shape of her breasts, which were straining out of her gown.

"Now I know there is a god! How else could such loveliness," he paused, raping her with his blue gaze, "have come into being?"

"Impudent bastard! Let me go!"

"She speaks! Watch out beauty, 'ere that saucy tongue of yours fire my blood."

She cried out again in frustration, struggling like a captured animal, but it only made him laugh. If only she had her dagger, she'd kill him now and avenge her father's murder!

"Let me go!" she ordered through clenched teeth.

"Bohemund, Duke of Taranto, does nothing without gaining something in return." He pulled her toward him and whispered in her ear, "What will you give me, beauty? Eh? What prize, what treasure, will you freely part with to gain your release?" His tongue darted out and licked her ear lobe.

Furious, she screamed, "Your life, bastard! I'll spare your life!"

He burst into laughter, charmed by her oath. He did not notice the dagger points flashing in Phaedra's eyes.

"By the Holy Virgin, you are a wild one, eh? And with a good sense of humor." He released one arm, but gripped her hard around the other when she attempted to fly. Eyes twinkling with amusement, he said, "I love a woman with a sense of humor. 'I spare your life,' " he mimicked in a high-pitched voice. "Hah! That's good! Very good! If I had more time, I'd carry you off and see just how playful you could be."

"A plague on you, you braggart!"

"The face and body of a goddess, with the mouth of a foot soldier. 'Twould make love play all the more interesting."

His blue eyes flickered at the deep hate revealed by her gaze. He stepped back, letting her go. Then with a smile and a great heroic gesture, he drew his sword from its scabbard and held it out for her.

Offering it to her, he cajoled, "Go ahead. Take it. Kill me now and be done with it."

She teetered on the brink of indecision. Christe! It was as if he knew of her death wish and was embracing it, she thought to herself. But he couldn't know. How could he?

She gripped the sword firmly and stepped back from him. It was beautifully wrought of blue iridescent steel, richly chased and keen-edged. She marveled at the feel of it, the lightness of the steel and its perfect balance. She held the deadly sword with the reverence it deserved. She could appreciate a good weapon as well as any man.

She looked up into Bohemund's face and noticed the flicker of concern amid the amusement as he noted the easy, familiar way she handled his weapon.

She smiled a slight, edged smile. "Kill him now," said a little voice in her head. No. It was too easy.

She was about to open her hands and let the sword fall to the ground when a voice called out, "Let him be, Lady Ancii."

It was Alexius, calling from below.

"He is a guest."

Phaedra opened her hands, and the sword clattered to the ground.

She stepped over it, toward the mighty Bohemund of Taranto. He chuckled uncomfortably. "Lady Ancii?" he emphasized. "You Greeks are a surprising lot. Of course, many Frankish noblewomen can handle weapons, but I thought you Greeks . . ."

"You'll have to forgive Lady Ancii her manners, Duke Bohemund," Alexius said, climbing the stairs. "She has not been feeling well."

Phaedra had Bohemund's interest, not just his lusty attention. By the stupid look on his red face, she knew she could have knocked him over with a feather, but she brushed past him, and felt his eyes on her backside as she moved away.

"You're mine, Bohemund of Taranto," she thought to herself.

Thirteen

Phaedra reined her horse to the right and urged him forward. They were southeast of Constantinople, a two days' march from the Seljuk capital of Nicaea on a slow journey to the Holy Land. Phaedra knew that if the cross-bearers were to reach Jerusalem, they must first safeguard the roads. Nicaea was crucial to the success of the campaign. Without Nicaea, the Turks would be a constant threat behind them.

Nicaea would not be an easy conquest. The Romans, who had built the city originally, and the Byzantines after them, had known its value and fortified four miles of walls with 240 towers. Not only that, but one of its walls to the west rose out of the Ascanian lake. Muscle alone would not be enough to win Nicaea. The emperor knew it. Therefore, he had sent a small Byzantine detachment of engineers with siege engines to help destroy its defenses.

The Byzantines were only a mile behind her, under the command of General Butamites. Phaedra had been riding with the Greeks since leaving Constantinople, under the pretense of traveling to Jerusalem to purchase supplies for her shop.

She heard the heavy thud of a galloping horse approach, but she did not look to see if it was friend or foe. She safely assumed that the Greek scouts who had combed the area for signs of the Turks had done a thorough job.

"Fools!" Vinicius muttered, joining Phaedra at her side.

She gave him a sideways glance, briefly noted his polished suit of armor and the blue felt cloak that fell back from his shoulders.

There was contempt in his gaze as he surveyed the scene of the barbarians setting up camp below them. "The tales of these barbarians being a disorganized, lawless, backward lot are false. They are worse than that! They are an embarrassment to anyone who calls himself a soldier." He paused and pointed west. "Look at that! Their provision carts are unprotected and in the rear! There are no sentries posted anywhere! What do they think? That God and His angels alone will protect them?"

Phaedra's mouth puckered as if she'd just eaten something sour. Vinicius was getting on her nerves. Ever since she'd left Constantinople, he'd been buzzing about. While Kasia and Gabriel had preferred staying in Pelecanum with the emperor, she had chosen, with Alexius's permission, to ride ahead with Butamites's detachment. She'd been warned not to go anywhere alone. Warned, not forbidden. Since she knew how to ride, had brought her own horse, and was confident of her skills with her dagger, she believed that the dictate wasn't serious. Vinicius had believed otherwise and had argued that if she felt compelled to be adventurous, he would be right there with her.

How had he put it? She scrunched her face trying to recall his exact words. Ah, yes . . .

"Just think of me as a watchful, caring husband," he'd explained when she accused him of smothering her.

"Husband? Would you permit your wife to accompany you on such a journey as this?" she'd inquired, her voice cold and full of doubt.

He'd paused before answering. "Why not? These Normans and Franks do. I could see the merit in having a woman close by to warm my bed," he'd said, winking.

She remembered telling him, "I'm sure the camp followers would be happy to oblige you and share their heat, Vinicius."

She never would have believed Vinicius's story about the barbarians' womenfolk, had she not seen them with her own eyes. It was true, many of them had followed their husbands. They'd been lured, like the men, by the thought of seeing the Holy Land and having their sins absolved. It had been ordained by the Pope himself who had proclaimed this holy war a Crusade, that anyone on a pilgrimage to Jerusalem could receive absolution.

An amazing trick, that. Like bartering with the devil, she thought with a wry grin. Shading her eyes, Phaedra looked down into the valley. They can't all be motivated by God, she thought. Greed. Land. Riches. A battle fought and won. These were all equal motivators, best kept to oneself and shrouded in the name of God, she thought grimly.

She caught Bohemund's scarlet flag fluttering in the wind. Even Alexius didn't believe Bohemund was on this campaign for the glory of God.

A trumpet's sharp tone broke through the trees and Vinicius looked over his shoulder in its direction.

"I have a council meeting with General Butamites. Are you coming?"

Phaedra shrugged. "You go on ahead. I'll only be a little while longer."

Vinicius looked over his shoulder at her. "When?"

She gave him her most trustworthy smile. "Soon."

He spurred on and rode away. When the sound of Vinicius's horse had died away, Phaedra reined Achilles closer to the edge. She dug in with her heels and clicked the horse forward to start down the slope. Unafraid, leaning as far back as she could to keep her seat, she gently coaxed the stallion down the rocky incline, into the valley.

Phaedra shielded her eyes from the sun and squinted at the human sea before her. Everywhere she looked, there were soldiers, "soldiers of God," marked with the red cross on surcoats and vests, their faces red and blistered from the sun. In their armor, they looked like giants.

Wave upon wave of sounds filled the air, the rattle of carts, the crowing and clucking of roosters and chickens, and the whine of stubborn mules. The sharp snap of flags flapping in the wind drew her eyes to the sky. She saw the crimson standard of Bohemund of Taranto. This was his camp.

Loosening her reins, she nudged her horse toward the camp. It was not Bohemund she hoped to catch sight of, but another. She could see Bohemund easily enough back in Alexius's camp, where he was being entertained. The wine and the gold had seduced him into sticking to the emperor's side.

As far as she knew, the Dragon did not know she was traveling with the Byzantine army on this campaign. She had not seen Brannoc since returning to Constantinople. After she'd received the emperor's summons to perform the ancient ritual to conjure up her vision of his future success, Brannoc had traveled with Phaedra back to the city. Since then, five days had passed. She had been under the impression that it was Brannoc's duty to guard Bohemund at all times. But the Dragon was not in Pelecanum with the Duke.

She frowned at the thought of the tall, red-haired giant. What need did Bohemund have for a guard? He was in the safest place in the world, at Emperor Alexius's side. Not one red whisker could be removed without the express permission of His Most Holy Excellency, she thought with a smirk.

She'd hidden her hair under a white head cloth, Arab fashion, and was wearing a white sleeveless tunic and loose trousers, which she'd tucked into her leather boots. Her Saracen sword glinted from her belt.

Her eyes suggested that although this stranger was dressed as a man, she was a woman. Her gold coloring and exotic eyes sent more than one man's head into a spin. The throng parted before her as if she were royalty.

Keeping to the fringes of Bohemund's camp, which seemed to stretch on to infinity, she moved quietly along until she believed her search futile and reined Achilles around to head back up the hill.

Just then, a woman, comely of face, with soft brown eyes and red-gold tresses, approached her. She carried a baby on her hip and smelled of garlic and cook fires. She was holding a cup of water, which she offered to Phaedra.

Phaedra reined Achilles still and dismounted easily. Nodding her thanks, she took the water and drank thirstily. Over the rim of the cup, she noted that the woman was looking at her strangely and trying to peek into her surcoat.

Phaedra stifled a laugh for it suddenly became clear to her why the woman was so curious. "Why, she doesn't know whether or not I'm a woman," she thought to herself.

Phaedra lifted her hand to remove the head cloth and reveal her identity, but suddenly stopped as she felt a soft quivering in the earth. She cocked her head and listened. At first she heard nothing save the abrupt, jostling sounds of the camp, but then, a sound unlike any other grew in intensity and might.

Horses, Phaedra thought. She took another drink, all the while listening to the low, drumming thunder caused by horses. She turned toward the sound and noticed that a billowy cloud of dust was moving closer and closer. Slowly, soldiers appeared rising out of the dust, their steel lances reflecting the dying rays of the sun. She made out the lone figure of a man on a black horse, leading at the center, riding apart from the others.

A scream cut through the thunder and chilled Phaedra to the bone. She blinked, and saw to her horror that a child had wandered into the field that lay in the path of the charging knights. No one moved. Everyone stood rooted to the ground.

Phaedra tossed the cup and flew across the field toward the child who continued to play. Seeing only the child in front of her, Phaedra darted straight in front of the black horse's path. The stallion squealed as it reared and pawed the air. Its steel-shod hooves hung above Phaedra like knife points. Oblivious, she scooped the child into her arms and flung herself out of the way. She hit the ground, rolling. Pain speared her arm and shoulder, bringing tears to her eyes.

The rider fought to regain control of his frightened animal. Within seconds, his soothing words calmed the beast. He reined it still and, shouting an order, dismounted. He was out of the saddle in a swift, smooth motion that denied the weight of the armor he wore.

He covered the ground in long, impatient strides, tearing the steel mesh gloves from his hands, then flinging them to the ground. He opened his long shirt of chain armor at the throat. Unaware of the child, he cursed the fool who had darted in front of his horse.

The boy was crying in Phaedra's arms. Her lungs burned. She couldn't catch her breath. Unable to speak, she soothed the child with her hands. But as her body relaxed and her lungs filled with air, a woman ran up and snatched the child away without so much as a word or look of thanks.

The knight stopped and swore at himself when he saw the child. The anger disappeared from his eyes as he watched the child's rescuer attempt to sit up. The sight stopped the knight in his tracks, and he wavered as if he'd just received a blow to his head.

The head cloth fell in rolls around Phaedra's shoulders, releasing her long black hair as she sat up. Every limb throbbed, and her head pounded. She reached to touch her forehead and felt the warm, sticky ooze of her own blood. She felt someone near, watching her. The ground darkened in shadow. She looked up then and saw the knight.

His suit of armor, from his helmet to his overshoes, glowed blood red with the setting sun. A great brass-studded belt encircled his waist, bearing his scabbard and sword. She blinked as her vision blurred.

Then she noticed his eyes between the slits of his helmet. They were blue. Blue.

"Are you all right?"

His voice was familiar, but before she had a chance to think, he lifted her to her feet. With his free hand, he pulled his helmet off and cradled it under his arm. A steel mesh coif covered his head and throat, framing his face.

"Phaedra," Brannoc whispered, aware of the prying eyes around them. "What are you doing here?"

His voice was strangely guarded, she thought. She stared up at him. He'd shaven his beard and mustache since the last time they'd seen each other. Phaedra liked the effect. The handsome planes of his face stood out boldly, his mouth even more suggestive.

"My lord," she replied. She winced as he squeezed her arm. "My lord! You are hurting me."

"This way." Brannoc said, and he wheeled her around with all the gruffness of a victor handling his captive. He used his body to break the wall of onlookers as he strode toward a yellow pavilion.

She rubbed her arm when he finally let her go. They were alone, but his touch and presence seemed to fill the pavilion with a dark rage foreign to her.

"What's this about? Why are you here?" He bruised her with the tone of his questions, and her eyes narrowed on him.

He removed his headgear and flung it onto a cot. His blond hair fell to his shoulders, matted with sweat. He wiped his brow and then stood there, his cold eyes boring into her, waiting.

Lest he think she had come to see him, she said, "I came because I wanted to see the famous armies of the cross-bearers."

He grunted. "Why?" He crossed his arms over his chest and waited for her answer.

She stood mute with her jaw at its most defensive angle. Brannoc's head tilted. "Well, Lady Ancii?"

"Well," she countered, angry at nothing and at everything.

"Now that I've seen, I can leave," and she pivoted to leave, but he was quicker and grabbed her by the arm again.

"Are you one of Alexius's spies?' he accused.

"Of course not!"

"Why else would you leave your home?" He paused to give weight to the last word on his tongue. "And Alexander?"

In his tone, she heard him fault her for leaving the boy. She pulled her arm free and backed away from his accusing glare.

Could a suit of steel change a man so? For she swore she did not know the brute standing before her.

"I left you safe in Constantinople. I cannot protect you here," he snapped, eyes darting to the tent's covered opening.

"I'm not asking you to protect me."

"There is the matter of a dream, a vow."

She responded quickly, senses alert now that she was dealing with a stranger, a lowly barbarian. "I relieve you of the vow," she said. "As for the dream, alas, I cannot change that."

He swore under his breath and walked past her, ignoring her. He swiped the curtain aside. "Tristan!" he shouted.

In a beat, a yellow-haired youth appeared in the opening, his sharp nose blistered and peeling. Brannoc's menacing gaze followed Tristan as he darted into the tent. At first he did not even notice Phaedra, so unnerved was he by Brannoc's stalking appearance. But his eyes finally fell on her, and he gasped, startled. His eyes flicked over her and on her hair.

"Forgive me, sir." Tristan swallowed, "but I was seeing to—"

"From here on in, I want you ready to attend to me when I return to camp, understand? Now help me out of this." He gestured to his armor.

"At once, Sir Brannoc," and he lurched forward to Brannoc's side, but in his zeal to set things right, he tripped over the cot.

Brannoc seemed suddenly bored with his valet's clumsiness.

Phaedra took Brannoc's preoccupation as a sign for her to leave, but once again as she began crossing the pavilion, Brannoc yelled, "Where are you going?"

She ignored him.

"God's wounds!" He slid out of his armor, leaving his valet to deal with its weight, and caught her at the entrance.

"Go back to Constantinople," he ordered. "To your son."

She was silent, eyes burning. "This is no place for a woman."

She walked around his body. "Out of my way, barbarian!"

Tristan's eyes grew wide at her insolent tone.

Brannoc stepped to the side, blocking her again.

She looked up. He towered over her, lofty and unreachable.

"Be forewarned." His deep voice trapped her. "You Greeks have no rights in this camp. Especially you, a woman," he pronounced the last word as if it were a death sentence, "unprotected. Any one of these men could mistake you for a camp follower, a whore, and theirs for the asking. Do you understand?"

A fire streaked in her belly. She stabbed her finger into his leather tunic and drove whatever desire and passion she might have felt for him to the brink of certain death.

"You be forewarned, Sir Brannoc. I curse your vows, your dreams!"

Afire, she turned and left, and did not stop until she was in the thick of the camp.

"My lady!"

The crowd parted as Tristan ran after Phaedra. She stopped and turned, but when she saw who it was, she continued on, desperate to find Achilles and leave this place.

"This way! This way!" he beckoned. And she froze, caught by his Greek.

"Where did you learn to speak our language?" she asked as she let him lead the way.

"The monks, my lady. Come!"

Phaedra appraised the transformed valet. Whereas in Brannoc's presence he'd been as nervous as a twitching hare beset by a fox, now he was calm, confident, even graceful she noted as he nimbly sidestepped the crowd before them.

"I was afraid for you! Don't you know who my master is?"

"What do you mean? Of course I know! He is Sir Brannoc."

Tristan cocked a brow and screwed his mouth in a face suggesting that she was too dumb to understand anything.

"Are you going to tell me, or is this some crude guessing game?"

He lifted his chin and used it to point at something in front of them. She saw Achilles, standing nearby, picketed beneath the shade of a cypress. She noticed she was being stared at and wished she had picked up her head cloth.

When they reached the horse, Tristan let out a long whistle of admiration. He smoothed Achilles's shiny coat and shook his head from side to side. "What a beauty," he sighed.

Phaedra put her hands on her hips and said impatiently, "Tristan."

He cast a quick look over his shoulder, then furtive glances to scour the area. When he thought they were safe, he said, "I was afraid that if you angered him, he'd turn you into a frog!"

"What?" She jerked her head back.

"Or a bird," he continued, ignoring her outburst. "Or some such creature. He has powers, you know." His eyes bulged with wonder and fear. He sniffled and wiped his nose on his sleeve.

"This must be a joke," she laughed carefully. "He sent you to find me, didn't he? And to scare me?"

"Nay!" His face fell as if she'd wounded his pride. "I came to warn you. Stay away from the man. They all do. For he is a sorcerer and he can see, hear, and do things no mortal man can. Did you not notice the tattoos marking his wrists?"

"Yes, but—"

"The markings of the devil, they are. Just ask Sir Tancred, Bohemund's nephew. Or any of the other knights!"

He saw the doubt in her eyes, clucked and shook his head. "For your own safety, doubt me not. I've seen him do things . . ." he let his voice fade. He shivered.

Christe! The boy was a simpleton, she thought.

She accepted the help he offered her, placing her foot into the cup he formed with his hands to lift her up. She swung easily onto Achilles's back, then, looking down on him, she said, "You don't even know who I am. Why do you think it necessary to warn me?"

"He is a beast of the night! It is my duty as a goodly, God-fearing man to warn you. So you can guard your heart and soul."

Oh, she most certainly would guard herself against Brannoc, but not because he was a mage or shapeshifter!

"He is the Dragon they say he is. Beware!" Tristan's eyes were wide and round with fear, as if he'd seen a ghost . . . or worse.

Phaedra rode at a breakneck pace through the darkening woods. Shadows were blue-black beneath the branches of the trees. She didn't dare to look at the sky. Red, the color of betrayal and dragons, hung over her head, and she knew it. She felt the fiery color seep through the branches and leaves. She thought that if it touched her, she would surely burst into flame. For the fury in her heart was a smoldering, hungry force ready to feast on anything that reminded her of HIM.

She hunched forward and low over Achilles's neck, breathed his scent, tried to forget.

Phaedra.

A man's deep musical voice, crept through her barrier of fury. She gritted her teeth and kicked Achilles faster.

Phaedra, come back.

Within her mind's eye she saw a figure, tall, blond, armored, the setting sun behind his back.

Phaedra.

"Betrayer!" she cried aloud.

For an instant, the forest went black and she was suddenly blind. Her stomach tightened in a knot and she slumped over Achilles as if she'd been stabbed.

The vision slipped through the darkness. She was in Brannoc's arms, locked in a fiery embrace, and they were loving each other fiercely. Their hands moved with hungry urgency. Their breaths came fast and short between the sighs and moans. There was no line between giver and receiver, just passion and desire . . . fulfilling and fulfilled.

Anger blurred the image and smote it into pieces like glass. She straightened out of her weakness, but tears glistened in the corners of her eyes.

"Damn you!" she cried, to the listening wood. "Why? Why?"

A trumpet blared. Phaedra emerged out of the forest and closed in on the camp of the Byzantine army. The contingent was small. The main army was still in Pelecanum. Nevertheless, the encampment was precisely laid out to recreate the camp of a Roman legion. There was no similarity to the camp of the barbarians. Order reigned here, with the traditions established by the greatest army in the history of mankind.

She saluted the sentry at his post and moved past a column of heavily armed cavalrymen of the empire. Phaedra sighed with relief that Vinicius was not among them.

Phaedra's own tent, dyed blue, occupied a position of honor close to the Strategus. After dismounting and caring for Achilles, Phaedra proceeded to her tent. At the entrance, she hesitated, sniffing the unmistakable scent of roses, musk, vanilla and sandalwood . . . Aphrodite's Passion.

Phaedra swore under her breath and tensed, bracing herself. The scent could mean only one thing. Closing her eyes, she yanked the tent flap aside and was immediately bathed in the fragrance Aphrodite's Passion.

"Phaedra!"

The Swan opened her eyes and found Kasia bathing in a large bronze tub in the center of the tent. The siren had turned her head and was now grinning at her. Only her red head showed above the steaming water, but now a lily-white arm splashed out and waved. A silver candelabrum, supporting dozens of lit tapers, illuminated the siren from its post on a table where Gabriel sat. He looked up from the papers spread around him and smiled.

Thoughts of Brannoc vanished like mist.

"Hello, Phaedra!" Gabriel saluted with his wine cup. "Surprised, no doubt? Thought I'd venture closer to the action, you see. And get on with my sketches. Have to finish my mosaic, you know."

"Darling," Kasia turned in her tub to address him, sending water over the sides and onto the rugs. "All of Constantinople has been waiting for over twenty years to see this masterpiece of yours." She turned back to Phaedra and rolled her eyes. "Artists!" she whispered.

Phaedra entered her tent. "What are you doing here? I thought you were in Pelecanum with the emperor."

"We were." Gabriel smacked his lips, relishing the wine. He explained. "Bohemund left today to join his forces. He's a subject for my mosaic. I thought I should follow him."

Phaedra turned to Kasia for her story.

Curling a wet strand of hair which had fallen from the coil atop her head, she said, "Hope you don't mind the intrusion, Phaedra dear. But Butamites is only now putting up our tents. Sour man, Butamites," she complained, wrinkling her nose.

Phaedra turned away and removed her surcoat. She tossed

it onto the pile of pillows that served as her bed. Hands on her hips, she turned again to the tub and its sole occupant.

"What is that you're wearing? By the saints, without your hair, you almost look like a boy!" Kasia tsked distastefully, but Phaedra chose to ignore her.

"How ever did you get that here?" Phaedra questioned, pointing at the tub which was wide and deep enough for two.

"Never underestimate a courtesan's charms," Gabriel piped in. "The emperor sent it along." The artist shrugged, his attention on his work all the while.

"He took pity on me," Kasia lamented. "I told him you'd probably appreciate it, too."

Phaedra turned away quickly, and a bolt of fire seared up her neck.

"By the way," Kasia continued. "Did you bring any of your perfumed oils? You know, your customers are still fuming over your decision to discontinue Pagan Desires," she droned on, but Phaedra was too deep in thought to hear.

She was in the Imperial Garden with Emperor Alexius. He was holding her in his arms. She felt his hands fondling her, and saw the heat in his eyes.

Kasia's green eyes flicked, absorbing everything. "I haven't upset you, have I?"

Phaedra flinched and masked the feelings with invisible veils.

"Come! How about a relaxing soak," Kasia cajoled, flicking her foot and splashing Phaedra. "I'm just about done and the water is soooo warm."

The woman could make a living selling rotten fish, Phaedra observed, so invitingly did she weave her offer.

With a great whoosh, Kasia rose to her feet, and the water streamed its last watery gasp over her luscious curves. She stood naked in the candlelight, Venus-borne.

Gabriel didn't bat an eye. He didn't even look up. Sighing with impatience, Phaedra jumped to look for a towel when there came a shout.

"Phaedra!"

Without pause, Vinicius pulled back the tent's flap and poked his head in. His eyes widened as Kasia turned in the tub to face him.

Oh." His eyes were like a sponge, wiping the wetness from her limbs.

Kasia smiled wickedly. "Hello, Genreal. Is my tent ready?"

"Ah, y-yes," he answered, his eyes dazzled by her opulent breasts. He tore his glance away just long enough to address Phaedra.

"There's someone here to see you."

Phaedra whipped her surcoat at Kasia so she could cover herself, and followed Vinicius out of the tent. Kasia's throaty laugh curled into the darkened camp.

Phaedra saw Sharif before he saw her. Her eyes lighted with joy at the burly, proud man. He was dressed in his old charioteer's uniform and holding a crested helmet beneath his arm. Golden sandals were laced up his strong legs. He was well into his sixty-fifth year, but he stood as strong and mighty as if he'd just won his first Golden Belt for chariot racing. And even though his hair was gray, it was thick and long.

Sharif was looking about approvingly. Phaedra began to race toward him, but something in his glance checked her enthusiasm and she slowed to a quick walk.

"Sharif."

"Lady," he bowed stiffly.

A small crowd of foot soldiers, on their way to receive their ration of bread and meat, slowed to watch their reunion. Phaedra drew Sharif away down a torchlit street of tents.

"Is everything all right at home?" she asked worriedly. "Alexander?" she inquired softly.

"Boy's fine," he replied. "He's taken to his role of master of the house surprisingly well!"

A smile quivered on Phaedra's lips as she recalled their farewell. Alexander rarely cried. Even when he was sick or hurt, the boy was stoic to the core. But that morning, hours before she was to join General Butamites and meet the ferry that would carry them across the Golden Horn, he began to cry. Then she cried, then Helena, and the entire household, except for Sharif. It was as if Alexander had saved every tear for that morning. She'd nearly backed down from going.

She hugged her arms to her chest. The memory of Alexander's arms around her pierced her heart. A wave of homesickness shook her. It was an ache of loneliness so real that she swayed. A knot of tears and hurt lodged in her throat. She swallowed them back and cleared her throat.

"Then why are you—"

Sharif stopped her abruptly. "When your father went away to fight the Turks, I vowed to him that I'd look after you. I'm here to fulfill my oath. If you intend to travel to Jerusalem to get your supplies and oils for The Swan, then I'm going with you."

"But, Sharif—"

"A promise is a promise, Lady."

By the firm set of his jaw, and the stubborn look in his eyes, she knew she would get nowhere arguing with him.

"Very well," she stated matter-of-factly. "But where will you—"

"I'm a charioteer, Phaedra. And although I'm four times the age of most of the men here, I can look after myself."

She lowered her gaze respectfully. "Of course."

Sharif clicked his tongue. "There's one more thing." Phaedra cocked her head forward and waited. "Alexander insisted I bring you," he paused, "a surprise."

News of her son's gesture made the sun rise within her. A wide smile broke across her features. "Where is it?" she asked, looking the charioteer up and down, wondering where he had placed the surprise for safekeeping.

"Ah-hem." He cleared his throat to buy himself time. "I had him—I mean—it, sent to your tent."

"Him? It?" she echod, leaning forward.

"Awghhhhhh!" A shriek of a decidedly feminine timbre nailed them to the ground and split the night in two. The noise drew soldiers out of their tents, and caused horses to stamp and snort in reply.

Phaedra started. It seemed to have come from her tent! By the saints, it was Kasia, she realized.

"Um, that must be it now. I assumed you would not be sharing a tent."

Phaedra, thoroughly confused now, broke into a run to see what "it" was and what all the screaming was about.

Sharif shouted after her, "It's the bear, Brutus, my Lady. Alexander sent it," he paused. Seeing that she was out of range, he said to himself, "For your protection." Scratching his beard, he grumbled under his breath, then set off after her.

"Forbidden! The gall of that man to forbid me from setting foot out of this tent," Phaedra lashed out as she paced back and forth like a wild animal in Butamites's pavilion. The sounds of trumpets, thundering hooves and armies of men clashing together could be faintly heard in the distance.

Kasia lounged comfortably on a divan that she'd insisted they bring for their confinement. She was eating grapes. Brutus sat at her feet, watching, his eyes full of hope as they followed the path of each grape to her mouth. Gabriel sat on an ebony chair, sketching. He would look up now and then to consider Kasia's profile, then sketch furiously. Occasionally, he would throw Phaedra an impatient look as if her constant motion were getting on his nerves.

By order of Strategus Manuel Butamites, Phaedra, Gabriel

and Kasia had been expressly forbidden from leaving the pavilion. There were armed soldiers posted outside to remind them of that fact, or, rather Phaedra, who was the only one who tested the boundaries.

Since Kasia, Gabriel and Sharif's arrival, the army had moved twice, always in the shadow of the cross-bearers, and always setting up camp in a superior, safer location. Such a minor consideration as defenses never entered into the Christians' strategy.

They were now camped in a low valley surrounded by pine ridges, well in sight of the yellow walls of Nicaea and the barbarian armies. The first blow had been struck that morning by a Turkish reconnaissance force from Kilidj Arslan, the Red Lion, Lord of Nicaea, in an attempt to push through to the southern gate of the city and strengthen the garrison.

The brunt of the attack had fallen on Count Raymond of Toulouse's army of Lorrainers, Gascons and Provencals, who'd been guarding the south. The count's army had moved slowly across Europe and had been the last Christian force to arrive. Godfrey and Bohemund had command of the northern and southern walls. The east fronted the murky, weedy Ascanian Lake.

And Phaedra was missing everything!

Gabriel reached into a small decorated box on the table, drew something out and, yelling Phaedra's name, threw it at her.

Phaedra looked up and reached just in time to catch Gabriel's "gift." She opened her palm and stared. "What is it?" she wondered aloud, frowning at the small, black and pointy object in her hand.

"A thorn from Christ's Crown of Thorns," Gabriel said seriously. "You can have it if you would just stop that god-forsaken pacing!" he said, losing his patience. "It's making me nervous."

"The Crown of Thorns? Oh please, Gabriel. And I assume

you have a splinter of the Cross, too?" Phaedra answered
sarcastically.

"I do!" "He does!" Gabriel and Kasia answered together.

Kasia then tossed her head back and nibbled on a grape
while Gabriel looked back into his rosewood box where he
kept his holy relics. Phaedra had recently learned that Gabriel
never traveled without them.

Phaedra crossed the room and laid the thorn on the table.
She peered over Gabriel's shoulder to what other holy relics
he had.

"You don't really believe that it came from the actual
Crown of Thorns, Gabriel," Phaedra said evenly. She was
beginning to believe her artist friend was getting a little soft
in the head.

"Yes, yes, I do. And why shouldn't I?"

"Gabriel . . ." It was a good thing Gabriel was a talented
artist. He never would have survived in the emperor's army
otherwise.

Unaware of the direction of Phaedra's thoughts, Gabriel
said, "And what's more, I have a piece of the lash that was
used on our Lord as well as a few bones from the virgin
martyrs, St. Agnes and St. Catherine, who chose death over
submitting to the attentions of Roman generals."

"Foolish girls," Kasia chimed.

Gabriel tsked. "You, dear Kasia, are not qualified to speak
on the merits of virginity and chastity."

"Thank God," she blasphemed for good measure.

Phaedra reached into the box of relics and swirled her
fingers around, touching the saintly bones, and the
"Cross." For a moment, she forgot her anger. She ventured
a glance at the sketch Gabriel had been working on and
had to bite her tongue to hold herself back from laughing
aloud. It was a picture of Kasia all right, but she had the
head of an asp.

"They give me comfort," Gabriel admitted, as Phaedra
moved away from the table.

"What are you so nervous about, Gabriel? Phaedra is here to protect us. Why, she even knows how to drive a chariot!" Kasia teased, turning on her side to get a better view of her friends.

"I applaud Phaedra's skill. She reminds me of the goddess Athena, or a Diana." Gabriel beamed.

"Yes? Well she, we, may need to turn ourselves into Amazons and bare a breast or two once our barbarian allies discover the emperor has snatched Nicaea out of their greedy fingers. I can't imagine they're going to be pleased."

"What are you talking about?" Phaedra asked as she bent down to pick up Brutus.

"You don't really think Alexius would let Nicaea fall to those oafs, do you?" Kasia sighed dramatically in the face of Phaedra and Gabriel's blank expressions and used her hands to help her explain. "Alexius, through Butamites, has entered into secret negotiations regarding the peaceful surrender of Nicaea. And if that doesn't work, the emperor is prepared to prohibit supplies from entering the city. He'll starve them out, but he doesn't want to. Nicaea's citizens are predominantly Christian."

A question was burning Phaedra's lips. "If it's a secret, how do you know?"

Kasia stuck her tongue out slightly, then bit her upper lip. "I just know."

"Where's the danger in the barbarians finding out?" Gabriel asked, scratching away at his drawing. "The emperor's actions will save men from dying needlessly."

Both Phaedra and Kasia exchanged knowing glances before looking at their innocent friend.

"You forget, Gabriel," Kasia said impatiently. "These men are no better than animals. In fact, wouldn't you say they're like wolves?" she said, turning to Phaedra as her voice caressed the word.

Phaedra shivered down to her toes as if a snake had suddenly coiled around her ankles.

* * *

While Gabriel and Kasia dozed, Phaedra sneaked out of the pavilion, leaving through a loose flap in the side that was unguarded. In the confines of her own tent, she removed a white linen bundle from her leather trunk. Her heart pounding, fingers moving quickly, carefully, she unwound the linen and revealed the tarnished surface of Maia's bronze bowl. Phaedra hadn't touched it since performing the ritual for Alexius, when she'd caught a glimpse of herself tied to a stake, surrounded by flames. Had it been a vision of her own death? She still didn't know. She'd been afraid to see any further.

Now she needed to know whether or not Kasia was speaking the truth.

The sacred bowl glowed in her hands. She could almost feel its power vibrating. She filled it with water and placed it in the middle of her tent.

While burning laurel and the scent of myrrh fingered the air, she removed the pins from her hair and shook it free. She combed it with her fingers and used the silence and solitude to gather her thoughts.

Kneeling before the bowl, she closed her eyes and journeyed to a place deep inside herself. For a moment, she thought she saw Maia. Feelings of comfort and strength washed over her. Smiling, knowing that somehow the wise woman was with her, Phaedra took a deep breath. She opened her eyes and waited for the water to shift and shape itself into the future.

Fourteen

At Pelecanum, Emperor Alexius Comnenus's pavilion of purple and gold shook with the timbre of mighty voices praising God. The candles shimmered with the raised breaths of Christian leaders. The Almighty had not forsaken them . . . Nicaea had fallen. Emperor Alexius's army had won the first arm of the Crusade.

"Victory to the soldiers of God and death to the unbelievers!" roared Bohemund at the ceremony to honor the soldiers of Christ.

"Deus le volt!" God wills it, cried the happy crowd.

"Deus le volt!"

On June 19, before Alexius's siege engines could do too much damage to the protective walls, and before the barbarian knights had a chance to bloody their swords further, the Turks surrendered to the Greek army. It was just as Phaedra had foreseen in the water. The Turkish nobility were safely escorted out of the city and treated with the utmost respect and honor. The city's Christian inhabitants were unharmed and the crumbling walls were rebuilt.

But the barbarians had been cheated out of an easy win. Glory had been snatched out of their hands, not to mention plunder. They grumbled and growled.

Before the wolfish horde had a chance to become too ornery to handle, Alexius promised each of the local leaders compensation for their disappointment. Coffers of gold and jewels, each destined for one of the Christian leaders, now lined the aisle in the emperor's pavilion.

Alexius had summoned Gabriel to record the event, and he'd wanted Kasia to grace the assembly with her magnificent presence.

He'd wanted Phaedra, too.

Like a bird of peace, Phaedra was dressed in white silk. She wore her beauty fiercely. Her dark hair, woven into a braid that crowned her head, called attention to her skin, which was a pale, cold ivory. But it was her eyes that hinted at the rage burning beneath the marble perfection.

She stood beside Emperor Alexius, who wore a purple cloak over armor of gilded steel. She had wanted to keep to the safety of the shadows, the gray fringes toward the edges of the tent where she could go unnoticed yet notice everything. But Alexius had drawn her to stand at his side like a wife. The position of honor sickened her. She'd never felt so unclean as she did now, standing beside him, dressed in white like one of Rome's vestal virgins.

There was nothing in the emperor's manner or voice that suggested he recalled the incident in his garden, but Phaedra could not be rid of the memory. It gnawed at her, eating her, and she hated him for what he'd done, and the silence he seemed to demand of her without uttering a word.

She wished the veil over her mouth covered her entire body as well. The power of imagining made it seem so, and for a brief moment she saw the Christian leaders gathered before her as if she were standing behind a sheer wall.

They were all wearing their white dusty surcoats with the red cross over their mail. They looked like a strange religious order founded on destruction instead of forgiveness. Instead of crosses, they carried swords. That God must have a dark side was so clearly evident that Phaedra shivered in the stifling heat created by so many fervent souls.

She had seen a few of the leaders at the oath-taking ceremony in Constantinople. She remembered the fair, broad-shouldered giant Godfrey of Bouillon, and his brother Baldwin, who was dark and built like a bull. Hugh of Vermandois, brother to the King of France, wore a dark blue mantle trimmed with ermine over his surcoat.

Her attention swept on, and settled on Bohemund, red-gold and mighty. The man wore his ferocity on his sleeve and the others stood apart from him as if they were fearful of being bitten. His heavy-hooded eyes were centered on the emperor. His right upper lip was slightly drawn back in a hook.

Bohemund caught her perusal of him and bared his perfect teeth in a wide grin. His eyes raked her from head to foot, then slid to the silk wall where Kasia stood veiled and resplendent in a crimson gown embroidered with gold knots. Phaedra watched as Kasia's green eyes shifted momentarily to Bohemund and caught him in a hot, heavy-lidded look. Bohemund licked his lips. Phaedra had no doubt Kasia was doing the same behind her veil.

One cross-bearer showed her nothing at all. Brannoc. A brooding silence enveloped him like a black mantle. She noted how the others regarded him, deference mixed with fear.

The others were Christian princes and knights who had arrived in enough time to bloody their swords with infidel crimson and witness the surrender of Nicaea. Later she would match the faces to the man.

After the ceremony, Alexius held a celebration dinner in honor of the Christians. The red pavilion thumped like a heart, for the wind was blowing the silk paneling.

Thick carpets as plush as beds covered the ground. Chairs of diverse woods waited around ebony tables arranged in a three-sided square. Silver lanterns were slung between tent poles and candelabrum glowed.

"Phaedra?" They were seated at the table, watching God's warriors ogle the women. Kasia curled in her seat and bent close to Phaedra's ear. "What remarkable insult did you inflict on Sir Brannoc? Why, the man looks like he wants to tear your head off!"

At first, Phaedra wouldn't look. Insult, indeed! But his eyes provoked her and she met his eyes fire for fire.

"Mother of God!" exclaimed Kasia. "This army doesn't need a blacksmith with you two around! A look like that could sharpen twenty swords."

Phaedra turned the look in question onto Kasia, who flinched back as if at knife point. Nose in the air, Kasia turned to Taticius and began to engage him in a discussion of strategy.

With nowhere to turn, Phaedra looked down at her gold plate. Unconsciously, she fingered the vial of perfume hanging like a pendant between her breasts.

Why did Brannoc hate her? she asked herself. What had she done? She had taken him as her lover. She had joined the campaign. And now the man was looking at her with the intent to kill gleaming in his cold blue eyes. Did he know she was considering using him to destroy Bohemund? But how could he know? It was impossible. Unless . . . unless . . . he could read minds.

She gasped. Her hand froze around the pendant. Impossible, she told herself.

But in the next breath, she wondered what kind of hold he had on her that could make her doubt herself. Frustrated and infuriated, she gnashed her teeth. With steel-like resolve, she banished her doubts and strove to ignore the music and the dancing girls, the laughter and lewd jests.

As two pink prawns in a cream sauce were being ladled onto her plate, Phaedra looked up. The room spun and her stomach tumbled with it, sickening her. With both hands, she clutched the seat of her chair and waited for the room to still. Her silence isolated her from the hungry, laughing men around her, and the women, dancing and weaving their bodies as if they were moving underwater.

And with the silence, terror struck. Fighting Maia's words to "let the vision be," Phaedra struggled to destroy the waking dream she knew lay in wait for her around the next breath.

But it was to no avail. She felt the vision move before her and command her to look. Finally she obeyed, looking down at her plate. She crumbled back, sucking the veil into her mouth with a gasp, as a severed, blond head rolled on the table in front of her. When it stopped, its blue eyes were looking at her. Its lips were frozen around a sound. It was the head of Tancred, Bohemund's nephew.

Phaedra shot to her feet, upsetting the servant behind her with his plate of skewered lamb and onions. He was able to right himself before dropping the food, but Phaedra stumbled. Gulping air, she hurried past the seated men, unaware of the inquiring eyes. When she thought she was free to stumble past the red folds of the tent's opening, an arm shot out and drew her back.

She cried out with a start, and found herself sprawled across Tancred's lap.

"Where are you going, beautiful one? Why, look, how pale you are," he said, stroking her bare arm.

"Let her go, Tancred," Bohemund grumbled, swirling the wine in his cup. He was sitting across the tent from his nephew. His plate was piled high, yet he hadn't touched a morsel of food. The music wove a mood that seemed to add to his melancholy.

Brannoc, sitting to his liegelord's right, looked up from his plate, caught the scene in a cool blue gaze, broke a crust of bread in his hands, and ate. But his disinterest and dispassion never penetrated Phaedra's consciousness. The vision of Tancred's severed head was still etched in her brain. And now here it was, talking to her! She felt sick when she should have felt angry at being handled like a whore. Tancred wasn't more than twenty, yet Phaedra was totally passive in his arms.

"Shall we have a look behind the veil? Hmmm?" Tancred said, fingering the edge of silk. Robert, Count of Flanders, and Stephen of Blois jostled for a better view.

"I said let her go, Tancred," Bohemund warned again. "She wasn't invited here to please you."

"That's why I want her, uncle." His fingers moved lazily down her neck and between her breasts.

Bohemund growled and slammed his goblet on the table. "That's enough!" He rose, upsetting his chair, and was pulling Phaedra out of Tancred's lap before his nephew even knew it. Bohemund hit the boy on the side of his head before leading Phaedra outside.

Leaning against a tree, Phaedra fought to catch her breath. Bohemund hovered in front of her, blocking the moon and torchlight.

He stopped. "Are you all right?" He bent down, frowning, and looked at her. "You're the nymph from the palace garden, aren't you?"

Now that she had her wits about her, Phaedra cast the barbarian a vindictive look over her veil.

"Whoa! Beauty! Don't flog me for rescuing you. By the way you handled my sword," he smiled lewdly at the hidden meaning of the words, "I would have thought you could handle my nephew." He narrowed his eyes when she didn't answer. "What happened to that saucy tongue? Has Alexius forbidden you from speaking to me, eh? That it? Lord knows he has the power to order a man to hold his piss until he says," he mumbled.

"Better watch what you say, barbarian. Even the night has ears."

He smiled his wolfish grin and she felt chilled to the bone. "Ahh, there she is!" He crossed his arms over his chest. His armor creaked as his muscles flexed. "Want to tell me about it, beauty?"

"You may address me as Lady Ancii," she pointed out tersely, and Bohemund responded with an apologetic bow.

"Lady Ancii." He tested her name aloud. "So you're the one traveling to Jerusalem for the perfumes and oils?" He scratched his clean-shaven chin as he watched her respond with a nod. "I trust my army will offer you enough protection on your journey, for it seems that Taticius's force and mine will be venturing out together."

"Yes, I know." And it gave her great delight to see the surprise on his face. Kasia had told her the news hours ago.

He cleared his throat and repeated his prior question. "Want to tell me what happened in there, Lady Ancii?"

"What do you mean?"

"Pale you may be, wench, er, lady, but in there you looked as if you'd seen a ghost."

Phaedra laughed, although his observation unsettled her.

"It was just a chill," she lied. "I'm quite all right now."

"Chill, eh?" He stepped closer, and Phaedra had to press her back into the tree so he didn't touch her. He raised his red-gold brows and gave her a sideways glance, then looked over his shoulder at the tent. Phaedra watched him compose his thoughts into words.

"Perhaps later . . ." he began, then, turning to her, "we could . . ." The proposition ended with a leer that caused his teeth to bare slightly.

Phaedra stepped deftly to the side and slipped past him. But for every step she backed up, he took one toward her.

"I trust you will follow the advice you gave your nephew."

A soft whistle escaped his lips as he stared at the limbs his ally the moon was wicked enough to reveal through her silk garments. Phaedra felt his stare like heat. It strengthened her. She had the power! "This is going to be easier than I thought," she mused to herself as she plotted his death.

Bohemund caught her fleeting smile. Thinking it was for

him, he stepped closer again. But something in her eyes, a
look he had seen on battle-hardened warriors, stayed him.

"Another time." He smiled and with a short bow, turned
to leave, colliding into Brannoc.

Bohemund and Phaedra cried out, for the man had appeared out of nowhere. Brannoc had taken root like a tree
and Bohemund had smacked right into his chest. They were
nose to nose, their eyes a bridge of lashes apart.

"Brannoc!" Bohemund said surprised, stumbling back.
"God's feet, man, you startled me."

Brannoc was dressed in mail like the others. How had he
been able to approach them without making a sound?

"I was wondering if everything was all right."

"See that Lady Ancii gets back to her tent, man." And
without a backward glance, Bohemund stalked away.

Defenses raised, Phaedra stared fixedly at Brannoc. Why
hadn't he come to her aid before?

But in the space of a heartbeat, she locked the question
away. With bitterness, she viewed the irony of being "helped"
by Bohemund, the Norman wolf. Now the Dragon had arrived.

What great twists and turns this quest is taking, she
thought cynically. And without uttering a word, or venturing
a glance, she lifted her gown and flew into the night, too
deep in her own thoughts to be reached by something as
fragile and elusive as a man's sigh.

Fifteen

The Christian army rumbled like a heavy-scaled beast. It destroyed trees, fields, even fellow Christians, women, children and civilians who were already weak from their journey to Constantinople. White bones littered the army's path, marking the way for stragglers.

From Nicaea, the beast followed the old Byzantine road across Asia Minor and headed for the Sangarius River. Bright banners rippled in the whirl of sunlight above the scales of lance tips. Crimson marked Bohemund's well-ordered army. With him marched the followers of Robert, Duke of Normandy. The knights and civilians of Hugh of Vermandois believed themselves specially blessed, because they followed the white and gold banner of St. Peter. It had been given to the Franks by none other than Pope Urban, who had promised eternal life to all those who destroyed the infidel and freed the Holy Sepulchre from the children of Satan. The elegant and handsome Godfrey of Bouillon and his brother Baldwin rode beneath the blue flag of Lorraine. Blue also distinguished the followers of Raymond, Count of Toulouse.

Phaedra rode alongside Sharif at the head of the Byzantine detachment, while Taticius and Vinicius accompanied Bohemund further afield.

Comfortable in her trousers, tunic and vest, she'd also taken to wearing the white turban around her head to protect herself from the sun. During dust storms, she would take the end that hung loose to her chest and pull it across her face to cover her nose and mouth.

Shielding her eyes from the white sunlight, she could barely make out the leaders on horseback. Before her gaze could distinguish Brannoc, she looked away, past him and toward the horizon which slurred into the blue haze of the sky. Unknowingly, she began rubbing the perfume-filled pendant around her neck. She shifted uneasily in her saddle.

Seeing Brannoc, Phaedra lost herself within the dream she'd had the night before. The memory of it made her breath catch in her throat. In that place between waking and deep sleep, she had seen herself laying beneath a white silk pavilion fluttering in the breeze. Brannoc had appeared dressed in white, his sword slung at his side. The stone in the pommel had glowed like a third eye.

In her dream, she'd risen to meet him wearing nothing but a gold circlet around her brow and the vial of perfume on its sparkling chain. Her hair hung wild and loose, combed by wind and sleep. As he drew her into his arms, she remembered not trying to fight the direction the dream was taking, for she knew in her soul that they would make love. His hands moved fluently through her hair and over her body. His kiss carried her into fire-blue waves of sky.

The earth was their bed. Fragrant grasses were covered with perfumed breezes of jasmine, rose and Pagan Desires. He drew her up and over him. It was like making love to the warm earth. Brannoc and the tasseled grass and the ground, the sounds of flowing water in the distance all were one. Held by the earth, centered and made whole, her fingers tore at the grass as she followed her mounting desires. Then came the sweetest death, and the feeling of being reborn in his embrace. She remembered his arms stroking her, his voice in her hair guiding her back to the living.

The dream had sought to rekindle long unsatisfied desires. It thought it could master her, but Phaedra was strong. Shutting her eyes, she banished the memory of it and saw herself as a tower of rock, unreachable, untouchable. Best to forget, she advised the pagan in her soul. This journey meant everything to her. Everything.

She opened her eyes just in time to see Bohemund cantering up to them on a tall, heavy-footed charger that kicked up reddish dust. Like his men, he was bronze-faced from the sun.

"Lady Ancii," he saluted. He reined his horse and whirled himself around to walk with her. He towered over her and she felt his heat like a raging bonfire lick her hands and face.

"Duke Bohemund." She gave him a nod, nothing more, but even that was too much for Sharif. Phaedra felt him bristle at the barbarian's attention.

"The river's just ahead, past the bend in the road. We'll stop there, give the horses a rest before continuing on to Leuce, where I'll be meeting the others in council."

"Council?"

"To plan our course to Dorylaeum. I'm going to suggest we split into two armies. We'll get nowhere traveling as we are. And we're an easy target for these Saracens." He wiped the dust from his mouth with the back of his gloved hand. "Will you share some wine with me at the river?"

"Thank you for the invitation, but wine, in this heat—"

"Water." He was not going to take no for an answer.

Keeping her eyes on the road before her, she answered, "Very well."

Regardless of her curt manner, he smiled. "How's the Lady Kasia?"

"Bored, no doubt."

The image of Kasia fuming and fanning herself brought a slight smile to Phaedra's features.

"Kasia had no idea campaigning was such an arduous bother," Phaedra said, mimicking the throaty voice.

Bohemund snorted. "And you? You seem to be taking it better than some of my men." He cast her an appreciative gaze as he pulled hard on the reins to keep his high-strung horse steady. "One would think that you were born in the saddle, Lady. Don't tell me your father was a soldier, or something of that sort?"

Both Phaedra and Sharif looked at Bohemund with a start. "He can't know," Phaedra thought. She lowered her eyes. She could feel Sharif studying her. Even the charioteer did not know her real reason for joining the cross-bearers. "Had Sharif figured it out?" she wondered. All he knew was that she needed supplies and oils for her perfumes. Until now.

"Well, perhaps I can amuse your friend for a while." Bohemund spurred his charger, yanking the animal around, and cantered down the moving column, searching for Kasia's white silk and gilded palanquin being borne as if it held the Queen of Sheba herself.

At Leuce it was decided that the army would, as Bohemund had wanted, divide into two. One section was to precede the other by a day. Bohemund, leader of the Normans of southern Italy and France, would be leading one army. Joining him were the Duke of Normandy and the Counts of Flanders and Blois. Taticius's Byzantine contingent would travel with them as well. Raymond and Duke Godfrey were chosen to lead the other army. All this would happen on the morrow. For now, the forces of Christendom camped on the banks of the Sangarius.

But Bohemund, Phaedra noticed, had ordered his own tent to be raised far from the river. It was as if the river represented a line, and now that he'd crossed it, he wanted to put as much distance between him and it as was possible. Phaedra knew this was true, because the water itself had told her that Bohemund would capture Dorylaeum by leading one of the two armies and then betray Emperor Alexius. She could only wait and watch as her vision came true.

* * *

When she'd knelt at the river's edge, it was with the sole purpose of quenching her thirst. Sitting back on her knees, she dipped her headcloth into the shallow depths and, after wringing it out, coiled it around her neck for relief from the heat. It wasn't until she bent forward again, to fill her water-skin, that the vision began to take shape.

On the water's surface she saw Bohemund stretching his arms to the sky with a mighty roar, clenching and unfisting his hands as if breaking invisible shackles. His thoughts rippled on the water, teaching her the workings of his mind. She saw him laughing in Alexius's face, raising a gold crown and placing it on his head, and riding into a walled city as if he were its king. It was clear that he had no intention of handing over the rule of the Holy Land to another man.

The vision had not surprised her. Had she not warned the emperor of the barbarian wolf's duplicity and black heart? But the water had more to tell. The surface seethed with dark visions, fates, fortunes and prophecies that chilled her to the bone. They drew her, like the hands of beckoning river nymphs, and for minutes she hung spellbound above the water. There were images of skulls and fires, blood and twisted mouths grotesque with screams that pierced the mind. She saw writhing bodies crying for mercy and carrion birds descending.

The water unleashed the scents of dust and decay, hot metal and baked earth, fires lit by dung, odors of the night and light, sweat and musk. And rising above it—jasmine. She couldn't stop the images. There was so much, so much that needed seeing and telling.

She flicked the water, enraged by the power that gripped her. Why did she have to see? To know?

The water tasted like blood and metal. She spat it out and rose quickly to her feet, stumbling. As she backed away from the mirror that had read the visions in her mind so well, she stepped back into a wall, no, not a wall, but a man who had been watching. Brannoc.

His voice never touched the wind, but she knew he called her name.

Phaedra.

Hours later, in her dark tent, she wondered how he'd been able to speak to her mind. Was he the great mage that Tristan had warned her of? A man who could change his shape into beasts? "Shapeshifter," Tristan had called him.

Brutus rolled onto his back and snored deeply. "Christe," Phaedra swore, jealous of the cub's ability to sleep.

She rubbed her cheek against the leopard skin that served as her bed and tried to shut out the noises of the camp, to bring images of home and Alexander into her mind. She tossed and turned. An image took shape. She thought it before she knew what she was doing. She imagined Brannoc moving above her, the weight of him, making love to her. She bolted upright. This was what she had to guard herself against. Lust. Desire. The ache in her body. The scent of him. She wanted to touch him again. And again.

She wrapped her arms about her and rocked. She was mad to be thinking such things! She was an Acominatus, daughter of the Leopard. She pulled on her boots and stormed outside.

The night air had been cooled by the river. She tiptoed around Sharif, who had taken to sleeping outdoors like the more seasoned of the Byzantine cavalry. A spiral of laughter and a flute tickled the night, while grumblings and owls and the crack of a fire made the dark serious again. Noticing a light on in Kasia's tent, she moved toward it. She hoped Gabriel was with her. The artist had a talent for taking her mind off personal matters. She was willing to concede to his belief that he owned a piece of the Cross and the bones of saints. Anything, she thought ruefully, to bury the visions behind her eyes.

Kasia's tent was the largest of all the Greeks' tents. It even surpassed General Taticius's and had been outfitted as if for a queen. Lamplight flickered through the silk walls. Phaedra hesitated at the threshold, hearing soft, murmuring voices.

Eyes on the ground, she waited for a pause in the voices, then eased back the tent's flap just enough to pass through.

The scent of Aphrodite's Passion assaulted her. It was so rich and thick she gagged. At first, all she could see before her were the beeswax candles in glass votives on Kasia's table, and the thick rugs she'd brought from her villa. A moan coming from the corner drew her attention. She looked and stepped back all at once, reaching behind for the tent flap. Laying upon the divan were Kasia and Bohemund. She was straddling the barbarian, riding him with control. He was holding her by the hips.

Kasia's hands were tied behind her back with a piece of silk.

She writhed and moaned with pleasure as he worked her body up and down. His eyes were full of lust and fixed on Kasia's breasts.

Phaedra began backing away, but froze when Kasia's eyes turned toward her. Kasia watched for a reaction as Bohemund cupped the naked flesh bobbing before him and began to knead her breasts with grabbing strokes and rough caresses. In the candlelight, Kasia had the lazy look of a coiled serpent. And for a moment, Phaedra was afraid to move lest she be the object of a venomous attack.

Phaedra backed into the shadows as Kasia moved with new vigor above her lover, and the sounds of lovemaking intensified.

Sixteen

It was Maia's voice which finally lulled Phaedra to sleep. It was a sound so sweet in Phaedra's mind that it had the power to distance her from the camp sounds, the snort and snap of tethered horses, and the last dying crackle of the fires.

The moon was a crescent in a blue velvet sky as the riding party rode beneath the open gates of an abandoned city. Its yellow walls were pockmarked and crumbling. The wind howled through the openings with a human, grief-stricken wail.

Phaedra reined Achilles still to stand beside Sharif and Vinicius, who held a torch aloft in his right hand to help light their way. Only six other men rode with them, but Phaedra only recognized Bohemund.

With a curt wave of the mighty barbarian's hand, Vinicius doused the flame. With no light save the sliver of moon above, they urged their mounts forward and into the empty streets. Just as Phaedra was thinking about exploring the city alone, she felt Sharif's steadying hand on her arm. She shrugged his warning off and urged Achilles into the first side street she saw. Feeling the burn of Sharif's gaze, hearing the clackety-clack of hooves on stone, she moved past the empty buildings and homes. In some places, only the foundations were left. It looked as if a giant had walked through, squashing the brick and stone into dust. She heard the soft play of water in a fountain and, before turning down the alley, looked over her shoulder to see if she was being followed, but the others had already moved on.

She was alone. Guided by the palest moonlight and her senses, Phaedra urged Achilles through the narrow passage. It twisted and turned like a snail's shell and Phaedra felt as if it were leading her below the ground. The street opened into a courtyard before a low wall. An iron gate stood open in the darkness beyond. An abandoned villa, she thought to herself. She reined Achilles around. She was surrounded by walls. It was a dead end. She would have to leave the same way she came.

But instead of taking flight, she dismounted and, leading Achilles, stepped through the gate. She found herself in another courtyard, but this one fronted a villa much like her home in the city. She tied the reins to a wooden post. Without hesitation, she pushed the bronze door open and proceeded through the villa, following the pools of moonlight that fell through the shattered openings in the roof.

In what was once the dining room, she found platters and goblets set on the table, ready for a feast. She touched a dish, swirling her finger through the white dust, and noticed that the dish was made of gold. She passed her hand along the carved back of a divan and felt a trailing vine bloom beneath her fingertips. She counted eight divans and stopped. With an animal's instinct, she knew someone was watching her. She clutched the back of the divan and squinted into the surrounding darkness. She thought she heard the soft thumping of drums, but in the next breath recognized it as the sound of her own heart. Gulping for air, she pivoted to see what lay behind her. Something, beast or man, moved forward out of the dark.

The last thing she saw was the velvet back of the divan.

* * *

Waking, she found herself in a long room lit by brass hanging lamps. The scent of jasmine roused her further. Pagan Desires? As she reached for the pendant around her neck, she noticed she was wearing a Greek chiton that bared one shoulder and her legs. Her hair had been combed to hang in serpentine curls down her back. As she reached to touch the earrings that dangled from her lobes, she noticed gold cuffs around her wrists. She froze. Hammered and molded into the cuffs were the coiled figures of dragons. Blue stones glowed for eyes.

She bolted upright and somehow found the will to swallow her unease and fear. There were pillows scattered about her on the carpeted dais. Green silk curtains hung at the four corners. Near her right foot was a silver bowl of fruit flanked by two silver goblets. She moved onto her hands and knees to look closer. One goblet was filled with wine, whereas the other was empty.

Seized by a desperate need to know what had happened to her, and to find the others, she swung her legs over the side of the dais and rose. The room tipped and she clutched the drapes to keep herself from falling. Her legs felt like water. Weak and lightheaded, as if she'd been confined to bed for days due to an illness, she stumbled forward in her bare feet. The room spun. Clutching her stomach, she began to fall when something swooped out of the shadows and caught her. The strong arms around her told her it was a man, but it was the mask of a beast, a dragon, that stared down into her face. No! She struggled against the Dragon's chest as he carried her back to the dais.

Phaedra.

She stiffened, recognizing the voice. After the beast eased her down among the pillows, she grabbed its wrists, stopping him. She looked into its eyes, boldly meeting the Dragon's blue gaze before turning her attention to his wrists. There, coiled around each hand, were the blue dragon tattoos.

And then he was gone, vanished, and she was left clutching

the air. She rose again and ran from the room through an open door to search for him.

Her search ended in a firelit, vaulted chamber of gray stone. Still wearing the mask of the beast, the Dragon was seated at the far end on a throne. Bare-chested, he looked like a pagan idol. She hesitated before venturing further. The gloomy, stone cold of the room and his concentrated regard of her chilled her to the bone. She was suddenly afraid. *Turn, leave now,* said a voice in her head. The Dragon means nothing to you. Let him be. And she took a step back. Then another. As she turned to leave, she caught the glimmer of bronze out of the corner of her eye. It was on the stone floor, before the throne. Although she was sure it wasn't there a moment ago, it didn't seem to matter.

The familiar shape and shimmer held her and drew her forward into the chamber with the power of an open hand and friendly smile. When she saw it was filled with water, she knew in her mind what she was meant to do here. She heard his voice inside her mind.

Yes. Perform for me. Tell me what you see. What will be.

She felt the Dragon ease forward on his throne with anticipation as she removed the jewels from her ears and the gold cuffs. She felt the power of the bronze bowl and her own strength beginning to come together. Finally, she looked him straight in the face.

He sat back. The way he relaxed his shoulders against the throne, the ease of his breaths revealed by his naked chest, and his open palms suggested patience to her eye. But the true test was yet to come.

Unadorned now, save for the perfume vial around her neck, she unfastened the gold mesh belt that held the folds of her chiton close to her body. It fell like water to the stone and was followed by the silky sigh of her chiton that slipped and pooled around her bare feet.

Naked before the Dragon, she heard his breath catch in his throat. She felt his eyes follow the path of the chiton's caressing fall, then travel slowly upward again over her every curve. She trembled slightly, not from the cold but from the appreciative, heated look in his eyes. Yet she continued. She ran her fingers through her hair and shook it loose. Now she was free.

She knelt before the bronze bowl and gazed into the water. The ripples revealed an image that shocked and riveted her because it was occurring in the present, in the chamber she was in now. Her hands were bound together with silk, held above her head and secured to a pillar. She could feel the smooth, cold stone against her naked back. There was no fear on her face, yet she could hear her breaths coming short and ragged. She saw someone standing behind the pillar. He reached out to cup her from behind. Then the hands strayed downward and stroked the insides of her thighs, touching her womanhood. She heard herself sigh deeply and trembled as the hands caressed the sensitive cleft of her sex.

The boundary between the vision and the present felt as if it was melting away, because, for some strange reason, she felt and saw everything as if it were truly happening to her now. It was the Dragon that stepped out from behind the pillar. She lifted her velvet lashes, and the heat of his gaze burned her. She felt a spiraling sensation of heat between her thighs and, without realizing it, she spread her legs for him.

He fell to his knees before her and delicately kissed the perfumed flesh offered to him. He pressed kisses upon the insides of her parted thighs in a sinuous trail that led to the essence of her heat. His tongue probed her gently, moving slowly, sending violent shivers of fire through her. Suddenly afraid of the sensations he was arousing in her, she struggled, clawing at the air, to free herself from the bindings. She tried to pull away, but he grabbed her by the buttocks and held her still.

His delicate tasting of her changed as she sensed his naked

hunger for her growing. Her vulnerability aroused his desires, and his lips and tongue drove her senses into exquisite riot. He teased her. Savored her. Branded her with the mark of his own heat and changed her forever.

She cried out with a great racking shudder. His mouth stilled, calmed her with kisses, then brushed up to feast on her breasts. She moaned again, seduced by the pleasure of his mouth and the idea of being held captive to his desires. As he rose to stand before her, she knew what he meant to do next.

He tore the dragon mask from his face and his mouth swooped down on hers. He caressed her chin as he moved to press himself between her legs. With his free hand, he gripped her bound wrists. His kisses echoed his need. They showed her no mercy and promised her that he was not finished loving her yet.

His hands moved to her buttocks. She felt him lift her off the ground and, with a throaty cry, she knew that all his hungry attentions were to prepare her for what he was about to do. She felt no fear. She wanted him.

Enslaved, yet in control, she surrendered to a heat more primitive, more dangerous, more spellbinding than any other. He drove deeply into her willing body, filling her, opening her to the pleasures of the world. He raised her passions, moving slow and deliberate, sheathing his maleness and drawing away until it became sweet, ecstatic torture. Wavering between the vision and the present, she lost herself in the spiraling tightness of her pleasure. She heard the echo of her cry moving against stone.

Spent, his whispers guided her back to him.

"'Tis no dream, what we have. I have bound you to me, Phaedra. And the Dragon is your slave."

The sun filtered through the tent. The sound of Sharif's voice woke Phaedra from her deep sleep. She had had such a strange dream, but she could barely remember it.

"Phaedra?" Sharif's voice was a knot of worry.

She stretched. Her head ached. "Where are we? Are we back at camp?" she questioned the charioteer crouched at her side. Her tongue felt heavy. Her muscles ached as if she'd been out riding all night.

"What are you talking about? The armies are just getting ready to march to Dorylaeum now."

She sat up and immediately felt a wave of dizziness and nausea sweep through her. She tried to explain.

"Last night. You, Vinicius, Bohemund and I rode to an abandoned town and . . ."

Sharif grunted. "A dream."

Confused and tense, she sank back against the pillows. She struggled to remember. There had been the city. The night. The crescent moon. The villa.

Brannoc.

She turned onto her side in an effort to sit up again. That's when she noticed her wrists. They were rubbed raw and marked with purple and blue bruises, as if they'd been bound.

Phaedra guided Achilles through the onrush of mounted knights and soldiers, their rein chains jangling and shields clanking above the sound of hooves. The shriveled heads of Turkish warriors who had been caught in skirmishes outside Nicaea ornamented many lance tips. The women rode together on mules.

It was not yet noon, but already the sun swirled like a blinding pinwheel in the sky. The rays of fire had proven to be one of their most brutal adversaries. Faces were red and swollen from the sun's heavy touch.

Under this blazing heat, the parched earth reflected up into the eyes, forcing Phaedra to squint beneath the canopy of her hand. She loosened the cloth over her mouth as she searched for the camp followers. These were the prostitutes who had joined the Norman army in southern Italy. Fair of skin and hair, many of them had children. She liked the women's direct manner. When she was with them, she never had the feeling that they were plotting to do something behind her back, which was usually the case with Kasia.

One woman in particular drew Phaedra's searching gaze. She was a tall redhead, built like an Amazon, with twin boys who were Alexander's age. The sun had blistered and burned their milky skin. Phaedra wanted to find the woman so she could give them some of her complexion creams and oils. Her saddlebags were filled with the cream that was protecting her skin.

"Eleanor!" Phaedra shouted, spotting the woman walking beside the cook cart. She kicked Achilles toward the slow moving vehicle that creaked and moaned like a small ship, maneuvering her horse through the thick stream of soldiers, braying mules and pack horses.

Eleanor, shielding her eyes from the glare, caught sight of Phaedra approaching. Her smile pulled the reddened skin taut, and she grimaced with pain. Her face was swollen, her eyes slits.

Phaedra reached into her saddlebags for the vials of healing waters. She held them down to Eleanor.

"Here, take these. You need to start using the healing waters now, or the sun will leave its mark on your skin forever. Dab it on with a piece of cloth if you have it, and you must treat the boys the same."

Nodding with understanding, Eleanor asked, "How about the others?"

"Administer it to anyone who asks. I have plenty." Phaedra tipped Eleanor's chin up to take a closer look. She gave no outward sign of the thoughts running through her head. "Once the blisters have healed, start using the cream." Phaedra reached into the saddlebags again for the terra cotta containers. As she slipped them into Eleanor's open palms, a holy man rode by, catching the friendly gesture, and pulled back hard on his reins.

Alerted by the malevolence reaching out to them, Phaedra looked up. It was Girard, Bishop of Berain, dressed in iron mail, like the knights, with a mace hanging from his wrist guard, as a sword was forbidden to all churchmen. Burly, with tufts of white hair sprouting around a bald pate, the cleric had bulging toad eyes and a pointy face marked with pits from a skin disease. His mouth was fretted with bitterness. Nowhere, to Phaedra's eye, did the man look touched by the hand of God or filled with His divine grace, light and wisdom.

His voice was guttural. "What brings you to this part of the camp, Lady Ancii? You have no business here with these tainted women."

"Your holiness, these women are suffering from the sting of the sun. I have brought waters and creams to help heal them."

"So they may better lure God's warriors to their beds? I think your gesture is ill-placed. Let the devil and Aphrodite take care of their own."

His lips spread over yellow teeth and bile rose in Phaedra's stomach. Eleanor reached out to stay any rebuke, but it was too late. Phaedra could not resist.

"We are all God's children, so the Scripture says! Was not Mary Magdalene pardoned from—"

"Fie, lady. Watch your preachy tongue or you will offend Our Lord and find yourself burning in hell for your sins."

"There is no worse hell than that which is made by man."

His toad eyes bugged larger and his skin mottled with rage. "You blaspheme, Lady." His gloved hand cut the air into a cross. "Spare this creature, for she is but a female and does not know what she speaks." He leveled his gaze at her again, and Phaedra shivered at the unholy lust she saw reflected in his eyes and the darting curl of his tongue as he licked his lips.

"By the grace of God, I can protect you now. Seek this

woman's company again and I swear you will fall from grace like Eve and assume their wicked ways."

With a start, Phaedra backed away. For his voice was full of hope for such a transformation. But before she could vent her scorn at such hypocrisy, he rode off to join another flock.

"Beware of him," Eleanor whispered, tugging on Phaedra's saddlecloth. "I know you are not fooled by his holy vows, but you must guard your tongue from sparring with him."

"I'm not afraid of him," Phaedra laughed, her gaze still following him.

"You should be," Eleanor advised. "There are women in our camp who are deathly afraid of him." Phaedra turned sharply at what was veiled yet implied. Eleanor continued, her eyes wide with fright. "Just ask the women he's used to satisfy his lusts." She paused. "Be afraid, Phaedra."

Later in the day, it was not fear of a lusty bishop's attentions that caused Phaedra's skin to prickle with foreboding, and her heart to hammer wildly beneath her breast. The dream was coming back. Not in full images, but threads of impressions. They were gathering in her mind, into a web. The smell of jasmine, plush darkness, the cutting bite of silk bindings around her wrists, the taste of a kiss, and a pleasurable heat between her thighs. Brannoc. She remembered the smell of his skin, the lamplight and fire flickering gold across his naked chest, the green scales of the mask that had revealed his mouth and the intense gaze of his blue eyes.

They were all too real to dismiss. And there were the markings around her wrists to prove that she had been tied and held somewhere, to something.

She shivered in the night air and slumped against the oak at her back. A breeze off the river curled her hair. She stood on the fringes of the Greek army's camp. Bohemund's forces were encamped nearby. The hills formed a circle behind them. Roman ruins rose above the rocky pinnacle, cutting dramatic shapes against the night sky.

The heavens were deepening to blue after the purple and orange sunset. She could hear the hollow grumbling of the oxen and the braying pack animals. Beneath it all, like the steady flow of water, was the ever present dull clinking of soldiers as they removed their mail coats and made themselves more comfortable for sleep.

"Innocents," she thought to herself. The army of the Red Lion was close by. She could feel them. Sharif believed that the Sultan Kilidj Arslan had had enough time to gather fresh forces from neighboring tribes and mount an attack. After his humiliating defeat at Nicaea, he would be anxious to prove himself. And he would be more dangerous than ever.

She rubbed her temples and closed her eyes against the ache in her head that had persisted all day. She knew she would be unable to sleep, as the dream would command her restless mind to seek out the truth. What did it mean, she asked herself over and over. She had to know. Did Brannoc also have the power to enter and command her dreams? Had it been a dream?

She looked up with a start. "Of course it was! Christe! What a fool you are," she grumbled aloud. "I'll know soon enough what it means. Too soon," she groaned.

She was about to leave and appease the hunger pangs gnawing her stomach when she had the sensation that someone very close was watching her. Instinctively, she flung a look over her left shoulder and saw the unmistakable outline of a man standing amidst the shadows of the trees. She swallowed a gasp and turned to face whomever it was.

The man emerged from the shadows and into the sea of moonlight, revealing his identity.

"I fear I've startled you, Lady Ancii," said Brannoc. "Forgive me."

"There's nothing to forgive," she replied curtly, alerting Brannoc that she might be speaking about something else.

Phaedra noted he had left on his shirt of armor, and that his sword, as always, hung at his side from the brass-studded belt. He was dressed for battle, not sleep. Phaedra could not mask the glimmer of approval in her eyes.

"I didn't mean to intrude. I know it's hard to find solitude when you're on campaign."

She openly ignored him, stepping to the side as he blocked her view of the cook fire. He breathed in and exhaled deeply, as Phaedra smirked at his obvious unease.

But it was a deep caressing voice, one that betrayed not a bit of discomfort, that uttered the words, "Pagan Desires."

She was wearing the scent. She wore it always now. It was Brannoc who had awakened her to the perfume's power.

She could feel him watching her. Waiting. Her lover.

No! She dismissed the thought and balled her hands into fists as if she meant to fight someone.

"That day, when you appeared in camp, you must know I—" he began to apologize.

But she was not going to let him make amends for the way he'd treated her. Not now. She whirled to face him, to silence him.

"I know all there is to know."

"Do you, Phaedra? Do you know how much I've longed to take you in my arms? To make love to you? Do you know that if I showed you any attention, the least regard, you'd be suspected of an evil as great as the Beast's? For it seems I've become the embodiment of evil to these simple souls. A monster."

"The beast?" she looked away and recalled Tristan telling her that Brannoc was thought to have the devil's powers.

"But they cannot harm you if I come to you in your dreams."

Her heart stilled. Her throat locked, strangling her voice. "What? What did you say?" She met his gaze uncertainly. He couldn't mean . . .

The silence was frightening to her. He reached out and

wrapped his fingers around her wrists. In a gesture that turned her knees to water and answered all the questions flooding her mind, he drew both hands up to his lips and kissed the bruised flesh.

The touch of his breath, the press of his mouth made the moment throb with intimacy.

"Whoa there!" whipped a shout through the trees. Phaedra and Brannoc froze. His lips were still pressed against her skin.

"Show yourself!" It was a soldier on guard duty. But instead of pulling Phaedra into the light to prove their innocence, Brannoc drew her hard against him and kissed her. His lips moved slowly, fanning fires he knew were waiting to be rekindled.

Phaedra closed her eyes, breathless and dazed at the powerful force that drew her to respond to him. His hands tangled in her hair. His mouth grew savage. It would not be still. His lips ignited the flesh of her neck, the soft spot behind her ear.

His tongue, which knew her name so well, inspired her to pagan thoughts.

"Whores!" Phaedra barely heard the mumble behind them and the fading footsteps, because Brannoc's hands were stealing up her tunic and spreading wide across her skin. His fingers moved, stroking her waist, her back, moving to cup the waiting fullness of her breasts.

A moan of despair caught in Phaedra's throat. Beyond her will, her hands caressed his shoulders and her fingers spread through his hair.

She was lost. Again. She had thought it was finished between them, that the Dragon and the Swan would never love again. But it was a lie. He'd pretended to hate her and had ignored her to protect her. Protect her from his dark, sinister image. Protect her from the cross-bearers.

And herself, she thought.

With a sigh of surrender, she gave herself over to the beast in her arms. His parted lips slanted across hers, devouring

her. The kiss was relentless and fierce in its search for the
sweet caves of her mouth. She answered his hunger with her
tongue and began to move against him in a rhythm that hypnotized them both.

In a feeble attempt to cool her inflamed desires, she drew
away and turned, but he followed, pulling her so her back
was pressed against his chest. He lifted the curtain of her
hair to bare her neck and nuzzled the jasmine column until
he found her ear, then touched it delicately with his tongue.

His hands wreaked havoc over her skin, his fingers mastering her, claiming her silky breasts as his domain. His
groan scorched her skin. She lifted her arms up and wrapped
them behind his head. While he felt like a pillar of strength
behind her, she was all wet with wanting.

She felt his hands sweep up her arms. "Tighter. Hold me
tighter," he whispered gruffly.

As she obeyed, his hands returned to her stomach, then
slipped beneath the waist of her trousers. His hands moved
cautiously, as if they expected at any moment to be stopped
by a word or a sign. But none came, and the hands drifted
over the warm skin of her thighs.

"No!" Phaedra gasped as Brannoc closed his hand over
the hot, damp place between her legs.

"Shhhh, beauty. Let me touch you. You want me to feel
you." He kissed her throat as his free arm snaked her waist,
trapping her, forcing her to let him touch her.

He moved his finger gently within her and slowly eased
it out. He entered her slowly again and felt her tighten around
him.

"No, Brannoc," she moaned. "Not here. Not now."

"Phaedra," he whispered to hush her. His voice was like
the play of wind in her ear. Trembling, she let him continue
stroking her. Veils of inhibitions fell and she moved against
his hand, searching for more, her tightening womb enslaving
her and him, demanding that he continue.

She was breathing more quickly as she strove to find the

release his fingers promised. Uninhibited, she moaned into the darkness. Lest they be found, Brannoc moved his hand to cover her mouth and barely caught the soft scream of her release.

She shuddered against him. He dropped his hand. Now there was only the heat of fire in her arms and a light that made her heart soar.

Seventeen

A ground fog christened the army with a silvery mist. Phaedra was securing a saddle cinch on Kasia's horse while the courtesan watched, tapping her slippered foot with impatience. The woman had finally seen the wisdom of abandoning the sedan chair. However, she hadn't had much of a choice as all of her chairbearers had deserted her.

Gabriel was sitting on a rock, scratching something in the red-brown earth. Around them, the Byzantine soldiers were busy preparing their own mounts for the march. Phaedra could hear the morning prayers of the Christians rising from their camp.

"There's something different about you." Kasia paused. "Of course, your skin is ruined. You should have ridden with me when you had the chance. Now it's as brown as a country strumpet's from the sun." She waited for some sign that Phaedra was listening. And waited. Impatiently, she drove forth. "No, it's something else. Hmmm," she angled her head. "If I didn't know any better, I'd say that you have a lover." Her mouth curved wickedly.

Phaedra was all business, securing the saddle cinches. Hair swinging behind her back, she walked purposely to stand on the other side of Kasia's horse, which had been lent to her by Taticius.

"Look, Gabriel. I think our swan is in love." Kasia's green

eyes glowed mischievously. She chewed a broken red fingernail.

"Hmmm?" Gabriel scratched his drawing of horses in the dust.

Kasia gestured with her hand, "Come look. Who is he, Phaedra?" she asked breathlessly. "A Greek general? Don't tell me it's Vinicius."

Phaedra steadied the horse with a touch. "There. She's ready." The memory of the way Brannoc's hands had moved over her body rippled through her, but she was damned if she was going to let Kasia know.

Phaedra tossed the reins to Kasia. As she moved past the nosy siren and toward Achilles, Phaedra couldn't help remarking, "You should find yourself a pair of trousers. It would be more comfortable for you."

"And ride like a man? Never!" Kasia's red-tinted mouth dismissed the notion as if such a thing were far beneath her station to contemplate. "The only beasts I'll ever have a mind to straddle are two-footed. You know that."

The lewd comment was meant to remind Phaedra of the night she'd stumbled in on Kasia and Bohemund making love in the courtesan's tent. Phaedra remembered, but not without blushing.

Astride Achilles, she went looking for Vinicius. All at once the stallion's ears went back, flat. Something was wrong.

In the distance, horns blew and sounded from diverse directions. She heard such a clamor and din rise from the Christians' army that it threw the Greeks' horses into a panic. It was at that time that Vinicius galloped into the camp. His stallion was frothing at the mouth. He called out for his other horse. In a single bound, he was dismounted.

Phaedra could sense his impatience as he paced the ground. She cantered forward to see if he had any news.

Vinicius looked up, catching sight of Phaedra. He always had a smile for her, but the weight of army matters had turned his face to stone. Over the past month, the life of a cavalryman had taken its toll, handsomely defining his face which was tauter and thinner than before. With his hawk nose, his profile took on a greater nobility.

"Kilidj Arslan is advancing," he said matter-of-factly. "There must be thousands of men." He grinned sarcastically and his dark eyes glowed with mirth. "Now these barbarians will have the day they've been lusting for all year. They'll dance with the devil, or die trying." He turned away and spat on the ground.

Achilles danced and Phaedra had to rein him steady. "There'll be no help from reinforcements. The Count of Toulouse's army is a day's march away."

Vinicius's eyes narrowed into hers. "Fools they were to divide the army. Now they'll pay." He looked around as word of the Turkish advance spread through the Greek camp. "I'm riding over to Bohemund's camp. They already know," he said over his shoulder as he mounted a white stallion. "General Taticius wants me to keep an eye on the rogue. Come with me."

Responding to the spurs in his sides, Vinicius's stallion bounded forward. Achilles and Phaedra were not far behind.

There was chaos in the Christians' camp. Everywhere, sunburned and bronzed liegemen were scrambling to stand beneath their lords' banners in preparation for riding out to face the enemy. As Phaedra tried to steer her way through the mob and the swirling dust, she noted that many of these men were not even fully armored, so anxious were they to fight the infidel. Water skins hung slack and empty from their saddles.

Along with the tramp of iron-shod hooves, the black robes were leading prayers, the mob murmuring their answers at a feverish pitch. Phaedra counted many devout soldiers kneeling and silently praying before planted swords. To her right, she could make out the army's womenfolk and children, the sick and wounded gathering around baggage wagons to peer beyond the misty plain to where the enemy had been sighted.

"Phaedra!"

She looked. Vinicius waved her over and together they watched a mob of knights in their red-crossed surcoats riding out of the silvery mist. Lance points and helms glittered. In the center was the unmistakable figure of Bohemund. To his right, like an iron beast, rode Brannoc on the black.

When next Phaedra looked, she and Vinicius were being swept into a sea of commoners, knights and barons, mounted and on foot, moving toward the front. "Christe!" She was trapped on all sides. A foot soldier grabbed her by the leg and tried to yank her off Achilles's back, but in an instant she had her dagger raised in her hand and waved it in front of the fool's face.

Bohemund brought order to his army, his imperious tone rising with orders. "Mounted men to the front! Everyone else, I want you to set up camp here," he jabbed his finger down at the ground.

Recognizing Lady Ancii, Bohemund urged his mount forward to stand at her side. "Lady Ancii," he exclaimed, surprised. He grinned his wolf smile. "Come to give us a kiss before we go?"

The suggestion flustered Vinicius and he turned red, but not Phaedra.

"You barbarians have the strangest customs," she casually replied.

Bohemund snorted. His voice carried mightily on the air, bringing Brannoc around to them.

"Surely you don't intend to fight, Lady?" He thrust his shaven chin in the direction of her sheathed sword.

"My bow and arrows are back at camp. I intend to use them, too." She noticed Brannoc and Bohemund raised their brows at that. "Just tell me where I should stand. Perhaps the rear, to protect the women and tents?"

"I appreciate the offer, Lady Ancii, but I think there are

plenty of men who would be honored to protect you. Don't you think, Brannoc?" Bohemund said over his shoulder to his mail-clothed guard.

All Phaedra saw was the cool gleam of his blue eyes through the slits of his helm. He sat as high as his liege lord. His shield was slung before him. And his sword, with the mysterious carved scabbard, was beneath his left knee, ready to be drawn by his right hand.

Bohemund and Brannoc, moving as if one man, raised their heads, listened, and seemed to sniff the air.

Bohemund grinned. "Ah, the time has come. Good thing, for my sword hungers for sport. Prepare your victory dance, beauty," he winked. "Bohemund never loses." He wheeled his horse around and, with a great jangle of the bridle reins, he was gone. Brannoc followed, but not as speedily as his lord. He allowed himself a final look at the dark-haired woman armed with her sword, who sat on her horse as proudly as any knight.

As the Normans under Bohemund and the Greeks under Taticius fanned out across the plain to meet their mutual enemy the Turks, Phaedra and Kasia set to work with the Christian women. They fortified the middle of the camp, shaped like a square, with baggage to shield them. They filled every available water skin with fresh water as the archers and jackmen armed themselves with pikes and axes.

True to his word, Sharif had remained behind to guard Phaedra. He grumbled as he readied his bows and arrows. He checked his sword, running his fingers along the edge.

"Mother of God, they've left us no protection! Do they think the Turks are too daft to notice that?"

"Wha-wha-what are you talking about?" stuttered Gabriel, who was pacing uselessly back and forth, fingering his saintly bones as he watched Sharif and Phaedra inspect their weapons. Sharif's white brows gathered into a storm cloud as he tossed a look over his shoulder. He nailed the artist still with his gaze.

"I mean we'll be cut down like sheep if the Turks ever take account of the poor state of our defenses."

"But surely they won't kill us. The women and children. Where's the nobility in that?"

"Hah!" Sharif grunted.

"Sharif," Phaedra cautioned, noticing that Gabriel's rosy face had grown pale.

Sharif continued. "You've had your head in that mosaic too long, man!" Gabriel winced. Sharif's face furrowed with guilt and he walked away to see to their horses.

"Phaedra?" Gabriel stood patiently waiting for Phaedra to finish twisting the white cloth that covered her head. Nothing about her movements or the look on her face betrayed her feelings.

"No harm will come to us, Gabriel," she promised him. Gabriel gave a wan smile, soothed a little by her calm and strength. But Phaedra knew she spoke the truth. Neither the water nor her dreams had revealed their deaths. With a motherly touch, she smoothed the tufts of hair behind his ears. A smile trembled on his lips and he moved forward so their foreheads touched.

"I need your help, Gabriel," she whispered, patting his arm. He nodded. "Find Brutus. He might be playing with Eleanor's sons."

Phaedra watched the artist slump away. He looked so lost without his familiar charcoal sticks and paper. She briefly recalled his mosaic in the palace, the glory of an empire surrounded by smoke, fires and armies.

And there was the matter of the dragon. And the swan. One in the air, the other in the water. Both moving away from Constantinople.

Phaedra blinked at the image and the play of her thoughts. Then reality locked into place. She stood transfixed in the shifting sea around her before her solitude was torn away by a thundering roar.

The sound mushroomed until the air quivered with the

tumult of pounding hooves and drums. Everyone in the camp froze. Even the children stopped playing and stood unnaturally quiet. The women stared at one another in dismay, wringing their hands. Priests prayed to the sky, their arms held wide in supplication. Without the proud, confident knights sitting tall on their stallions to make them feel safe and protected, an uneasy quiet swooped over them. Fear entered the camp on the wings of imaginary carrion birds.

The beat of death and doom curled up Phaedra's legs and grabbed her like skeletal hands reaching from the grave. The years of practice in learning how to wield a sword, use bow and arrow and fight like a man were about to be put to the test. Was she worthy of being an Acominatus? Would the Leopard's daughter honor the blood of her forebears?

A rolling tightness in her stomach made Phaedra wince. Nevertheless, she fingered her sword sheathed within the red velvet scabbard at her side. The tightness came again. And again. Sweat beaded her brow. Her nerves stretched taut against the next wave as she identified the cause of her illness.

Not now, she wailed to herself as the blackness that came with the sight of her visions descended.

"Phaedra! What's wrong?"

She heard her name called, a voice through a fog. It sounded like Sharif. She felt the charioteer's strong arm wrap around her shoulder and lead her away.

"Out of my way, Kasia."

There was safety in the feel of muscles and might beneath her head. She closed her eyes and gave herself over to the power, just as Maia had instructed.

The vision came . . .

At a pounding gallop, his surcoat streaming, Brannoc swept across the plain of Dorylaeum. His mouth was a grimace of death, teeth bared, blue eyes hard on the waves of Turkish horsemen that surged down the slopes toward him. Their voices carried across the earth.

"Allah! Allah!"

Phaedra saw the Turks through Brannoc's eyes. They wore silver helmets and carried bows, already strung, and round shields. Defying the speed of their small horses, they stood straight in their stirrups and aimed.

Brannoc ducked behind his shield as a storm of arrows whistled past. The points tapped like iron hail against shields. But the unprotected horses plunged to the ground as the arrow tips thudded into their sides. The beasts screamed and threw their riders into the dust. With a light touch of the reins, Brannoc guided his protected horse through the falling sea of horseflesh, spurring his beast to weave around the dead and dying. He reached for his lance as the distance between the approaching forces closed.

A pound of hooves crashed through Phaedra's skull as the armies moved forward and crashed into each other at full tilt.

She watched Brannoc spear two Turks off their saddles before he found himself caught in a press of Christian and Turkish soldiers. Too close to be of any use to him, he threw his lance aside and reached for his sword.

"By the blood of the Dragon," he cried, and the gates of heaven and hell opened. He pulled back the reins of his war stallion, who reared up and lashed out with iron-shod hooves, destroying the smaller Turkish horses.

The field was a packed, whirling sea of soldiers of God and Allah. Crimson and blue banners flew amongst standards of green dyed horsehair tipped with golden crescents. Death screams were muffled by the clash of iron and the crush of mounted men seeking escape from the tight melee.

With each downstroke, Brannoc's sword sheathed itself anew in flesh and bone. He wore no gloves, as he preferred the intimacy of his flesh against his weapon. Phaedra could feel his callused palm gripping the leather hilt. She could hear the great heaving gulps of air he stole between thrusts and slashes of his mighty arm. She felt his chest on fire. For an instant, he became his namesake, the Dragon. The smell of death seemed like an aphrodisiac to him, and he roared like a crazed creature. Brain and blood spattered as he moved with deathly precision.

His mighty wrist seemed alive with the spiraling, winged, hissing serpents. The Turks, catching a glimpse of the blue tattoos, fell back, away from him.

The plain was flooding with sun, dead horses and men. And still the Turks kept coming. Through Brannoc's eyes, she saw the dismay in the Christians' eyes. She heard their labored breaths and groans as the sun beat at them.

From the hills, on both sides, fresh horsemen appeared, adding their might to the Red Lion's forces. Bohemund, now at Brannoc's side, watched them coming. "Bloody Christ!" He spat blood to the ground and with the death-defying resolve and blood hunger of a wounded wolf, he threw himself back into battle. And Brannoc followed.

The shrieks and screams of women, the soul-piercing cries of children, and the clash of metal. Sounds jarred Phaedra out of the trance. She sat up, caught her breath and looked around her. Sharif was gone. She climbed out from behind a toppled pile of baggage and gaped in horror as Turkish horsemen rode through the camp, toppling tents, snatching women and children off their feet, slashing men with scimitars and sending heads rolling like cabbages.

Without a thought for her own safety, Phaedra scrambled in a half crouch to find her bow and bag of arrows. The touch of her weapons renewed her. Scanning the area, she noted white-robed Turks racing through a defenseless rift in the Christians' makeshift defenses. There was an overturned oxcart nearby. From here, she thought, she would make her stand.

With her satchel of arrows strapped to her back, her sword at her side, she ran toward the vehicle, eyes focused before her, instinctively sidestepping the flayed animals and speared bodies that marked the way.

Eyes tearing from the smoke, she climbed atop the cart. She booted a Turk who reached from below to pull her off. Kneeling behind the dead bodies of two jackmen, Phaedra aimed an arrow and sent it whistling into the face of a man pulling one of the camp followers by the hair. With cool, deadly precision, she singled out her prey, and like a trained assassin, brought them down one by one.

It felt as if days had come and gone. But the sun's position, a fireball above her head, told Phaedra she had been fighting for less than an hour. Already her right arm was trembling. She stopped to rest. The onrush of Turks had dwindled to a slow trickle. Down in her bones she knew they would be back. This was not the end.

What of the iron men? Brannoc? There must be news, she thought and, with her bow in hand, she climbed down the cart and turned to rush into the camp.

The sight that met her eyes turned her legs to rope and forced what little food was in her stomach to rise in a heated rush. She stumbled forward and fell atop a priest whose eyes and tongue had been cut out. She scrambled quickly to her feet and picked her way across a carpet of corpses until her tears made it impossible for her to see. Wavering on her feet, she looked all about her.

The camp had become a valley of death. Amidst pillars of gray smoke and shreds of tent were the ravaged naked bodies of women and children. Priests lay crucified to the ground, their entrails in a heap beside them. Archers and jackmen were speared standing to the earth. She turned, hoping for life, a sign of hope, but everywhere she looked there was death. She could smell blood, burned flesh, and the fear that came with knowing the end was near.

Swallowing back the horror, she moved on. Her eyes widened with shock at the scores of cross-bearers trudging across the plain and back to the camp. Many bore the weight of their comrades over their shoulders. Those who still had horses led them slowly, murmuring encouraging words to their faithful mounts.

With shaky breaths she recalled her own words: There is no worse hell than that which is made by man.

"Help me! Oh, God, help me, please!"

Phaedra looked down at the blood-stained soldier at her feet. On bended knee, she gently rolled him onto his back. Quickly, she removed her turban and pressed the cloth against the deep, bleeding wound in his side. He needed a surgeon. The wound had to be cleaned and sewn immediately.

Frantic for help, she looked around, hoping to spot the familiar figure of a surgeon. Then she remembered the westerners hadn't had the foresight to bring any. She thought of her own healing waters. Perhaps . . .

"I can help you," she said, and she began to rise to her feet.

"No! Don't leave."

His frightened plea pulled her back and she knelt beside him. Torn between leaving and staying, she smoothed the sweaty hair from his brow. It was only then, as the soot and the blood came off on her hands, that she noticed he was just a boy not much older than Alexander.

The boy smiled at Phaedra and closed his eyes.

No! She crumpled to the earth and placed her hand over his heart. As if she were moving underwater, she pulled him into her arms and held him as he went on his final journey.

When next she looked up, she saw Brannoc, his helm under his arm, walking his war stallion into the camp. In the wavering sheets of sun, through the glisten of her tears, she saw he was pressing his hand over a wound to his right shoulder. Fresh, hot tears spilled. She wasn't sure if they were tears of joy that he was alive, or tears of fear that, once again, a vision had come true.

Sharif found her next to the dead boy. He tried to help her

to her feet, but she shrugged his hands away. The flow of
her tears had cut pale streams down her soot-covered face.
Her eyes flashed with anger.

She rose quickly to her feet. "The boy didn't have to die!
Look at his wound, Sharif! It's nothing a good medic could
not have repaired!"

Sharif bristled at her tone and passed a blood-caked hand
over his brow to wipe the sweat. "Phaedra," he sighed, too
tired to say anything more.

Her gaze landed on Bohemund, who was locked in conversation with his knights. "Bloody bastard," she swore. Her
rage pounding through her, she covered the open distance
between them. She didn't stop until she stood before him.

Ignoring the grief reflected in Bohemund's eyes, Phaedra
launched herself at the barbarian, startling him. But the man
was a rock in his chain mail and did not flinch. His knights
simply stared in shock as she hit him again, and again. Then
she threw herself against his unresisting body as if he were
a wall and hit him harder. Finally, they pulled her away.

She kicked out, catching Bohemund in the shins before
they yanked her back and off her feet. "Fool!" Her voice
felt like a lash.

Bohemund winced, then clenched his features so tightly
he trembled from the effort. Struggling against the weight
on her arms and shoulders, Phaedra smote him with words.

"You left them unprotected! You left them with no one to
see to their wounds! Monster! How could you!" Her eyes
raked the knights around him, Robert, Duke of Normandy,
and Tancred. "How could all of you be such ignorant fools!"

Robert stepped forward and cuffed her with the back of
his hand, tearing her lip open and drawing blood.

Phaedra licked her lip, tasting blood, and smiled. "Impo-
tent bastard."

"Why you—" Robert lurched forward again, but Bohemund reached out and pulled him back by his shoulder.

"Let her be," he said gruffly. "She's mad from the battle, no more."

His cold, brutal gaze had no effect on her. She spat on the ground at his feet and would have done it again had Sharif not dragged her away.

Phaedra's disgust and rage at the cross-bearers' shortcomings renewed her strength. She threw herself into the task of helping as many of the wounded as she could, cleansing their wounds with myrrh and cedarwood oil which were known for their healing properties. The women who had survived eased water skins to blistered lips and urged food on hollow-eyed soldiers who had lost the will to open their mouths to eat. The prayers of the priests weaved like incense. A few children played in the dirt with Brutus. They were the lucky ones who had hidden with Eleanor and her children when the battle had begun.

Although surrounded by the dead and dying, Bohemund and his men did not wallow in grief. Like Phaedra, they drew strength from adversity. Their faces and bodies were taut with anger. Their spirits fed off the blood of their comrades. They were anxious to return to the field and destroy the men who had had the audacity to prove the iron men's mortality. They were all prepared to fight to the death.

Once again the cross-bearers took to the field. They rode their surviving horses, baggage mules and asses. Many had become dismounted during the battle and trudged singly and in packs beneath religious banners and the flags of their lords. Servants with no one to serve, and freemen, seeing an opportunity, joined the ranks. They armed themselves with the spoils of the field, swords, helms, and shields, and turned themselves into fighting men in an afternoon.

While Phaedra bandaged the shattered ribs of one of Bohemund's sergeants, Sharif limped across the field, leading his horse toward her. Waving away the flies, she chanced to see him approaching. She had only to look into his face to know his intentions. It had that hard, proud, far-away look of a warrior. He's going to join the cross-bearers, she thought to herself.

Phaedra quickly handed the bandages to Eleanor, who was the only woman to approach her after hearing of her bout with Bohemund, and met the charioteer halfway. Confusion knotted her brow. He had promised to stay with her! He couldn't leave her now. He was her friend, her family.

They stood apart, looking at each other for a spell long enough to call up years worth of memories. Phaedra saw the young, burly charioteer with Samson curls howling with laughter over one of her pranks. She saw the man who had taught her how to race chariots, to use bow and arrow and defend herself with the sword she now carried. She saw the thunder-browed protector who had driven away the suitors who'd descended on the villa after Jason's death. And she saw the scent-tester who wiggled his nose over her every creation, describing each with the same, "Humph!"

She did not see an old man.

Sharif cleared his throat. His horse stamped and shivered at his side. "I've come to ask that you release me—"

Phaedra flew into his arms, giving him no time to finish. Hesitantly, the charioteer raised his arms to hold her.

There was no need for words, for the silence between them had always been rich with meaning. She felt his strong arms tighten around her and she buried her face in his neck.

"Remember everything I taught you," he whispered stiffly.

She nodded as she continued holding him tight.

He patted her back once, then held her away from him. Looking down into her face, he said, "I've asked Sir Brannoc to watch over you in case something happens to me."

"What!" She stiffened and tried to pull away in his arms, but his fingers dug into her arms, steadying her.

"You'll need someone to watch out for you. Keep you out of mischief," he advised.

She rolled her eyes and shook her head vehemently. "I can take care of myself. For you see, I've had a wonderful teacher who's taught me everything I need to know," she said lightly, although every word carried the weight of a thousand truths.

"Not everything," he countered, looking around at the battered camp. "I did not teach you about this."

Phaedra swallowed. "Then you better come back," she said softly, and she could not suppress the quiver that hung over the edges of her words.

He pulled her to him one last time and, holding her face between his hands, kissed her gruffly on the forehead. He chucked her on the chin when he saw the tears.

"Be the Swan. Rise and fly from this as soon as you can. And take care no one learns of your powers."

She narrowed her eyes, saw that he knew, had always known about her dreams and visions. He'd never mentioned them to her. Never.

And with that, with words cast to protect her power to dream and see, he let her go and led his horse onto the plain.

Phaedra felt herself caving in, but righted herself in case Sharif should chance to turn around and look at her. Taking a deep breath, she lifted her chin and prepared herself for what was to come. She smiled when Sharif looked over his shoulder, catching her gaze. She bowed her head in salutation, then pivoted on her heels and returned to help the cross-bearers. Yes, she thought to herself, he'd taught her well.

Again the endless din of the enemies' horns and drums and the demon cry of the mounted, turbaned archers and lancers rushing like a white foam wave. Again the confident shouts of "Deus le volt!" and the majestic screams of Christian trumpets firing blood. Jangle of bridle. Thunder of hooves.

Mounted on Achilles, Phaedra watched from a knoll near

the camp. Where once the field had been a sea of men, now there were great gaps in the phalanx formation Bohemund was employing to charge the Red Lion's army. Narrowing her eyes, she watched Sharif galloping among the westerners, his red-crested helmet visible between the towers of iron.

The armies clashed. A third appeared, a fresh force of Turks. Phaedra watched in horror as they moved to attack the Christians from behind.

Sharif!

The Acominatus blood in her rose as she realized the peril Sharif and the others were in and, without thinking, she urged Achilles forward, toward the battle. The black stallion reared and bounded into full gallop. They flew across the field, Phaedra's black mane coming loose from its bindings, alerting the Christians in the camp that they were watching a woman ride out to meet death.

The sound of her heart thumping wildly in her ears, she checked the satchel of arrows over her shoulder. Trained like the Turkish archers to shoot from horseback in full gallop, she readied an arrow for its first mark.

Moving up behind the Turks, she took down three men in quick succession before she was spotted and challenged to fight. Using the same tactics as the Turks, she darted in to attack, then rode away, stinging the enemies' flank again and again.

Spying Sharif surrounded by the enemy, she whirled Achilles around to go to his aid, then watched the charioteer slump to the side, stabbed by one sword thrust, then another, just as she rushed in to help him.

Her mind denied what she had just witnessed as she continued forward. Sharif's assailants sensed her, turned to face her and charged.

She had time to aim and shoot twice. She missed the first, but the second arrow did not disappoint her. Instincts ruling, she slung her bow over her back and unsheathed her sword.

"Remember a blade is like a living creature," came

Sharif's voice in her head. "It has a soul. It becomes part of the arm that wields it."

She gripped the hilt firmly. She did not fight the feel of the metal, rather, she concentrated on letting the purity of the steel wash through her, strengthening her, so the weapon became an extension of her might and not the might itself.

Focused on the riders streaming toward her, she chose the assailant to the far right, and reined Achilles at the last moment in an effort to surprise him. She screamed and slashed through the Turk's belly. Then whirling Achilles left, she quickly cut down another man.

Her eyes stung and her vision blurred as the sweat streamed down her face. The sun hammered her. Her battle was against nature, too. But the sight of Sharif's still body fired her blood, and she released a bloodcurdling yell that announced her commitment to destroy her friend's attackers.

She warded off a lance point that was hurtled toward her side and counter thrust before the man could retreat, delivering a death blow with the flashing steel. But when next she looked to gauge where the other riders were, she saw that they had surrounded her. As her mind grasped for a way out, she heard thundering hooves and saw someone coming to her aid. A knight broke through the circle and, with a clean, powerful stroke, beheaded a rider like a flower from its stem. The remaining Turks charged, and Phaedra spurred Achilles to engage.

Without stopping to see who it was who had come to her rescue, she rode Achilles to Sharif's side and slid to the ground. She felt for his life force, but found quiet and calm instead. She looked into his eyes before brushing the lids closed.

The din and clamor of drums and horns, cymbals and war cries echoed in the far recesses of her mind as she held Sharif to her, cradling his head in her lap. Submerged within her grief, she moved slowly, touching his face with her fingers and the back of her palm.

Racked by sobs, she huddled over the body, unaware that Achilles had galloped away. She did not see the red-bearded Turk moving toward her. He was hanging over the side of his saddle, his arm out, ready to grab her.

Startling herself into the present, Phaedra looked over her shoulder just as the Turk's arm shot out, hooked around her middle and yanked her off the ground. He slammed her, face down, across his saddle. Her chest burned and she gasped, unable to breathe. But just as he let out a savage howl and began to gallop away with his prize, the horse bucked and plunged, throwing Phaedra and her captor into the dust. Without thinking, she scrambled away. She slipped over the blood-soaked bodies of men and horses. The haze of heat and dust boiled like a cauldron about her. She rubbed her eyes. She could not see. She stumbled onto her knees, was swept up into the air again and found herself sitting across a knight's lap.

Fighting and screaming, she tried to tear herself free of the arm that held her pinned against an iron chest. She turned to look, saw the blue eyes burning fiercely to either side of the iron slits. She saw death in those eyes.

"Brannoc!"

"What in Hades are you doing here?" he shouted.

"Sharif . . ." Her words were lost in the thunder of the battle.

"What?" The horse reared and Brannoc fought for a moment to bring him under control.

"Sharif! He's dead."

Arrows whistled past their ears. Without further talk, Brannoc spurred his horse to a leap. His blade arced and hissed through the air when the enemy appeared at his side, and both Brannoc and Phaedra received a bloody shower of bright scarlet from the Turk's neck where it had joined his shoulder.

Out of bow shot and away from the main battle, Brannoc reined his destrier. He pulled his helm off and, before she

knew what was happening, Brannoc was kissing her. His
mouth was brutal and hard on hers. His tongue raged like
an iron-hot weapon. All she could do was cling to him. She
could not give him anything in return, for his power was too
strong and had swept her into a darkness of his own making.
There was no feeling of light in the man. He was a warrior.
An instrument of death.

Phaedra struggled against Brannoc and, as she pushed him
away, her vest and tunic fell open to where the Turk had
ripped the cloth. Phaedra looked. At the sight of her clothes,
her body, she made a small sound, like a wounded animal.
Her breasts were raked with scratches and splattered with
blood. Hands shaking, she fumbled to keep her clothes together.

Brannoc gently pulled the fabric closed. He kissed her hair
as she collapsed against him.

Seconds of calm passed before Brannoc whispered,
"Look!"

Phaedra straightened in the saddle and followed his gaze.
The blue banner of Lorraine rippled above the hill, leading
the armies of Duke Godfrey, Robert of Flanders and Hugh
the Great. Weapons sparkling, they swept down the hill and
took the Turks' left flank.

The onslaught of fresh armies of men drowned out the
Turks' drums and cymbals. When another army, led by the
Bishop of Le Puy appeared on the hill behind the Turks,
the Red Lion ordered his men to retreat rather than be
caught between two armies.

It was a miracle. Even the cross-bearers who had fought
all day had found the will to pursue the Turks back to their
camp. The iron men fell upon treasures of gold and silver,
silks and brocades, weapons and spices. Victory was theirs.
Many a man had looked death in the face and cuffed it aside.
Others were not as brazen. Their dead bodies lured carrion
birds out of the sky.

Circling down patiently, the vultures took to the fringes

of the plain of Dorylaeum, and the great flap of their wings ushered in the night.

As the sun faded, Phaedra picked her way across the field to find Sharif's body and then bury him. Everywhere she turned, there were bodies and horses prickled by arrows. The earth lay buried beneath broken lances, shields and swords, blood-stained clothes and empty, dented helms.

She found the bear Brutus next to Sharif. Somehow, the bear had escaped the camp. The animal had been shot through the heart with a green-feathered arrow. As she cut the steel point out of Brutus's flesh, she remembered the day she found the cub at the Hippodrome. It was Sharif who'd shown Alexander how to care for and feed the bear.

The memories wrapped her in pain as Phaedra wiped Sharif's face and strong hands with a cloth fragrant with myrrh and rosewood oils. She sat with his head in her lap, looking at him until the cook fires snapped to life. It was Brannoc who found her lost inside herself. Brannoc who helped her bury the charioteer and the bear on a small rise. When they were done, she could not move. She stared and stared at his final resting place as if the power of sight could raise him up from the dead.

Brannoc did not reach out to her. But his eyes were like hands, strong and warm. His voice was like the sea.

"He's gone, Phaedra. Mourn him. Swear to avenge his death in the next battle, but let him go."

That night, alone in her tent, she stripped off her garments, which reeked of blood and death. To the wails and moans of the wounded, the sobs of the survivors lamenting departed souls, she cried herself to sleep. She cried for all of them: Sharif, Jason, her mother and father. Cried for the girl she had been. A girl who had known the love of many.

But what had she given in return? She cried to herself.

Eighteen

Days had passed since the battle of Dorylaeum, and the cross-bearers and the small contingent of Greeks had camped in the fertile valley outside the walled city of Iconimium. It was the Garden of Eden in comparison to the desolate, hostile terrain they'd just crossed. Its green smell was the scent of living things. It was a welcome relief to the dust-dry smell of blood, marshes and baked earth.

Phaedra and Kasia, bathed and refreshed, were passing the time with Gabriel beneath the green tent. It was just one of the many prizes that had been claimed as booty from the Red Lion's camp.

"By the saints, Phaedra! You should have seen what I saw!" Gabriel exclaimed. A blow to his jaw during the battle of Dorylaeum had knocked out five of his teeth.

Phaedra slumped back in the chair and closed her eyes. Kasia, however, leaned forward. The silk folds of her gown rippled. She was dressed for a state banquet. Now with only one servant to tend to her, she wore her hair in a simple coil behind her head. Even without the paints and tints of color on her face, her features still had the power to lure. Her eyes, with their exotic slant, provoked desires.

"There you were, Phaedra," Gabriel began, "riding out to meet the Turks as if the hounds of Hades were after you. With your bow and satchel of arrows, you were the image of Diana! And when you reached for your sword, I swear the sun's rays reached out and bathed you in the most golden light, and I had to blink, for it seemed to my eyes that you'd grown into that stately, deadly goddess of might, Athena."

Phaedra opened an eye and regarded the babbling artist cynically. The blow to his head must have been worse than I thought, she mused to herself. She leaned back once again and groaned when Gabriel took a breath to continue.

"Those images are locked in my mind. Such heroics! I may have to work you into my mosaic, Phaedra."

"Please, Gabriel." If only he knew she was already represented as the Swan, she thought to herself.

"Stop it Gabriel," Kasia sighed with boredom. "You're embarrassing her."

Gabriel turned abruptly to Kasia. "How? She fought the enemy like some immortal creature. It's the stuff that gets written into song!"

Phaedra jumped to her feet, upsetting her chair. Startled, Kasia and Gabriel looked up at her.

"Enough," she said simply. She did not see the battle the way Gabriel described it. And she would have laughed had Gabriel told her that he thought her more beautiful now than ever before. Her new-found strength made all of Gabriel's comparisons to goddesses valid in his mind. Ever graceful, she now moved with a confidence and authority that was queenly. Even the bronzing of her glorious ivory skin enhanced this new Phaedra who had emerged from the field of Dorylaeum.

And yet, they sensed she had grown colder and more withdrawn since Sharif's death, and rightly so. A transformation had occurred. For just as the perfume Pagan Desires had the power to awaken her senses, so did the scent of death that clung to Sharif have the power to destroy them.

Phaedra crossed her arms over her chest and, leaning back on her heels, managed a stare that dared Gabriel to continue.

"No," Gabriel defied, raising his chin. "You would have

made your father proud, Phaedra. There's no mistaking you're the Leopard's daughter."

Phaedra's face closed up at the compliment.

"If you find that offensive, then, then, well, I don't care anymore."

So absorbed were the trio, that they did not notice a hulking shadow pause to listen at the entrance of their tent.

Phaedra sighed and walked up to Gabriel. Patting his shoulder, she said, "I'm honored, Gabriel. Really, I am. Thank you. But please leave me out of your mosaic."

He touched her hand. "Done."

"How touching," Kasia droned, her deep voice laced with honey.

"I have another favor to ask of you," Phaedra said. She took a deep breath. "I was hoping you'd have an empty scroll that I could write on. I would like to send a letter to Helena and Alexander."

"Of course! Of course! Here," and Gabriel reached down to the carpet beside his chair and handed her a scroll.

"Thank you," Phaedra said gratefully with a smile.

"Lady Kasia!" shouted a voice outside.

"Enter," Kasia answered.

Brannoc swept back the tent's flap and, holding it open behind him, stepped inside.

"Duke Bohemund will see you now."

Phaedra's eyes flicked over him. He wasn't wearing his long shirt of chain armor, but a sleeveless leather vest, chausses, his sword belt and sword. His long hair was white gold from the sun and tied back with a piece of leather. The fiery rays had also bronzed his face and arms.

With a wicked gleam in her eye, a secret edging her smile, Kasia rose and winked at Phaedra. At the tent's entrance, she stopped and ran her fingertips up Brannoc's muscular arm. Brannoc met her flirtatious gaze with a hard, cold look.

"Will you take me to him?" Kasia asked with a tilt of her head.

"My lord's squire awaits you outside."

She ran her fingernails down the same arm, then put her finger into her mouth and struck a pensive, pouty pose.

Holding the flap back, Brannoc moved to the side and let her pass. He didn't leave just yet. Casting a look at Phaedra, who had turned away from him, he asked, "If I might have a word with you, Lady Ancii?"

Following Brannoc out, she left Gabriel's inquisitive stare and turned at the last moment to look at him and shrug.

Brannoc and Phaedra hadn't spent a moment together since Dorylaeum. There had been rumors regarding his ferocity on the battlefield. The talk proved to the Christians that he was a mage, or worse. And Brannoc had been concerned that his reputation would hurt anyone he came in contact with. Especially Phaedra.

He stopped near the trees where he, Bohemund and fellow knights kept their horses tethered. The animals snorted and tossed their heads at the intrusion. Brannoc turned to Phaedra. Blue eyes narrowed on her.

"Your father was General Nicephorus Acominatus?"

Phaedra stepped back, thrown off balance by his question. Brannoc closed the space she had opened and asked her again.

"Yes," she finally answered, cool as the north wind. She met his gaze, wondering all the while why he wanted to know. Her hand tightened around the scroll.

"I've heard the song around your campfires. 'The Leopard,' they called him. They said he led a Greek army against Bohemund and was murdered by the Norman 'Wolf,' " he emphasized.

She felt her heart lurch beneath her breast. She ground her teeth. Had he guessed her plan? Her motive?

Brannoc's voice interrupted her thoughts. "You wouldn't be thinking of avenging your father's death, now, would you?"

As if caught in a web, she stood unable to move. "Of

course not," she hissed with false scorn. Her eyes slipped away from his scrutiny.

He arched his brow. It was obvious to her that he did not believe her. He walked around her, eyeing her as if he had already found her guilty.

"Antioch. Is that where you'll do it? Or has Alexius ordered you to wait until Jerusalem?"

She laughed. "I'm a businesswoman on a journey for supplies, not a murderess in the making."

"Good." His tone chilled her to the bone. "Because he would kill you first. The man is protected by a force greater than anything I've ever encountered. Even the great El Cid didn't have it. It's not Bohemund's time to die."

Oh, now, this was interesting! "How do you know? That it's not his time to die," she added.

He put his hands on his waist and looked away, at the war stallions. "Look into the water and you'll see."

Ripped of yet another veil, she began to back away from him, but his hand closed around her arm, stopping her. How could he know, she raged to herself.

Then it was as if he could read her mind, for he said, "I've always known you had the gift of sight." He felt her tremble, and he rubbed her arms up and down. "That is even more dangerous than any desire you might harbor to kill the Duke. If the fools were to find out that you could divine the future, they'd tie you to a stake and burn you as a heretic."

His knowing was too much. She hid her fear beneath anger and tore herself free. "You're making all this up to scare me!"

A storm cloud seemed to cross the Dragon's face. The light disappeared from his eyes and his face grew somber. "Phaedra," he said with mighty patience. "Why would I? How? Even a field of armed Turks is not enough to scare you. Nay. I'm here to protect you, remember?"

"Then protect me," she ordered between clenched teeth.

Had the words been a sword blow, she would have unarmed him, so taken aback was he by her demand.

She thrust at the heart of his pledge, and used it to attack him.

"Make certain no harm comes to me until the cross-bearers take Jerusalem."

"Protect Bohemund's assassin?" His words held a hollow, deathly ring.

"Why not? Or are you offended by the idea that your lover might actually desire to kill a man?"

His face was cold and still. Either he had grown, or she had shrunk. The Dragon towered over her.

"The Dragon is bound to the Swan, remember?" she whispered.

Brannoc's cool mask cracked a little. Phaedra smiled. Nothing mattered now save the fulfillment of her quest. She'd witnessed atrocities that no mortal should ever see. Sharif was dead, and so, to a point, was she.

With a final look that made her step back, Brannoc said, "He didn't kill your father."

All thoughts of writing Alexander a letter flew from her mind as the sting of Brannoc's words echoed in her mind.

"He didn't kill your father."

The words taunting her, she paced like a caged animal beneath the hot shade of a parasol pine. Of course Bohemund killed her father, she raged to herself. Every citizen of Constantinople knew how her father had died. Brannoc didn't know what he was talking about! He was protecting Bohemund.

She dropped to the ground and leaned back against the tree. She didn't know what to do. She wanted to tell someone about the lie, but who? Kasia? Gabriel? She toyed with the scroll. Absentmindedly, hands shaking a little, she unrolled it. She made a face as she noticed that the scroll was already

covered with Gabriel's scribblings and drawings. She began
to roll it up again and put it aside, when her eye caught her
name. She stopped. Part of her felt like Pandora about to
open the box and release evil into the world. The other part
was too curious to care. She read the passage:

JUNE 30

"Phaedra was an angel of mercy. She treated and
mended the various wounds of many soldiers and
knights. She did not shun anyone, but helped all, the
royal-born and the peasant. She set the broken bones
of many, including Sigurd de Bouverier, liegeman to
Baldwin and Godfrey, the brother knights from Lorraine. I watched him follow her with his eyes when she
was done. I believe the man is quite taken with her."

JULY 1

"Perhaps I should capture our Phaedra in my mosaic? What would the emperor say to that? What can
he say? Throughout the ages, our empire has been
shaped by women as well as men. It distresses me
greatly that her formidable knowledge of weapons and
battle strategy, combined with her ability to heal, has
caused many a tongue to wag that she is a sorceress.
And it doesn't help her image that she consorts with
those women skilled in the arts of Aphrodite. She gives
generously from her supplies of perfumes and creams
and they purr like cats. The wives of the Christian
knights, however, eye her with scorn.

"No, it's the simple souls who may be the ruin of
her if she continues the path she's taken. Poor dears,
they have artichokes for brains, but they are feverish,
ruthless, and unwavering regarding godly matters. The
rabble has power, too. Collectively they add up to one
giant threat. They don't know their right from their left,
but they know a sorceress when they see one, by God!

Masters of riots, they must be reckoned with. Thank the saints no one knows about Daniel's accusations! Phaedra must be warned, and she must take care."

JULY 2

"The aftermath of Dorylaeum. The cross-bearers buried their dead and sent the prisoners speedily along to join Allah. They beheaded the Turks with swords or axes as befitted their mood. The Christians took great sport in this, and laughed at the heads that rolled on the ground. It sickened me. And Phaedra. Kasia, cruel bitch, watched it all and never said a word."

Phaedra looked up from the scroll and frowned. She continued reading his entries. They ended on the date July 13. She sat wondering why she figured so prominently in Gabriel's writings, when a shadow fell across her lap. She heard a sigh and wrinkled her nose. She glanced up. It was Sigurd. The rough-haired knight stood blocking the sun. His mouth was disfigured by a small scar at its corner. Other than that, his broodingly handsome features would have swelled the heart of any maid. His arm was in a sling and his powerful body was encased in a suit of scale mail that fell back in a loose coif about his short, thick neck that came down to his knees. His brow glistened with sweat.

"At last, I've found you!" he said in Latin. "Ah, my dearest," he sighed. Phaedra winced. "We must talk."

As Sigurd squatted to sit beside her, Phaedra jumped to her feet, snatching the scroll. He shadowed her movements. He had begun following her like a puppy dog ever since she had healed his wounds one day after a fierce battle had been fought and he'd been badly injured.

His heavy-hooded eyes regarded her thoroughly. With a smile pursed on his lips, he reached out for her hand. Before

Phaedra could snatch it away, he raised her hand and kissed her fingertips.

"Sigurd!" She pulled to free her hand from his paw. Coarse black hair bristled over his skin. His one arm had the strength of two and he would not let her go.

"Hear me, then you may go. Yes?"

She lurched back at the stink of wine and meat on his breath. Annoyed, Phaedra nodded.

"Your touch has made me a new man," he said, lifting the arm swathed in a sling.

"It was only a broken bone," she reminded him. Christe! He made it seem as if she had brought him back from the dead!

"I can now fight with the power of ten men!" he bragged. Phaedra rolled her eyes. "And I will be your protector."

"What?" she snapped.

"Yes." The paw tightened. "You need a protector. Surely a woman of your beauty and grace cannot expect to survive outside the safe sphere guaranteed by a valiant knight."

Phaedra's shoulders bobbed as she suppressed the laughter that threatened to erupt. She cleared her throat behind her free hand. She soon regained her composure.

"I can promise you that the attentions of my fellow knights will never trouble you again or give you cause for concern." He spoke in a tone thickened by intense feelings.

"The attentions of other knights?" Phaedra repeated. "I can safely say that no one has ever—"

His gruff voice cut her off. "Trust me, m'lady, your plight is on every knight's lips."

"How foolish! I'm not a young, wide-eye innocent school girl. I can take care of myself."

As she pulled to reclaim her hand, she did not see his face redden over the claim that she was not an innocent. He hung on to her greedily and squeezed the delicate bones of her hand until she screamed in protest.

"Sigurd!"

He dropped onto one knee. "By the grace of God, his son our Lord, and the Virgin, I vow to defend you to the death!"

An intimate audience was beginning to form around Phaedra and the knight. She could hear them chuckling and poking one another in the ribs. What a spectacle Sigurd was making of this! And as she looked up, her gaze caught Brannoc standing tall among them, grinning from ear to ear as if he were watching a performance at the Hippodrome.

Turning back to the knight on bended knee, she ordered, "Get up, Sigurd." He had closed his eyes and his lips were moving in prayer. "Now, Sigurd."

His eyes flashed open as he rose. A victorious smile shone on his face.

"It is done. God has agreed to release you into my protection."

She narrowed her eyes at the buffoon before her. She hated the fact that Sigurd had surprised her with his ridiculous notions, but she had never dealt with someone so pig-headed, someone so beyond the realm of reason.

"You are mine, beauty. You need never fear again. Sigurd will protect you!" He released her finally and reached out to stroke her chin. Phaedra recoiled from his touch, but the knight was too starry-eyed from his conversation with God to notice.

Finally, Sigurd took his leave, walking as if a pathway of billowy clouds had been laid to cushion his step. The crowd dispersed. Only Brannoc remained. He stood with his arms crossed over his chest, running his eyes over Phaedra.

"I believe the man is in love with you."

"How could you stand there and do nothing? I thought you had sworn to protect me!"

"Are you sure you want me to protect you? Sigurd looks to be the better man for the job. Don't you think?"

She glared at him and thrust past. His soft laugh hovered after her like the barest hint of a caress.

Nineteen

Fed and rested, the army moved on from Iconimium, winding its way like a great beast, limping and groaning. In the evenings, it dreamed of a land of milk and honey.

In the middle of August, the army took Heraclea by overwhelming the Turkish garrison. Red from the sun and bellowing like Mars, Bohemund led the attack. But the Turks had no stomach for a serious battle and fled, abandoning the city. A comet lit the night sky and the holiest of holy crossbearers believed it was a smile from God.

That night they dined on lamb spitted and roasted with garlic and rosemary, which was plentiful in the fields. Kasia and Phaedra's cook fire was far from the others. The best cuts of meat spattered over the flames, sending succulent veils of smoke into the air, curling like fingers, teasing the nose.

Phaedra sat on her heels watching the flames, a cup of wine in her hand. The scowl on her face darkened as she thought of General Taticius. He had barred her from attending another council meeting with the barbarians. Never mind that she now knew enough of their barbaric tongue to act as an interpreter. No, she'd been refused because she was a woman. That glorious fact had never stopped her from doing what she wanted before, she thought to herself. Why should it start to matter now?

She drank, never taking her eyes from the fire. The wine

was sharp to her taste, almost sweet, but strong. It steadied her, and it calmed her nerves.

A loud, dramatic sigh coming from behind demanded Phaedra's attention. She looked. Kasia. Phaedra's eyes swept over her, the gown of pleated silk, the hair loose and waving over her shoulders, the gold arm bracelets and sandals. She looked as if she were about to host one of her dinners.

The sphinx's eyes seethed with boredom. "Oh, how I miss the city! And my bed! My cook! My things!" She paused and gave another sigh. "Phaedra, you never warned me it would be like this," she whined.

Phaedra turned her back on Kasia just as the courtesan began to pout. Phaedra sipped her wine and rolled her eyes as Kasia took a breath to continue.

"Sleeping on the floor! The bugs!" Phaedra heard her squirm. "The noise. And the stench! By God, the stink of these people turns my stomach."

"I warned you that this would not be a pleasure trip," Phaedra said.

"I thought you were only trying to frighten me into not coming."

"Frighten you?" Phaedra laughed. "Kasia, nothing frightens you. Don't tell me you're getting soft?"

Phaedra heard Kasia approach and kneel down next to her. "I'll tell you what does frighten me," the courtesan said. "Spending another night with that red-haired brute Bohemund! He's built like a stallion, but damn if he knows what to do with it! He's yet to think of my pleasure. Animal! I have to do everything."

Laughter curled in Phaedra's throat, but she restrained it from rising further.

"Then why do you bother with him?" Phaedra asked, even though she knew the answer.

"He talks in his sleep," Kasia confided with a shrug. "The others would skin his hide if they were ever to hear him, for he boasts of getting the better of them and how someday he will be king."

She then turned to Phaedra. Her green eyes glittered wickedly. "I already know what they're discussing at the council meeting. And I know what Bohemund's plans are." She paused, biting her upper lip and arching her brows. "They're deciding on which route to take to Antioch. Bohemund intends to secure the city for himself."

Phaedra looked away in an effort to downplay the news. Her thoughts whirled. "So the wolf was planning to reveal his true self. But so soon in the march?" Phaedra thought.

"Taticius won't permit it, Bohemund naming himself King of Antioch, that is. Acting on behalf of the emperor, our General will appoint someone prince of the city." Kasia shrugged. "But, then again, Taticius is planning to return to Constantinople as soon as we reach Antioch. Who'll stop Bohemund after he leaves?"

"The knights, Raymond or Godfrey, one of them will stop Bohemund."

"Perhaps. If they ever get into the city. I'm sure those gray stone walls can withstand whatever these barbarians have in mind. Antioch will stonewall them. Hah! I'm so clever." She grinned. "The walls are thirty feet high, Phaedra. And there are sixty towers guarding them. Fools!" she snickered.

Phaedra cocked her head back and looked at Kasia as if she'd suddenly grown a beard and turned into a man. Since when did Kasia pay attention to such things? From whom did she learn this information?

As if reading Phaedra's mind, Kasia tilted her head to the side and said, "Taticius told me. Now there's a man whose prowess isn't limited to the battlefield," she said. "And he doesn't talk in his sleep," she divulged.

"How else do you think I've been able to alleviate my boredom? Since we're on the subject . . ." the siren continued, "I don't mind telling you that I've had my eye on Sir Brannoc, the one they call the Dragon. He's very mysterious, don't you think? And he appears to have taken a liking to you," she said, unable to prevent the shock of her voice from making its presence felt. "So, tell me. Are you lovers? Mother of God, I hope so. It's time you took someone to your bed."

In spite of Phaedra's warning look, Kasia continued, speaking slowly, as if she were reciting poetry. "The Dragon and the Swan. Oooh! It gives me chills!" she shivered, and her breasts bobbed from side to side. "You were turning into such a nun!" Kasia complained.

She must have sensed Phaedra prickle, for Kasia rose to her feet at once. "More wine?" she suggested. "It isn't Cyprus, but it will do."

Later, staring into the cup, watching the reflection of the flames, Phaedra had a brief image. It was of a man and woman, making love. It was Bohemund and . . . At first she thought she saw Kasia, but then she realized the woman in the barbarian's arms was herself!

Shock blurred the image and shattered it.

"He'll die before he touches me!" she vowed.

When Kasia led Phaedra in to see Bohemund, he was sitting back in his chair, studying his wine. He lifted his gaze from the amethyst liquid he swirled in the gold cup, and greeted her with a nod as he licked his upper lip. He had been drinking deep. The scent of wine hung over him. He had the lazy look of a wolf after it's eaten.

Bronze lanterns cast an eerie light within the canvas tent, breathing with the wind. Bohemund's eyes held Phaedra's.

"Lady Ancii," he said.

Phaedra stopped before him and said nothing. What did he want with her, she wondered. It was late and the wine had made her sleepy. She was barely aware of Kasia, who stood off in the shadows, silent and still.

The red-haired giant stretched his legs before him and the

leather seat creaked. Rubbing his jaw, scraggly with several days' growth of hair, he said, "I haven't had the chance to tell you how much I appreciate your help in caring for and treating the wounded. My men are my family."

Phaedra arched her brow as she remembered the scene on the plain of Dorylaeum, when she attacked him for not being better prepared for treating the wounded.

"Then you must despise your blood kin. If the lives of your men were that important to you, you would have added surgeons and doctors to your staff."

Kasia's breath hissed between her teeth at the criticism, but Bohemund lifted his hand to silence further outbursts.

"Yes, you are right. I should have planned better. How fortunate that I now have you." His gaze intensified, then slipped to sweep the length of her. He shifted in his chair again as if his muscles were sore and he was aching to stretch.

"You've taken very well to your soldier's role. I watched you fighting at Dorylaeum. Where did you learn to fight like that? One would think that you were the daughter of the god Mars himself. Blessed Virgin, but you can shoot a bow as fine as any Turk."

A muscle in her jaw twitched as she regarded the beast sprawled before her. He was tempting her to reveal herself, laying a trap. She could sense it, thinly veiled beneath his words of praise.

"You didn't ask me here to tell me how much you admire my fighting skills, did you?"

"Skilled at killing a conversation, too."

"I didn't realize I was an enthusiastic participant in something as meaningful as that!"

He rubbed his nose and glanced at Kasia as if he didn't know what to do about the stubborn woman before him.

"May I go now?"

"No." The answer was quick and clipped. He drained the goblet in a single gulp, then sat forward and rested his arms on his knees. His eyes fixed on her as if they would devour her.

"Share a cup of wine with me."

Phaedra heard a command, not an invitation. "Just say the word and a thousand men will eagerly line up to share a cup with Bohemund the Mighty. Alas, I don't care to."

A smile broke across his face. Phaedra tightened her lips in annoyance.

"Kasia!" he bellowed. "Bring Lady Ancii a cup of wine," he demanded, inclining his head toward a table of goblets and an earthenware jug.

The courtesan did his bidding. When she handed the goblet to Phaedra, it was with flashing eyes and a slight grin.

Phaedra took the cup, held its cool weight and waited.

Without words, just the lift of his chin, Bohemund ordered Kasia to leave. Soundlessly, she crossed the tent and left them. Alone.

Outside, the wind howled.

"Go on," he urged. He smiled, baring teeth. "It's the last of the wine your emperor Alexius sent us when we were near Iconimium."

Phaedra sensed it before she smelled it. There was a drug in the wine. Something sweet. Potent. She looked into the cup, swirled the liquid as if she were getting ready to drink it, then froze.

The vision in the wine cup! She and Bohemund, lovers.

With a start, she looked up. Bohemund rose in front of her. The barbarian wolf was trying to drug her so that he could . . .

"Is the wine not to your liking?" he courteously inquired.

She looked up into his face and had the prickling sensation that she was staring into a wolf's den. Suddenly, she had an idea.

"Your cup's empty," she exclaimed as she quickly tossed the drugged wine into his goblet.

"Wait!" He pulled away, but it was too late. The poisonous

liquid sloshed and spilled into his cup and over the Turkish carpet, staining it blood red. The wind snapped at the tent. The wax lamps flickered out, throwing Bohemund and Phaedra into darkness.

"God's bones!" Bohemund swore.

Phaedra jumped back just as she felt him reach out to grab her. He snorted when he clutched the dark. Instincts guiding her, she moved away until a chasm stretched between them. She heard him stumble. The goblet fell with a dull clang. She could feel him reaching out, embracing the dark over and over again.

"Lady Ancii? Where are you?" he cried out with thirsty lips.

Phaedra threw back the tent flap and a wedge of light sliced through the darkness. Bohemund's head snapped toward the light, like an animal stopped suddenly in its tracks.

He glared at her standing there, calmly silhouetted against the light of a star-lit sky with a moon to make the wolves mad with wanting. In her most obliging voice she asked him, "Shall I inform your squire to bring his lord candles?"

His eyes flashed hot with his answer.

The afternoon's heat roared in the fertile valley of Heraclea. Phaedra brushed the sweat from her brow with the back of her hand as she removed the bandages from a pilgrim's arm. A burly, wide-shouldered sheep farmer from Lorraine, the pilgrim was one of many who had joined their more noble lords, knights and fellows in the battle of Dorylaeum. At the start of the journey, he'd had nothing but a shepherd's staff. Now he owned a suit of mail, battle mace, helm and shield, all spoils from the battle.

The pilgrim watched Phaedra intently. Smiling, she brushed his arm as she drew away the last of the bandages and the poultice of herbs. The wound was a deep, clean gash caused by the thrust of a lance. She patted the red flesh around the stitched wound and nodded her head, impressed by her own handiwork. She dipped her fingers in a wooden bowl containing oil of Balanos that had been mixed with myrrh, and dabbed a small amount around the wound.

After wrapping the injury in fresh bandages, which were nothing more than strips of canvas from a tent, she sent the pilgrim back to bask in the metallic glow of his new possessions.

Phaedra sat back in the grassy field and sighed. She'd been ministering to the sick and wounded since daybreak. She ached with fatigue. She reached with one hand to massage the back of her neck and quickly pulled away at the sticky feel of unwashed sweat. She winced. She contemplated taking a knife to her hair and cutting it off. Even with it tied back, it was burdensome, another layer of heat.

She closed her eyes and tried to envision a shallow pool of cool water sprinkled with rose petals. As the image took shape, and the water turned a beckoning shade of blue, she smiled to herself. The chaotic sounds of the camp fell away. The scent of rose petals lapped her senses. A soft moan escaped her lips.

Then it assaulted her, a smell. Unmistakable, that scent, she thought, wrinkling her nose. It called to mind the smell of the crowds on their way to the Hippodrome on racing day. It was the sharp scent of a mob feverish for a spectacle.

She opened her eyes and noticed swarms of cross-bearers and pilgrims hurrying toward the crimson banner that marked Bohemund's camp. The pennant hung limp, defeated by the windless heat as if it, too, were sticky with sweat.

What was Bohemund up to, Phaedra wondered. She hoped that they would be breaking camp soon and moving on. A man like Bohemund was even more dangerous when he was idle and had time on his hands.

Wiggling through the crowd, angling her body this way and that to slide past the press of bodies, Phaedra worked her way to the front of what was a circle. Knights marked the circumference, standing like sentinels. They were posted five arms' lengths from each other. A gladiator ring? There's going to be a fight? A duel? But why? Over what?

Knights were always challenging someone to a fight. The wrong look, a curt reply, or the curl of a lip could prompt a hot-headed westerner to take drastic measures.

There was a break in the circle across from her. An aisle formed and through it walked Sigurd, bare-chested, dressed in nothing but his armor and his thick, nail-studded belt from which hung his sword. He moved with a flexed swagger that suggested he was proud of his powerful physique.

She caught hints of conversations around her. Most of them she couldn't understand. But in the net of words she knew, she heard "duel," "woman," "protector" and "devil."

Her senses turned keen as an element of foreboding rippled through her. Already standing at attention, she stood taller still. She clenched her jaw. She waited, knowing the prickling in her back would not subside until—

She gasped aloud as Brannoc, stripped to his chausses, moved into the circle. A circlet of gold around his brow was his only ornament apart from the pommel of his sword which flashed its ruby eye at the crowd.

Pressed by the crowd, Phaedra rocked back and forth on her feet as everyone moved forward, jostling one another for a better look. Pushed, she stumbled into the circle. She righted herself quickly and, heart thumping wildly, watched Brannoc, caged within the circle, move as easily and gracefully as a wild animal. His muscles were sun-darkened to a bronze-gold. She remembered the warmth of his chest and the feel of his hair, which was like the finest silk. She noted the mark of a wound that colored his side. She had healed him. In her home.

And in the quiet of a jasmine-scented night, he had healed you, too.

Phaedra shook her head. The thought had sneaked up on her. Best not to remember, she thought.

But the sight of his body demanded that she remember.
Shoulders, arms, all she could see with her eye seemed
carved by a war master's hand, not from stone or marble, but
something hot and alive. She felt the heat of him. Or was it
the press of bodies behind her?

The blue tattoos which marked his wrists looked even
more frightening now that he was stripped to the bare essence
of his strength. They had a power unequal to the finest steel
sword. They made their presence felt, for as the pilgrims and
the foot soldiers laid their eyes on what must surely be the
marks of the devil, they lurched back, away from the heathen
images.

Transfixed, Phaedra had not noticed as the pilgrims drew
away from the man they believed to be the Prince of Darkness. She stood alone now, exposed, and within the circle.

By the time she realized the sea of eyes were on her as
well, it was too late. She looked over her shoulder at the
crowd standing away from her, and in that moment, Tancred
wrenched her forward and dragged her across the circle.

"Let me go!" she screamed. She tried to pull herself free,
but his hand around her upper arm was like an iron manacle.
Her struggles brought her nothing but sharp shooting pains.
A sadistic glimmer lit the knight's eyes.

"This way, please, Lady Ancii. My uncle has a surprise
for you."

Tancred escorted his unwilling companion to his uncle,
Bohemund, who was standing apart from his knights. His
arms were crossed over his chest, and his wide legs straddled
the earth. Watching Phaedra, he possessed the same fiery
look on his face as he'd worn the evening past.

With a wolfish narrowing of his eyes, he signaled to Tancred, and the boy threw Phaedra at his uncle's feet. Bohemund made no move to help her. He flashed a smile that
chilled her to the bone. He crouched down and, lightly wres-
tling her to her feet, whispered, "You and I could have enjoyed one another's company, Lady." He held her before him,

her back pressed against his chest like a shield and continued. "I could have been your protector. But now you must deal with this and," his breath was wet on her neck, "play the prize. For he who wins this day will be your master."

She wriggled, hooked by his words and the vindictive intent in his voice. Grimacing beneath the weight of Bohemund's hand, she noted Brannoc and Sigurd staring at her. Now that she understood that this was indeed a duel over her, she flushed. Color welled into her neck and features. The sudden rush of heat angered her all the more, but she was powerless.

"Protect me," echoed her demand in her mind as she recalled her argument with Brannoc. Christe! What a fool she'd been. She'd baited the Dragon and he had risen to it with a vengeance.

"Hear me!" Bohemund roared, and the murmuring crowd fell silent. "You see before you two knights, two warriors. Both seek to 'protect' Lady Ancii," he shouted. He gave Phaedra's shoulder a squeeze, inspiring a look of such hate that many a pilgrim and knight crossed themselves in case such fury be misdirected their way.

"I'm not chattel to be disposed of at your will!" she said between clenched teeth. "My protector since childhood has been my father's man, Sharif. Before he died in battle, he gave me into Brannoc's care."

"Hush, my sweet, or you'll ruin the fun," Bohemund warned, digging his fingers into her shoulders. "Besides, who else can swear to that?" She winced, yet she still tried to pull away. But the wolf held her trapped between his arm and his chest.

He cleared his throat. "I cannot choose one over the other. I am not the ruler here."

Guffaws and snorts rose behind Phaedra and Bohemund at his last words, but it did not stop the barbarian. "So a duel must be fought. To the victor shall go the right as master.

PAGAN DESIRES   249

And Lady Ancii will be well protected and served through
the remainder of our campaign."

With a nod to Tancred to proceed, Bohemund drew Phaedra back to stand before the wall of Christian might—Baldwin, Godfrey, Raymond, the Bishops of Berain and Le Puy,
Stephen of Blois, Robert of Normandy and Robert of Flanders. The Bishop of Berain's holy eyes slitted like a lizard's,
and he stared into space as if he were devising a new scenario
in which he figured prominently.

Upon Bohemund's signal, a trumpeter raised his horn and
sounded an earsplitting blast. Brannoc and Sigurd's squires
dashed out into the circle carrying long, kite-shaped shields.
Sigurd's shield displayed steel bands radiating from a center
boss. It was edged in metal, with a series of rivets, just like
Brannoc's. However, the Celt's black shield bore two winged
serpents that resembled the tattoos around his wrists.

Shields in place, the warriors eyed one another. Sigurd
rocked from side to side with impatience. Brannoc looked
as if he were barely breathing, so still was he. They were
both waiting for the signal to proceed.

The shrill blast of the trumpet sounded and both men drew
their swords. With a flourish, Sigurd raised his weapon and
shouted, "For the glory of Lorraine."

"This is madness," Phaedra thought. Brannoc was just
standing there, waiting for the man to strike. She could not
see his eyes, could not know what he was thinking. It made
her stomach buck with worry.

Sigurd took the offensive, running toward Brannoc, arcing
his blade to strike. But the Dragon took the blow in the shield,
sprang to the side and came around from behind. Sigurd
whirled on his feet and raised his shield just in time to fend
off a blow so vicious, Brannoc's blade sank into the iron-
faced wooden shield. Sigurd, with a startled grunt, tried to
wrench his shield free, but it was Brannoc who, with the
slightest tug, withdrew his sword as if it had been embedded
in a roll of silk. Sigurd wasted no time and delivered a rasp-

ing blow aimed at Brannoc's unprotected right side. The Dragon parried, and the rasp of blade against blade carried over the field and the quiet crowd.

A rain of strokes was deflected and parried as the duel progressed. Sigurd was red in the face and breathing heavily. Brannoc showed no signs of fatigue. In fact, she noted the fiery glimmer in his eyes, the semblance of a smile shadowing his lips.

The Lorrainer charged at Brannoc, slashing horizontally. Brannoc backed away, parrying, protecting with his shield beneath the onslaught that threatened to throw him off balance. With an inside jab, Brannoc turned the tide and now pushed to send Sigurd reeling back. But the Lorrainer was a bull and stubbornly stood his ground, meeting and deflecting Brannoc's blows with Herculean might.

Neither one had drawn blood yet. The crowd began to grow restless in the heat. They pushed and shoved. They wanted a show, a diversion, but the skillful sword fighting was beyond their realm of appreciation. They wanted blood. They grumbled with dissatisfaction and, between jeers and whistles, accused Bohemund of staging this fight. This was to have been a battle between God and the devil, between a good Christian knight and the devil's spawn.

Both Bohemund and Phaedra, of one accord, tore their gaze away from the warriors and swept the crowd, noting movement, frowns, hard eyes and faces slack with boredom.

"You'd think they'd had their fill of blood by now," Bohemund snorted.

Phaedra sensed the danger. She felt the mood of the crowd shift from excitement to a lust for blood.

"Stop it now, Bohemund," Phaedra warned. She tried to look over her shoulder at him, but his arm snaked her neck. He bent his head to whisper.

"Keep still."

"They're not interested in sport. They want blood!"

"Quiet!"

Brannoc had landed a blow on Sigurd's shield with such force that the Lorrainer reeled back, visibly shaken. The upper brace that secured the shield to his arm broke, and fell to the side. Brannoc, seizing the opportunity, peeled a flurry of blows in quick succession as Sigurd attempted to discard his hampering shield. The crowd was now urging Sigurd not to give up, but to avenge himself and destroy the Dragon. The force of their voices and the swell of support empowered the Lorrainer with the strength of ten men, and with a bellow that split the heavens, he tossed his shield aside. Gripping his sword in both hands, Sigurd attacked Brannoc.

Sigurd had the advantage now. It was easier for him to move, and he had the strength of two arms now behind each stroke. Brannoc smiled as if pleased with the change, and quickly tossed his own shield aside. Now both men gripped their swords in two hands. The weapons, easier to manage, were deadlier than ever.

With the ferocity of animals, the two warriors circled about the field, stalking, slashing and hacking at each other. Sweat coursed down their backs, arms and chest. The ends of Brannoc's hair were wet and dripping. Sigurd's hair was plastered against his head. Their grunts and groans could barely be heard above the hoarse yells of the crowd, ecstatic over the quick change in the duel.

To Phaedra's eye, it seemed Brannoc could have killed Sigurd many times over. Brannoc was holding himself back. She frowned, troubled by his strategy.

The vision attacked her senses with the ferocity of a bird swooping into her face, talons extended. She started and, lifting her arm to shield herself, cried out at the sight. For on the field, Sigurd was battling a beast, a dragon breathing fire. The serpents around his wrists had come to life and were circling the air.

Her strange behavior was hard for Bohemund to ignore. He looked down at her, a puzzled look on his face. Her skin

had paled and her eyes were tightly closed. But a blood cur-
dling yell forced his attention back to the warriors.

Phaedra looked, too. Sigurd had caught Brannoc on the
left shoulder, and the Celt was yielding ground as he pressed
the bloody wound with his sword hand. Phaedra couldn't
believe he'd dropped his guard to permit such a thing. Sigurd,
sensing victory and buoyed by the whistles of the crowd,
smiled as he fought for breath.

So full of the moment was the Lorrainer that he did not
see the black look that crossed Brannoc's face like a moving
shadow. But Phaedra saw it.

She felt Bohemund press his lips against her hair and whisper.

"Be glad your protector will be the Lorrainer and not
Brannoc. I would fear for you otherwise."

Phaedra swallowed. Was she the only one to have seen the
deadly intent in those eyes? Brannoc was going to win, not
lose. It was Sigurd who would die a horrible death. He had
no chance against the beast, and she was to blame.

Sigurd executed a series of slashing cuts, but to the chagrin
of the crowd, each was warded off by Brannoc. With a bellow
of rage, Sigurd struck again and again, but Brannoc would
not go down.

Sigurd's arms were bending beneath Brannoc's parries and
he was losing his strength. He wobbled a little on his feet
and even his wide, comfortable stance could not support him.

Brannoc fought like a man possessed, viciously hacking
at his opponent. Phaedra felt Bohemund's arm loosen around
her. No doubt he was wondering if Brannoc was so battle-
crazed that he would be unable to stop once he unarmed
Sigurd. It was considered a sacrilege for a man of the cross
to kill a fellow Christian. But a quick glance over her shoulder told her she was wrong to think such a thing. Bohemund's
face was alive with interest and wonder. It was as if he were
watching Brannoc fight for the first time.

"What they say about him is true then . . . he is the son of Satan, for never have I seen . . ."

The words were lost in the shouts and screams of the crowd as Brannoc sent Sigurd sprawling into the dust, his sword spinning through the air. As Sigurd struggled to rise, the Celt lowered the point of his sword to his neck.

"Kill him!" the crowd howled.

Bohemund's eyes swept the mad crowd. Tancred moved restlessly at Bohemund's side, hand on hilt, ready to rush in and stop Brannoc from murdering the Lorrainer.

"Kill him!"

Drawing breath in painful, shuddering gasps, Sigurd looked up with blood-shot eyes and pleaded, "Mercy! She's yours, man. She's yours." Spent, he collapsed onto the ground.

Brannoc sheathed his sword. Disregarding the mob pressing forward, he pivoted on his heels and crossed the open ground that separated him from Phaedra. Sweat- and blood-stained, his breath ragged and labored, Brannoc halted before the man who continued to hold his prize possessively close.

"Well done," Bohemund complimented. "Now let's see if you can handle this," and he pushed Phaedra toward the victor.

Brannoc's arms came around her, stopped her from falling at his feet, and lifted her up before him. His hold tightened. The battle madness still clung to him, she could see it in his eyes. He cupped her jaw with his bloody hand and swooped down to kiss her.

She bit him, and Brannoc smarted. Looking down at her, he licked his lip and tasted his blood.

"Accept me or there will be more fights for your head," the Dragon warned.

"No."

"Phaedra!" his voice snapped.

Jaw stubbornly set, she glared at him. She opened her mouth to refute him but his mouth claimed hers again.

To great hoots and cries of laughter, Phaedra struggled to push him away, but he grabbed her firmly by her buttocks and nailed her to him. He opened his mouth to taste her and used his tongue like a weapon. Incensed by his crude, public display, she slapped him. The Dragon caught her branding hand and wrenched her arm behind her back. She screamed with the pain of it, and the Dragon, a hard look on his face, studied her anger. With the hint of a secret gleaming in his eyes, he abruptly picked her up and threw her over his shoulder, knocking the wind out of her.

Beating him with her fists, she wiggled and fought to be put down. Brannoc slapped her on her buttocks to quiet her.

"Beast!" she cried. To think that she'd been concerned for his life! Fuming, she continued to kick and pummel his back. "You've won nothing," she screamed. "Do you hear? Nothing!"

Brannoc turned a deaf ear to her, grinned and slapped her again.

Twenty

"How dare you!" Phaedra screamed at Brannoc.

She was alone with him, in his tent, where she would be expected to sleep and stay while he tended to army matters. She turned her anger into a weapon and attacked him.

"Fighting over me as if I were a piece of furniture!"

"Humph. A useless piece of furniture."

Her eyes shot daggers upon hearing his jest.

"Listen to me," Brannoc encouraged. Bathed and cleaned of sweat and blood, he closed the distance she'd erected between them.

Phaedra stepped back from him. He continued his pursuit, and she kept retreating until she found herself against the wall of the tent. She reached for her dagger, then remembered he had taken it from her.

He stopped an arm's length away. "It was the only way. Sigurd was serious about making you his."

"Better him than, than, you!" she answered.

"You're angry because I took you seriously. 'Protect me,' you said. Now, in the eyes of all cross-bearers and these simple pilgrims, I am your protector. No one will dare come near you since you're the Dragon's!" He arched his brows sardonically, mad with hope that she would cease her tantrum.

But she was stubborn and held her anger like a drawn sword.

"If you think I'm staying here, then you're soft in the head."

"I do. And you will."

"Never!"

He loomed over her, glowering, but she didn't feel threatened. Nor did she feel trapped. He would listen to reason. He must! She refused to compromise herself before the eyes of the westerners. Once he learned how serious she was, he would have to oblige her.

"Never?" he echoed.

"I see the duel did not damage your hearing."

"Don't bait me, Phaedra. I'll use force if I must."

"Oooh, I'm trembling," she said sarcastically, clasping her hands over her breasts.

"By the gods!" he swore, turning his face away from her. "If only we kept our women in harems!" he mumbled to himself. He shook his head and turned back to her. "Like it or not, for the remainder of the journey, you are my responsibility."

"What about your pledge to Bohemund? To guard him?"

"He's relieved me of it, as he knows I'll have my hands full with you." He paused to weigh his words carefully. "Actually, I'll still be guarding him. So long as I keep an eye on you, I'll know the whereabouts of his assassin."

Phaedra swallowed uneasily.

"You won't be able to stop me. It's fate."

"So is this," and before he'd finished, he reached for her and drew her unwilling body against his.

The shock of his heat caught her off guard, but she found the strength to resist. Amber eyes flashing, she used her arms to brace herself and pull away. But he wouldn't let her go.

"No!" She stomped on his foot with all her might.

"Phaedra!" he lashed with mashed teeth.

But she was well across the tent and darting for freedom. He reached her just as she was about to run outside, and yanked her back. She answered his ill-timed grab with a blow to his stomach, followed by another, then another.

"Enough!" the warrior ordered. But the humiliation she'd just endured, coupled with her anger, and the grief of losing her one true protector, Sharif, overrode her senses. She was lost in a pain of her own creation and she could not stop.

As he backed away from her pummelling fists, Brannoc tripped over a bowl of fruit and fell sprawling to the carpeted ground. She threw herself on top of him, scratching, hitting, and hissing like a cat. They rolled across the floor entangled and entwined until, finally, Brannoc managed to pull her on top of him and grip her wrists between his hands to stop her.

By the time she realized what had happened, it was too late. She found herself straddling his hips. Her hair had come undone and the folds of her tunic had opened. The vial of perfume dangled between her breasts.

Breathing heavily from the tussle, she twisted to release her hands from his grasp. But Brannoc's manacle closed harder still, turning the flesh around her wrists white. She stopped.

Brannoc's eyes, blue and bottomless, met hers.

"By the laws set by Bohemund in this camp, I am your protector. Now you can either return to Constantinople or stay. Or, perhaps you'd find the harlots' campfire more to your liking? For that is what the men will make you out to be if you refuse me."

She snarled and spread her fingers to scratch him, but he held her too firmly for her to hurt him. "Better that than stay here with you!"

His eyes softened. "Why?" he whispered. "You assume that I desire you and that I wish to make love to you." Brannoc read the confusion in her eyes. "That is, unless you *want me* to make love to you."

Holding her gaze in his, meeting no resistance, he drew her captured hands to his mouth and pressed a kiss into one palm, then the other. Phaedra bit her lip, barring the gasp that welled in her throat from finding release.

Gently but firmly, he set her hands on his chest. Again, she didn't fight him. With his large hand he cupped her head, while with the fingers of his other hand he tenderly touched her face and sent sweet sensations down her spine.

He whispered her name. She answered with her hands, moving them down his chest, feeling the fluid slide of muscles, his warmth and strength beneath his tunic.

Unaware, as if in a waking dream, she went on touching him through countless breaths. She watched her hands moving over him as Brannoc smoothed her hair off her face, caressed her neck, and the sensitive soft spot behind her ears. He drew his fingers across her cheek with a stroke that reminded her of feathers. She turned her head into the sensation. His fingers moved over her mouth. She parted her lips to taste him, and when he moved one wet finger between her parted lips, she met him with her tongue and sucked what was offered.

His moan drew her back. She stopped and jerked away from him.

"What is it?"

Nothing, she said to herself. Only that I want you. Hot breath, knowing hands, the weight of you atop me.

"Complicated woman," stole a voice inside her head. With a start, she turned back to Brannoc, for it had sounded like him!

"This can't be," came the words and for a moment she didn't know if she was referring to his ability to read her thoughts or her desires.

He rested his hands on her knees and began to massage her flesh.

"We can't go back to being lovers," she said, stopping his hands. "Because they, especially that, that, wolf who calls himself a soldier of God, will know."

Brannoc caught the vial of scent between his fingers and

laughed deep in his throat, amazed that the woman astride him should be such a child to care for what others thought.

"Why do you care? Do they matter all that much to you? Are they so important, Phaedra?"

Stung by his laugh, she bucked to rise, but he pulled on her necklace, stopping her. She put her hand over his to release the alabaster vial. When he wouldn't let her go, she looked at him with hate in her eyes and he winced. Not once had a look of pain crossed his features when he was fighting Sigurd. But Phaedra had the power to hurt him dearly.

Holding the vial hostage in his hand, he began to pull her back to him. She had no choice but to surrender or else risk breaking the gold chain.

"How can it be that the woman who created Pagan Desires cannot fulfill her own desires?" With the perfume vial hidden by his fingers, the chain enmeshed around his hand, he forced her to look him in the eye.

"That woman is gone, barbarian. Now let me go."

He released her, but not before fingering her mouth again. She bit his finger soundly between her teeth.

Free, Phaedra rose and flew, clutching Pagan Desires to her breast.

Evening brought her heart nothing to quiet the onslaught of feelings Brannoc had raised within her again. She raised her face to the stars. Standing before Brannoc's tent, aware of the dart of eyes, the snickers and pointed fingers singling her out, she tried to dream a little on her feet. But all thoughts turned in, like a snail's shell, leading her back to her present state. Back to him.

After leaving Brannoc, she'd gone in search of Gabriel and Kasia. Surely she could stay with one of them, she'd thought. But both of their tents had been empty. She'd waited until the bruised light of dusk spread and filled the sky.

Driven by impatience, she returned to her "protector's" tent with the intention of stating conditions for her protectorship.

But Brannoc's tent had been empty as well. She decided to wait for him outside.

The night made her think of her gardens, her oils and perfumes. Her fingers ached to measure and pour the essential oils and drops of precious scents. To create the indescribable. Moods, feeling, lusts, desires, love—all were within her power. The Swan could manipulate them all through the secrets of scents.

Her thoughts brought her to laughter. What was the Swan now, but another "helpless" female who needed the protection of a man? "Christe!" she swore under her breath. When would this journey cease its endless twisting and turning, surprising her at each turn? Perhaps in Jerusalem, she hoped. With Bohemund's death. Then she could go back to Alexander and become the Swan again.

Alone in the tent, she forced herself to stay awake so she could listen for Brannoc. But the heat of the day, the heart-pounding horror of the duel, her subsequent shame and anger weighed her down, and she drifted off to sleep.

Sometime during the night, she sensed him standing before the tent. She heard him lay down and stretch out on the ground. So that is how it will be? Near, yet far. Separated, because it was what she desired. She heard herself sigh. Heard his breath as if he were beside her. Sleep's arms beckoned and she rushed as if into her lover's arms.

Twenty-one

Phaedra's desires were Brannoc's command. She'd told him that they couldn't be lovers, and he'd accepted it.

No, she mused alone at night, he'd done more than accept her conditions, he'd made them his own. For days after the duel, she hardly ever saw him. And when she did, she noted he was careful to keep his distance, his eyes averted. And yet she could feel his presence whenever she went to the stream to bathe or tend to the wounded and sick. Somehow, her protector had made himself invisible.

But over and over, she caught herself thinking about him. She'd stare out over the water, her head filled with visions and memories of him. She'd recall the feel of his embrace, his lips on hers, his mouth whispering his desire for her. These thoughts unsettled her with a fierceness that shook her to the core.

"What is happening?" she asked herself. What magic had he spun to make the very thought of him enflame her?

She felt unveiled and more vulnerable than ever. But more importantly than that, she was amazed he had the power to touch her without ever coming near her.

Progress to Caesarea was slow as most of the army was now on foot. Phaedra was fortunate enough to still be able to ride. Achilles had proved himself to be as invincible as his namesake. There were knights who would have bartered their souls, or worse, for a chance to call Achilles their own. Phaedra felt their covetous eyes following her. Jealousy was a hard thing to mask, and the sunburnt faces she encountered staring at her were stiff with it.

She could sense their dirt-caked fingers itching to grab their daggers as they contemplated murdering her. Only one thing kept them from performing the actual deed, and that was Brannoc. She rode at the Dragon's side. To kill her and secure her mount, they would have to kill him first. Phaedra knew that Brannoc's duel against Sigurd, his fearsome tattoos and his reputation as the devil's own spawn robed Brannoc in something more powerful than the finest armor. Which soldier of God was fool enough to wrestle with the power of darkness?

Brannoc guarded her well. And that was all. Phaedra's stubbornness had built a wall between them. She could feel it even in the dark of night. All she had to do was reach out from her pallet, toward him, and her fingers seemed to brush up against an icy ridge of set stones. She could tell what he thought of her by that alone. He hated her enough to keep himself locked up in a tower of his own devising.

Some dreams know no bounds. Even as she turned in her sleep, she knew she would remember this dream always. There was darkness and a whirlpool of fear that swallowed her heart. A pair of eyes, brown, liquid eyes, beseeching and fatherly, soon became the eyes of a beast. No, a bird. Glassy and gold-speckled, hooded and watchful. A flutter of wings and the air rushed past her face as the bird rose before her. It was an eagle, brown, black and gold. Magnificent and royal, it beat the air, cooling her face. It hovered, talons stretched.

Then it dropped like a stone. A blur of feathers and a cry, then it swept up again, but with something caught between its talons. A bright, gold thing. Not a coin, but something round like one. She squinted to see better, and beheld a medallion shaped like the sun. A medallion like the one her father used to fasten his cloak.

Phaedra flinched and shielded her eyes with her arms as if they could keep the dream at bay.

But again, the eagle dove, this time so close she felt its feathers brush her cheek. It rose, rushing to her face, and in the dream she crouched to move out of the way. It soared over her head and into the sky. She followed it and watched something fall. This gift from the eagle dropped at her feet.

She tossed, battling against seeing, for she knew instinctively that it was something so horrible . . . She looked: it was a hand, a man's hand, bloody and freshly severed from his arm. Phaedra squeezed her eyes shut. "I won't," she said aloud, refusing the dream, and she raised a barrier to it. She stretched out her hand to keep it away.

But the eagle cried out, and it startled her, forcing her to open her eyes. And for a moment, all she saw was a man's hand with a ring of gold. The jewel was set with an amber-colored stone striped with jet through the middle, like the eye of a tiger, or a lion.

Or a leopard.

Her father's ring, cried her memory.

"No!" she cried aloud.

She felt hands on her arms, a body drawing her close.

"Shhh, Phaedra. It was only a dream."

A deep, sheltering voice. She wanted to hide in that voice, lose herself as if in a cave of warm stone. The eagle would never be able to find her there. She felt herself trembling, gasping as if she had been running or battling giants, clutching at the warmth, the quiet strength beneath her hands.

"Shhh," soothed the voice. She pressed her cheek against the warmth of a living fire, and heard the vibrations of sounds. She clutched the perfume vial and held on as if it, too, could save her.

His hand smoothed her hair down her head and back. And the halo of awareness spread. It was Brannoc. Her protector. He would protect her from this, the dream, the eagle.

She listened to the strong beating of his heart. From somewhere came the flutter of wings, and the arms tightened. And the sound was gone.

Brannoc said nothing. And she was grateful for that. The arms which held her, the hand in her hair told her everything she needed to hear. He drew her down to lay in front of him. She settled, the long curve of her against him. She touched the arm protectively held around her and ran her fingers over his wrist. She felt him press a kiss into her hair. That he knew enough to let the quiet heal her.

Another kiss. At the touch of his fingers draping back her hair, she swallowed and finally closed her eyes to sleep. Let the eagle beware, she thought. Nothing could hurt her now. Nothing.

Twenty-two

Phaedra woke from a deep sleep without dreams. The camp was still. She was afraid to move for fear of waking Brannoc. He was still holding her against him. She dropped her gaze to his arm, his wrist, the tattoo that curled there, guarding her. She sighed. He stirred. She knew he was thinking of her.

If he had the power to enter her thoughts, could he use that power to let her in? She wished to tell him that she'd been wrong to turn away from him. They were lovers. The Dragon and the Swan. Maia had intimated at the inevitability of their union. The waters of prophecy had shown her, too. They told the truth. Nothing, not even this journey, could change that.

Closing her eyes, she thought to herself, "I want to be alone with you. Make love to you. Brannoc, hear me."

With a touch that took her breath away, he turned her face to look at him. She saw by the searching look in his eyes that he had heard.

"How can it be?" he whispered.

"I, I don't know. I thought you—" He shook his head once.

He traced the line of her cheek from brow to jaw. She shivered. Her heart was beating hard. She imagined them already entwined, kiss answering kiss.

They were on their feet. She had no memory of rising.

Holding her hand fast in his, Brannoc led her out of the camp. She flew, hardly aware of the snoring figures curled on the ground around her, or the mantle of sky as it prepared to greet the dawn.

At the touch of his lips on hers, she lost all sense of who she was. There was only this, the heat of his mouth, the scent of him, the press of his body, the pulse of his blood. Wanton deeds unfolded in her mind. Pagan desires yet to be fulfilled.

Before he could master the flood of his own desires, she knelt before him and, for his pleasure and her own, took him in her mouth. He groaned and cradled her head. She moved her mouth and her hands over him, relishing the sacred heat, the power of his need. His hands dove into her hair.

The wet of her lips and tongue drove her on. She loved the taste of him. Wild and gentle, she sucked him, drawing him deeper into her mouth, then, like the tide, easing away until the end where the taste of him was the greatest. Her tongue whipped circles before her lips paused to begin the ascent again, then again. She felt him watching her. She felt him shudder with the ebb and flow of her every onslaught and wickedly slow release.

The hands cradling her head made demands. Turning her face, she took his fingers into her mouth and sucked them, too. She controlled him, prolonging the inevitable with a mastery that made him moan to the sky like an animal gone mad. He grabbed her hands and held them stretched above her head, permitting only the touch of her lips and tongue. The line between slave and enslaved disappeared. In the quiet of the woods, her mouth answered his thrusts, peaked his pleasure and finally brought him the release she prized.

They lay within each other's arms in the warm hollow of the earth, their clothes scattered, their skin glistening in the spilled light. Their mouths were soft, lips plump as if slightly bruised. Her mouth was wet from tasting him. His lips shone, for he too, had satisfied his hunger for her.

Phaedra awoke to the scent of rose and jasmine, and the feel of Brannoc's finger as he brushed her nipple. He'd opened the vial and was anointing her body with the fragrance. From her breasts, he drew a line to her stomach. He bent his head. She felt his mouth against her skin as he drew his tongue across her nipple, first one, then the other. His breath was warm and coming fast.

He was gentle, caressing her as if she were some delicate thing, a rose of opening velvet petals. She felt herself arch back as the pleasure shot through her body like a spear of fire. His senses attuned to her, knowing that she desired it, he sucked harder, his mouth greedy above her writhing body.

Phaedra felt the hot sun of full morning lash her thigh. She sat up with a start. Her hair spilled over her golden shoulders.

"Christe! We've got to go. What if they come looking for us?" she asked worriedly.

He tried to hush her by smoothing her hair behind her ear. "They're still asleep," he reassured her, but the look she cast him was one of disbelief.

"How could they be? They must be ready to march."

"Trust me," he whispered.

His face, calm and strong, was eloquent with meaning, provoking her to wonder as to whether he had anything to do with their "sleep."

"Trust me," he repeated. "There's time."

He reached his hand up to fondle her. She caught his wrist. She could barely wrap her small hand around him. She swooped down for a kiss, letting that be her answer. She felt him shiver beneath her touch. He plunged his free hand into the dark waves of her hair and cradled her head, keeping her there, above him, kissing him. The scent of her worked in him like strong wine, and the flaring heat of his desire returned with an intensity that took his breath away.

Phaedra curled against her pleasure-giver, rubbing her cheek against his chest. She felt him shift beneath her. He stroked the hair from her brow. She lifted herself to look down on him. She touched his cheek, following the line of it down his jaw to his neck.

Blue eyes caught hers. "Tell me about the dream," he whispered. "I want to know." He watched the darkness move into her amber eyes and hugged her close.

She took a deep breath. "There's an eagle," she said softly, lest the bird hear her now and swoop down to hurt her. "It follows me. Brings me . . ."

"What?"

She could not say it. "Things."

He moved, rising above her and easing her back against the ground. "How can I help you if I don't know what it is that's frightened you so?"

"It was a dream, Brannoc. Nothing more."

He sighed a cynical laugh while looking up at the leaves. "The greatest seeress since Troy's Cassandra, and you think it's nothing?" He lowered his gaze back to her and his blue eyes made her feel suddenly cold.

"I'm no prophet—"

He stopped her with his finger. "Believe it, Lady. I'm beginning to think that one of the reasons I am here is to protect you from your own sense of powerlessness!"

She laughed, uncomfortable with the twist of his conversation. But his words needled her. She knew she was powerful. She had used her power on Alexius to agree to let her join the cross-bearers. She used it every time she created a scent. But to have someone else know it too, hold the thought up to her as if it were a mirror, made her uneasy. And afraid.

She bit her lip. "I don't want to talk about this," she mumbled, and she moved to rise and run, but he loomed over her, barring her way, forcing her back.

"What does the eagle mean?"

"I don't know."

"What did he bring?"

"He?"

"You know who he is, don't you?"

"No!" she answered angrily. If Brannoc meant to push her into a corner, then she would push him back. Hard.

"Of course you do," he pressed. "And what did he bring?"

"Stop it."

"What did the eagle drop at your feet, Phaedra?"

"I said stop!"

He rubbed her pearl earring between his fingers and said nothing for a long while. "Whoever he is, he can't hurt you if I know."

Stiffening beneath him, she asked, "Why do you insist that the eagle represents a man?"

He looked into her eyes. "Then tell me it's not."

Her mind locked in resistance. "I can deal with this on my own."

He smiled faintly, painfully. "You've become quite the warrior, haven't you?" He reached for her hand and brought it to rest against his cheek. She did not fight him. "I'll be here when you're ready."

She couldn't help answering. "It will be a long time, barbarian."

"I've already waited a lifetime for you." He turned her hand and, looking into her eyes, pressed a kiss into her palm.

Brannoc had spoken the truth. The camp was just beginning to stir when he and Phaedra returned. Cook fires flickered, and yawns rose and fell amidst grumblings rolling out from the knights' tents.

With the blond Celt at her side, Phaedra moved through the camp to prepare her mount for the journey. She shook her head in amazement at the slow-moving actions of the iron men. She knitted her brow. It was as if some enchantment had befallen the camp.

It wasn't until much later, when they were mounted and moving toward Caesarea, that she realized no one had even noticed them. No one had looked at them or spoken to them. Even Gabriel and Kasia's stares had passed right through Phaedra as if she were invisible.

She knew in her bones that it all had something to do with Brannoc. She didn't understand how, but the Dragon had woven a mantle of invisibility around them. In plain view of the knights and Bohemund, Brannoc would reach for her hand, or caress her arm, or kiss her. No one raised a brow at the intimate gestures. Under the canopy of stars, sleeping an arm's distance from soldiers and knights, Brannoc pulled her into his arms as if they were utterly alone together. He touched her in ways that made her forget where she was, who she was, and her quest to destroy Bohemund. With Brannoc, Phaedra forgot the world. And after three nights, she began to believe that this was the greatest enchantment of all.

The journey continued. The army plowed the earth, defeating troops at the village of Augustopolis, and finally reaching Caesarea at the end of September. The iron men took the city without a fight, for the Turks had deserted it. Nevertheless, the Christians celebrated as if they had fought the bloodiest, deadliest battle yet. The splendor of victory was less sweet without the spill of the infidel's blood, but a victory just the same.

Through it all, Phaedra dreamed. She had hoped Brannoc could ease the fearful visions her night mind imagined, but even he could not fend them off. When she awoke, she could remember one thing only, the eagle. She grew to hate sleep.

Somehow she knew the dreams had nothing to do with the journey to Jerusalem. This went deeper. The eyes of the eagle reminded her of someone, a man, just as Brannoc had said. And she knew they were the key. They were trying to tell her something. If only she could remember.

The days fled by, and Phaedra's thoughts turned to Alexander. Gusts of homesickness shook her again and again, chilling her to the bone. She ached, wanting him near. In the quiet of Brannoc's arms, listening to his heart beating, she yearned for Alexander. What was he doing now? And she'd imagine him playing with his wooden sword, his bow and arrows, riding and laughing with the wind.

As if Brannoc knew the turn of her thoughts, his arms would tighten around her and hold her more closely. Proud swan, she would bury her face in his chest and hide her tears under the cover of night. Her throat hurt from keeping the tumult of her feelings inside.

Finally, a day's ride from Comnana, feeling her pain for her child as if it were his own, Brannoc said, "Go back to him."

She looked up at him, startled. It was morning. They were sitting apart from the camp which was a babel of noises. The sun was gentle in the first hours of its birth.

"Go back to Alexander," he said again. "Go back to the city and care for your son."

She turned away. "You know I cannot."

"Why? Because of Bohemund? Because of a childish oath to avenge your father's death?" He paused and watched her wince as if she were being pricked by thorns. "The man won't die by your hand. Look into the water and see."

"It's what I've lived for!"

"You've lived for death?" He laughed. "To feel blood on your hands? What about life? Joy? Love?" He paused to give weight to his words. "Your son?"

"In time."

He sat back, assessing her. "Taticius is sending forces back to Constantinople. Go with them."

"You ask the impossible, barbarian. My destiny is here. Tied to that murderer."

"But he didn't do it."

She closed her eyes against his lie. "You don't know!"

He took her hand and squeezed it as he said, "You have the power of sight. Why won't you use it to see into the past?"

Her eyes flew open. "I have seen enough!"

"Not the truth. You see only what you want to see. Go, Phaedra. Your work is done here."

"It's just beginning!"

"Not where Bohemund is concerned."

"With who then?" she taunted with a lift of her chin.

He didn't answer at first. "With me. It's beginning with me. And I want you safe."

She felt her heart, a cold clenched thing, melt and open.

He leaned in closer. "Bohemund plans to ride after a band of Turks out of Comnana. I'm to go with him. I don't want you here, alone and unprotected. Return with Tacticius's men."

But the Swan couldn't fly. Not now. In Jerusalem she would get her chance.

"I can't! Don't you see?"

"Your pride has made you blind," he whipped out, and released her hand. But in the next moment, he reached for his dagger and unsheathed it. He held it so the hilt faced her. "Take this."

"But I have—"

"Will you fight me at every turn, woman? Take it."

She lowered her gaze to the metal blade that sparked the

light. Two entwined serpents were carved into the gold hilt. She reached out to touch it.

"This was given to me by a powerful swordsman in Cordoba," he explained as she ran her fingers over the carvings. "The man was reputed to be a sorcerer. I doubt it not. That's why I want you to have it."

Mesmerized by it, she took the dagger from him and turned it over in her hands. In the blade were flame patterns. She'd never seen anything like it before. Just then her eye caught a reflection at the tip, but it was neither of herself or Brannoc. Her spine prickled. She thought of Maia's bronze bowl and its power to reveal the future. Could she use this dagger the same way, she wondered?

"Keep it with you always. And this," he said as he tilted her face up between his hands and kissed her.

The way he held her, with her face cradled between his hands, and the gentle touch of his lips on hers, she was sure his words were more than the hollow shells of sounds. It was his soul speaking to her. And after, as his eyes searched hers, waiting for her answer, she knew a simple vow to do as he asked would never be enough for him. It was a commitment he was after. Something that would transcend this moment.

She closed her eyes, afraid and unafraid all at once. To bind herself to another man, risk wound to heart and soul, how could she?

The answer was there, beneath her lips. Warmth. Desire. Flame of truth.

She tucked the dagger into her belt, then pressed her hands over his, adding her power to his.

"Always," she said to herself, for she didn't have the courage to say it aloud.

But she forgot Brannoc's power to hear the turn of her mind.

"Always." The word bridged the chasm she'd taken such pains to build between them. She shuddered with the breath

of it in her ear, the feel of it inside herself, joining her soul
to his.

It was a lion-colored afternoon in the city of Comnana
when Bohemund gave the order to fifty of his knights to
prepare to mount. He was itching for a battle, and if the
Turks would not come to him, then he would seek them out.
Dressed for war in his armor and helm, he paced, restless,
hungry, his great hands opening and closing as if they were
crushing human heads.

Phaedra had been talking to Kasia and Gabriel. Gabriel
had a chest filled with sketches and scrolls of notes for his
mosaic. He had lost the bones of St. Agnes and felt his luck
would not hold up after Antioch. Kasia, who was now without anyone to attend her, had been driven to care for herself.
Her once voluptuous mouth was hard and brittle. She smiled
at the sight of the red-gold barbarian as he prepared to leave.
Now, at least, she whispered to Phaedra, she would not have
to put up with his sexual advances and pretend to enjoy what
little lovemaking skills he possessed.

But Phaedra didn't hear. Her eyes, all her attention, were
on Brannoc. Seeing him standing in the light of the sun, the
rays turning his mane of hair to gold, dressed in his suit of
armor, she was moved beyond reason. Her heart in her throat,
she looked at him, hoping he would approach her to say farewell.

As the thought turned in her head, Brannoc turned. He
looked across the field and caught her amber eyes in his
gaze. She felt her heart leap beneath her breast. Unable to
bear the intensity of his attention, she looked away. But out
of the corner of her eye, she caught him moving to Bohemund's side, then whisper something in his ear. In the next
moment, he was closing the distance between them. Without
stopping, without a word, he took her hand and led her away
from prying eyes.

Into the shadow of a city wall with the mountains looming around them, he stopped suddenly and turned to her. His gaze dipped to her waist where she'd tucked the dagger he'd given her beneath her belt. Looking at her face again, he sighed and nodded.

Phaedra knew the answers to all the questions whirling in her mind, still she had to ask, at least just to set them free and listen to the sounds they made on her breath.

"Now that I know. . . . Now that I've accepted this . . . this . . . feeling we have, do you have to go?"

Brannoc ran his finger from her ear down and around her jaw. He leaned down and kissed the spot between her brows to smooth the lines that had furrowed with her question.

"A week, or two. Then Bohemund will have had his fill."

A trumpet sang its silvery tone. It was time to leave. Phaedra took Brannoc's face between her hands and looked at him as if she would never withdraw her eyes again. She rose on her toes and kissed him, a soft and delicate kiss with a melancholy sting that made him shudder.

She let him go, stepping away. He followed her and drew her back into his arms. Just holding her close to him seemed to ease all the wanting in his heart.

But Phaedra, her head against his armored chest, warm from the sun, could not help but feel something break inside. Shutting her eyes, barring the tears that threatened to destroy her facade of calm, she began to convince herself that life was better the other way, when she had been alone in her tower of stone, cut off from this feeling that made her tremble and her breath catch in her throat.

Somewhere in time, whether it was a breadth of days or more, they would stand close like this again. Heart to heart, soul to soul, kiss answering kiss.

She turned in his arms and leaned back against him. She lifted her chin and closed her eyes for a moment. She felt his acceptance of her flourish as he possessively curled his arm around her. He kissed the top of her head. She put her hand over his on her shoulder, and felt his warm strength answer hers. They stood, locked and silent.

The Devil Mountains. It was the name Phaedra had learned from the city's inhabitants. And they did not say it without a shuddering glance, for the mountains stood out like the handiwork of a demonic force that had a desire to keep mortals out.

But even with the strength of the Dragon at her back, a wave of unease suddenly spiraled through Phaedra. She did not need to use her power to see what lay ahead in the mountains. Whatever it was, it was poised and crouched, ready to spring.

Twenty-three

The army was now led by Raymond, the Count of Toulouse, Godfrey of Bouillon and General Tacticius. But they were no match against nature and her forces. The advent of the autumn rains secured nature's victory. The men of the cross were powerless against the muddy, steep paths up inclines and around precipices. The horses and pack animals slipped and fell, dragging each other into the abyss. Provisions were lost. The cold wind, slicing through the gorges, made effigies of the sick and wounded. More men were lost along the sides of the mountains than in battle against the Turks. In one day, 500 soldiers died. The mountains were no longer laughing. They were roaring with glee.

Full moon. Phaedra tucked herself close behind Gabriel for warmth. He was snoring softly as if he were camped on the shores of a pleasure lake and not on a wind-swept ledge in the bowels of hell. There were other snores, louder, but she kept her mind focused on Gabriel's and took comfort in the familiar rhythm of his breaths.

She fidgeted on her side, then rose to pat the earth beneath her head as if it were a pillow. She lay down again, but as soon as she tucked her arm to cushion her head, she noticed strange markings on her arm, around her wrist. She squinted in the light. As it had been days since she'd last washed, she

278   *Veronica Ashley*

thought it was dirt embedded in her skin. She rubbed. Smudges of dirt came off on her fingers. She spit into her hand and rubbed more fiercely, but the grimy marks would not come off.

She sat up and turned her arm in the moonlight. There appeared to be a pattern to the mark and, unless the light was playing tricks, it looked blue. She attempted to follow it with her finger, but a dark, foreboding wave made her stop. She sat with her hand in her lap, refusing to look.

She swallowed. She could hear her heart pounding in her ears. Without looking, she touched her other wrist and rubbed it, too. And she knew instantly that the pattern was there, beneath her fingertips, on her skin. A stain. Blue.

Like a tattoo.

The thought knocked the air out of her, and she coughed as she fought for breath and control. Gabriel muttered something in his sleep. Phaedra looked up in alarm.

"It can't be! It's an illusion. Because of the cold, the lack of food, and sleep. I must be ill," she tried to convince herself. But unconsciously, she brushed her fingertips over the pattern around her wrist.

"Here's the dragon's head," stole a voice into her mind.

In the light of dawn, she looked at her arms. She saw markings, faint but visible around both wrists.

Brannoc's dragon tattoos.

While crossing the Devil Mountains, nothing touched Phaedra. Neither the cold, the rain, not even the petty hate and fear the barbarians wallowed in along with the mud, had the power to displace the one thought that governed her days. Somehow she'd been marked with the sign of the Dragon. Day after day, the tattoos grew darker and darker.

She'd never feared the cross-bearers before, but now, marked as she was, knowing how the westerners loathed Brannoc and attributed his tattoos to the devil, she knew she had to be careful. So she bound her wrists with strips of brown leather. Kasia had thought nothing of the leather bands. She'd thought Phaedra had crossed the line of respectability in Dorylaeum, when she'd joined the battle. The sphinx believed the leather guards were just another of Phaedra's many attempts to mold herself into a man.

Still clinging to the devil's back, but within sight of olive groves and sesame plantations, the cross-bearers decided to rest before beginning their descent. Their relief unfurled like new banners. The soldiers relaxed and laughed and reassumed whatever quotient of civility they'd had before the passage through the mountains began. Hands which had clenched to batter and bruise now closed in friendly tests of strength and skill.

They were within sight of the land of milk and honey! They had surmounted the obstacles the devil had placed in their way and were about to be rewarded. The air hummed with their excitement and the glory that would soon be theirs, but, for once, they did not mean to rush into it. The mountains, the sun, and the rains had aged them. The fact that Eden lay within their path was enough to gladden their hearts and raise their spirits.

In the city of Marash, a great feast was held to celebrate the return of God's warriors to the main army. Spirits were high due to Bohemund's gifts, the wine flowing as freely as water, and the fact that Antioch, the jewel of the East, was only a few days march away.

The fabled city of Antioch had given birth to the name "Christian," and at one time had been the third largest city in the Roman Empire. Titus and Diocletian had planned its greatness. King Herod had built a pleasure palace there. The great caravan routes passed through her white walls, bringing rice, papyrus and cotton from Egypt, silk and ivory, rugs and jewels from as far away as Cathay. As the mistress of the spice trade, Antioch received camphor, oil of sesame, myrhh and perfumes of rose and aloes laid at her feet.

In Marash, Phaedra had spent the day in the waters bathing. Its warm, scented liquid worked like a magical elixir. She could not forget Brannoc's silence and distance. It had been two days and he had not even asked after her well-being. She knew Brannoc was aware that she'd been staying in Gabriel's tent. But he had yet to seek her out and bring her back to his.

Skin glistening with sesame oil, and body clothed in white trousers and tunic, she returned to Taticius's camp and Gabriel's tattered, battle-torn tent. The smells of roasting meats, garlic and onions spilled through the air, but they tempted her to do nothing more than draw a long, appreciative breath. The sounds of revelry, of spirited drums, laughter and song tangled her thoughts. Fingering the leather cuffs that hid the dragon tattoos, she believed it wise to stay in the Byzantines' camp, far away from the bold, measuring stares of Bohemund, Baldwin and Sigurd. Even Brannoc. She especially had no interest in seeing him.

But such a lie as this mocked her. Alone in the tent, she paced like an animal that was tame enough to stay within its walls, but still wild enough to stretch its limits. The quiet of the bath vanished like water under the hot sun, unmasking her confusion and hurt, her anger at herself for letting a thing like a man consume her thoughts.

Unconsciously, she reached for the vial of Pagan Desires around her neck. She had anointed herself with the perfume at the baths. The scent seduced her memory and caused the image of Brannoc, holding her, his hands on her skin, to capture her now.

But somewhere between a breath and the magical haunting of his hands on her, he was there, standing in the tent's opening, blocking the light and the noise of Bohemund's camp.

Once again a beard covered the planes of his face, though

now it seemed thicker with silver than wheat-colored hairs. She noted that his shirt of chain armor was brown from tarnish and that it fit him more loosely than before. His belt was cinched tightly at his waist. He was as sleek as an animal in the wild that survived by being faster and more cunning than its prey.

His lips pursed slightly with an unspoken question as his gaze swept over her, stopping momentarily on the dagger at her waist and the leather cuffs on her arms, before indulging in the sight of her face, and the wild, beckoning mane of hair.

"Gabriel said I would find you here."

Phaedra said nothing. She lightly fingered the hilt of Brannoc's dagger.

"Why you're here, I don't understand." He paused. "I've been back for two days."

Phaedra's eyes narrowed on him. "He expected me to simply return to his tent and sleep with him as if he'd never left," she mused to herself.

"So. My protector has returned," she said aloud.

Brannoc caught the edge of cynicism in her eyes and replied, "I should have come for you. I did not expect—"

"You and Bohemund were victorious, I trust?"

He shook his head and finally entered the tent. He looked around. Gabriel's reliquary box was missing from the familiar surroundings, as was the furniture, which had fallen over the side of a cliff during the frightening journey through the mountains. All she and Gabriel had left between them were her horse Achilles, Maia's bronze bowl, the tent, the vial of Pagan Desires, and Gabriel's chest of art renderings and writings.

As there was nothing to study, Brannoc quickly returned his attention to Phaedra and caught her looking down at her hands.

He was standing in front of her before she'd even realized he'd moved. She jumped back with a start. The forced intimacy was too much for her to bear, but he quickly reached for her hands to restrain her.

The shock of his touch was like the first time. It was as if a blue flame had leapt between them. She knew he felt it too by the way he looked at her hands in his, then at her face. Her heart stopped.

He squeezed her wrists. "Show me," he whispered, massaging her flesh through the leather bindings.

He knew about the dragons! She shut her eyes for a moment, then did as he asked. She unlaced one binding, then the other. She stepped back and held her arms out before her.

Drawn to the pagan markings, Brannoc ran his fingers over the familiar blue shapes. Without meeting her gaze, he said, "They'll protect you when I can't."

"But how?"

He bent over like a devout supplicant and kissed each arm lingeringly, drawing a moan from her lips. For a moment she thought she saw the dragons move. They seemed to twine more tightly around her wrists. And something inside her, older than time, told her that there was something fitting in her having been so marked.

He drew her to him and moved his hands up slowly to touch the nape of her neck. He paused to savor the light of desire in her eyes before he bent to taste her. Tenderly, he brushed his lips against hers. The scent of her breath, her perfumed skin and hair bound him closer. She pressed herself against him and offered him her mouth as if it were a ripe fruit. Hungrily, he accepted and enjoyed her at his own easy pace, but her delirious, darting tongue teased him mercilessly and shattered his control.

With a ferocity that did not surprise her, he lifted her off her feet and finally gave his wanting full rein. With a moan like an animal's, she answered his need with the might of her own and grew warm and lush in his tightening embrace. No place for words. Just hands and mouths. Smell of rose and jasmine and sandalwood. Taste of sun on skin, metal and perfumed water. Skin like silk and a body hard with relaxed power. Fingers lost in a storm of black hair. Palms remembering the pleasure places of the back and thighs, the curve of a breast.

No place for words. Just this, moving her body over his. And this, the thrust of him, the heat. And this, the touch of his tongue, his hands cupping her, holding her. They were hands wiser than all the greatest minds that ever lived. This was everything in the world. Phaedra embraced it with a lift of her arms, a cry from her soul.

Later, laying side by side, Brannoc did not see the shadow lurking at the tent's entrance. He was fingering her hair when he sensed something and turned. But he saw nothing. No one.

Phaedra let out a long, deeply satisfied sigh and Brannoc raised his head so he could see her face. He grinned, she smiled back and drew his head so she could softly kiss his mouth. Then, touching his beard, scraggly and rough from lack of attention, Phaedra teased, "I suppose you think I'll obediently return to your tent now."

His laugh was deep and low. "I do." He nuzzled her neck. "As your protector, I order you to."

"Hmm, I don't know. Gabriel is a very undemanding tent-mate. And," she arched her brows dramatically, "he doesn't snore."

"Very well," he said with a dismissing shrug. He sat up and moved to gather his clothes. He heard her sit bolt upright and smiled to himself.

"Time with Bohemund has made you very complacent, barbarian."

The face Brannoc turned to her was serious. "You may sleep anywhere you like, Phaedra."

He was teasing her, she was sure of it. "Liar," she whispered, and she reached out to fondle him.

Brannoc let out a long whistle at the touch of her hand around him. "Phaedra!" He looked down and watched her hand caressing him. "Woman. You can't make me change my mind. You can sleep—" he swallowed his words as she moved to kneel between his legs and lowered her head to take him into her mouth. At the feel of her lips tasting him, he drew a shaky breath and arched his back. "You try my patience, Phaedra."

He pushed back the curtain of hair that hid her loving of him, saying, "Your protector commands your presence in his tent tonight. And tomorrow, and . . ." he groaned as her seductive fingers swept over the hard powerful length of him. She took him again into her mouth. And the last word he had the strength to utter was, "Forever."

Velvet night lit by a splinter of moon, stars and torchlight. The moment Phaedra and Brannoc entered Bohemund's camp, a mob flew at them, like harpies, brandishing burning sticks and stones.

Their voices shouted all at once. "There she is! It's her! Just like the other one. Spies! Greek whores!"

Brannoc drew his sword, warning the mob back.

"A spy?" Looking puzzled, Phaedra turned into the sea of angry faces. She felt Brannoc's arm around her waist, pulling her back. Someone was accusing her of being a spy?

A red-haired giant moved through, pushing people right and left. "Get out of my way," boomed the voice, and the mob, prodded as if by lance tips, jumped aside to make way for Bohemund.

He raised a golden brow at the sight of Brannoc's unsheathed sword. He frowned and shook his head.

"That won't be necessary, Brannoc. It's just a little misunderstanding regarding the Lady Kasia. Nothing more."

The frown deepened when Brannoc did not immediately lower his weapon.

The red giant opened his palms and capitulated. "Very well. Just follow me." He turned and snarled until an opening was cleared for them to pass.

Twenty-four

The moment they entered Bohemund's faded tent, Kasia threw herself into Phaedra's arms, knocking her off balance. Phaedra reached out to keep from falling.

"Oh, Phaedra, thank Mary Mother of God you're here!" the sphinx moaned, hugging Phaedra with relief.

A loud, wet snicker of contempt drew Phaedra's attention. Looking over Kasia's shoulder, she saw that the entire council was present. As she pulled away from the hysterical woman's clutches, Phaedra swept the pavilion with one look. There was the peacock, Hugh the Great, his lips parted to launch another snide noise. Beside him stood Stephen, Count of Blois, who nodded courteously in her direction. The serious Godfrey of Bouillon towered next to Raymond, the one-eyed graybeard who was still ghostly pale from his illness. Baldwin stood rigidly at attention, his stern mouth in its familiar down-curving arch.

The two cousins, the slothful Robert of Normandy, and the fair and young Robert of Flanders, stood on opposite sides of the tent. And there was Bishop Berain, who stood with his arms crossed over his pigeon chest, looking as smug as if he'd just come from a meeting with God. She felt his gaze on her wrists.

The only leader missing was the Byzantine General Taticius.

"Count Bohemund?" Phaedra's voice commanded his attention. But at the lack of a response, she turned and watched Bohemund stalk to a table set with wine ewers and goblets.

"My lord . . ." She bristled as he continued to ignore her.

Bohemund finally looked over his shoulder at her, but he did not stop.

"What is the meaning of this?" She heard the edge of exasperation in her voice and winced at the slip in her control.

"Go now, all of you." Bohemund gestured the onlookers out with a sweep of his great hand. "I'll see to this myself."

"I told you not to trust these Greeks! Especially the women!" Hugh spat at the ground.

"I'm certain the Lady Kasia has an answer for her, er, dalliance in Bohemund's tent," smoothed Raymond, ever the gracious courtier.

But Hugh was not so easily convinced. "Dalliance indeed! She was spying!"

"But wait!" The bishop held Godfrey back as the Lorrainer turned to leave. Phaedra felt her heart stumble and stop. "What of the markings I told you about?" His head swung wildly to take in the whole company. Then, lastly, his look settled on Bohemund. "Don't you want to see them? They're the sign of the devil, I tell you!" The bishop turned his toad eyes to Phaedra and they slitted venomously.

"What are you talking about?" Phaedra asked with a honey voice. She looked at Bohemund. "His holiness sounds feverish. Perhaps it would be best for him to take to his bed?"

She didn't hear Brannoc's hand move to rest back on his hilt. Nor did she hear him move to stand directly behind her. It was his heat that told her he was prepared to protect her. The warmth of his body reached out to melt the chill that had risen protectively around her like a battlement wall at the sound of the bishop's slippery voice.

She felt their eyes on her. Like a pack of wolves, the bishop, Godfrey, Baldwin, Raymond, Hugh, Stephen and the two Richards stood in a semicircle before her. Bohemund held the center and watched her over the rim of his cup.

Kasia, breathing more comfortably now that she was no longer the center of attention, eyed Phaedra curiously, too.

Phaedra felt the bishop move even before she saw him. She felt the air yield to him as if he were moving underwater. But before he could touch her and claw the protective leather cuffs off her wrists, Brannoc slipped between them.

The bishop grunted a groan of frustration and, pounding his fists against his thighs, peered around Brannoc's arm.

"Her wrists! Her wrists! I tell you she's marked."

"Your holiness . . ." Bohemund grumbled impatiently.

The bishop lanced him with a heated look. "See for yourself!" He thundered his order.

Bohemund sighed and, after scratching his chin, drank the last of his wine in a gulp and put the goblet down.

"Truly you don't believe him, my lord?" Phaedra said as she arched her brow.

The red-haired leader turned to Phaedra and opened his arms to his sides. "Lady Ancii," he began apologetically. "His holiness is convinced that there is something marking your wrists." He gave her a sheepish look that almost made her laugh, for the mask was a total farce. He stepped toward her. "May I?"

The bishop clicked his tongue and mashed his features sourly in the face of Bohemund's proper little dance. "Force her! No need for gallantry. She's a Greek whore." He looked up at Brannoc and, baring his yellow teeth, sneered, "Concubine to the devil."

"Enough!" Bohemund bellowed. The bishop shrank.

Phaedra looked down at her hands. *"Show him,"* said a voice in her head. With a startled breath, she looked up and gazed at the waiting men poised on the balls of their feet to catch a look. She steadied herself. Swallowing, shielding the pain caused by her dry throat and mouth, she unwrapped the protective leather around her right wrist. There was no dragon tattoo. Fighting the trembling, she quickly unwound the other and revealed a wrist as immaculate as the other.

"What?" The bishop tore around Brannoc, but the Celt caught him before he could touch Phaedra.

"But it's impossible!" He tore himself out of Brannoc's hold. "According to my sources, they were there only days ago," he gulped to Bohemund, who shook his head and turned his back to pour himself more wine. "I swear on the sanctity of the Virgin Mother," the bishop said as he turned, wide-eyed toward the others.

"Please, your holiness," Count Raymond cautioned.

"But my men did see them!" He stomped his sandaled foot. Patches of red mottled his face. He wheezed, then whirled to face Phaedra again.

"Bitch! Whore!"

Phaedra leaned forward to throw herself at him, but Brannoc held her back by her arm. "How dare you defile my name!"

But it was as if he hadn't heard. "What trickery is this? How dare you play games in the sight of the Lord," he brandished, shaking his cross in her face.

Embarrassed by the unholy display, Raymond jumped forward, took the bishop by the shoulders and led him from the pavilion, leaving a string of oaths for the others to dodge on the way out.

Phaedra shrugged off Brannoc's hands and, a victorious gleam in her eye, looked from Kasia to the red-haired Duke. "Now, shall we get back to the real reason I was brought here?"

Brannoc crossed his arms over his chest in a gesture that told everyone he was staying.

Bohemund ignored him and dropped into his leather chair. With the goblet poised between his fingers, he began, "Well, Kasia."

Kasia glided serenely across the room as if she were hosting a dinner party. She raised her chin. "I wasn't spying, but merely looking for my earring," she stated matter-of-factly.

"And did you find it?" Bohemund baited.

"No."

The red-haired giant, with menacing eyes narrowed and intense, gazed over the rim of his cup at Kasia. "It's been a long time since you've visited my tent. I've missed your wicked little mouth." He licked the beaded rim of his cup. "Brannoc!" He continued, "You really should try the Lady Kasia's mouth. Or does it belong to Taticius now, hmmm?"

"My lord, Duke," Phaedra rebuked. The tight edge in her voice lured Bohemund's predator eyes.

"Lady Ancii. How dear of you to stand by your friend." The look in his eyes did not change as he turned again to Kasia.

"Have you told her yet, sweetness? That you and I know about her secret?" He gestured with a nod of his head.

Phaedra felt an ominous chill move up her spine, but she shrugged it off. "What are you talking about?"

"Will you tell her, Kasia, my pet? Or shall I?" Bohemund then drank deeply of the wine in his goblet.

Kasia stamped her foot and crossed her arms in front of her. "Stop this behavior at once! I won't stand for it! Do you hear?"

Brannoc's brows pricked up. Bohemund broke into peals of snorting laughter.

"You are hardly in a position to give orders," Bohemund commented. "Now, fetch me more wine." Kasia simply fanned herself with her hand.

"Now!" Bohemund bellowed, shaking his cup.

"You see, Lady Ancii," Bohemund began, lacing his fingers together. "Kasia has told me about your gift."

There was a kind of savage pleasure in his last words. Phaedra looked at Kasia in wonder. The sphinx stood in profile, frozen at the table, wine ewer raised in her hand. Phaedra watched as a fiery stain of color appeared on Kasia's cheek.

Before Phaedra turned back to Bohemund, she composed her features to reflect the blank dismissal of his accusations.

"She's told me you have the gift of sight, prophecy," Bohemund continued with a meaningful, sidelong glance at Kasia.

Phaedra felt as if all the air in the pavilion had been sucked out. "And you believe her?" she asked, finding breath.

"Oh, yes." He leaned forward, preparing to pounce. "I heard the holy man, Daniel, speak of your powers, too." His eyes held a distinctly wicked sparkle as he waved his knowledge before her like a scarf.

But she refused to believe he knew. "A crazy man's mutterings."

"Kasia?" His voice was suddenly silky. It leashed Kasia to him.

"Kasia," Bohemund repeated. "Tell Lady Ancii what you told me." He was sitting forward in his chair like a creature that was half man, half beast. "Ka-si-a!"

The binding twisted and the sphinx blurted, "She can look into the future. She has the power."

Brannoc reached for his sword, but Bohemund, ever the animal, caught the move and bellowed at him, "Don't insult me, man! I don't want to hurt her." He collapsed back into his chair and gracefully opened his arms as if preparing to dance. "I just want her to tell me what she sees!"

Bohemund's eyes flicked back and forth between Phaedra and Brannoc. He noted how close, and yet apart, they stood. Accustomed to gauging the weaknesses in her defenses, he now pondered the strength of their love. He worked his jaw back and forth. His heavy-lidded wolf eyes glinted jealously.

Suddenly, he smiled. The change was startling. He eased back into his chair. He let the silence build.

"You've taken your role as protector to heart, my friend. But you, too, advised me to seek out the lady's powers. Remember?"

"What?" Phaedra spun on her heels to confront Brannoc.

Her gasping exclamation stabbed Brannoc like a knife blow. "He's baiting us, Phaedra. It's not true." Brannoc lifted his gaze and looked over the top of Phaedra's head at the wolf, who was hiding his delight behind his cup.

"Come, Brannoc. You can be frank with the lady now. Your time of service to me is nearly over and you'll be on your way."

The room reeled beneath Phaedra's feet. Believing Brannoc had betrayed her, she took trembling steps away.

"Phaedra!" Brannoc reached out to stop her, but she flinched at his gesture and increased the distance between them.

"Let her be, Brannoc. I think Lady Ancii is willing to relieve you of your duties, eh, Lady?"

But she did not have the strength to look at Bohemund. A dagger, wielded by her lover, was cutting away at her heart, bit by bit.

"Shall I order him to leave?" Bohemund was suddenly standing over her, lifting her chin up to look at him.

"Say the word, beauty. And it shall be done."

Taking her silence for a resounding yes, he waved his hand and ordered, "Go. Both of you!" His eyes darted to Kasia, too.

But when Brannoc did not move, he bellowed for the guards.

Three burly cross-bearers latched on to Brannoc like steel burrs and dragged him from the pavilion. "Phaedra! Don't listen to him! It's all lies!"

Hollow-eyed, a shell, she permitted Bohemund's hands to trail up and down her arms in what he must have thought were soothing caresses.

"What an astonishing woman you turned out to be! Warrior. Healer. And, lo and behold, a prophetess, too, right under my nose!"

She tried to look away but his eyes would not let her. They held her, hypnotizing her. "What a journey this has been, don't you think? And now you will tell me how it will end."

With your death, she thought to herself. She turned her back on him with the force of a slap and began walking away.

"Refuse my request," he called after her, "and your little spy friend dies."

She stopped. "I'll do as you ask," she said over her shoulder, "in Jerusalem." You'll die then, barbarian.

But the Duke shook his head. "Nay. Tonight." He closed the ground between them in two steps, laid his heavy hands on her delicate shoulders and forced her around to look at him.

"You and I. No one else need be present." His eyes flicked over her, appraising her beneath the loose boyish clothes. "And wear something . . ." he waved his hand in the air, "womanly. See that Kasia finds something suitable for the Swan to wear."

He met her shock with a grin that raised the hairs on the back of her neck.

"The Swan must be perfect. I command it."

There seemed no escaping Bohcmund's devouring gaze. Phaedra, standing in one of Kasia's gowns, barely breathed so as not to draw attention to her breasts. The white silk gown was cut low, off the shoulders, and revealed the full, round weight of her flesh. The silk poured smoothly over her stomach, hips and thighs like melting candle wax. The bell-shaped sleeves hung past her fingertips.

Phaedra had refused Kasia's help to paint her face and dress her hair. She had not anointed herself anew with Pagan Desires. Still, the wolf practically licked his lips in her presence.

Incensed, she knotted her hands, then in the next breath, she tried to calm herself. The sooner she did his bidding, the sooner she could fly free.

She watched the wolf, dressed in his tunic and a clean white surcoat, move about the pavilion, snuffing out the candle flames between his fingertips. He was slated to die at her hand, in Jerusalem, once the cross-bearer had assumed command of the city. Of course, she couldn't reveal this to him. She'd have to make something up. But then maybe the water would tell her something she didn't already know.

When there was no light save for the small flicker of the candle beside the bronze bowl at Phaedra's feet, Bohemund seated himself in his chair. Phaedra lifted her gown and knelt down. The noise of the camp did not touch the pavilion, as if it had been ordered against doing so on pains of being put to death. Could he order quiet as easily as that, she wondered. She shook her hair off her face and breathed in the pungent scent of laurel burning in a small dish next to the clay ewer of rainwater. She opened her fists resting in her lap, and felt her hands grow light. She closed her eyes, pictured the flow of her breath, and followed it.

Cleansed, aware of everything and nothing, she opened her eyes and poured the water into Maia's bowl. The sound of falling water rose and filled the pavilion, comforting her. Her task complete, she sat back on her heels and stared into the dark shine of water.

"Show me Bohemund, Duke of Taranto," she thought to herself. "What does the world hold for him? What is to be?"

The vision came to her like the ferocious leap of a beast, and with a gasp, she arched back. She touched her neck, as if the beast had bitten her, and beheld the shifting shapes on the water . . .

"What is it? What do you see?" Bohemund thundered.

Phaedra saw Bohemund seated on a throne. Someone, a knight, was standing before him, holding a man's severed head by the hair. She heard Bohemund's great snorting laugh and saw his lips twitch into a wolfish leer. He reached for the head as if it were a toy, then the water shifted and shaped itself anew.

The white walls of Antioch . . . Bohemund's crimson banner waving in the light of a rising sun . . . the mangled, defiled corpses of men, women and children, knee-deep in the streets . . . the rot of flesh steaming in the heat . . .

In an unfocused voice, she said, "Antioch has fallen. And you are its prince."

"Hah!" Bohemund slapped his thigh, but Phaedra did not hear.

"The citizens shall die at your hand, even those who pronounce their fealty to you. Even the children." She swallowed the cold, hard lump in her throat. "Even the children are put to the sword."

"What of Jerusalem? What of Jerusalem?" he asked anxiously.

She shook her head in disbelief over the telling water, her gaze locked on the image of him bidding farewell to the cross-bearers as they journeyed on to the Holy City. "You will stay in Antioch!"

The significance of her words and the images on the water made her pause for a moment, but the full realization of what it meant had not yet taken hold. She continued, her voice shaped by seeing.

"A long, bitter battle will be waged and there will be suffering that will make them all wish they'd already died and been sent to hell. But Jerusalem will fall to the cross-bearers. Blood-mad, they will massacre the city's inhabitants. News will spread and your homelands will all rejoice over the blood that has been spilled for the glory of God," she said in a failing voice.

She continued. "The throne of Jerusalem will be offered to Raymond—"

"What?"

Phaedra talked over the outburst. "—But he will refuse, claiming that the true King is Christ. Godfrey of Bouillon will assume the power and the title of Defender of the Holy Sepulchre." A vision rose from the water, then splintered as Bohemund's voice rang out.

"But what about me? After Antioch, what? Jerusalem must be mine!"

Phaedra narrowed her eyes at his biting impatience and began to look up to quiet him with a scornful look, but an image forming on the water, like a mosaic, drew her waning attention. And it made her smile.

The water showed her the mighty Duke of Taranto in prison, manacled to a stone wall, guarded by not one, but four Turks.

"You will be captured by the emir and languish in prison for two years. Upon your release, you will find your nephew Tancred seated on your throne."

"Bloody Christ!"

"You will return to your lands in Italy. Then in Rome, and at the Court of France, you will seek recruits for a campaign against all of Byzantium and the emperor Alexius. But Alexius will have grown in strength and might, and the imperial army will surround you at sea."

The news propelled Bohemund out of his seat and he stood, glaring down at her.

"Disease and lack of supplies will cripple your ships, and you will surrender. You return to Italy to die. The story of your life will die with you."

With a mighty howl, Bohemund kicked the bronze bowl, sending the water spilling across the carpet.

"Aahhh!" Phaedra screamed as Bohemund twined his paw in her hair and yanked her to her feet.

As fire-red as the forge of Mars, Bohemund screamed in her face, "You lie!"

Glassy-eyed, Phaedra stared up into his face as he dragged her down by her hair. She blinked, and when next she opened her eyes, she was looking into the mangy jaws of a wolf.

She swooned and would have fallen had Bohemund not caught her.

"Bloody, stinking Christ!" he swore. He lifted her in his arms and carried her to the tent's opening, which he kicked open. On the threshold, in the half light of a purple dusk, he dumped her on to the ground at his feet. He looked around, caught Sigurd standing by, and roared, "Get this piece of baggage out of my sight!"

As if he had just been commanded to accept a chest overflowing with countless treasures, Sigurd grinned and leapt to do Bohemund's bidding.

Twenty-five

It was a small rat, gray, with a tail which curled behind on the stone floor like a drawn-out spiral. Its nose quivered over an empty copper plate of crumbs, the remains of a simple meal that had included a torn piece of unleavened bread, crumbly goat cheese and roasted cubes of lamb.

Phaedra laid upon a bed of straw in the gloom of a corner, watching the rat. On his level, she noted the pink of his nose, the black obsidian eyes. She watched him reach for a crumb, then stop.

Rain. A soft hush lured her attention to the square window that was set too high to offer hope of escape. The beams of sunlight that had been moving across the floor, tickling the dust motes, diminished in intensity. Phaedra sighed. She felt the cold stone reaching up to entomb her.

She stretched her foot. She barely felt the iron manacle around her left ankle anymore, or the weight of its rusty chain that was secured to the iron ring on the wall. For ten days, Sigurd had kept her locked up in the prison cell. She knew it had been that long by the markings she'd etched with the chain on the wall. Ten days in Edessa. Before this, she'd spent a month in a prison in Ravendel. And before that, a month in Turbessal. She was becoming quite accustomed to the prisons in the cities along the Euphrates and its valley.

She sat up, startling the rat, sending it scurrying for cover. Her back against the stone, she hugged her knees to her chest. She focused on the opposite wall, only four arm's length away, and, as she did every day, replayed the series of events that had brought her to this prison in Edessa in the valley of the Euphrates. For just as her body was imprisoned, pinned to a wall that had probably been standing since the birth of Christ, so was her mind held prisoner within a block of time.

After hearing her revelations, Bohemund had turned on her like an animal that had been denied the choicest piece of a killed prey. She remembered the brutal attack of his hands as he'd lifted her and thrown her from his tent. Drugged by the burning laurel, still rising from the sensation the visions always caused, she vaguely recalled Sigurd picking her up, dusting the dirt off her gown and fussing over her as if she were a discarded toy. The memory of the cross-bearers camp and that night ended there. It was as if she'd been swallowed by the dark. When she awoke, she found herself strapped across the back of a horse.

The details slowly fell into place like pieces of a mosaic set in the most haphazard fashion. From Marash, while the main army was set upon a southward march to Antioch, Baldwin, Sigurd and a hundred horsemen had set out along a parallel road with the intention of venturing into the valley of the Euphrates and the lands beyond. Once again, Sigurd had thrown his lot in with the younger brother of the Duke of Bouillon. Had Sigurd kidnapped her, Phaedra wondered again and again. Or had he taken her with Bohemund's blessing?

And what of Brannoc?

Unconsciously, her hands reached for the vial hanging from the gold chain around her neck. She rubbed the curves of alabaster. She had no intention of opening it and breathing in its luxurious, sensual scent. Pagan Desires belonged to someone else. It was the scent of a woman in love, a woman who knew that the strength of that feeling could be as subtle as the fall of a veil.

Her defenses rose quickly to banish the thought and the path it was about to take. She stiffened against the wall. Her lover had proved to be a traitor. She played with the truth back and forth as if it were a ball between her hands. She caught the flick of the rat's tail sweeping the stone in the shadows. While listening to the rain's underlying music, her thoughts played on in her head.

Brannoc had defiled her trust. He'd told Bohemund about the most sacred part of herself, her gift of sight. The Dragon had used her. But for what? What did he stand to gain by telling Bohemund?

With a frustrated growl, she let go of the pendant and stared up at the ceiling. It was stone. Yellow. She felt as if it were collapsing down upon her and stiffened, squeezing her eyes shut.

She rocked herself back and forth. How much longer did Sigurd intend to keep her locked up like this? But she knew the answer. Speaking to the wall and the rat, she said, "As soon as I decide to give myself willingly to Sigurd, I'll be free."

She crossed her arms over her chest and continued to rock. She pictured Sigurd's big, flat hands, with their coarse black hairs like a boar, moving over her body. She grimaced. Sigurd had made it clear that she would have to come to him willingly. With a snicker, she recalled when he'd tried to force himself on her. She looked down at the tattoos and caressed a dragon with her finger. Although they had disappeared in Bohemund's presence, they'd reappeared the second night of her captivity with Sigurd.

They'd been encamped near Aintab. In the dark of night, amidst the groans of his tired and sleeping comrades, he'd attacked her. He'd used his weight to pin her arms to the ground above her head, and had just thrust his knee between her thighs, when the dragon tattoos suddenly came alive and attacked him. They darted and flew about his head like little demons. Horrified, he'd tried to bat them to the ground. They just hissed, but when they began to breathe plumes of fire at him, he jumped to his feet and ran.

When next she'd looked, the dragons were still, blue and beautiful around her wrists. Sigurd instinctively knew the dragons would attack him again if he tried to take Phaedra by force. That was why he'd made it clear that her freedom was dependent on her coming openly to him.

"Is everything all right in there?"

A steel panel scraped in the heavy wooden door, and a pair of eyes peered in at her.

Phaedra looked up, swallowed, and met the brown eyes gazing at her. They were soft and possessed a slightly vacant look, like a trained brown bear.

"Lady?"

Phaedra snorted. Sigurd had instructed the guard to call her that. And to make sure she was well fed, the palace kitchen prepared her food and the guard's, too. "I like my women to feel like women, not birds, all delicate and bony," Sigurd had boasted.

"I'm all right, Abu'l. I just wish . . ." She let go of the thought of a bath. What was the use? She was imprisoned, caged, and filthy.

She slumped, unable to bear the weight of her thoughts and laments. She heard the panel steal back into place. Sound of jangling keys and the clickety-clack of one in the door.

She arched her brow as the door squeaked open, away from her. Abu'l filled the entry, menacing in his steel armor breastplate and black tunic. His sword was as large as the Normans' two-handed weapons, and it was sheathed in a plain leather scabbard across his left thigh. But the froth of brown curls on his head softened the giant's appearance, as did the beard, which haloed a mouth of such delicate proportions, that it seemed incapable of shaping a blasphemous oath. And his gentle eyes held a question creased in the corners.

"I've been ordered to escort you to the palace," he said, clearly dumbfounded by the order.

"What's Sigurd up to?" she wondered to herself, as Abu'l entered the cell and knelt to unlock the manacle around her ankle.

The palace garden had been designed to be a sanctuary of beauty and calm. Square in shape, it was contained on all sides by stone colonnades. A round pool with a spraying fountain ornamented its center. There were orange and lemon trees as well as tall cedars, pines and roses.

Cloud tendrils veiled the sun, and yet the light blinded Phaedra. She had become accustomed to the gloom and the miserly fingers of sunlight that moved through the high window of her cell. Squinting, her hand cupped over her eyes, she turned on her bare feet, crunching the raked gravel walk. Rain droplets clung to the leaves and shone like diamond chips.

She closed her eyes and breathed. The air had been scrubbed clean by the rain. The dampness heightened the natural perfumes of the flowers, trees and grasses. But on the wind, she furrowed her brow as she caught a dank, malodorous smell. It was animal-like, with the ashy hint of death about it. She drew a shallow intake of air. As she winced, she suddenly realized that she was the cause of the foul odor.

She looked down at herself, at her dirty trousers and tunic, her filthy feet and hands. Ashamed by the harsh realization, she caved in, dropping her shoulders. She prayed for the earth to open and swallow her.

Footsteps on the path behind her alerted her and dragged her away from her thoughts. She whirled around, automatically reaching for her dragon dagger, but her fingers clutched at nothing. Sigurd had taken the weapon from her months ago.

Her eyes flew up to see Sigurd. He stood with his arms crossed over his bull chest, his legs spread wide as if he owned the earth beneath his feet. His freshly barbered chin was thrust at a proud angle. His tunic was pure white, a color she never thought she'd see again. She coveted it. Her fingers itched to touch it.

"Lady Ancii," he hailed. He lurched to a stop and grimaced. He brushed his hand in front of his face. "Mother in Heaven! What is that smell?"

Phaedra felt the color rising in her cheeks and was grateful that the dirt on her face hid her embarrassment.

"Must be something dead in the trees," he sniffed. He stopped before her. Phaedra backed away. "So!" he blurted. "Have you decided anything?"

His pomposity was like a poke in her ribs. "I've decided that when I'm free I will spare your life."

Sigurd retorted with a throaty laugh. "Indeed, Lady? I think I'll be an old man, eager to die, when that day finally arrives." He stepped closer. "You have only to say the word, say that you'll be mine," he whispered feverishly, "and you may have anything you like."

His excitement gave her pause to wonder, and a full-blown plan was born.

"Look at me, Sigurd. I'm a filthy, detestable creature. How could you possibly want me?"

His eyes widened with interest and his nose edged forward like a dog that has been thrown a bone.

"You are beauty born, Lady Ancii. Do not speak of yourself so! I'll not have it."

"Look at me! Even the rats stay away from me." She laughed, but it brought a wince to his face.

"Stop!" He looked at her keenly. "I could arrange a visit to the baths, of course."

A bath! Phaedra steeled herself from jumping with joy.

"Would that help you make up your mind? It will give you a taste of what could be yours if you decide to come to me."

She knotted her hand into a fist. She had a mind to strike

the foolishness from his head. All she wanted was a bath, not to be turned into the Queen of Sheba.

"I'm a powerful man, now that Baldwin rules."

"Wha-at?" Caught off guard, she stood there, shocked. "What do you mean, Baldwin rules? Edessa has a ruler."

Sigurd shook his head. "Thoros was murdered. Poor old man. He was torn to pieces by his own people. There was a conspiracy by members of his assembly. His troops deserted him. The old man locked himself in the palace and, when he tried to escape, he was captured by the citizens."

He paused for a look of comprehension to cross her face, but when it did not, he went on. "The people have asked Baldwin to govern and he has accepted."

The thought of bathing had flown from her mind at the mention of Edessa's political situation. "Impossible. Since the city belonged to Emperor Alexius before the Turks, it is covered by the oath Baldwin swore at court. He must turn its rule over to Alexius."

Sigurd snorted and dismissed her observation with a wave of his arm. "It doesn't concern you, lady." He tapped her under her chin. "Now, all I want you to think about is how you're going to demonstrate your appreciation for my generosity." He winked. He bowed before her. "Your bath awaits."

I don't need a bath, Phaedra thought to herself as she walked past Sigurd and followed the path. I need paper and ink. Someone to carry a message to Taticius.

All along, the Byzantines had been afraid that Bohemund would carve out his own empire. Baldwin was a more immediate threat than the wolf. It was obvious that Baldwin intended to establish a barbarian principality right under the emperor's nose.

Phaedra stopped suddenly. Sigurd stumbled into her. I need to take that message, she realized. So intensely did she weave scenarios for her escape that she did not feel the stones cutting into the soles of her feet.

* * *

Although she refused to remove the gold chain and vial of Pagan Desires, Phaedra did submit her body to the lavish attentions of the servants in the bath. The tattoos did not alarm them, but, rather raised coos of surprise and admiration as if the dragons were cuffs of precious blue jewels.

Phaedra arched with a whimper of delight at the first touch of the water cascading down her back. It was warm and fragrant. It washed the grit and sweat of the desert, the bone-rattling cold of the mountains, and the dust and dirt of the prisons from her skin. Cupping their hands, the servants guided the precious water to Phaedra's shoulders, back, arms and breasts, and let it fall. Like the ebb and flow of different oceans, the hands moved to their own rhythms.

Stripped of the journey's dirty layers, she stepped into a pool of bright turquoise decorated with a peacock-colored mosaic. She lost herself in its glassy depths, skimming along the bottom, brushing her fingertips against the glass tiles. She relished her freedom before the soft, experienced hands reached out for her again.

They dried her hair with silk and her body with feathers. They scrubbed a thick paste of almond meal and honey over every inch of her body until her skin turned pink. Their oils and massage creams conjured visions of Nefertiti and the queens and princesses of the Euphrates born to wear the crown.

She rose reborn, white-gold from the sun, her hair a night cloud that hung to her waist. But before they dressed Phaedra, the servants presented her with a gold belt from which dangled hundreds of small, sparkling coins.

"A gift from the master," they told her.

Phaedra twisted her mouth and waved the belt away. She had seen one like it on a dancing girl in Turbessal.

The servants shook it in front of her and begged her to put it on, or else they would suffer the bite of Sigurd's lash. Phaedra whipped it out of their hands. Seething with anger, she vowed she would force every last coin down Sigurd's throat if he so much as touched her!

Phaedra followed the servants through a candlelit stone hall, moving as gracefully as possible, imagining herself a cloud slipping through the sky lest she set off the coins around her hips their twinkling laughter. She despised the belt, the suggestive way it swayed on her hips, and the delicate strand that hung between her thighs. The God-fearing knight who had once looked at her as if she were the Madonna, had forgotten his holy worship of her somewhere along the journey. He had turned as decadent as a hedonistic pasha with a feather-stuffed pillow for a brain.

What was the point of wearing clothes, she thought, glancing down at the violet velvet bodice, cut short to reveal her waist, and the lavender silk pantaloons? The gold belt around her hips told her precisely what role she would be expected to play.

She touched the perfume vial for comfort and stepped into a room dripping with rich fabrics, covered with plush rugs and pillows in every size and color. Soft candlelight and the play of light and shadow shrouded the room with mystery.

"Christe," she swore under her veil. It was a room suited for only one thing, a seduction. She swallowed nervously, taking in the silver dishes of food arranged on the low polished rosewood table. Tendrils of fragrant steam weaved in the air.

Her kohl-shadowed eyes widened at the provocative sound of a curtain being whisked aside. Phaedra turned on her gold-slippered heels and watched Sigurd step through the draperies. She slyly noted her dagger was tucked inside his belt.

The sight of her dagger gave the evening new meaning. She drummed her fingers against her thigh with anticipation.

"Well, Phaedra?" He cut a glance at the thick gold cuffs which hid the dragons around her wrists, and licked his upper lip.

With only one thought on her mind, the repossession of her dagger, Phaedra answered, "I'm here, am I not?"

"But what about . . ." Sigurd finished his thought by pointing his bearded chin at her wrist.

"You're safe as long as I'm safe, Sigurd," she smiled demurely beneath her veil.

"Very well then." He held his hand out to her. The simple gesture opened the way to a memory, an afternoon by a stream. The recollection turned her to ice. Gritting her teeth, she put her hand in his. She felt the burning warmth of his skin, the slippery remains of the perfumed oil he'd worked through his beard and hair, the carefree hook of his fingers as he led her to the table.

Sigurd lifted one domed cover after another, revealing plate after plate of fragrant offerings. There was roasted pigeon on a nest of cresses and a whole baby lamb roasted with garlic, onions, peppers and tomatoes with saffron rice. The loaves of bread created their own perfume. Purple, green and black olives glistened. There were shelled pistachios, figs, raisins, green grapes and candied dates.

Phaedra helped herself to a grape as Sigurd filled her plate. Sitting on her plump red velvet pillow, she noted how easy it would be to take him by surprise, wrest her dagger away, and leave him to the dragons.

Sucking the sweet juice from her fingertips, she knew she could do it. But he knew she could do it, too, and that was the reason why she made no move to free herself. She'd be dead before she even stepped from the room. She knew it in her bones as surely as she felt the spying pair of eyes watching her, watching them.

She lifted her hand to remove her veil, but Sigurd stopped her.

"Let me." He caught the fragile silk in his thick hand and ripped it free. He lifted her chin with his little finger and set a chaste kiss on her lips. Phaedra smelled wine on his breath.

"We can marry, if you like," he whispered, resting his forehead tenderly against hers. "Baldwin has granted his permission."

"God's foot!" she swore to herself using the barbarian's favorite oath. His sweetness was sickening and rang so falsely as to sound off clanging bells in her mind.

"Shouldn't we eat first?" she jested, turning her head toward the table. "I've not seen so much food since . . . why, I cannot remember when I was present at such a feast."

Phaedra failed to see Sigurd's face turn hard. "I've seen to it that you received meals fit for a queen!"

Hearing him salvage his pride, Phaedra turned with a start. His eyes were beaded on her, like a boar. With a grunt, he swept the table with his arm, sending platters clattering and food flying.

I could placate him, soothe him so easily, she thought. But why? He's kept me locked up for three months! Which queen was he thinking about? The entombed Cleopatra?

Emboldened by his fury, she glared back at him.

"I'll not stand for your ingratitude, woman. You'll see. When we're married, I'll set things right." He grabbed her by a gold cuff and squeezed, causing her to wince. "I'll cut the beasts out of your arms." He smiled malevolently, let her go, and thrust a goblet of wine at her.

"Drink this before I take you back."

She shoved the cup back at him, sending the amethyst wine flowing over the sides, puddling the table. Words poised on her tongue, she crossed the line.

"You think that by freeing me for one day, bathing me, robing me in silks and this slave belt, I'll swoon at your feet?" Her voice struck out like a slap.

But Sigurd did nothing. He tossed the remainder of the wine down his throat and rose to his feet in one move.

She felt her wrists grow warm and felt the dragons move, awakened from their sleep. And she was not afraid.

Twenty-six

Sigurd held the serpent dagger at Phaedra's throat as two stout guards chained her to the stone wall in her prison cell. The weapon pricked her, cut her skin and bit her again when she bucked away from the cold press of the stone against her breasts. But Sigurd pushed her back with a snarl.

She was kneeling, her face to the wall, arms above her head with her hands cuffed together and chained to an iron ring in the wall. Her silk bodice and pantaloons were ripped, and baring her bloody scratches. She felt Sigurd standing behind her, breathing heavily. She sensed the guards were gone. She turned her head to see, but the position of her arms made it painful.

Sigurd began to beat the pommel of the whip in his hand against his thigh. The leather lashes swished against the ground. With every slap, Phaedra worked harder to find a way to slip her hands free. Frantic, she looked up at her hands. The dragons!

Sigurd laughed at her futile struggle to escape. "Where are your protectors now, eh? Your dragons." He spat at the ground and cracked the whip. "Perhaps I've discovered a way to control them. And you."

With her face to the wall and her arms held above her head, Phaedra was unable to see the blows coming. At the first bite of the lash, she arched, pressing into the stone wall. She'd barely taken a breath when the lash came down again.

The pride she mustered to remain silent did not long endure. So frantically did she writhe that she nearly turned completely around. As a result, Sigurd was able to whip her belly and the front of her thighs as well as her backside. The silk garments were ripped into shreds, until she wore nothing but the gold belt around her hips.

With every flick of the whip, Sigurd's breathing grew heavier and heavier, until, crazed with lust by the sight of the belt dangling around her hips, he threw himself at her, kissing the nape of her neck and the welts on her back. Cupping her buttocks, he moaned her name. Groaning with his desire, he quickly unfastened his chausses and pressed himself against her. She screamed, and it was as if the angels answered her back, for there was a great whirring sound, like wings, that filled the cell and echoed in her ears.

So great was the sound, she barely heard Sigurd cry out in terror. She felt him jump away, but in his hurry to flee, he shoved her head against the stone wall, and a darkness swirled and swallowed her.

Phaedra hung on the wall until Abu'l returned to duty. Finding the cell door open, he ventured inside and began to weep at the sight of her bleeding and helpless. Her head was cocked at an ugly angle, as if someone had broken her neck. Through his tears, he untied her and cleansed her wounds on her back with water and a sponge. He bandaged her head, swaddling her brow with strips of white linen. When she moaned, he gave her his wine mixed with water. He positioned her on the stone floor, on her stomach, in a pose he hoped was comfortable for her. At the darkest hour of the night, he covered her with his own blanket and watched over her.

Pain tugged at the end of Phaedra's unconsciousness. In her head, a sharp persisting throb became increasingly stronger, like a workman's chisel striking glass tiles. She awakened with a start, her head splitting in pain. It was dark, black. The space weighed heavily on her, and at first she thought she'd been buried alive in a crypt.

She lifted both hands at once as if they were still bound together. She still felt the manacle. She could not see her hands. She moved her fingers, groping at the darkness, but saw nothing. She moaned, touched her brow and felt the wet sticky blood on her hand.

She heard the squeak and scamper of a rat close to her head. Was she still in her cell, she wondered. Then where was the light? The window?

She turned to look, but the pain bolted her to the ground and she stiffened. She felt the wounds on her back opening, oozing. She whimpered and heard the rat squeak in agitation.

As her eyes grew used to the darkness, the crypt softened to a dull metal gray. There was light, and a window above her head. She pictured the stars framed in the sky and cried with the pleasure of knowing that she was in her cell, her home for the past month, and had not been buried alive.

She felt spiritually emboldened and turned onto her side. Through the wall of tears, she saw it, a gleam in the corner, like polished metal. It had the dangerous wink of something sharp.

Could Sigurd have forgotten the dagger, she wondered.

She reached out, but the dagger was too far. She willed herself to move and, with the same determination that carried her across Devil Mountain, she crawled the two arm's lengths necessary to reach the bold gleam in the dark.

At the sound of approaching footsteps, Phaedra grabbed the serpent hilt between her fingers and returned to her position on the stone floor, her body racked with pain as she bit her lip to keep from crying out. No sooner had she slipped the dagger under the straw near the wall, then the door creaked open and the cell flooded with torchlight. Her arm flew up to shield her eyes from the painful light.

"Well, now. Awake, are we?"

That wasn't Abu'l, she thought.

"Who are you?" she whispered hoarsely in the direction of the gruff voice on the other side of the wall of light. "Where's Abu'l?"

"Been promoted, lucky bastard. Serving the new king as bodyguard. There's been rumblings. The barbarian has enemies and he's afraid." He paused. "You his woman?"

"No." Cautiously, she lowered her arm and opened one eye to venture a look at the guard. As if anticipating her need, he lifted the torch up and behind him. He was squat, built like a brick, with one savage dark line for a brow.

"They say you have powers."

Phaedra snorted. "Would I be here, like this, if I had powers?"

"And that you have the beauty to charm the scales off a dragon." The light swirled around her as he waved the torch. "You don't look like much to me."

Her mouth curled with a half smile at the blunt observation. Though gruff, there was something in the man's voice, a begrudging tone of kindness, that made her think of Sharif.

"You flatter me, sir." She bit her cracked lips. "Now, do you think I could have something to drink and eat? Or do they intend to starve me to death?"

"Water, bread and some cheese, if that's to your liking. Don't think you could stomach much else."

She breathed with relief and dropped her arm to her side. "It is a feast, sir. A feast."

The guard's name was Hakim. He was Armenian, with a fondness for chess to rival Sharif's love of the game. They played every afternoon after their lunch, splitting a dark red wine that Phaedra compared to ambrosia.

He dressed her wounds for her, too, paying special attention to her back. Under Phaedra's direction, he created a healing salve, comprised of oil of balanos and myrhh that she had used on the cross-bearers.

Hakim was caught between the years of early manhood and old age, a wide span of time that could easily be nothing more than a waiting game. He was a soldier, but he had dreams. Hakim revealed to Phaedra how he'd often imagined that he was master of his own home, with a fine wife and children playing in the sunlight beneath date trees. He wanted to start a business, but he was at a loss as to what, for most occupations were closed to him as he'd never learned any trade skills. His father had been a professional soldier, too. But Hakim had openly admitted to Phaedra that he'd never had the stomach for killing.

She looked at him as if she were listening to the play of her own thoughts. How alike they were, both prisoners. The only difference she could see was that she no longer dreamed. It was as if the prison's walls were too thick and high for her to leave them even in her sleep. Even the nightmare of the eagle did not touch her here.

She no longer felt connected to her gift of sight. There was no bronze bowl to help her make that journey. But more importantly, she didn't feel any need to see past the walls. What was the point in seeing what you couldn't have? She already knew Bohemund was not fated to die by her hand.

Seated in the corner, she rocked herself for hours, thinking how cruel it was that the one thing that had occupied her thoughts and energy for her entire life would not come to pass.

It was not her fate to destroy Bohemund.

What was she supposed to do now? Why had she been permitted to come so far? If there was a God, why couldn't he give her the one thing that mattered to her the most?

What if her whole life had been lived for nothing?

Phaedra's despair pushed her deeper and deeper into a place inside herself as walled as the prison tower. Hakim was at a loss over what to do. The squat, steady soldier watched her through the opened grate as she stared listlessly ahead in the light and the night. He tried to be more entertaining during their games of chess, but as her interest waned, the opportunities to spark a change in her mood decreased. He brought her figs and dates and sugared rose petals. Only the regular offerings of lavender oil and a brass tub filled with hot water for bathing brought a gleam of interest to her eye, the hint of a smile to her face. He wrung his hands with worry, and was afraid that she would will herself to die.

Hakim didn't know she had her dagger. She held it in the dark, palming the familiar weight. It was the only thing that made her feel a part of something. She likened it to a branch, or a hand. She felt as if she were dangling above a sea of darkness, and the cool metal, with its fierce shine and fiercer serpents, was the only thing preventing her from falling.

"Promise me that you'll remember to keep it with you always," Brannoc had said. She remembered. But there was more. She felt the memory of his hand cradling her face, the gentle touch of his lips on hers, and his eyes searching for some sign of a commitment from her. Bending herself to him, she had risked wounding her heart and soul. And he, in time, had hurt her in a way that made light of all the pain she'd suffered at Sigurd's hand. Brannoc had told Bohemund about her gift, and had broken her trust.

Or had he?

She had chosen to believe Bohemund over Brannoc. Why? She beat herself with the thought that she may have been wrong. She felt her hands slipping and the blackness licking her soles.

But on a star-filled night, the twentieth day of her captivity in Edessa, as the scent of orange blossoms drifted on the breeze with the rain, Phaedra saw something, like a reflection, move on the dagger's blade. She peered more closely without even trying. Her eyes were as used to the gloom as a night creature.

She saw a figure ripple across the blade's surface.

"This was given to me by a swordsman in Cordoba," echoed Brannoc's voice in her mind. "The man was reputed to be a mage. If there's magic here, you may be able to use it to help you. Promise me you'll remember to keep it with you always."

Reverently, she set the blade before her on the stone floor, and eased herself onto her knees. Before she realized what she was doing, she focused on the shiny stream of steel and said, "Show him to me. The figure in the dagger. Show me."

Unconsciously, she reached for the vial of perfume and held it. The image settled. Cast upon the surface of the blade was Brannoc. The tall, fair-haired Celt had his sword in hand and was engaged in battle. The dagger glowed red as if it had been touched by a spume of Greek fire. She watched him match an unseen opponent blow for blow. She watched, drawn to the blade, drawn into the steel as easily as if it were a pool of water held within the bronze embrace of Maia's bowl. She knew what was happening and let herself go to the place the vision wanted her to see. The walls fell away and she soared.

Twenty-seven

She saw a swan flying through the night sky. She stared at the creature and knew instinctively that she was looking at an image of herself. As she watched, she recalled Kasia's dinner party and her vision, when all the dinner guests had been transformed into beasts. She shuddered, thinking of Kasia, who had turned into an asp. The Varangian Guard had become a lion, Vinicius a hawk, the Senator an ass, and Brannoc, a dragon.

The image of the swan wavered.

"No! I must stay calm," she told herself. "Clear my mind of everything except the swan."

A strange sensation flowed up her spine. She eased into the feeling of power that it brought. A feeling of weightlessness rippled through her hands. Involuntarily, she shivered. She believed she was the swan in the sky feeling the cold night air.

"Take me to Brannoc," she whispered.

In her mind, she formed an image of Brannoc. She reached out and touched the dagger. It was as though a greater force was passing between her and the blade, a force powerful enough to strip away a veil of the real world and cast her into the realm shining before her.

She saw Brannoc looking out at the sea awash in moonlight. The water thundered, rolled and foamed on the beach. White spumes reached out like fingers eager to trap him and carry him away. But he had a look in his eye that warned the water to beware.

A swan circled above him and cut its shadow into the moon. Brannoc looked up, saw the swan and turned. His quiet gaze followed the creature.

"Free yourself and return to Constantinople for Alexander. But after that you must not stay. GO. Anywhere. I will find you."

She knotted her brow. "But I don't understand," she said to herself, even though she heard him above the roar of the waves as clearly as if he were standing before her in the prison cell.

"Flee Constantinople. But beware. The eagle will be watching. Escape. Pagan Desires will set you free."

The eagle? What did he mean by Pagan Desires? How could a fragrance free her?

"Brannoc!" Her mind cried out to him.

The image reached his hand out to the swan in the sky.

"Always." The unspoken word bridged the chasm between them. She shuddered with the song of it in her ear, his rich deep voice rising above the waves pounding the shore, and the enormous beating of beautiful wings.

"Always." She felt it moving inside of her, joining his soul to hers.

"Hakim!" she shouted the following morning, startling the rat that she had named Sigurd.

"Hakim, I'm going to make you a rich man! You will have your dream."

I know what I must do, she thought to herself, fingering the alabaster vial. Just as Brannoc had said, the perfume *was* the key!

She rose to her feet and pounded on the prison door with her fists. "Hakim! I need paper, an ink horn and a quill. Quickly, man!" She pressed her ear to the door and listened for his steps. Hearing his heavy, shuffling gait, she smiled. She did not step back but waited against the door.

"Stop that screaming, or you'll get me thrown in there with you!"

The iron grate in the wooden door lurched, got stuck, then batted aside. A pair of eyes widened at the amber orbs staring directly back.

"What?" He blinked with shock at the change in Phaedra. The day before he had found her rocking herself in the middle of the floor, staring listlessly at the wall.

"Paper! Quill! Ink! Riches await, my man. Your dream is so close I can smell it!" She laughed and twirled in the cell until she became dizzy.

When he'd brought her everything she needed, she settled down in a pool of sunlight and wrote:

Aphrodite's Passion
Oil of Damascus Roses, Musk, Sandalwood,
Oil of Balanos

Her hand moved quickly across the paper as the ingredients and measurements rushed from her head and into her fingertips. She relished the feel of the quill between her fingers, the scratching sound it made across the coarse cream paper, the black characters appearing almost magically before her eyes.

She continued.

Cleopatra's Seduction
Mistress Of The Night
Athena
Bacchanal
Aegyyptium

And as she wrote, revealing the treasured secrets of the Swan, the scent of each perfume bloomed and filled her cell.

Writing became a power as great as the actual creation of the scent. It unveiled the mystery and defined something that could not be seen, tasted or touched.

Damascus roses, she wrote. She could feel the rose petals between her fingers.

Lavender. She saw herself in the field, picking the long, purple stemmed flowers.

Cinnamon. She tasted it on her fingertips.

Lush with sensation, giving birth to her perfumes again and again, she unleashed that which was wild and pagan about her soul and grew into her power. Maia, in her sanctuary between the water and earth, had hinted at Phaedra's powers. With the mixture of each perfume, Phaedra unveiled her strengths and bloomed with a force that made the walls holding her disappear.

Phaedra worked until the perfumes covered the stone floor from end to end like a paper mosaic. Only the spot where she sat remained clear. Sitting in the middle of her mosaic, nearly finished, she set her quill down and looked around. The torchlight flickered in the wall sconces, fingering light across the papers as if the flames were reading, too. A wicked gleam came to her eye as she glanced at the page closest to her. It was the description for the emperor's hair pomade, something she'd created for him alone. At the top of the page she'd written, The Emperor's Secret.

She smiled and swept her gaze across the floor. Her life's work. It would buy her and Hakim's freedom, for there was no way Sigurd would allow the guard to live after she escaped. The perfumes would make Hakim wealthy beyond his wildest dreams.

Only one perfume remained to be captured and added to the mosaic, Pagan Desires. She opened the vial and the scent of rose and jasmine laced the air. The perfume unlocked the poetry of a moonlit night spent in Brannoc's arms, and she became lost in the memory, in the heat of her desires.

The memory stirred her, and yet, it brought tears. With the pleasure came the pain of not knowing if she'd ever be with Brannoc again. Would Brannoc succeed in finding her? If not, would Pagan Desires forever tease her as it carried her back into his arms?

She bit her lip to stop her trembling. Brutally, she wiped her tears with the back of her hand. "If that is to be the case, then I will easily give up Pagan Desires," came the martyr's wish inside her mind.

And yet . . . She drew a deep breath, filling her lungs with the scent, and slowly exhaled. She slipped the alabaster stopper back into place and pressed the vial against her heart. And yet, to give up Pagan Desires would mean she was giving up on herself and the wildness of her soul. Pagan Desires was the essence of who she was. She could no sooner give it up than give up her feelings and identity, the wild stirrings of her heart, every sense that made her feel alive.

"No," she decided, looking down at the vial in her hand. She closed her eyes and saw the truth. Unlike the other perfumes, the mystery of Pagan Desires would be known only to her.

Apprised of the details regarding her escape by Hakim, including that she would be traveling with a caravan, and posing as the caravan leader's daughter, Phaedra finally permitted herself to relax in her cell. On her back, arms bent beneath her head, she contemplated the craggy stones above her head as if they were puffy clouds. She could already feel the sun upon her face and the wind in her hair.

It would be heaven, she thought, snuggling into the straw. It would not be the angelic abode the Church patriarchs raved about, but heaven none the less.

It was her last night in prison. She'd proven to herself that she had the power to bring down the walls which had been holding her back, and this filled her with new strength. But her power had also made her vulnerable. For the walls had protected her like the stoutest guards ever imagined.

Now they were gone. And there was nothing to shield her from the eagle of her dreams.

Twenty-eight

The eagle's brown liquid eyes fastened on her as if she were prey. The great wings beat once, twice. The bird plummeted through a blue sky, talons stretched. In the dream, she raised her arms to shield herself from the attack. The eagle clawed, shredding her skin, scratching the serpent tattoos and drawing blood. It rose, circled, and dove again, this time as if to pluck out her eyes. It flew off, came back, and circled.

She knew the eagle was biding its time, waiting for her to drop her guard. Incensed by its haunting return, she curled her lip and decided in a breath to confront and destroy it.

She dreamt that she unsheathed the serpent dagger and gripped the hilt so tightly her knuckles turned bone white. With the same steely resolve that had marked her features the day she rode into battle to face the Turks, she looked up into the sky and waited.

The eagle swooped with a piercing cry. Just as its talons parted, as if to rip off her head, she ducked and attacked the bird from behind, plunging the dagger between the wings.

The eagle fell to the ground with a cry that split the sky. Startled, Phaedra glanced up, sure that hundreds of eagles were circling above her, ready to avenge the attack.

But in the dream there were no avenging eagles in the flame blue sky. There was only the dying creature at her feet. Its feathers were an iridescent rainbow of browns and bluish purples peaked to white at the tips. The dagger, with its hilt twined with serpents, rose out of its back.

Both hands on the hilt, Phaedra turned the eagle over and crouched down beside it. Its beak opened and closed soundlessly. In the gray-brown spheres of its eyes were flecks of gold and amber. She peered closer, lured by her own reflection, and something more.

Like Maia's hammered bronze bowl and the dagger's flame-marked steel blade, the eagle's eye gave a glimpse into another world and, without any warning, revealed a vision. Phaedra's eyes squeezed shut against it, but the vision blazed within her mind.

She saw her father, Nicephorus Acominatus, dressed in his silver armor. He was astride his war horse, Theseus, looking out over what may have been a battlefield. It was deserted. His proud noble features were unmarred by worry lines. His steel-gray eyes focused on something in the distance.

Her stomach rolled as she became dizzy. She blinked. This time, she saw her father with his sword raised in his right hand, engaged in battle with a tall, raw-boned opponent with flaming red hair. The man fought with the vigor of a boy unafraid to die, and the skill of a man who knew he was invincible. She looked closer with her mind's eye. The red hair, the strength, the ice-blue and devouring eyes all told her the man's identity was Bohemund.

The realization made her flinch, and she drew a shaky breath. The past was unfolding before her, a time she'd never had the courage to open herself to. She began to turn away, but stopped as if held on a short tether. Her hands hung lifeless at her sides, weighed down by invisible iron manacles.

The battle unfurled even though she fought against it. She didn't want to know. She saw her father lead his men through a pass in the hills. The Normans, yelling their war cries, flooded down the rocks, surprising her father and his men, massacring the soldiers, and, in the end, surrounding Nic-

ephorus. Her father challenged the barbarians to a fight to
the death, but no one stepped forward. Not even Bohemund.
As ten men held her father still, the red-haired giant slapped
manacles around his hostage's wrists and led him away.

There was a white pavilion. The crimson banner told her
it was Bohemund's. The cloth waved beneath a sun blood-red
like a wound in the sky.

Inside, chests of gold gaped open-mouthed at her father's
feet. Bohemund ran his fingers through his hair, snorting
with bewildered laughter. He dove his hands into a chest,
scooped the coins between his paws and showered the pavilion with gold. He unrolled a document written in the emperor's hand, signed with his seal. The giant arched his brow,
and Phaedra saw a puzzled look cross his face. Faint furrows
appeared on his brow.

Something was wrong, she told herself as she watched
Bohemund unlock the iron manacles around her father's
wrists. She remembered a conversation she had overheard
as a child between two patricians talking in the palace garden.
They'd said that after accepting the hostage money from Emperor Alexius, Bohemund had murdered her father. "Bohemund killed him in cold blood." That was what they'd said.

But that was not what the vision unveiled. She saw her
father astride his horse, leaving Bohemund's camp. There
was a movement in the trees and four Varangian Guards attacked her defenseless father, stabbing his body again and
again and again.

Varangians. Alexius's personal guard. They obeyed no man
save the emperor. They took their orders from him alone.

Alexius's men. Alexius's orders. Alexius . . .

Murderer.

Suddenly, the eagle shuddered, dislodging the dagger, and
with a great movement of wings it rose into the air. Phaedra
looked up. The emperor's brown eyes peered down at her.
There was no beak, but a mouth, with lips shaped thin and
etched fine like Alexius's. They seemed pursed around a se-

cret, a private joke. The eagle opened its human mouth and pushed something out with its tongue. It was a bit of gold, a ring, with a stone like a leopard's eye, her father's ring.

Phaedra screamed and the vision broke. She found herself back in her cell. She clutched her side as her stomach heaved. Somehow she found the strength to drag herself to the corner before the sickness took command.

The sour smell of her retching overpowered the perfumes' lingering scents. She crawled to her bed of straw and lay flat, with her cheek buried in the musty smell.

She could not stop shaking. Her anger held her in a grip so fierce she could hear her bones rattling in her ears.

The emperor Alexius Comnenus, the great Basilieus, Autocrator, the Thirteenth Disciple, had sanctioned her father's death. Commanded it. Blessed it.

Bohemund was innocent. The barbarian, the wolf who had moved through her waking and sleeping dreams, was not the beast she thought he was.

She closed her hands into fists. The emperor Alexius had used her. He'd taken her anger and innocence, her strengths and weaknesses, to demonically bind her to him. Had she carried out her vow to avenge her father's murder, the barbarian's death would have been on her hands only. *Think of the power he would have had over you then,* she thought, teeth chattering in rage.

She clutched at the straw and froze, paralyzed by the foul memory of one of their last encounters when she'd caught the emperor fondling her. The memory went deep, and she knew, in her bones, that there were other memories waiting to be unveiled.

She became sick again. Half-blind, she crawled in a circle, her hands searching for something. Her fingertips brushed up against cool metal. "Yes, the dagger," she thought. Of their own accord, her fingers caressed the blade and the sharply honed edge pricked and cut her, but she neither pulled away nor cried out. She felt her blood trickle and mix with the steel in a pattern of red. Her fingers slipped down the length of it until she came to the hilt where they traced the dragons, moving over them affectionately. Her hand curled around it, lifted it in the dark, and tightened, ready to plunge.

With a full-throated roar, she unleashed an anger that stretched back many years. She'd spent her entire life cherishing certain beliefs. Now she knew they were false. Where there had been light, there was now darkness. She did not even try to understand.

The truth surrounding her father's death, and the reek of abuse at the emperor's hands, now threatened to keep her from moving forward, toward freedom. Held in the grip of evil, she lay wounded, passive, but oddly at peace. All of her anger drained into the stone floor and wall. She hugged the dagger and the darkness to her breast.

It was Alexius's dark, laughing face which sparked something inside her. She imagined his beard glistening with her oils. He was crownless, and a pearl dangled from his ear. His eyes were afire with a dark, pleasurable secret.

No! She rose onto her hands and sat back on her knees, still clutching the dagger. She was not going to let him win this, she told herself. She had the power to stop him. She could control her own life. Use the sight. Trust herself. It was all within her power.

"Go back to Constantinople, get Alexander and flee. Quickly. Anywhere. The Eagle . . ."

Brannoc's words. He had known about the emperor all along. The Dragon had seen the truth and had warned her. Wherever he was, he was still trying to protect her.

She looked around the cell. It was dark like smoke now. "It will soon be dawn," she thought.

No more walls.

Her hand tensed around the serpent hilt of the dagger.

There was one thing she had to do before she left. With her free hand, she smoothed her long hair over one shoulder and coiled it into a curl that fell to her waist. She grabbed the rope of hair and pulled down on it. The steel winking in the waking light, she set the edge of the blade against her hair and cut it off by her shoulder.

She tossed the heavy rope of hair onto the floor. She stared at it. There was no misgiving in her eyes. But then a thought came to her. The blood of an Acominatus singing in her veins, she picked up the long black curl of shiny hair and draped it through an iron manacle hanging closed around an invisible wrist on the cold stone wall.

The caravan moved to the slow and sluggish rhythm of sun-struck lands. Camels trudged on, laden with silks and spices, carved chairs of ebony and chests of rosewood. There were horses, too, Arab ponies, small but fast, riderless and intended for market.

It was a world without walls, until the caravan entered the cities with its inns and the squares where goods were sold and new treasures bought.

Phaedra had chosen to ride a horse over a camel, a tall gray gelding which Hakim had "borrowed" from the court stables. She rode astride in Arab dress, cuffs around her wrists, her face veiled. She was the daughter of Matthias, the seller of spices. At their first meeting, Matthias had clicked his tongue at the sorry sight of her butchered hair. Yet, washed and wearing clean, white linen robes, she was, at least in his eyes, presentable. And lest any merchant think the gangly old man could be easily swayed to barter a treasure for a night with his daughter, they had only to note the damascene scimitar winking beneath his robe.

They were two days out of Edessa, following the Euphrates. After four months in prison, she was too glad to be free to feel the heat, the dust of the road and even the biting flies. The smell of camel dung, sweat, and the lush curtain of Hakim's spices did not give her pause either. Nor did the lack of money. She had nothing of value save the dagger, gold cuffs and her vial of Pagan Desires. She'd left the gold slave belt locked in the cell. It could have fetched a purse heavy with gold, but its glaring shimmer and the music of its coins would have needled her nerves. She didn't wish to be reminded of the harlot role she had been expected to embrace.

Not once did she look back. Her eyes were always on the open road ahead of her. She was free. She was alive.

After the sunrise prayer on the third day, they were preparing to mount, when a cloud of dust in the near distance alerted Phaedra that they would soon have guests.

A cutting glance from Matthias ordered Phaedra to hide herself for her own protection. As the caravan's leader, Matthias's word was the law, and although she wanted to obey him, the yoke of subservience was beginning to chafe and she did not move so far away that she could not keep an eye on the approaching riders.

The dust settled around the hulking frames of ten mounted knights on their way to reinforce the army at Antioch. They were Franks, judging by their fair looks. Their swords sparkled, helms gleamed and their shields bore not a single scratch. They were untried, yet their eyes glittered, betraying visions of exciting battles, treasures and glory. Phaedra watched from the shadows as the barbarians looked about, their mouths hanging open, eyeing the camels piled high with the caravan's goods. She caught their fingers tickling the hilts of their unbloodied swords. Two silver-haired giants exchanged sly glances as eloquent as battle cries.

Of its own accord, her hand reached for her dagger. No sooner had she slipped it free then all ten knights unsheathed their swords. With a bellow to wake Hades, they fell on the caravan.

Most of the merchants were armed with simple daggers,

nothing like the heavy swords that flashed before their faces
now. Like sheep, they fell to the wolves. With no heart for
defending the caravan, Phaedra raced for her horse, tearing
the veil from her face as she ran, and leaped onto the gray's
back. He whinnied and stamped in alarm at the sudden fall
of weight and the hard tug on the reins, alerting the Franks.
Three gold heads turned and froze in shock at the sight of
her face. She had enough time to see their wolfish grins,
hear the smacking of their lips, before she turned her horse
around and, in a leap, headed east.

The gray gelding had been sired by the wind. And Phaedra
had been taught to ride by a master. The combination netted
them an advantage that made the Franks' pursuit laughable.

But Phaedra did not take her pursuers lightly. The journey
had taught her that the westerners were fiercely stubborn
and inspired by challenges. They would run their mounts
into the ground before they gave up the chase.

The sun was at its zenith, merciless, lashing the ground,
before Phaedra pulled back on the reins and slowed the gray
to a trot. She'd lost the Franks long ago. It was impossible
for them to catch up to her now, she thought. She snorted
and shook her head. One skirmish and the knights were already rich. The horse answered her mocking laugh and she
patted its neck as she shrewdly calculated that Matthias's
spices alone could outfit a troop of twenty men with new
armor, horses and weapons.

Yes, more weapons. And more bloodshed, she thought
cynically as the horse shortened its gait to a walk. She reined
the gray to a stop and, shielding her eyes from the sun, looked
to the right then to her left. She tugged to the right and set
out in a northerly direction, back to Constantinople. Antioch,
with its promise of bloodshed and impending reign of Bohemund the Mighty, lay behind her, to the south.

The eagle lived in the north.

She narrowed her eyes and pressed her thighs into the gray's sweaty flanks, urging him back into a trot. White robes flying behind her, the Swan flew home.

The need to know more about her father's death prompted her to set the dagger on the hard ground before her one night. She willed herself to see. Abruptly, she found herself elsewhere.

Where? See . . . the pattern of moonbeams streaming in through parted curtains between marble columns . . . The light skirting the marble floor that glows like the foam of the sea. And there . . . Gabriel's mosaic, bright and dark with its unfinished story, longing to tell its tale. And standing before it, in purple robes, Alexius Comnenus.

There were dark circles under his eyes, and the lines radiating from the corners had deepened. She noted his hair was mussed as if he'd just risen from bed.

He was staring at the swan in the mosaic. He reached out to touch it.

"Murderer," Phaedra thought to herself.

Alexius jerked his hand back with a start. He looked about the cavernous room.

"You killed my father."

He turned. Phaedra felt herself shrink back. Even though she was miles away, it seemed Alexius could sense her standing before him. He frowned and muttered something under his breath.

Suddenly bold, she moved closer. "The Leopard died at your hand. Your most loyal servant. Why?"

Alexius stepped back and glared straight ahead of him, as if he'd sensed her presence. Nervously, he brushed his hair back with a thrust of his hand.

Enough, argued a voice. She didn't hear it, but felt its command in every nerve of her being. *Let him be.*

She heard herself say, "He robbed the world of a good man. He robbed me of my life!"

His secrets will kill him. But not now.

She started to say something again, but a darkness pressed on her, and she was unable to breathe.

"No!" she lashed out. She raised her arms and suddenly she saw that the dragons were twining about her wrists. She felt the fear in every bone of Alexius's body, saw the reflection of the dragons in his eyes even as she felt the strength of will that had brought her to this place fading.

She awoke to find herself lying on the ground, before the dagger. Over her the wind howled. It sounded like the frightened screams of a madman.

"There! Look!"

Her muscles tensed at the sound of the voice. Phaedra pushed herself up into a kneeling position. The air buzzed in her ears, the earth danced before her eyes. She wavered, rocked with dizziness and nausea, then felt a stabbing sensation in her arm followed by a sudden flow of heat. She looked. An arrow had pierced her upper arm near her shoulder.

As she moved to pull the arrow free, she heard and felt the slap of sandaled footsteps approaching. She didn't stop. Gritting her teeth, she tensed her hand around the shaft and yanked the arrow out of her arm. Her face went white. She swooned forward, pressing the bleeding wound with her palm.

Through the cloud of pain, she smelled the coarse, wet smell of cloth and the rancid sweat of clammy skin. Slowly, she lifted her head.

The Bishop of Berain's grin was as menacing as a sword pointing between her eyes. "Praise be to God that we found you!"

The bishop and twenty of Bohemund's knights had been on an expedition in search of food to take back to their starving comrades when they came across Phaedra. The cleric had given the order to wound her, to keep her from escaping.

Also at his request, they'd tied her hands and feet together. And one of them carried her across his saddle back to Antioch. By the time they returned to Bohemund's camp, the wound had festered and she felt as if her body was on fire.

"Where is she?"

Phaedra heard the wolf's bellow through the fever's scalding walls. Suddenly the tent blazed with torchlight. The heat fueled the flames licking her skin and she flinched and moaned on the muddy ground.

"God's bloody feet! What has she done to herself?" Bohemund stood over the huddling, filthy figure at his feet and shook his head. He crouched down and lifted a curl of her short hair. He sighed deeply as if the loss of her beautiful mane saddened him.

He brushed matted curls off her face. At the feel of her skin, burning with fever, he pulled away in alarm. He drew his brows together.

"How bad is she?" he asked, looking up at the bishop. His eyes reflected another kind of fever, one borne of worry.

The bishop's bulbous eyes closed for a moment as his hand cut the sign of the cross in the air. "She's in God's hands now," he lamented icily.

Bohemund cocked a brow at the chilling tone and caught the smug look on the cleric's pocked face. The barbarian straightened and crossed his arms over his chest. He looked down on the holy man and the worry in his eyes vanished in the blaze of anger that gathered there.

"I want her to live. Do what you must."

"Only God—"

Bohemund snorted, cutting off the whiny response. Sounding out every word in the bishop's face, he ordered, "Then start praying, man. I want her alive."

Phaedra moaned. The bishop crouched beside her and stabbed a gnarled finger at her wrist. Studying the tattoo, he said, "They'll believe me now. They'll see the devil's markings." He bent close to her and whispered, "Death by fire is the only way to cleanse the world of the devil's harlot."

Days, weeks, years passed while she lay and her fever burned. She thought she saw Maia, robed in black silk, standing in the pavilion. She saw Brannoc in her dreams.

The truth was that Bohemund had sent Brannoc to St. Symeon, a port within a day's ride from Antioch. Sensing the cross-bearers' fear and hatred of the Celt, the duke had sent him to secure supplies and weapons from ships that hailed from Constantinople, Genoa, and ports as far away as England. Still she yearned for him.

"Sweet merciful God."

Phaedra turned toward the familiar voice, Bohemund's voice. She must have fallen asleep, her fever ravishing her body and her mind.

His gaze swept over her robes and her hair. With an approving nod, he noted that her blue-black mane, though the same length as his, curled in a becoming manner around her face. The pale coloring of her skin had returned, due to her illness and the lack of sunlight.

Phaedra looked behind the red giant. Knights thronged at his back. She saw Richard and Tancred among them. Their gaunt faces no longer shocked her. She'd heard tales of how the armies had been reduced to eating weeds, thistles, dead horses, asses, camels and rats. They were forced to dine on animal skin soup and various broths concocted from boiled fig leaves, vines or bark. There were also reports of cannibalism. The rabble, led by a Norman knight who had taken the name King Tafur, had been digging the graves of Turks and boiling the bodies in cauldrons heated over fires.

It was mid-March and they had been camped before Antioch since October. A long time to go without decent food.

"You continue to regard me as if I were the devil. The
bishop has been busy spreading lies through the camp."

Bohemund fidgeted and nervously cleared his throat.

"Don't tell me you believe him, too? You?" She laughed.

She heard his footsteps behind her, climbing up the steep,
rocky incline.

"Then tell me how this," he reached out and grabbed her
wrist, "happened." He held her arm up so the tattoo was in
her face. "Did Sigurd do this to you in Edessa?"

She met the wild look in his eyes and answered. "No."

"Then how?"

"Let's say it was a miracle."

"The bishop claims they're the mark of Satan."

She scoffed at him and pulled herself free of his possessive
hold. "Such a wild imagination our bishop has, eh?"

Concubine to the devil, she mimicked to herself. She knew
she should be afraid, but what good would fear do her now?
She couldn't arm herself with it. Fear was empty, useless. It
made more sense to wear her confidence like an impenetrable shield, she mused.

She turned her back on Bohemund and resumed studying
Antioch's fortifications.

The city clustered at the foot of Mount Silpins. It was
surrounded on the north, east and west by walls that were
well fortified by towers, 400 it was told, spaced so that every
yard of them was within bow shot. The walls rose out of the
marshy ground of a river bank, and ran along the summit of
a ridge. The south was guarded by the earth herself, an in-
hospitable, precipitous terrain that looked impossible to
cross.

"So the stories about Antioch were true." She paused.
"You'll never get inside by breaking down her walls, Bohemund. Only deceit will work. But you already know that,"

she said over her shoulder, referring to what the vision had foretold.

"Quiet!" Bohemund barked, afraid someone would hear.

She smiled. "Shall I start calling you *Prince* of Antioch?" He glowered at her, but she could not stop. "It is your fate, barbarian. Accept it. You know how long you've waited to hear it . . . *Prince*," she dragged the word until it slithered.

"Come back with me now. Henceforth, I don't want you to leave my camp for any reason. It's for your own safety."

Her brow arched. "My safety? I'd rather try to get across that," she gestured with her chin to the rough terrain that guarded Antioch's western face. "With you I'm as safe as a lamb in a den of wolves," she mocked.

Bohemund scratched his shaven chin, then thrust his arm out to her. He opened his hand. "Come. You're still weak on your feet. Your thoughts are muddled."

"My mind has never been clearer, barbarian."

During Phaedra's stay, while the leaders of the cross-bearers saw to the blockade of Antioch and prepared themselves for the inevitable battle against Kerbogha of Mosul, the bishop preached to the starving, sunken-eyed followers that Phaedra was the cause of all their ills. He stood in open fields, brambled woods, and on sharp rocks, pummeling his fists against his thighs as he spoke of the "devil's concubine." She had caused the earth tremors and the torrential rains of the previous months. With a lift of her hand, she had lit the night sky with strange flashes of light. The harlot had made all of the available food in the area disappear. She was evil, he cried, foaming at the mouth. She needed to be punished. She deserved to die.

Twenty-nine

"She must die!" the bishop snarled, using his voice like a whip. He swung around to look at the men gathered in Bohemund's pavilion: Raymond, Godfrey, Stephen, Hugh and the two Richards. "Your subjects demand it. God demands it," he whipped. White spittle dribbled from the corner of his mouth.

The leaders glanced nervously at one another. They were in council to decide Phaedra's fate. The people believed her to be the image of evil, gifted with black powers, and they were ready to take matters into their own hands. The camps were set to erupt at any moment. They were unconcerned with the coming of the most formidable army in all the East. They had become a danger to themselves, their leaders and to their mission to rescue Jerusalem.

The quiet in Bohemund's tent cut each man off from the other. Raymond of Toulouse pulled his eyebrows down as far as they would go and tugged sternly at his beard. Godfrey shifted his weight from one foot to the other. Hugh the Great bit his lower lip. Bohemund sat still in his chair, a wine cup frozen at his lips. Stephen observed the others as if he were taking notes for the letter he would soon be writing home to his wife. Only Richard appeared relaxed and ready to carry out the bishop's wishes.

The bishop clicked his tongue in disgust.

"Can you not see that God's bidding must be obeyed? The Greek whore must die. Satan has entered her filthy sou he can only be cast out one way." He lowered his voice as if he were telling a fabulous tale to children. "But there remains hope for her in the life hereafter. Will you deprive her of life everlasting?" he demanded.

Godfrey, the fair-haired knight, caught the bishop's eye. The cleric made it all sound so honorable. But Bohemund and Raymond continued to ignore him.

The bishop extended his arms toward the unconvinced leaders.

"Mighty knights. Defenders of the True Faith." Bohemund and Raymond looked up and caught the feverish gaze leveled at them. "You have traveled great distances in the name of Our Lord. You have risked death to banish the dark from these lands and bring people back to the one true God. You are leaders of His army on earth. You are the light. Now, shine it on the infidel within our midst, the whore who has infiltrated this great army of true believers. Cleanse and purify your people before it is too late!"

The gray-beard Raymond swallowed and cut a glance at Bohemund, who heaved himself out of his chair. The duke's disapproving frown deepened. He curled his lip at the man of God who had cornered him like an animal.

Once the council had decided to proceed with the bishop's wishes, the cleric from Berain himself saw to Phaedra's arrest. He had her chained to a stake in the center of an empty tent. He denied her food and water. However, he lavished her with his presence, a punishment worse than Sigurd's lash. He would visit her throughout the night, subjecting her to a litany of her abominable acts. Phaedra saw the curls of flame ref᷄ected in the bishop's eyes when he forced her to look at ᷂᷄᷄᷄ she knew that as punishment for her "lascivious ᷂᷂᷂an ways," they were going to burn her at the stake.

* * *

The wolves were coming for her.

On the third day, she heard the great tramping footsteps of the soldiers, moving across the earth, coming to take her to her death. She struggled against the leather restraints that secured her arms to the stake. It took six soldiers to hold her still, while two more unloosened the bindings to free her. The bishop, incensed by the men's inability to control Phaedra, plunged into their midst and slapped her twice across the face, stunning her long enough so that the trained warriors could finally tie her up again.

Meaty, callused paws forced her head back so they could force wine down her throat, but she smelled the pungent bite of herbs meant to drug and subdue her spirit, and spit the liquid out. She thrashed wildly until the bishop, again, pushed them all aside and kicked her in the stomach with his dirty sandaled foot. She coughed and he held her jaw open between his hands while they poured a river of wine down her mouth.

When they were done, her linen robes were so stained that she looked and smelled like a drunken beggar. But her face told all that it was a lie, that her clothes were but a costume, and that she was still a power to be reckoned with. Even as they yanked her to her feet, she tilted her chin up higher still. Her eyes blazed with fury. Not even the bishop's sadistic cackle and the clap of his hands could quell her resolve to survive at all costs.

The wine worked quickly. One moment she was walking sure and steady, and in the next, she was stumbling as if the earth beneath her feet was as yielding as water. The tent walls were quaking. Hands tied in front of her, she dragged herself forward, but when the bishop whipped the tent flap to the side, inviting the sunlight, she froze at the sudden flood of blinding light. She squeezed her eyes shut in pain and turned her face away. White stars danced behind her eyelids.

A sharp poke in her back ordered her to move on, and she stepped forward. She slipped, but quickly righted

When the bishop stepped outside of the tent, the crowd let out a cheer. From all of the camps they had come to see the "Devil's Consort." The cleric's coarse brown robes, wooden cross, heaven-directed gaze, and prayerful mutterings conferred upon him a holy status. The sheep parted before him in two waves.

Great hoots and whistles rang out when Phaedra appeared. The bishop stopped the procession and let the people gaze at the great whore of Byzantium. He wished they could see her tattoos, but her arms were covered now with leather bindings. She stumbled, and the crowd roared with laughter as if she'd done it for their amusement. Slowly, carefully, she set one foot before the other. She could not feel the ground. She blinked and the fiery crowd wavered like heat shimmers. Her stomach bucked and she swallowed the hot bile that rose, searing her throat.

Above the jeers, the taunts, and the frantically whispered prayers cast her way, she heard the pulsing of her veins, like some deafening music, fill the camp. But it helped keep her awake. Whatever they'd put in the wine was trying to seduce her into sleep. It took all of her strength to stay awake, until she saw the pyre of wood and the stake rising from its center. Then her eyes widened with panic. She felt the kick to her thighs that told her to keep moving. She hadn't realized she'd stopped. But instead of moving forward, she whirled on her feet and attempted to kick the soldier who had touched her. The smell of a deadly spectacle perfumed the air, and the crowd roared and waved fisted hands as Phaedra landed blow after blow on the cross-bearer. At the wave of the bishop's hand, soldiers moved in and dragged her to the stake.

㎰s and legs unbound, she fought off the force of the ㎰te men whose job it was to secure her to the stake. ㎰blows and kicks sent three of them crashing ㎰pyre, the pile of branches snapping and cracking ㎰weight as if they were already aflame. ㎰and red, the knuckles raw and swollen, but with angry yells that seemed to come from some strange creature inside herself, she fought with men twice her size and landed a punch to a nose here, a jaw there, all to the consternation of the bishop, who had thought his drugged captive would be as docile as a newborn baby lamb.

The mob roared with gut-splitting laughter, amused by the soldiers' clumsy handling of their victim. More men were thrown into the fighting melee until Phaedra was finally subdued. They strapped her to the stake.

The bishop, flailing his arms at his sides, wrestled to hush the crowd and bring it back under his control. When the laughter had quieted, he turned toward the stake, rammed his arm toward Phaedra and pointed a gnarled finger at her.

"Damned you are! Whore of Byzantium. Damned are your crimes against man and God. Your consort awaits you. The Devil. He hungers again for your touch. Fly to him, I say. Go, evil one, and may your charred remains scatter to the winds."

The cry of the crowd closed in around her like walls. "Brannoc!" her mind cried out, looking for him.

She thrashed in an attempt to escape, but it only served to make the straps around her shoulders, arms, and knees cut into her skin.

Her gaze cut through the crowd, looking for her only hope, Bohemund, but she did not see him anywhere. "Coward," she muttered under her breath.

"Renounce Satan so your soul may live and God find it in His heart to forgive you," the bishop cried. "Do you renounce the devil?"

Phaedra spat in his direction and the bishop stiffened with rage.

"Thou shalt burn in hell!"

There was a momentary respite from the holy speech as the bishop looked about for the soldier he had given the to to. Gasping for breath, fighting her fear, she look the sky. She searched the cloudless dome of b some portent that would tell her that her life would not end here. But not even a bird marred the perfect sky.

She slumped, chin to her chest and was about to close her eyes when she felt it, a low rumbling, like a mighty animal, a beast that even the gods could not master, moving toward her. The pyre creaked, the stake shuddered. The sign she was looking for was rising from the earth!

He was coming!

Without using the sight, she knew it was Brannoc. She slammed her eyes shut and saw him now, riding hunched forward and low over the sleek, shiny neck of an angry black stallion. His men were two horse lengths behind him, breathing the clouds of dust thrown up by the mad pummeling of the black's iron-shod hooves.

She felt her wrists grow warm. The dragons stirred. As her captors hadn't bound her wrists, she was able to move them freely behind her back. She was aware that something was happening to the leather straps around her arms. It felt as if they were growing slack, yet they didn't slip or come apart with her next breaths. She heard her heart beating in her ears as if it could somehow beat its way free. She felt it fluttering beneath her breast. And all the while, beneath the low murmur of the crowd, she heard the earth moving toward her like a great scaled beast.

She blinked, and there they were, a detail of soldiers, with Brannoc at the fore, red cloak flying behind him like a sheet of fire. The sun was low and to their backs. They looked as if they were pulling it behind them.

The men had the torch now in hand and cocked his head to the tumult of the earth. His eyes grew wide, and drained of all color as he gestured to one of his torch, quick! quick! A bright orange malevolent sneer twisting his mouth, the pyre with the lighted torch held vic-. The crowd cheered, caught in a euphoria sparked by Phaedra's impending doom, oblivious of the men flying to her rescue.

Phaedra bit her lip. She cast glances back and forth between the Dragon, thundering toward her, and the bishop, who was about to set her aflame. Frantically, she worked her arms at her sides. The straps fell free. Just as the bishop grazed the torch to the pyre, she tore off the bindings around her hips and thighs as well. She noted the burn marks where the straps had come undone.

The wood crept into flame. She heard the crackle of it as it moved upward to her feet, still bound. The smoke rose, boiling black, trapping her within walls as thick and impenetrable as a castle tower. Coughing, sputtering, she fought for breath. Her eyes burned. Her thoughts whirled, caught up in their own darkening storm, with visions of Alexander, Brannoc, her home appearing in bright flashes of light. Brannoc! Where was he? How could it end this way? There was so much to say! To do! To feel!

It was her anger that kept her alive now. Like an invisible shield, it protected her from the flames, the smoke and the hatred of the crowd that oozed toward her like a widening pool of poison.

Cut off by the smoke, Phaedra was unaware of the horsemen riding at full gallop through the wall of flesh, scattering the screaming mob right and left. At the sight of Brannoc thundering toward him, the bishop froze as if he were face to face with the devil himself. Brannoc did not alter his course. He spurred his horse on with a beastly yell and, at the final moment, before the hooves reached out to trample the bishop, horse and rider took to the air and leapt over the cleric's head.

With a mighty stride, this beast, this man-horse cut through the flames and the wall of smoke. There was a sensation that made her feel as if she were being lifted out of herself. For days to come, her dreams would tell her the story

of her rescue. How his arms, like dragon wings, had reached
out to carry her to safety.

But for now, the world suddenly fell silent. Against a powerful shoulder, she permitted herself to close her eyes and
embrace the darkness that so eagerly wanted to claim her.

The next several hours proved to be an exhausting ordeal
for Phaedra. She'd been fully awake and aware of their plight
for some time now. They had veered off the direct road to
the port of St. Symeon to confuse their pursuers, and as a
precaution against falling victims to an ambush by the Turks.
They'd been riding as though the hounds of hell were after
them. The mad, obsessive glint in Brannoc's eyes revealed
his resolve not to stop until he believed the woman he held
in front of him was out of danger. But Phaedra was so tired
she could barely keep her eyes open. She slumped forward,
chin to her chest. She was ready to collapse over the horse's
neck. But when Brannoc reined his black stallion to a sudden
halt, it jarred her upright, and off balance. Instinctively, he
tightened his hold around her waist.

"We'll rest here," he ordered, reining the black horse
around to face the other men. They were Celts, four in all,
and they towered in their saddles, like Brannoc. Phaedra had
never seen them before. They were dressed plainly in tunics
and chausses, short black cloaks flung around their necks.

With his free hand, Brannoc impatiently tugged his helm
off and tossed it to one of the men. With a kick, the Dragon
urged his horse away from the others, then reined it still
again.

"Phaedra," he whispered into her hair. No one ever said
her name as he did.

Sensations ruled her. Fear, exhaustion and hunger had un-
dermined her strength and she felt everything now with such
force—the sound of his deep caressing voice, the feel of his
arm protecting her, the warmth of his body against her

back—that she trembled. Overwhelmed, she began to cry silent tears. The world blurred. She closed her eyes to hinder the quiet tears, and when she opened them again, the world was a glistening mosaic of images and tears.

She could not stop shaking.

"I love you." Brannoc wrapped his free arm around her. She felt his lips in her hair. She listened to the flow of his breath, moving in and out of his powerful chest. She tried to steady herself and find solace in his strength. She struggled for control, but it was as if a single tear had the power to crush her resolve. Her entire body shuddered with a great wracking sob. The pain and confusion she'd suffered over the past four months finally surfaced in a cry of such animal intensity and pain that the men all turned at once to look.

Brannoc did not try to stop her or hush away her pain. He was a man who understood the cleansing force of tears. Without a word, he turned her and cradled her shuddering, sobbing form in the protective embrace of his arms.

Until this moment, she had not realized how much she'd needed him to hold her. Sensation bred sensation, and her cries tore her apart.

A wave of emotion engulfed Brannoc, the mighty warrior, gifted with the powers of the Dragon, the most afeared man of all the cross-bearers. As he smoothed her wet hair off her face, he closed his eyes to capture the glistening sting of his own tears.

It was ink black when they stopped at a whitewashed inn with a flat roof, nestled along a street with identical buildings. Herbs, rosemary and bay, grew in terra cotta pots on either side of the plank wood door.

A gray-haired man with a thick beard and wide shoulders stood at the entrance, guarding the inn's welcoming light. He smiled in greeting and hurried to Brannoc's side. The light spilled into the street.

"We'll spend the night here," Brannoc said. He helped Phaedra down into the innkeeper's waiting arms, then dismounted. "Lest Bohemund and the others think they can take you away from me, we sail tomorrow." He nodded, dismissing the innkeeper, and resumed holding Phaedra.

Sail? Tomorrow? Her mind in a fog, Phaedra nodded. She knew she would fall on her face if Brannoc let go of her now. His hands held her by the waist, and she knew he could feel her trembling. He didn't mention her pitiful condition, and continued to allow her to hold onto his arms until she could make her legs stop shaking.

Phaedra's red-rimmed eyes flew about the room. It was small, white, with a simple bed covered in a cream wool blanket. A fire glowed in the bronze grate in the corner. Two unadorned lamps of glass and copper shed twin circles of light.

Brannoc's presence overtook the room. When two servants brought in a bronze tub of steaming water, the room shrank further. But the closeness, the tightness of space reminded Phaedra of Maia's cave, and it soothed her spirit.

She stood with her back to Brannoc as he undressed her, starting with her baggy, dirty trousers which he slid gently down her hips, then the tunic, which he lifted over her head. She heard the sharp intake of his breath as his eyes beheld the crisscross of white scars upon her back and the tops of her buttocks. She felt his hands move like a breath down her spine. She cringed at the delicate observance of her wounds.

His touch made her feel healed and afraid all at once. Did he find her ugly now? Deformed? Did he pity her? She could not bear it if he did.

She stood quietly, afraid to breathe. She watched their shadows on the walls, saw him move forward to kiss her back, and all her fears disappeared.

Silently, he lifted her and set her into the tub of warm

water. He washed her hair with soap that smelled of camo-
mile, and sponged her clean of the dust and dirt and degra-
dation of the cross-bearers' camp. With Maia's bronze bowl
he rinsed her body. Understanding its value, he'd taken it
from Gabriel and had been keeping it in his saddle bags.
Now, with each fall of water from this ancient bronze bowl,
the scars to her body and soul began to heal.

They had to speak of everything that had happened over
the last months. But it was as if Brannoc already knew and
had experienced it firsthand. So when he drew her back into
his arms, her body glistening wet, her cut hair a wild tangle
around her shoulders, it wasn't so he could mend their sepa-
ration with words, but with a kiss. Then another. And another.
Each kiss, though quiet, deepened into sound inside her body,
like a whisper of love, moving through her veins and making
her glow with life from the inside.

With his mouth and hands he praised the beauty of her
breasts, the hollow of her stomach, the curve of her thighs.
He sought the alabaster vial laying in wait against her skin
and opened it. Treasured oil glistening on his fingertips, he
anointed her as he had the first night that they came together.

His worship of her began at the insteps of her feet, then
moved up to the backs of her knees. He traced patterns across
her stomach, the hollow of her back. He lavished his touch
in the cleft between her breasts, then on to the backs of her
ears, her elbows, and the dragons entwined around her wrists.
All the while he bided his time, until the scent of rose and
jasmine mixed with her heat and the heat of his wanting,
and she bloomed and became the scent Pagan Desires.

They moved onto the bed as if into smooth water. At the
sound of her name on his lips, his touch, all the wanting
within her rushed against the burning warmth of his arms
and chest, his thighs and legs. Unveiled, she moved, rising
above him, then arching beneath, mindless and lost, fulfilling
her own pagan desires. Listening to his moans, moving in a
sea of sound, she moved her tongue along the pleasure places

of his body until he stopped her wet assault with his hands and fingers. Then his mouth. He pulled her above him, her thighs straddling him and held her hips securely so as to satisfy his hunger for the ripe, glistening fruit of her sex. She bucked and clawed the wall she'd been forced to face, fighting and not fighting his firm hold of her, the flaming spear of his tongue as his mouth sought the essence of who she was. She succumbed, answering his mouth by moving her hips in such a way as to encourage his assault. Wild, all desire now, she moaned and begged, "Enough!"

With a barbaric groan, he grabbed her and drew her down on the bed. Her spiraling need began anew, lifting her. She writhed, demented, blind, soaring upward from her flesh. His hot weight anchored her or else she would have flown away.

The morning was fierce. The wind blew strong and cold off the sea, snapping Phaedra and Brannoc's cloaks, whipping their hair as they stood watching the water, the sailors, the ships. The sky was a dull gray lined with low clouds with a greenish cast like old metal.

Phaedra lifted her face to the sky and grabbed a fistful of her unruly hair. The dark smudges under her eyes made her delicate skin look bruised. Although she'd been well fed and well loved the evening before, she had not been able to sleep, as thoughts of Alexander, his health and welfare, had kept her stomach in knots.

The whip of the wind threatened her balance. She caught Brannoc's hand, anchoring herself to it. Staring out at the sea, she was falling under the spell of the crashing waves when she innocently asked, "How long will it take us to sail back to Constantinople?"

Brannoc's hand tightened around hers as he answered, "We're not going to Constantinople."

"What?"

The exclamation was like a blow. Her eyes were feverish

with accusations, but he neither wavered nor looked at her. "By now, Gabriel has Alexander and Helena safely on the way to Greece."

"What?" she said again.

She yanked her hand, pulling it free. Hands on her hips, she looked up and by sheer presence alone, forced him to look at her.

"Is that all you can say, 'What?' " he echoed, knowing full well that he was about to catch the full blast of her fury.

"Brannoc!"

Her hands opened as if she meant to tear him limb from limb.

"Before Taticius, Gabriel and Kasia set sail for Constantinople, I asked Gabriel for his help. I knew the emperor would never let you leave Constantinople once he became aware that you knew the truth about your father's death."

"How would he know? It was a vision! My vision."

Brannoc laughed low in his throat and shook his head once. It incensed her all the more.

"What is it? What don't I know?"

"Dreamer of Dreams. You couldn't help going back, scaring him, could you?" The hairs on the back of her neck stood up.

"It cost you, you know."

She swallowed. "Well I know that you have powers beyond mine, but Alexius—"

"—is not a fool," he finished for her. "The man lives as much by instinct as by his wits, Phaedra. His secret has been unveiled. He can feel it."

"No." She turned her back, shutting him out. But her anger was over her own foolishness. The thought that she may have imperiled her son's life made her tremble.

Brannoc's steadying hands on her shoulders reassured her that Alexander, Helena and Gabriel were safe, but she could not put aside the power of the shame laughing inside her. What a fool I am, she thought to herself.

"No you're not," Brannoc whispered into her hair as he kissed the top of her head. "Your power is young. You will learn to use it wisely."

His calm, soothing voice was beginning to brush away her unease, but then a new thought bullied its way through. She whirled around to him, her eyes wide with visions of a harsh reality.

"But if I can't go back . . . The villa . . . My shop . . . Everything I own is in Constantinople. Look at me! I have nothing. I'll have to build a new life. But with what?"

His blue eyes softened at her distress. He held her face between his hands. "Everything you need is right here. You can recreate the Swan's perfumes anywhere in the world. You are mistress to a treasure beyond anything you have in Constantinople. I will help you obtain everything you'll need, spices, oils . . . I only ask," she stiffened for she knew everything had a price. "I only ask that you never create Pagan Desires for anyone . . . except yourself."

She breathed with relief, then caught herself.

"You wish to be my partner, barbarian?" she said gruffly.

"In all things."

"I can be a stubborn, short-tempered, demanding person to do business with."

"Well I know it." He smiled, and it was as if a thousand suns had suddenly brightened the sky.

"You're not afraid?" She arched her brow. She felt her heart quicken beneath the warm, loving regard in his eyes. "You should be. The Swan bends to no—" Brannoc swooped down, stealing the last word from her mouth, sealing their fate with a kiss that echoed his need and love for her. She wrapped her arms around his neck and answered, matching him kiss for kiss, desire for desire.

They set sail in a ship bound for Genoa, where Brannoc had made arrangements to meet Gabriel. The wind finally had the good sense to mend his gruff ways, and the sun had decided to show himself. It was a circle of fire, but it melted into the water, quenched by a power greater than its heat. When the moon, pale as cream, showed herself, the sky was the color of violets.

Together, Phaedra and Brannoc watched the power of one thing yield to the power of another and create something new. She was resting against his chest. He smoothed his palm across her stomach, and had Phaedra chanced to look up at him then, she would have caught the secret playing at the corners of his mouth, and would have asked him to tell her what was obviously filling him with so much joy.

But she didn't look. With a sigh, she eased herself back, closer, and all her panic left her, melted. And there was only the sun and the moon, the hush of waves, the creak and slap of oars, the song of the wind in the sails.

There was only the Dragon and the Swan. And the scent of Pagan Desires.

About the Author

Veronica Ashley lives in Chicago.
Pagan Desires is her second romance novel.